A Kiss in Winter

By Leah Banicki

D0048365

Book 6 of Wildflower Series
Published by Leah Banicki

© 2018 – Written by Leah Banicki

https://www.facebook.com/Leah.Banicki.Novelist

All bible references are used from King James Version, used with permission from Bible Gateway. All verses can be found at https://www.biblegateway.com/

Acknowledgements

This journey has been such a wonderful gift.

I thank God for His many blessings.

The friends I have made that have helped me along this path are so very precious to me.

God bless you all for everything you have done for me.

Liz, Leslie, Jeff, Emma, Mary, Gene, Kathie, Ernie, Estelle, Reen, Meri, Rob; You all have helped in your own special way.

Thanks!

Book 6 of the Wildflower Series.

This is book six of the series. I wrote these as a continuing story. Though you may be able to pick up this book and be able to follow along there are a lot of characters and stories that you have missed. I highly recommend you go to the start with Book 1 - Finding Her Way.

The stories start in 1848 on the Oregon Trail and each book adds new stories and characters as the town of Oregon City grows as do the people we meet along the way.

I hope you enjoy the long journey as loves are lost and found, as faith in God is renewed and discovered.

Chapter 1

Saturday - September 2, 1852

Galina Varushkin's Birthday

Sometime in the night Galina awoke in a cold sweat with the memory of bleeding in the snow and watching her brothers' crying in the light of the cabin, spilling out of the doorway.

Her father's ugly work boots in front of her, his snarled and angry words rasped out into the cold puffs of air.

She remembered the feeling of her own warm blood dripping down her face and into her eyes and the cold of the slush and snow on the ground.

The fear went through her and she had an awareness that she was dreaming.

She had prayed then, in that horrible moment of blood and cold, and she would pray again now.

Lord help me forget, she asked. She shook and burrowed deeper into the warmth and heaviness of the blankets, willing herself to put those memories back deep within herself. It did no good to dwell on the dark times.

The yellow face of her mother and baby brother who had died in the Yellow Fever epidemic or the angry lines that crisscrossed her father's forehead right before he captured her hair in his fists that fateful night.

These two events were months apart but somehow in her nightmares they merged, her two unhappiest memories in the dark and twisted tangle of thorns and broken bones.

She muttered a verse softly while buried in the cocoon of her blankets. It was Isaiah 41 verse 10.

"Fear thou not; for I am with thee: be not dismayed; for I am thy God: I will strengthen thee; yea, I will help thee; yea, I will uphold thee with the right hand of my righteousness."

She was finally calm after repeating the verse several times. She couldn't comprehend how God could calm her so completely when moments before she was shaking and fearful but the prayers had

5

settled her.

She fell back to sleep, with better dreams.

❖ ✦ ✦ ❖

She woke up dreaming of a kiss. *It had a been a promise.* Galina mused as she stretched in her bed. The sun was rising outside and she heard the birds singing. It was Indian summer and the warm morning was a delight. Her nightmare had been terrible but her dreams had changed after her prayer and she was peaceful, even hopeful of the day now.

Galina leapt from her bed and felt the excitement of the day dawning. It was her sixteenth birthday and Warren had promised to kiss her.

It had been a few months since they had sat on the river bank, and he had been bold, his sweet face with that hint of a stubborn jaw and that small flirting smile.

'I plan on stealing a kiss on your birthday,' he had said.

She grinned and dressed in her daily work dress. She was feeling so very much better than a few months ago. Her ribs and body had healed.

She slipped on her lightest petticoats and took a few extra minutes brushing out her long dark hair. She let her wavy hair frame her face a little and then did a loose braid down her back tying a dark blue ribbon at the end to match the dark sprigs of flowers on the dress. She may be working this morning, but she felt pretty in the cap sleeved dress that Marie Harpole had made for her.

Galina saw the little table in the corner. She had a short story she had been working on over the last few months and she wondered if she would get a chance to read it through later in the day. She had a few candles for light if she wanted to write at night when she was alone after her duties. It wasn't something that she did all the time, but sometimes it gave her some joy to think up stories. Since moving in to the Greaves' household she had been spending a lot of energy learning this new job. It was definitely different than just taking care of her family home. Galina had been just about survival after her mother's death. Keeping the laundry clean and food on the table was the main focus. Being a housekeeper was more about a schedule and maintaining things. She was enjoying her job here at Ted and Angela Greaves' home for the last several months, though it had been challenging at times. Most of the challenges she had made worse by her own silliness and immaturity, she had learned.

She had started the job here, learning from Edith Sparks and Angela, when Angela had injured herself a few months ago. With a broken ankle and past injuries Angela Greaves, a sweet friend, was just not able to do as much as she would like. Galina had needed a task and working for these good people seemed a chance for her to branch out. It would also be a good living for her. She was a little young for a housekeeping position normally but these people were friends and were willing to deal with her young age because they knew she needed to find her own way, since her father had put her out of his house.

Edith Sparks was kind. She was living in a cabin on the property with three children and a large garden she grew nearby. Edith had a produce stand that sold a range of vegetables and fruits to the neighbors during the year at harvest time. Edith was helping Angela but Galina knew that eventually the workload of trying to run two households was going to affect Edith as well.

Galina had heard amazing stories from Angela about Edith's generous heart and found everything to be true. Edith was warm and funny, with a gift for teaching Galina what she needed to know in a way that made Galina feel like she was thriving. Galina took many notes and was blessed to have Edith so close by, if she needed help. After a few weeks Galina was allowed to continue most of the workload on her own, to see if she had learned the basics. In a way, Edith was a missing piece in Galina's life. Angela called her Mama Sparks and slowly Galina was feeling the same way about her. After her mother's death last year Galina still needed someone to show her love.

Ted and Angela were truly lovely. Both of them gave her the praise she needed to find her confidence after a rough year. Galina tried to pretend the last year had never happened, the death of her mother and youngest brother to yellow fever, then the beating her father had given her in a rage, that had broken bones and broken her heart. Galina was learning though, that she could not pretend any of it away.

Edith Sparks, was very thoughtful about teaching her all the little tricks to keep organized. Galina had pages of notes, learning all the little things of maintaining cleanliness.

This week Edith had taught her the many uses of tea. Brewing tea then using the wet tea leaves, sprinkled over the rugs and then using a brush over the rub to gather up the dirt and grime. Galina was surprised at how well that worked.

In the back washroom there was a tub full of Ted's dirty work clothes that were soaking to release the caked-on mud. Edith and Galina both agreed to take on some of the work clothes for Earl, the land manager, and Warren the other work hand and they were soaking too.

She walked down the stairs and saw Edith in the kitchen with Angela there with her walking cane.

Edith Sparks lived in a cabin with her husband Henry and their three adopted children. Edith was broad through the middle, with bright friendly eyes and a broad smile for everyone. She just had this way about her. She had good folksy wisdom was always a good listener. She wasn't surprised that Angela and others called her Mama Sparks. She had nursed Angela back to health a few years before after a horrible accident on the trail west. Angela finally came west. Edith and Henry followed soon after, bringing the three children who had been orphaned on the trail. There were a lot of stories of loss and heartache in the valley. Galina knew that she was not the only person to have loss and pain in life. Having someone like Edith around made things a little easier. She never judged when things came bubbling up to the surface.

Galina said hello from the top of the stairs as she made her way down. Angela smiled up to her sweetly.

"Happy Birthday Galina!" Angela said. Her red hair was hanging in a long braid down her back and her dressing gown hung loosely around her. Her belly was swollen with child a little. She had recently stopped wearing her normal dresses and had to go with a more loose-fitting day dress to fit comfortably in clothes.

There were white roses on the counter in a vase.

Galina joined the women at the counter.

"I have got cinnamon buns in the oven and they will be ready soon." Edith said and widened her eyes a little. Her friendly ways and gestures were infectious, and Galina couldn't help but respond with what could only be described as warmth and acceptance.

"I could have made breakfast." Galina said and lowered her chin a little.

"Not on your birthday." Angela said and limped over a few steps, her cane thumping across the hardwood floor. There was a part of Galina that wanted her friend and employer to rest, to not over do things, but the other part of her knew from her own time of healing that one had to get up and keep moving, to gain strength.

"How's your ankle doing?" Galina asked with concern.

"It is good today, I'm just using the cane to keep steady." Angela seemed to be calm and not concerned or in any serious pain. Galina was relieved to see it.

Sometimes when she had watched Angela in her healing process it would remind her of her own struggles. That dark time over the early summer when the 'incident' had happened with her father. It was something that Galina fought hard to forget.

Galina leaned over the counter and sniffed the fragrance of the white roses.

"I had another bad dream last night," Galina shared, feeling safe and loved in the company of two women that cared for her.

Angela nodded thoughtfully and crossed to her, in the silence, with a few thumps of her cane. Angela ran her hand soothingly across Galina's back.

"I still get them sometimes too." Angela said, her eyes sympathizing.

Edith nodded as well. She had her own bad memories.

"You seem calm," Edith said, though it almost felt like a question.

"Yes," Galina said lifting the corners of her mouth in a hint of a smile. "I prayed and thought of good Bible verses while I shook off the trembling and nonsense. I have to remind myself often that I am safe now."

Edith was thoughtful and quiet as she checked on the cinnamon buns in the oven. "I am trying to give reminders to the children of that, when they wake up from their own nightmares. It is a struggle, when in the grip of the bad memories, to remember that God has brought us out of that into a new place." Edith was also looking into Galina's with caring.

Galina took a deep breath and felt at peace. She didn't want to dwell on the bad thoughts but sharing with Edith and Angela had lifted a little of the heaviness that usually lingered after bad dreams. She wanted to focus on good and happy things for the day. She would enjoy this day and all the promises that it held for her.

"I love you both," Galina said, trying to keep emotion from her voice.

Angela and Edith both were hugging her a few moments later. It was just what she needed.

"No, you may not go." Her mother said for the third and final time.

Sophia Greaves felt the inner rage and walked to the window seeing the sun shining and wondering how her mother could be so stubborn.

Why can't I visit my friend on her birthday? Sophia wondered sometimes if her mother just didn't want her to have a friend and be happy.

Their home in town was a pretty little townhouse. There was a nice parlor in the front, with a big paned window that overlooked the street. There was a door off to the southern side that had a glass oval frame that showed the Lace Shop where customers came in and bought their lace goods here in Oregon City. A local woman was working the counter. Normally, Sophia enjoyed her life spent mostly in this room, with its fancy wallpaper and the soft furniture that she worked in. But too much sitting was making her anxious, even more so today.

"Is there any chance that you could explain your logic to me?" Sophia asked, forcing herself to be calm. She was wringing her hands in agitation.

"Well, I wanted you to come to the lady's lunch at the church with me." Her mother, Amelia Greaves, said with a no-nonsense tone.

"Mother," Sophia said with an exasperated tone. "Those women are your friends, not mine. It is Galina's sixteenth birthday and I would like to have family dinner with Ted and Angela as well."

"You can go in a few days. It'll keep." Her mother didn't even look up from her lace work. Her red gold hair pinned up fancy in preparation for the church luncheon. Sophia felt her angst rise up painfully in her belly.

This parlor, so pretty and perfect for their work was beginning to close in around her. All she did every day was work and make lace. She would pop into the lace shop, add her work to the pile, say hello to Mrs. Hammerstein who worked the counter and then go back to work.

She had a nice little savings account that grew every month, but she never did anything with her money except buy some little thing as a gift for someone. Her life was so very dull.

Her education had ended at ninth grade, as was the norm for someone her age and social standing. She enjoyed her books. But suddenly she was standing here gazing out the window on the world of sunshine and early fall and felt so trapped. Her mother held a tight grip over her and she longed to be out. She wished that she could ride the country side or walk along the river, anything to be out in nature.

"Mother, I am going to lose my mind if I am forced to stay inside anymore." Sophia was trying to explain her feelings while also being cautious.

"We will be heading out to the luncheon soon. You will get some fresh air then." Her mother gave her a pert little smile that said, 'get back to work.'

"Why can't I go out for a bit on my own?" Sophia knew that she was pressing the issue but the tension inside of her was rising to a boil.

"Because you are a young girl and this place is full of men and danger." Amelia set her hands in her lap, looking away from her work.

"I didn't realize that we had moved to such a den of iniquity. You make Oregon City sounds like some wild place with hooligans and criminals." Sophia sighed in frustration.

Her mother gave one of her sighs as well. It was usually followed by a lecture. Sophia was ready for it.

"When you are older you will understand my caution. You are a beautiful young girl and do not need to be out walking alone. You have a good occupation and you are well taken care of. You are not slaving over domestic chores every day. I wish you could just be thankful for the life you have instead of always wishing for something else." Her mother's tone was low and annoyed.

"I don't want another occupation. I would just like a chance to be outside more. You lock me in this parlor working every day with no freedom." Sophia argued.

"A woman's life is about work and anyone who says otherwise is a fool." Amelia retorted.

Sophia opened her mouth to argue more but knew that it was pointless. Sophia loved her work but sometimes she needed a break from it.

She went through every woman she had in acquaintance. They all worked very hard but took moments in life to enjoy nature and friendships. Sophia only saw Galina, the only friend she had that was her own age, very rarely.

The funny comparison was that Sophia's mother Amelia saw her friends all the time. They were constantly having some kind of church club function at least once a week. Sophia didn't mind seeing them on occasion, they were nice enough, if a bit gossipy, but they had their own interests. Sophia was in a different place in her own life and wanted to spend time with young people her own age. The town was not going to boast on its vibrant collection of young folks. The few people her age were spread out far and wide. Sophia was feeling penned in and frustrated, but she said a few little prayers to calm herself. There was nothing for her to do but to obey her mother and wait to see Galina until her mother considered it appropriate.

She wondered how long that would be. Sophia gathered up her collection of bobbins and started back to work feeling frustrated and aggravated. There was nothing else for her to do but continue her work.

She began making small ribbons of lace, something easy that she didn't even have to think much about while she moved her fingers in the motions that they knew by heart. Internally she fumed.

Her life was starting to feel like she had these invisible walls going up around her and she was tied to the ground and could not see a way over.

Chapter 2

Galina Varushkin

Galina felt her impatience grow as the night ticked by. Her disappointment of not seeing her dearest friend Sophia had been a hard pill to swallow. Her employer, Ted, had ridden to town to pick his sister up and bring her to dinner and had brought back a note from Sophia.

I am so sorry my friend, my mother would not let me come.
I am wishing you the sweetest of birthdays, with the promise to see you as soon as I can.

Sincerest apologies,

Sophia Greaves

Galina had no good reason to complain about her day, her brothers had come, with some sneaky diversions on the part of their new stepmother and Galina had spent more than an hour with them outside. The two youngest Sparks children had joined them for a game of hide and seek and Galina felt so good about the precious time she had with her brothers. Guadalupe, the new stepmother, came by for them just before dinner time to get them home before Galina's father came home. Hopefully, he would not know anything about the visit and no major angry outburst would take place.

The family dinner was lovely with Edith and Angela pampering her and forcing her to visit with the guests while they prepared dinner. It hadn't taken much force. She was feeling pretty special about her day.

Galina had a pile of gifts at the end of it all and now with dusk approaching she was waiting. She tapped her foot as she peered out the back window, looking for a sign that Warren was anywhere she could see. Had he forgotten? She had reminded him after Sunday service a few weeks before, about her birthday. She had blushed beet red at the suggestion.

Edith and Angela had a conversation weeks ago, over canning jars, about how silly young women and young men were about attraction. They counted themselves in the conversation as well, since they had once been young.

'Why young folks are so afraid to let someone know that they are interested is beyond my understanding. Now that I am older I realize that shyness is just a waste of time. How is someone to know iff'n they like you back until you give them a little poke?' Galina had been a casual observer to the conversation, but it had planted a bit of a seed.

She had attempted, on several occasions, to stop being so shy around Warren. It didn't mean that it wasn't extraordinarily uncomfortable but she did notice that Warren had stopped being quite so shy around her once she had broken through her initial discomfort over making him aware of her attraction. It was an interesting thought to ponder.

The day was passing and Galina finally let Angela and Ted know that she wanted to go for a little walk.

It was dusk and the sky was streaked with orange and purple across the mountain range. There were sounds of the summer bugs chirping around her as she took a stroll to enjoy the warm evening breeze when Warren found her. He walked alongside her for a few minutes, asking her about her day. She enjoyed the look of him. He was barrel chested, with wide shoulders and everything about him was well toned, his arms and legs, from all the hard work. His father must have been a big man too. Warren gave her a smile and she admired the sweet way he looked at her.

"Angela gave me her horse and saddle today. Since she is no longer able to ride. Marie Harpole gave me two new dresses." Galina was feeling very well spoiled and her heart was light. All of the impatience and frustration of waiting had melted away.

Warren was attentive and listened. He was always a good listener. She glanced at him a few times as she spoke, enjoying the way he responded to what she said.

She finally forced herself to pause from her chattering, giving the quiet a chance to settle around them. She felt her heart beating a happy thump in her chest.

"Well, I made a gift for you as well," Warren said. He smiled boyishly, charming her completely.

He pulled something out of his pocket and in a bold move grabbed her by the shoulders and turned her to face him. Galina's eyes went wide just as he leaned down to kiss her briefly.

"I did make a promise, but I didn't want to steal it." He smiled at her as she stared up at him.

In an unspoken way she nodded, giving him the permission he wanted to kiss her.

She had been expecting it, but he had still managed to surprise her. She found her voice. "Thank you." Once she said it she felt silly but once it was said it was gone, out into the world, free to roam.

He brought his hand out and opened it. She looked down and saw a braided leather necklace with a turquoise stone attached.

"I found the stone in the creek this summer. The blacksmith in town set the stone," Warren said. He seemed to be a little nervous about whether she would like it.

Galina was more than pleased and gushed about it for a long moment. She let him do the honors of placing it around her neck.

He didn't kiss her again that night but the sweet looks between them had been more than pleasing. He was charming and honorable.

They had parted ways that night with a small understanding between them without speaking much about it. In her heart and mind he was her beau.

She had a few weeks in September of happy memories. Galina would do her work during the day and a few nights a week, during the early fall, they took walks along the creek. Everyone knew about them, that they were courting.

Corinne Grant

"Good morning my darling," Lucas Grant said cheerfully as Corinne sat up in bed and stretched.

She looked at the cabin window and saw a tiny edge of frost on the glass. The colder weather was starting, and Corinne frowned.

"Hmm... good morning." Corinne said.

"You are frowning," Lucas smiled and turned to face her while he was buttoning his work shirt.

"Oh, just frost on the windows." Corinne said and shook her head. He knew that she wasn't particularly thrilled about colder weather. It made everything harder.

"I will head over to the greenhouse and get the woodstove stoked up." Lucas offered.

Corinne smiled. Lucas was thoughtful and after a few years of marriage they had a routine that worked for them.

Lucas would get the woodstove going in the greenhouse and the lab, then come back for breakfast at their cabin. Corinne would check to see if the children were awake and start the feeding process. Debbie would take one, and Corinne take the other. Since the adoption of her cousin's child, Caleb, a few months ago the cabin had taken on a few new routines. It was crowded and a little manic some days, but they were working through the issues together.

"Thank you, sweetheart," Corinne said and forced herself up from the bed. She was fighting off the urge to sneak back under the covers for a few more minutes of warmth and rest.

"I have the materials and the crew is ready. We're going to start work on the cabin today," Lucas said. He held his arms open to her as an invitation to join him for a hug.

Corinne accepted and stepped into the offer. She rested her head against his chest for a long moment, glad for the comfort of his arms. It was almost as warm as the bed. She mused.

"Are you certain that we won't have snow in the cabin if you start now?" Corinne asked as she pulled away a minute later.

Lucas gave her a solid nod. "I will do everything I possibly can to make this as quick as we can."

Corinne nodded. She had seen the plans to add a second floor to the cabin. There had been talks about it since they adopted Caleb but Corinne wasn't really certain how it all would work. She was always distracted by other thoughts in her mind; her children, her home, her business and she let Lucas have his plans about the land and maintaining the property. They had a partnership.

Right now, Corinne was wondering if she hadn't paid as much attention as she should have.

"I know you are a little apprehensive." He kissed her on the nose.

She gave him a look that told him that he was coddling her. He chuckled in the way of men, knowing he was trying to ease her mind with a kiss or a cuddle. Corinne raised an eyebrow and Lucas put up his hands in mock surrender.

"I am apprehensive, but I trust you." Corinne said and gave him the smile that he wanted to see.

His countenance changed and he smiled boyishly. The look his eyes was the same look that had first attracted her to him years ago when they met.

"I will see you at breakfast. I love you." He said and then snuck out the bedroom door.

Corinne found a blouse and skirt and dressed quickly trying to avoid getting chilled. The temperature was getting colder for certain and the habit of stoking the fires would have to take more of a precedent. It was not summer anymore.

She felt silly as the day passed the frost on the windows melted and by mid-afternoon the sun was warmer than expected. A warm breeze started up and the windows of the cabin were opened.

Corinne went about her work in the lab with her partner Dolly. They were grinding out herbs for making different ointments but Corinne was thinking about the days ahead while she worked.

Her husband was working hard with the crew of laborers and her house would be torn apart over the next days.

She was praying for some patience throughout her work. By the time she walked back home down the path towards the cabin some changes had taken place. She carried her wool coat but no longer needed it in the warmth of the late afternoon.

There were piles of lumber and logs beside her home. Her heart leapt in her chest to see Lucas standing on the roof. He was pointing to some other men who were up there with him. She was certain that men somehow enjoying scaring the wits out of women by standing in dangerous places.

She passed by without trying to catch his eye. She didn't want to distract him and cause him or anyone else to fall.

Corinne helped Debbie and Violet as they prepared dinner and got the children settled into their evening routine.

Lucas finally came back into the cabin after the women and children had eaten. Corinne warmed him a plate and they sat in the small parlor as she listened to him chat about his plans.

She still felt apprehensive, but she listened without interrupting. She put on her bravest smile. Sometimes being a wife was about trusting, even when she wasn't sure that she fully understood. She prayed quietly in her mind for God to take away some of her fears.

17

A thought dawned on her right before bed.

When they first were courting, she had been brave and told Lucas about her ideas for a business. He had listened and had trusted her. She had wanted to plant lavender fields and have a lab to made medicinal oils. It certainly had not been a normal kind of farming pursuit but he had trusted her vision and over the last few years they had built up her dream together.

It was her turn to see her husband's vision and trust him.

Corinne said a thankful prayer in her mind to God, He had shown her the way.

Chapter 3

October 18, 1852

Galina Varushkin

The evening was still warm when Galina stepped outside after dinner was served. Galina had been upset throughout the day. Angela and Ted must have sensed it because they gave her the evening free to get some fresh air during the warm weather.

The last few weeks had been a mixture of joy and sorrow.

She had been learning her duties and that part was going well. But, more often than she should, she would go to wandering to find Warren. Just a quick and unnecessary trip to the barn. Warren would spend the morning there caring for the livestock. She would get to say hello or something and then Warren would need to go. He had given her a few glances. He was always kind but then he would have to remind her to get back to her work and he would do his.

It happened more than once that she would go looking for Warren and not find him but find Ted, or Earl Burgess, the land manager.

She would act flustered and leave quickly, that inner reminder that she had work to do.

Angela and Edith had sat her down and talked with her gently. They all knew about the courtship and they understood her desire to see Warren throughout the day. But she needed to remember that Warren had work to do too. Angela had even shared that she had to learn that lesson herself. To let her man do his job during the day. Unless Ted was needed for some reason, Angela would let Ted have his own space to do his work. Galina felt like a fool for having been caught wandering the farm on multiple occasions, but the urges came about again, and she was caught a few more times over the last week.

Galina was frustrated that Warren had been gone the last few evenings and they hadn't walked together in nearly a week. His mother and sister lived out of town and he had been called away to help them with something.

The trees would be turning colors in the next month and

Galina was eager to spend some time with him. He was such a good listener and she wanted to regain the closeness that she cherished so much.

Galina had given an unhappy glance to Angela and Ted who were doing the washing up after the evening meal. They were cuddled up next to each other, being adorable and sweet to each other while they worked on cleaning the dishes.

It made her feel so lonely and agitated.

She wasn't sure if she would ever have that.

Sure, Warren has been flirting and had been sweet when he had the time but Galina was upset that he had been busy most evenings.

Galina left the house and crossed the wooden bridge over Spring Creek. There was a destination she had in mind as she plodded over the road. The sun was going to set in a few hours, but the yellow sun still had some warmth left in it.

The tree-line was still the dark green of summer but if Galina looked really hard she could see in a few places that there was a hint of fall color showing up on the tips of a few branches.

Galina took deep breaths of air as she passed by all the houses that she knew so well, her friends and neighbors. They almost all went to church with her every Sunday. There were still a few that traveled to town when the weather was fine to go to the fancier church there.

Galina finally reached the rural church. It was a simple white church building with a small little steeple. Galina walked through the empty yard, seeing the line of flowers out front and she knew that her friend Corinne had probably helped plant those there.

Everything out here was connected to her friends. They all had their lives together. They knew who they were. Galina felt like she was lost.

She reached the cemetery in the back and quickly found her mother's grave site. It was marked with a simple stone.

Magdalena and (baby) was on it. Galina knelt before it. She didn't care if she got her work dress dirty. She was needing to talk to her mother and she also felt the need to be close.

"Hello Mother." Galina said, her throat tight with the sudden emotion of missing her mother so desperately.

"I am a foolish girl. I am certain to disappoint you on every turn," Galina confessed and placed a hand on the grass over the grave.

"I need you sometimes, maybe more now than ever before. I feel that strange feeling again. It feels like a growing thing inside of me. Just this overwhelming need to lash out. Perhaps that is why father doesn't love me. Because I cannot control this part of me. I get so frustrated and then I do things that I regret." Galina was upset and wiped away a few tears but she was accepting of the tears as well. They were little badges of truth, admitting that she was broken.

"I don't want to be this way, but I cannot seem to stop myself. I have this boy... well young man…that I am seeing, Warren. You would like him mama. He is a hard-working, sweet-tempered kind of man. He is not like papa. He is patient with everyone. He works for the Greaves. He kissed me on my birthday, and sometimes we go walking together, or even ride horses around the valley. He is a good listener. Well, his mother was feeling ill and he went to make sure they were doing well. He has responsibilities that he takes seriously." Galina sighed, "I have been messing up." She admitted. "Since I haven't seen him for our normal walks I started looking for him during the day when I should be working. Everyone is upset with me now. They haven't yelled at me or anything like that. But the disappointment in their eyes is tearing me to pieces. So, I behave better for a few days then I get that feeling again. That I-want-to-be-happy and do-what-I-want feeling. Then I disregard everything and go out looking for Warren again. I just don't know if I can convince myself to stop making these mistakes." Galina let out a big breath and sat in the stillness. She was not expecting to hear from her mother. Galina was not superstitious but sometimes pretending her mother could hear her the way God could was comforting. Galina prayed a little while as she sat there. It was quiet, and she felt better than she had in days. The quiet was like a blanket over her.

"Dear God, please show me how to be better." Galina said to the silence.

Angela had been trying so hard to be encouraging over the last few weeks. Instead of yelling at her, which Galina totally deserved, she would talk about the journey that she had to make to learn her place.

Angela had a hard life and was extremely patient with Galina and her growing pains. But she wondered if the patience would eventually run out.

Galina got up from her place on the ground. Her skirts only a little damp from the grass and dirt.

It was time that she got back to the house. She would endeavor to do better. That was all that she could do.

⬥•◉•⬥ ⬥•◉•⬥

Galina Varushkin

Galina warmed up a pan of water on the hot stove and shaved some of the hard soap, into the basin she used for washing the dishes. The pleasant scent of lemons wafted up as she poured the warm water in. She splashed her hands in the water to encourage the bubbles to form. The few dishes and pans were cleaned up in short order as she daydreamed and watched out the window for a glimpse of a certain someone in the yard below.

She saw the young man she had been looking for and let out a small sigh, as she did every morning. She couldn't help herself, truly. He was still a weak place in her heart. She wondered if he ever saw her and sighed, like she did for him.

She had messed things up in a royal fashion, she knew. He had made her a promise in the early summer, perhaps, to kiss her on her sixteenth birthday, and he did. She had waited all day, had a special lunch with Ted, Angela and the Sparks family. Then she had a visit with her neighbor Corinne and her little ones. She had been given extravagant gifts by all her friends. Her young brothers, Milo and Pavel had come by later in the day after they had finished their chores to give her birthday hugs. It had been a good day, but she had been waiting, breathless and anticipating a chance meeting with the strapping young man who had been slowly earning her trust and friendship.

Galina had had longs talks with Edith, Angela, and even Violet Griffen, a neighbor who was also a housekeeper. She was happy, even contented in her new life.

Things had changed after a few weeks, though, when she began to act foolishly. She got impatient again.
Those persistent feelings kept invading her thoughts. She would go to feed the chickens and she would try to catch a glimpse of him in the barn nearby. If she saw him she would interrupt his work. A few times it was not a problem, just a moment to say hello. But then she would make longer trips, wandering to the orchard while he was up a ladder, checking on the apple trees with

22

Ted and Earl, the farm manager. She felt the glares from the men, they were wondering what she was doing in the morning hours, wandering around.

Angela and Ted had had a word with her, to remind her to give the men space to get their work done. She took that advice to heart, realizing she had been foolish, but a few days went by and she had missed getting attention from Warren and sought him out again.

She had found him on the edge of the fence line, helping a sow, who had her hind leg stuck somehow, between a fence post and a large rock, probably trying to escape.

Warren had been covered in dirt and grime, having been obviously exerting himself, to get the animal free of the entanglement.

"Hello Warren." She had said sweetly.

He only gave her a momentary glance. He put his attention back to the animal. "I don't have the time to talk right now, Galina."

The sow grunted loudly in protest and Warren grabbed the sow by the hips to give her a pull.

Galina tried to keep quiet, watching and waiting for him to get this finished so she could talk with him some more.

It was about ten more minutes of Warren wrestling with the pig before the back leg was free. Galina clapped happily as the pig was picked up, and with an inelegant grunt from Warren, was deposited on the correct side of the fence. Warren slapped the loose dirt off of himself and then finally looked at Galina again with a frown. He paused a moment.

"Don't you have any work to do?" He asked, his tone frustrated.

Galina took a step back? "I just fed the chickens," she said defensively.

Warren pressed his lips together and sighed.

"That was rude Warren…" Galina had said with a pout.

"But gawking at a man while he is wrestling with a pig is not?" He had asked. He didn't look as mad her father would sometimes get but seeing even the hint of any kind of anger triggered her own.

Galina lowered her eyebrows and stared at this young man, all the sweet feelings that had been growing for him had escaped and she saw him as she saw her father, just another man that was cruel

23

and rude.

She gathered herself and huffed. "Don't ever speak to me again!" She said and marched away.

She had cried all through the afternoon that day, while she prepared dinner and washed the linens. Angela, who had been having a rough day, trying to get strength back into her healing leg, had tried to comfort her; consoling her that men were different from women, 'you needed to give them space.'

Galina had escaped the house after supper and sat on a rock by the edge of the creek. The wind had picked up and Galina could smell rain in the air, but she ignored it and enjoyed another good cry in her quiet place.

Warren had found her just as a cold rain started.

"You should get back to the house, it's supposed to storm." Warren said gruffly. Thunder rumbled off in the distance to prove his point.

"I asked you to not speak to me again." Galina said, she angrily wiped at her wet cheeks. She had a headache from crying and she didn't want to hear from him.

"You are acting like a petulant child." Warren said in a softer tone. His words did not help her mood. She felt a little like a child, but she was too angry to deal with her own emotions.

"You were cruel to me, earlier." Galina turned her head around and looked to his face. He was calm, and the thoughtful look in his eyes said that he was listening. But his patience was annoying just then. She wanted to be upset. It angered her that he looked relaxed as the rain fell softly around him.

A cold gust of wind reminded her that his advice to go inside was perhaps wise, but she was feeling stubborn and wanted to ignore him as much as possible.

"You know that I work for Ted and Angela. I need to be responsible and pay attention to my tasks." Warren sat down next to her, a few feet away giving her a little extra space.

Galina looked away from him, still angry. She didn't want to say anything, so she didn't.

"I cannot just stop working whenever you get it in your head to come and talk to me." Warren said.

"You haven't had a walk with me in days." Galina said quietly.

"My mother needed me in town, I have been away most evenings." He said without apology.

"You could have told me." Galina said.

"I am sorry to have disappointed you Galina, but I have responsibilities to many people. I have filed for land, I have my job here, I have my mother and young sister to care for. I am trying to get my own homestead soon and as much I would love to spend time with you every day, you have to realize you are expecting a lot from me. I need my job, to raise funds to build a cabin, and start my own farm. How would I do that without this job?" He asked.

Galina tried to listen and be understanding but she failed.

"I guess I am too much of a petulant child to understand such noble thoughts and schemes." Galina said harshly.

Warren stood, he reached down and tried to coax her into taking his hand.

The wind gusted bitterly, and the rain started to pour down with force. The fat raindrops slapping against her skin. She pushed herself up to standing, ignoring his outstretched hand.

"Don't worry Warren, I'll leave you alone to pursue your goals. I will focus on my work." Galina said, her tone hurt and unforgiving.

"It doesn't have to be that way between us, Galina." He reached for her.

"Don't touch me." Galina pulled away from him then ran away toward the house.

Chapter 4

November 1, 1852

Violet Griffen

There was something about the mornings for Violet. It was quiet and the day was new. The kitchen was her domain, her kingdom, and she enjoyed the time there. The gentle glow of the lamp that sprayed the golden light over her counter top. The soft hissing scratch of the white phosphorus match and the small flame that she used to light the tinder in her stove. The quiet time she had as she sat at the kitchen table while the stove brought the room to a steady warmth. Sometimes she would read her Bible in the lamplight, then pray quietly to herself. Then she would make her little plans for the day. There were mouths to feed, and neighbors to greet. Her life as a housekeeper was fulfilling. The house may currently be in chaos once the sun came up, and with it all the souls that lived within it, but for now the house was hers.

Her pale blond hair was still hanging free down her back and she would wait to pin it up until the rest of the house was stirring. If she had been a housekeeper in a different house there would be different rules and expectations. Perhaps it was because it was in the West, where people had a different mindset of equality, but her employers were more like family to her. She was a good employee who never had to be told to work hard, or when to make breakfast, or scolded to redo some task that had been done in a poor or negligent manner. Violet had a certain integrity. She believed whether you work for yourself, or work for others it all was as unto the Lord.

She gathered up all the ingredients for breakfast and pulled the butter and cream from the cold storage in the root cellar behind the back door. She was quiet on her feet and rarely woke anyone with her steps. She had to scrape the bag of sugar in the pantry with a pronged metal scraper to loosen up the crystalized clumps, then she filled the sugar bowl.

Violet would lug in water from the water barrel by the front door and get some heating up on the stove, then start two pots of coffee. Lucas Grant, her employer would finish off at least two cups before he would start his day. His wife Corinne would drink almost two herself, though she said at least two times a week that she should cut back on drinking so much coffee, but she never did. Whatever coffee was left after breakfast Violet would peek out the door and offer the leftover brew to the men working on the addition. They would gladly help her finish it off.

Within an hour the day had begun for everyone else. The babies, Trudie and Caleb, would be fed and Debbie, would tie Trudie in a sling around her and tidy up the house. Sometimes Violet would put Caleb in sling around herself while she pounded out bread or washed the breakfast dishes, he was quiet and sweet and was good company. Today Caleb was taken by his mother, Corinne, to her greenhouse and she would care for him while she worked. She was a good mother and Violet was proud to see her employer handling motherhood and her calling in a special way. It could not be easy.

There was joy found in the sweetness of simple things.

The simple pleasure of the friendships that she had and the visitors that came to the door during the day.

Pepper, the gray and white shepherd dog from next door, still gave the door a scratch once a day to come and visit after his boy, Cooper Harpole, was safely deposited at school. Usually someone left a scrap or two from their plate of bacon or eggs and she sometimes gave this to Pepper as daily treat, but she would never tell.

Violet was happy that Debbie had taken over some of the house cleaning duties and she enjoyed the laundry, which gave Violet more time in her beloved kitchen.

It was an hour past breakfast when the knock came on her door and Reynaldo Legales gave her the warm smile that she loved seeing so very much more than she wanted to admit.

They had been courting for a few months and he took little opportunities to surprise her.

"I was in town delivering some new horses to the livery and stopped in at the grocers" he said, once she had invited him in.

"You want some coffee?" Violet asked, hoping perhaps he had the time to sit and chat with her while she peeled potatoes.

"I cannot stay but I brought you a sweet surprise." He went back outside and brought in two big jugs. His dark eyes brightened, and his skin glowed in the way that Latinos do

27

sometimes. "The last of the season's apple cider."

Before her husband Eddie passed away in the gold fields she would have kissed him for making such a generous and sweet gesture, but Violet just thanked Reynaldo with her expressions and gratitude, but she felt the loss of touching. She had only been a married woman for six months but she had known the intimacy of having a husband to dote upon. She wished she could have been bold and kissed him as a thank you.

"You are most welcome." Reynaldo said as she took the jugs and thanked him several more times. They chit-chatted about the cabin renovations for a few moments and she said goodbye, wishing again for more time as she always did.

How could she feel so happy and strangely empty in the same moment?

A few minutes later Violet sipped hot spiced apple cider. The tart flavor was a delight on her tongue and she closed her eyes a moment to savor it. There was frost on the windows as she looked out, but she could see the far-off barn and the dark shapes of the mountains beyond. The white picket fence that went around the property next door was charming. The horses were wandering the fields and huffing out air that came out in frosty puffs. The grass was turning the drab brown of winter and she knew that soon there would be a blanket of snow.

She thought of Reynaldo again, every little thing about him was making her think of their relationship more and more. The way he tried to teach her Spanish words. The stories of his childhood that he shared with her on the walks they took at night during the summer months. The majority of the memories she had of him were in the light of dusk.

Violet scolded herself whenever she let the old feelings resurface, that he was too good for her, or that she didn't deserve such a handsome man after all that she had been through. It had taken many a prayer for her to accept herself, and therefore, also accept that a man could love her again. Though they hadn't said it, she knew that it was growing between them. Someday soon the words would be said, and Violet would have to face one of the hardest choices of her life. For now though, she could pretend the choice away and just enjoy the growing relationship. His visits were a highlight to her days and she would face the future another day.

She peeled potatoes after she had savored every sip of her mug of cider. She daydreamed a little while she worked, thinking of how she and Reynaldo had begun to court.

It had been several months since they'd begun their relationship and every week he would do something sweet for her. Usually they would walk together along Spring Creek when the weather was fine. He had even ridden over on horseback and worked with her on her riding skills.

Reynaldo was funny and charming and she enjoyed watching him work with the horses at the ranch next door. He was the ranch foreman for a reason. He had patient, adept skills, and for reasons that she couldn't fathom, he was courting her. His dark eyes held deep compassion within them and he always looked at her with respect.

The potatoes were finished, and Violet refilled her cup enjoying another sip of her cider. The cinnamon was warm and fragrant, and she enjoyed the aroma. She set the cup down and got busy with her work. The bread should be kneaded and set into the oven to proof before she finished the lunch she was making for the family.

The cabin at Grant's Grove was bursting at the seams. There was a lot of ruckus as the building was expanding to accommodate the new additions to the family. Debbie Travis was now Violet's righthand, Debbie was a joy to have around, with her quick humor and hard work ethic.

Baby Trudie Grant was about eleven months old and toddling around. Baby Caleb, recently adopted, was almost six months. Debbie was brought on, when Corinne and Lucas had to make a trip to Portland to help Corinne's cousin. She ended up staying on when Corinne and Lucas came home with her cousin's child, after he had been abandoned. It had been heart-breaking to Violet, to know that a woman could do that to a newborn child. But the delight of Caleb was the silver-lining to that dark cloud. He was well loved here. Violet enjoyed each baby in the house and was looking forward to watching them grow up.

Lucas Grant was keeping busy, building on the southern side of the cabin, adding a second story for more bedrooms and a front porch that wrapped around the addition. The parlor would be bigger as well. There was a lot of noise and chaos, but Violet took it in stride. She savored the sweet quiet moments and did her work with pleasure. She was finding her joy again after a few years of hardship and confusion.

She knew change was on the horizon, though, for wasn't it always when life settled in that you knew something would change?

Violet saw Debbie through the door of the parlor, sitting on the floor with Caleb and Trudie, playing with little toys and blocks. They would be having their nap soon after the lunch feeding and then Debbie would join Violet, and they would work and visit. It was a daily routine that Violet enjoyed. Corinne would come back from her morning in the greenhouse and her laboratory and help with the feeding time. Violet was so impressed with Corinne's unending drive to run her business and also be a good mother. Perhaps many would judge her employer, as trying to do too much or going outside what a woman was expected to do. But Violet knew that Corinne was following God's calling in her life. Violet knew that calling trumped all opinions of anyone else.

Violet kneaded the bread dough, enjoying the way it felt in her hands, and the earthy scent of the dough. Her neighbor, Marie Harpole, would be coming by later, with freshly churned butter to trade for a few loaves of fresh bread, also a weekly routine.

She was making an extra loaf now, every few days. She would get to take a walk across the flagstone path and find Reynaldo with the horses. Their eyes would meet, and they would have pleasant things to say to each other, then the next day he would stop by and bring back the tea towel she had wrapped the bread in. It was something to look forward to every day, and she found herself taking a little extra time each morning making sure she looked her best. Debbie was becoming very skilled at braiding Violet's hair and pinning it up attractively whenever Violet would ask. They had some of the best morning talks with a few steaming cups of coffee in the early morning, before the babies would wake. Debbie was full of spunk and had a strong faith, and she fit into the Grant's house with ease.

Violet shaped the loaves and checked the Dutch oven with her hand and slid a few loaves inside. She had a rhythm to her baking and it was second nature to her now. She slid another few loaves in the other side of the Dutch oven. There was another bowl of dough on the counter, to repeat the process once the first loaves were done. She would take a few loaves over to her other neighbor, Angela Greaves, and get in a short visit with Angela and Galina next door. She would get a few eggs in trade and everyone would be happy.

She tidied up the counter and swept away the flour that always found its way to the floor. She wiped at up counter and then washed up the few dishes before she started on the gravy to go with the roasted turkey she had been baking of the oven in the cookstove.

She opened the window after a while, since the heat from all the stoves going made it sometimes feel like a furnace in her kitchen. She enjoyed her space it was where she was needed and fruitful.

Galina Varushkin

Everything was ruined, and she knew that she was to blame.

She was cleaning up the breakfast mess and peeking periodically through the window.

Angela's pregnancy had been causing her to have some sickness in the mornings, so Galina had the quiet house to think a little more often then she liked.

Galina had relived that last conversation with Warren in her mind a thousand times. It had been more than a month of silence between them. She got up every morning, Warren delivered the milk early to the counter. Every day she saw the buckets there and she thought of him, dutifully doing his work, and her pining for his attention but unwilling to apologize.

She knew he had been right, about everything. She had become just like a silly female, chasing after Warren like a fool. She knew she was in a good position, earning a decent income with room and board. Her every need was met, better than she had ever before. She had risked all of that by being irresponsible in front of her employers. She had talked things over with Angela one afternoon, apologizing for her behavior. She was facing the fact that she had a lot to learn about life. Somehow, though, she had never tried to talk to Warren again, to apologize to him. A small part of her still felt that rebellion rise up every time she thought to go out for an evening walk, which she hadn't done since that day weeks ago. Now the weather was turning colder and she had missed the trees turning colors and the mild fall weather because of her own stubbornness.

She finished up the dishes and looked out the window again, seeing the shape of several men far off near the orchards. It was probably Warren and Ted doing some work together. She felt that pang of regret.

Galina heard Angela, with the thump of her walking cane, come nearby and Galina turned and smiled, ready to talk with her.

Angela was wearing a loose dress, her belly large with child. Angela's red hair was loosely braided, she smiled at Galina warmly.

"You are moving better today." Galina said sincerely.

"The cane that Clive found for me is becoming like an extension of me finally. I do despise it sometimes though." Angela made a face in the direction of the cane to be funny.

"Well, you are doing better, that is good news." Galina tried to stay positive with Angela, knowing how hard the recovery process was sometimes. Angela had had several injuries over the last few years, and a recent ankle break over the summer months had put her back in a wheeled invalid chair for more than a month. Being pregnant had added a challenge to the situation as well, but Angela was walking more every day. She had a pink healthy glow to her cheeks and Galina was glad to see it.

"You should get outside today, Ted was told that we may get some snow in the next few days." Angela suggested.

This week she had started a new habit, of taking the horse out and riding the property. Her stubborn refusal had affected more than just herself, but the horse she had been gifted was wasted by sitting in the barn day after day. Ted had given her a few gentle suggestions at dinner and she finally conceded that he had been right. She just didn't understand why, when someone gave her kind and thoughtful suggestions, it always made her want to do the opposite. She enjoyed her horse and there was no reason she shouldn't go riding. Her riding skills were still pretty basic, but Dolly had shown her how to ride over the summer and early fall. Galina always timed it so when she went to the barn she knew that Warren was going to be off doing some other work. It was just easier that way.

"I will go ride once I dry the dishes and get them put away." Galina offered.

"I might go outside with a jacket and sit on the front porch. Get some of the brisk breeze before we get locked inside with the winter coming so soon. I do wish it stayed warm all year." Angela said wistfully.

Galina nodded and got busy with her work. She felt a moment of happiness thinking of riding again, it had been a few days. Yesterday had been busy with laundry. The day before she had been over at Edith's for the afternoon, canning up vegetables and sauces for the pantry. The pantry was full to the brim with winter stores. Ted and Angela had sold many bushels of apples from their trees to the neighbors and the grocers in town. They still had many bushels left over so, Galina was promised another round of canning to do tomorrow. She was going to learn to make apple pie filling and they were going to can that up as well. Violet was going to be joining them and sharing some of her recipes. Angela's kitchen was bigger and so Edith was bringing everything over. The children would be coming, and even a few neighbors said they might stop in. Galina was looking forward to the fun of all the learning, talking and carousing.

Galina was headed off to the barn a few minutes later. Her wool coat kept her warm in the chilly fall breeze. She was excited to get away from her own thoughts for a while and just enjoy nature before a blanket of snow came to the valley.

Sean Fahey

Sean was pleasantly surprised to find out that he enjoyed his new life. He had that small worry for a few months after he arrived in Oregon City, if he was always going to be the wandering kind of man. The thought that a nice cabin and a piece of land was going to make him feel idle and he would disappoint himself and his sister when he got the urge to wander again. He had come to Oregon to reunite with her, after he had so callously sent her away a few years ago in San Francisco. Now, after a few months he felt their relationship was growing. He felt that God had led his steps, through a long path that went from the California Territory, to Ireland, and then back to the western territory of the United States.

He handled a few chores in the barn. There was a small window and the light shown through the paned glass spreading and showing off his tidy space. He grabbed a pitchfork and spread out some fragrant hay in a stall then patted his horse Shipley on the nose. He took a good look around to make certain everything was in its place. It had taken him a few months but with some hired help his small barn was built. He had been told by several new friends and neighbors that they would gladly help him with a barn raising, but he actually enjoying paying them for the help. He had the money and knew they all could use the funds for emergencies or to be able to add to their own farms in some way, be it more livestock, or extra food from the grocer. He hung up the pitchfork and put away the few tools on a newly built table. A new friend in town, Amos Drays the carpenter, had built it for him and Sean was pleased. He hung a kerosene lantern, unlit, on a hook near the front door of the barn. It would be there, if he needed it.

His barn was just big enough. There was room for a wagon, which he needed to purchase, instead of the one he kept renting from the livery, and his horse Shipley, and an extra stall in case. He had spent a good amount of money at Clive's store getting new tools and even a new hunting rifle just last week.

He had set up a few empty tins on a fence post and fired off a few rounds to check his aim. He was very excited to know within a few days he would have some company at the house. His cabin was cozy, and he enjoyed his time there, but the nights were quiet; perhaps a little too quiet as his thoughts seems to bounce off the logs. His thoughts weren't always good ones, and he really missed having his companion. The death of Ol' Willie had been such a dramatic change and was the impetus of many changes in his life. Most of them were good changes but the loneliness was real. When he spent so many hours alone his thoughts began to stir, and all his mistakes would weigh heavy on his heart. He wondered often if there was any way to have another companion is his life. Recent news was circulating that his hopes were about to be fulfilled. With winter approaching he knew that he could use some company to keep the walls from closing in on him. Thankfully, his friend Clive Quackenbush was doing something about it.

Clive had been a busy man over the summer and had a few dogs on order from several sources on the East Coast. Word around the communities nearby was that there was not enough dogs to keep the breeding stock healthy. Too much inbreeding from the few dogs available was causing sickness. Several dogs had been put down because of it. A meeting of the local communities got together and worked with Clive and his contacts and a massive project was undertaken. Along with a livestock order several orders for companion and working dogs was placed via telegram to states back East.

Clive Quackenbush, the local purveyor of many good things, was telegraphed last week that the first of several orders would be arriving by ferry. Young dogs, of many breeds as well as stock were arriving all along the Oregon coastal towns. There were promises that each community was receiving dogs that were not siblings or related in any way in order to prevent any more health issues with animals.

Sean had plunked down his money eagerly to get a young beagle from Michigan. Sean's close friend and neighbor, Mack, was well versed in the breed and ordered one as well. Mack got the female and Sean got a male with the promise of teaching Sean how to train the creature to hunt and obey commands.

"Beagles are pretty good to have around too. They keep your feet warm." Mack chuckled.

Sean was anticipating having some company around. He had visitors sometimes during the week, and of course Shipley his horse, named after his old friend, went with him on long rides through the rugged landscape; however, his cabin was growing quieter and quieter every night. He felt lonely for company and a dog was a good start. He felt that nudge in his chest that he had other thoughts, but he ignored the sensation. He was still new in town. His sister was nearby and he had budding friendships to be thankful for. There was a great church down the road a piece too. He was blessed... but he couldn't help thinking for a moment of that certain woman who intrigued him more than any other.

***

Dolly Bouchard

She set the pen on the cloth to clear the ink from the tip and then set it into the cup on her small writing desk. She had three new jars of ink next to her, a recent purchase from the fancy goods store. She would have to scrub her blackened fingers from the drips of ink that always found a way onto her fingers even though she was careful.

She was happy that the book was near completion. The woodworker in town had a friend in Portland who was making the woodcuts for the drawings that she had done. Corinne had done a few but once she saw Dolly's drawing, she had been given the task to do most of the artwork for the book. They would soon be sending the woodblocks and the copy of the printed material to Boston. They were being sent to a publisher there who had agreed to publish a limited run of their book. It was an exciting time.

Dolly cast her mind back to that fateful journey she had made to return to her home in Oregon City. She had been chosen amongst the Shoshone tribe to travel with Corinne Grant almost four years before, to learn from her and also to teach Corinne about the herbal and plant medicines of the Shoshone tribe. It made perfect sense for Dolly to go with these white people, according to the tribe leaders. That meeting had been very intense. They had just been under attack from a rival tribe the day before. She had been so young, but when she heard that they wanted someone to go; Dolly, who was normally silent at these meetings, spoke up forcefully. She knew a few words of English from her mother, and she was one of the best of the young people at finding plants for medicine. There had always been a part of her that knew that she wanted to explore the white man's culture, since her father was white. The surprised faces of the chieftain and the others had been comical. Dolly could still remember the nerves she had when she stood up and volunteered to travel with the wagon train.

"I will go and learn and teach others of what I have been taught." She had spoken in the Shoshone language.

They had agreed and some discussion was brought up about coming to retrieve her once she had spent a few years in Oregon. Dolly, whose name was Bluebird, had taken on the name Dolly when she arrived in Oregon City, since it sounded similar to her name in the Hopi' language of her mother. Her mother had been rescued, as a young woman, by the Shoshone. She had married a French trapper. Dolly had felt for a long time that she hadn't really belonged to any tribe. She was not really Shoshone nor was she white. She was something in between.

The tribe had fulfilled their promise and sent two Shoshone tribesmen to retrieve her the year before. Dolly had gone with them but it had been a mistake. One of the tribesmen had grown violent and Dolly had escaped, having to find her way through the wilderness back home.

To many she may indeed be a half-breed, she thought. But in her heart she knew that she belonged in Oregon City. She had a purpose here, even if she flitted from home to home. She was feeling more and more like she belonged here. Her faith in God was what kept her mind at peace. She wasn't sure that she could ever live the Shoshone tribal life again.

She heard through rumors and newspaper reports that many missionaries and ministers were here in the West, teaching different tribes about what the Shoshone called 'White man's God.' They were offering schooling to the children of the tribes. Dolly prayed daily for her tribe and hoped that someday they would understand why her faith was so important to her. Someday, maybe a child that had grown up in her tribe would see her book and learn from it, reading the words and thus fulfilling her promise to share her knowledge with her former tribe.

Dolly and Corinne had spent several years putting these pages together and it was a good start, but Dolly knew that she wanted to know more. There were always more things to learn and she felt like she was finally doing the work that God intended for her.

She no longer had any doubts. The Shoshone tribe that had raised her was forever in her thoughts, but they were her past, not her future. With every drawing and page she wrote, she was honoring what they had taught her but now she finally felt free.

When Dolly had escaped from the Shoshone men who were taking her back to the tribe, she had been so frightened and confused. The more she prayed and leaned on God the more she realized that she was allowed to love her own life. She still enjoyed some parts of her past; the hunting and enjoying every part of nature but now she saw it differently. She saw God in every living thing, His divine creation.

She dipped the tip into the ink a little, closed the ink with a cork and dabbed at the pen after she drew in the final few lines of a stem. She was pleased with the drawing of the milk thistle. It would probably be a good one for the book and she would allow it to dry overnight.

She had told Corinne that she would go into the lab today

after lunch, she had a bowl of mash that would be ready today to make the alcohol they used for distilling the oils they would make over the winter months. Corinne and Clive had worked on a deal with a citrus grower in the California Territory, to send oranges, limes, and lemons to Oregon City. Even boxes of peels would be useful. They expected a shipment to arrive by ferry in the next few weeks. They didn't talk about the alcohol they made for the lab, since it was for lab use, but they had informed the sheriff. He gave them permission to make it, as long as none of it was used for consumption. Corinne and Dolly had fervently promised, and it was always kept well hidden from anyone who was hired to do extra work in the lab during the busy lavender harvest time.

Dolly fetched some warm water from the kitchen stove and chatted with Chelsea Grant, who was quietly churning butter while the kids were busy with their father, Russell, in the barn.

"I am heading out soon to the lab." Dolly said. She grimaced and held up her stained hands for Chelsea to see.

"If you use the lemon soap and add some salt, it may help to scrub it away a little better." Chelsea chuckled a little. "Did you have a good morning?"

"Yes," Dolly smiled. "I think I finished a drawing. I had to start over six times, getting it perfect is a lot harder than I ever expected. I do not want the woodcarver to fix my mistakes." Dolly always spoke carefully and her grasp of English got better every day.

"Are you leaving tonight to stay at the Greaves?" Chelsea asked. She stopped her churning and rubbed her shoulders and shook out her arms.

"Yes, I was invited to stay a few days, they are doing some canning and I want to learn more recipes. My cooking is getting better every time I do these kinds of things." Dolly said. She pulled down the lemon soap as Chelsea had suggested. She carved off a chunk and set it to the side of the bowl, she then got a spoonful of the salt from a canister in the cupboard. She dunked her hand in the warm water, sprinkled it with the salt, then placed the soap chunk in her salted hand. She then dunked her clean hand in the water and began to lather up the soap. The salt was gritty, and she was pleased to see the foamy soap turning grey as the ink stains were getting

38

smaller. "The salt is helping." Dolly couldn't help but smile.

Chelsea laughed a little and went back to her butter churning. "I am glad it is helping. I will be going to the canning party myself. I have some pantry goods that need canning, it has been difficult to get everything done this fall. Knowing that the kids won't be underfoot will help to get things done. Usually I go over and do some with Violet but with their cabin getting an addition it is even more chaotic over there."

Dolly did a second round of scrubbing and though it wasn't perfect it was a vast improvement. Her hands smelled like fresh lemons.

"I saw that they are tearing a portion off of the roof when I was there a few days ago, they have logs piled up and are adding a…" Dolly paused searching for the word. "Is it story? That doesn't seem like the right word."

Chelsea smiled. "A second story, yes, it means a second level to the house."

Dolly nodded. "Words that have two meanings always bother me." She frowned.

"They bother me sometimes too." Chelsea was always so good at helping Dolly understand things. Dolly appreciated her patience.

Dolly ate a simple lunch and packed up a few things for later and said goodbye to Chelsea. She rode her horse Clover, a gift from Corinne Grant, over to the lab a mile down Spring Creek Road. She led the horse to the barn and waved at a few of the ranch hands that were working near the barn. The air was cold, but she didn't think it was going to snow yet. It would be soon though. She glanced to the east and saw the light gray clouds, and then to the west. No dark clouds were on the horizon.

The Grant cabin was a different sight, with men working on the roof, three logs already forming part of the second level. A pile of logs was near the cabin and a few windows were set against the side. Men were making a racket with pegs and hammers. Lucas waved as Dolly rounded the corner of the fence-line of the Harpole property. Dolly waved back.

Her boots crunched over some dried leaves and she shoved her hands in her pockets to keep them warmer. Her mittens were old and not as warm as they were the year before.

She saw Violet, standing outside the front door, scooping water from the water barrel.

"Hello Violet." Dolly said with a wave.

"I have warm apple cider on the stove." Violet said with a smile and a wave.

Dolly couldn't resist the offer and was a few minutes later to her task than she intended. Corinne wouldn't be concerned, she was inside enjoying a cup also. They had a lovely chat amidst the chaos.

Corinne handed Caleb to Debbie, who was now working for the Grants as wet nurse and helping around the house. She placed a kiss on his sleepy head.

"He is definitely ready for his nap. He was up so many times last night. He is getting a tooth." Corinne said. "I don't know how well he will sleep with the racket on the roof but we can try."

"Oh, Corinne, you are just being stubborn again," Violet said. She was smiling as she poured out a cup of the apple cider and handed Corinne a cup, then one to Dolly.

"I know." Corinne said with a tired smile.

Dolly was confused. "How is Corinne being stubborn?" She asked carefully. She wondered if she was mistaken to ask after the words were out of her mouth. Dolly frowned.

"Oh, I am stubborn as a mule sometimes. Marie was just here, offering me a chance to stay with them while the men get the job finished on the roof. I declined and then instantly regretted it." Corinne took a sip and closed her eyes. "This is so good." Corinne sighed.

Dolly smiled and sipped her own mug. The spiced cider was delicious and was the perfect remedy for a cold day. She thought about Corinne, who was always so willing to admit that she was wrong. It was a strength that she appreciated, they had been friends for over four years, and Dolly was always inspired by Corinne's strength.

"Marie was kind to offer." Dolly said. She was trying harder to speak more, to let people know her, though it was a challenge. She would often forget to speak, even though her mind was always so full of thoughts.

"Yes, she was kind." Corinne said. Dolly was sitting next to Corinne and was happy when Corinne reached over and grabbed her hand in a gesture of friendship.

"You know, it wouldn't be a terrible thing. It is not like it will be a huge imposition to walk down the path to get there. Marie would be over the moon kissing on her grandbabies." Violet said with a smile.

Dolly was amazed that Violet could be so honest, even with a mild criticism. Dolly had seen this kind of thing before here in the Grant house. Violet was family and was able to voice her opinion as an equal. It was good to see how these people worked together.

"Let me finish my cider, I will walk over and talk with Marie. Just for all your sass you get more work. I will need some help getting the children's things hauled over there." Corinne gave Violet a well-meaning glare.

"I was already planning what to tackle first. Since my room no longer has a roof and I am sleeping at Chelsea's tonight I can finish up my cooking here this afternoon and leave the cabin to the men." Violet put her mug into a bucket of sudsy water. "I will be helping Chelsea get ready for the canning party."

Dolly finished her mug and Violet swiped it away before she attempted to wash it.

"Thank you for the treat, Violet." Dolly said. She turned to Corinne. "I will be in the lab this afternoon."

"That is great, I checked, and our project is ready to go." Corinne gave Dolly a wink.

Dolly smiled as she bundled into her wool coat and mittens. She would enjoy her work today.

Chapter 5

Clive Quackenbush

It was certainly a pleasure to be alive after having such a beautiful woman bid him farewell that brisk morning. Clive gave his dear bride Olivia a sweet goodbye kiss as he broke for town in the early morning. He was expecting the ferry to arrive today, and it was no surprise when the ferry whistle blew as Clive was just a few steps away from the livery in town. He gave his horse a pat on the rump as he left him with the attendant.

"I'll just be a few minutes, I'll need a wagon. Let a few of the guys around know I will need some help down at the ferry today. All hands needed." Clive knew the word would spread fast. Clive always paid well and the young men would gather to be useful. The town was certainly buzzing in anticipation, knowing the cargo that was coming in. Even those that didn't have an order in might be heading over to see the hullaballoo.

Clive had left a stack of leather collars, ropes cut for leashes and a few small crates for any of the small pets that came along. There was always a chance for a few odds and ends to arrive from his suppliers. They knew that Clive would pay for any extras things they sent along, Clive enjoyed the surprises. His customers did too.

Clive's son JQ was leaning against the counter, a steaming cup in his hands.

"Heard the whistle, should be quite a day." His son, now in his early forties, said with a grin.

Clive chuckled identically. "Let's hope for the best."

"I had a dream about chasing dogs through the woods last night." JQ said and took another slurping sip. "Ah, hot..."

Clive laughed good-humoredly at his son. He could have said something, but instead he just smirked for a long moment. JQ set his cup down and stood up straight and stretched.

"You ready to wrangle some dogs?" JQ asked with a smirk of his own.

Clive gave a nod to the affirmative and was ready after he took a few more sips of coffee. This was going to be quite a day.

All of Clive's and JQ's suspicions were realized when they reached the edge of the river docking area. News had spread quickly once the whistle had blown and the crowd gathered was larger than usual. Clive was glad for a few extra hands as JQ handled the paperwork.

Clive was busy looking at dogs, checking their sex and breed, while JQ checked his orders. Millie had come along and was writing out tags for each leash or crate for the names of the owners of the pre-ordered canines. Sean Fahey was there early as well and joined in while helping. The yapping of dogs, wagging tails and general hubbub was exciting and chaotic.

A few extra wagons had been rented from the livery and the beds of two wagons were filled within an hour. A few families were excited to see that cats had arrived as well and fresh orders were placed, first come first serve. Several of the cats would be used as house cats, but a majority would be used for a much more practical purpose. Keeping barns free of rodents was a high priority. Cats on a property kept the bunnies out of gardens and mice and birds out of the barn lofts.

Clive was so pleased with the extras he had received from his suppliers back East. Three brass bed frames and mattresses were paid for cash on delivery, and Clive happily plunked the money down for them, knowing they could easily sell to a few people in town. A shipment of fancy glass lanterns, 3 crates full, was a pleasant surprise as well, since he hadn't had those in his shop since the previous spring.

Sean took charge of the dogs in the wagons and headed back to the storefront with them while Clive mulled over the crates with the ferry operator. Every crate had to be inventoried before being signed off on.

Clive looked through boxes of buttons, ribbons, flatware, reams of cotton fabric, linen, spices, silk thread, colored dyes in glass bottles, matches, a few pieces of jewelry, 5 gold watches, packets of flower seeds, bulbs, and three separate crates of tools without handles. Clive dove into the work, trying hard to get the paperwork done in short order. He knew in the back of his mind the chaos that waited for him back at the store. Everyone in town and in nearby communities would be interested in this shipment of goods, especially the canines. This was likely the last big shipment to arrive before the winter snows set in.

Clive settled the payment with the ferry operator and loaded the crates into the last two wagons with a dock worker's help. The crowd had cleared considerably by the time he was finished. He was likely to see that same crowd that just left, waiting for him in town. Main Street was probably going to be congested.

Clive pulled the scarf out from under his wagon seat as the cold wind picked up on the ride back into town.

He heard the barking and crowd noise as he got closer to town. He saw there were at least thirty people gathered around the wagons in front of the store.

It was going to be a long day.

Sean Fahey

It was strangely exhilarating to spend the morning gathering and herding dogs and cats with Clive and JQ; it was so very different than his normal existence. He was beginning to get accustomed to homesteading and he enjoyed some of the freedoms it offered. It was different than he suspected as a younger man. His years trapping the Snake River with Ol' Willie had led him to live a rather nomadic existence. Having neighbors and set chores was never something he had thought much about. He had thought for years that living off the land meant something far different than his new reality was showing him.

He still had time for things he enjoyed, like trapping and hunting. But he also enjoyed some of the new activities. He had planted a few fruit trees that he had purchased from his sister's friend Corinne at her greenhouse. He knew the peach and pear trees would eventually bear delicious fruit. He spent a good portion of time chopping wood to stockpile for the winter months. He also delivered extras to the shop workers in town, who did not have time in their schedules to do this kind of work. The dense woods had plenty of deadfall and he never had need for chopping down any living trees so far. It gave him plenty of opportunity over the summer and fall to get the lay of the land.

Today felt like a big day. Getting a new companion for his quiet cabin was going to be a big change. He was not worried about the added work, because he knew, in the long run, he would be better off having a dog for a variety of reasons.

Clive finally arrived, and more chaos followed. Sean helped to expedite getting dogs to owners. Mack had given Sean a pat on the back when he picked up his female beagle. Sean handed over the leash and Clive checked the name and dog off of his list.

"I will meet you at your place in a few hours, Sean. We can start on the basics," Mack promised. "I am happy to see that both our dogs are old enough to start breeding next year." Mack laughed and chatted for a minute about the adventures of raising pups from birth, a daunting task to be certain.

Mack had purchased all the necessities for his dog and said he would be stopping by the butcher shop for some extra meat and bones with a promise to grab a few bones for Sean's dog. Sean thanked him and waved as Mack walked away with an excited dog; her white-tipped tail swishing happily.

Once every name was checked off the list Clive gave him the go ahead to get on home with his new companion. Sean tried to pay for the extra leashes and a clay bowl for watering, but Clive declined.

"You earned it today. I appreciate your help." Clive smiled in that way that always managed to make him feel a bit taller. He was a man that Sean hoped would be a life-long friend.

Sean saw there was a stack of smaller crates still in a wagon, with a few of the cats, and several smaller dogs still inside. He shrugged, thinking that Clive had a plan for these. Sean went to the side of the wagon where his own dog was waiting.

"JQ is heading out to make some deliveries of cats and dogs to some out-of-towners that had placed orders. Millie will hold down the fort here." Clive gave Sean a wave and his head bent to look over his list one more time.

Sean walked around the side where Clive had told him to go to retrieve his own dog. Sean was happier and more excited than he had been in a long while.

The dog looked up at Sean with big brown eyes. He was sitting rather patiently until Sean came closer. Then he started tugging and jumping up, eager for some contact.

"It is okay fella I'm taking you home," Sean soothed. He reached and gave the pooch a pat on the head. He calmed and sat at Sean's feet, his tail swishing along the ground.

Sean was trying to think of a name, but his mind was a blank after the chaos of the morning.

"I will give you a name soon fella." Sean gave the dog a scratch behind his ears and was rewarded with what could easily be ascertained as a doggy grin. Sean couldn't help but get attached. This was a pleasant feeling.

Sean headed home and by tying the long rope to the saddle horn, he let the dog follow along. His horse Shipley had been nervous at first but then adapted to it well. Sean kept the riding pace slow and was happy to get all three of them home safely.

Sean had tied the dog up to the edge of the fence and got Shipley settled into his stall. The dog was whining and chewing on the rope he was tied with. Sean was pleased to see the dog drop the rope when he got closer.

"Alright, boy, let me give you a quick tour." Sean felt more than a little foolish at first, talking aloud to his dog, telling him about the property.

"This is my garden. It is rather pathetic at this point, but I plan on planting a few more things in it this next spring. Try not to dig anything up, alright?" Sean laughed at the happy expression of the dog. Who seemed to be enthralled by his every word.

"This is the barn," He started but stopped when he heard some chuckling.

He turned to see Dolly Bouchard standing a few feet away.

"Are you giving the dog a tour?" She asked, she always spoke slow and pronounced every word carefully.

"Well, yes," Sean said, and was surprised to realize that he was blushing. This woman perplexed him at every turn.

"I heard the dog delivery was coming today. So, I spent the afternoon doing a bit of hunting. I have a meal or two for your new friend here." Dolly said simply. Her face was always so calm, it was hard to tell what she was thinking.

Sean wondered if he should think anything of her gesture. "That was kind of you." He said and brought the dog closer to her. The dog was very interested in sniffing her.

She handed the linen bag over to Sean and knelt down to give the dog her full attention.

She let herself be sniffed and gave the dog's head and neck a thorough scrub with her fingers. The dog was in heaven. Sean could have watched her petting his dog all day, just so she would stay. He chided himself for always wanting something from her, especially since she seemed to deem him as a friend only.

46

"Do you plan to use him for hunting?" She looked up to Sean, her lips formed a grin and her brown eyes were sparkling in the sunshine. He was distracted for a moment before he could answer.

"Uh, well… yes… Mack, my neighbor, has experience with this breed, so he will be teaching me the basics. We intend to breed our beagles next year." Sean said. He wondered if women did this on purpose, look at a man with smiling eyes so they lose their wits.

"Oh…" She said, nearly singing it. She turned her attention back to the dog. "I think I would like a puppy. Though I wander a bit too much for keeping a dog. Perhaps I will just have to visit this guy often." She planted a kiss on the furry head of the dog. The dog responded by rolling to his back, so she could rub his belly.

Sean chuckled. She had completely taken over the dog at this point. "You know you are welcome any time." He meant that more than words could express. He could have said. 'Come stay forever,' but that would have scared her off for certain.

Dolly looked up at him for a moment, that smirk still on his face and she locked eyes with his for just a flicker of a second. She was considering his offer, to come any time, and perhaps she was considering him too. It took his breath away. He certainly hoped that his jaw wasn't gaping open like an idiot.

"You found yourself a keeper here." She gave the dog one last pet and stood.

Sean nodded. "Thanks for the game." He lifted the linen sack she gave him. He wished he could say something sweet to her. Something that would express that he was interested in her, but he remained quiet.

"Let me know when you are wanting to take this guy on a hunt, I would love to tag along and see him in action," she smiled.

Sean nodded dumbly.

"You be sure to keep an eye on him today, in the cabin I mean. Every time he sniffs the ground take him outside. Otherwise you will be cleaning up a lot of messes." She looked to the dog. "You be a good fellow for Sean, now."

The dog was looking up to her with adoration. Sean was just pleased to hear her say his name. He felt like a silly boy.

"Mack told me similar information. It should be an interesting few days." Sean laughed.

"You boys have fun together, I am heading back to talk to

Corinne, I am thinking of gathering up some pine boughs and doing a batch of pine oil. We are running low and with winter coming on the oils can help with colds and lung complaints." She said.

"You have a good ride, looks like snow is coming soon." Sean was amazed at Dolly and her knowledge of things that he knew little about.

She waved and walked to her horse that was tied up to the hitching post he had in the front of his cabin.

She wore a green dress, a simple frock really, not the full bell gowns that women wore to fancier events or to Sunday service. Her skin was a pretty brown tone that showed her Hopi heritage. She looked good in everything she wore, from a fancy dress to the leathers and trousers she wore while hunting. He knew while watching her ride away, that he was a lost man.

Once she was gone he finished the rest of the tour with the dog. He was pleased to see the dog do his business in the grass and gave him some praise. He kept the leash on him and took him inside the cabin.

"Okay fella, you heard the lady. You need to learn to hunt, so we get to spend some more time with her. I am counting on you." Sean closed the front door and let the dog off the leash. He placed the game on the counter and let the dog wander and sniff everything. Sean enjoyed watching the dog's tail swish frantically as he discovered his new home.

Sean lit a fire in the fireplace and then one in the cookstove. He was going to cook up the game and have a bit to eat for lunch and give some to the dog once it cooled enough.

Sean put down the clay bowl that Clive had given him and filled it with some water and the dog lapped it up. After about an hour he was sniffing around, and Sean took him outside to the patch of grass beside his cabin. Sean gave him praise and brought him back in, unbuckled the leash, and the process began again. Mack had told him the best way to train a dog is by being aware and consistent. The first few days would be the most important for creating good habits or bad ones.

Mack came by a few hours later with his dog. She had similar colors, the dark chocolate brown with black around her legs. Sean's dog had a few more white patches with a white triangle on his head. The dogs were happy to see each other, and Sean's dog was enthusiastic about Mack too.

"My dog seems to love everyone." Sean said with a chuckle. He told Mack how Dolly had been by earlier and was well loved by the dog already.

"She promised to come hunting with us if he learns to hunt." Sean said and couldn't help but smile.

Mack had known about Sean's interest in Dolly. It was obviously to anyone who had seen him around her.

"So, you get to be Cupid and bring your sad owner a chance with the pretty lady." Mack gave the dog some affection.

"Indeed, he might just help me out on that score." Sean thought hard for a minute. "Perhaps I should just call him Cupid."

Mack laughed, deep in his chest, and Sean couldn't help but join in.

The dog seemed to like the name well enough and both dogs danced between the two of them, getting their leashes all tangled.

They got them untangled and began training in the open area in front of the barn. It was an hour well spent. Both dogs were responsive and willing to be obedient. Sean was very pleased.

Mack promised to come back again the next day. Sean and Cupid went back inside. Sean was able to get Cupid to sit and wait for his supper by his bowl. His dog's brown eyes looking up to him. It was a great feeling. This decision had been a good one.

Sophia Greaves

Sophia Greaves heard the bell in the shop ring in the room next to her. There was a glass door between the parlor and the shop and she enjoyed glancing over while she worked to see who was stopping by. Sometimes she was fully immersed in the details of the lace she was making, and she would go hours without looking up, but today she was distracted. She was making simple lace ribbons and she found herself wishing she was able to leave. She had been cooped up all week, and she was tired of these walls.

Sophia moved the silk thread and pin cushion out of her lamplight to the table beside her. She stood and stretched, letting out a small squeak like a cat.

"You seem antsy today, dear."

Sophia looked over at her mother. Her mother was frowning,

49

and she had spectacles on her nose, just for when she was doing fine detail work. Her mother's blond hair was done up extra special. She was going to a church meeting later on.

"I was wondering if I could go and visit with Ted and Angela." Sophia needed some fresh air.

"It is cold out." Sophia's mother said curtly.

Sophia looked out the front parlor window, to the main street of Oregon City. The bushes in the front of the shop weren't moving so it wasn't too windy.

Sophia fought the urge to sigh in frustration. She looked to her mother. Amelia Greaves was an intense person on most days. She was opinionated and ever since she had been widowed she had an edge to her moods. Sophia wondered if a day would come when her mother didn't try to run her life. Sophia was sixteen now. There would certainly be a day when Sophia was trusted enough to make her own decisions. The last few months had been tense, her mother reigning her in more and more as the leaves changed. Sophia had barely seen her friend Galina since the early fall and now with colder weather threatening she knew her mother would get even more protective. Had she always been this way, or just since they moved out West? Sophia wondered if her mother still thought of her as a five-year-old girl.

"The weather is chilly, but I think we'll have a little break before the snow falls." Sophia said and wanted to mention that once the snow falls they would be trapped inside for a long period.

The bell rang in the shop next door and Sophia looked over. Her mother looked up and took off her glasses. Sophia noticed her mother's face was stern and she was winding up to lecture. Sophia knew her mother's moods and faces, so she prepared herself for the lecture that was coming.

A moment before Sophia looked away Clive Quackenbush was looking through the glass door between the parlor and the shop. He knocked politely. Sophia smiled, never being happier to have an interruption.

"It's Clive!" Sophia waved him in with a smile.

Sophia looked to her mother, her demeanor completely changed. They all loved Clive. She was so happy that Clive had come in and married her aunt. He was such a good man. He had given them such an incredible opportunity to sell their lace here to the ladies of the west. But also, he lifted their spirits in so many ways.

50

"Greetings to all, on this fine day." Clive said, as he took off his hat. "Much ado about town today." His silvery hair was laying long over his ears. His mustache smiled to match the one he always had on his face.

"We are always happy to see you, Clive." Amelia Greaves said, her voice was all honey coated and sweet when it wanted to be. Sophia noticed that she saved that tone for everyone except her lately.

Sophia took a few quick steps and gave a bear hug to Clive. He was just the person to cheer up her mood.

"I wasn't sure you all heard about the news around town." Clive was gestured to sit in a parlor chair and he gladly took a seat. Sophia sat in the chair next to him.

"I noticed that there were a lot of people on the road this morning." Sophia said. She had found herself wishing she wasn't always stuck working when things were happening in town.

"Yes, well, the ferry came in today. All the dogs I ordered finally arrived. A lot of folks now have a pet of some sort. I got a few cats as well. The barns in our valley will have less critters mucking through the hay bales." Clive smiled. "That is why I came. I got a surprise for my dear Olive, and I was wondering if I could steal Sophia for a few days. She can stay with us." He looked hopefully to Amelia.

Amelia grinned and gave a look to Sophia. "Well, I think perhaps it is good timing. Sophia is needing a change of scenery. She is a bit distracted lately."

Sophia was glad, but felt her mother's gaze, even behind her smile she was annoyed with her daughter. Sophia wasn't sure what she could do to keep her mother happy.

"If she wants to pack up a few things I can chat with you for a few minutes." Clive winked at Sophia but turned back to Amelia for approval.

Sophia saw that her mother nodded. Sophia wordlessly got up and headed for the staircase. She did need a change of scenery. The thought of being cooped up here all winter long was giving her the blues. Her mother was perpetually in mourning. First, she had lost her husband. Then Ted got married to Angela, now her sister Olivia was married. Sophia felt that she was her mother's last person to cling to, and the clinging was going to be the death of Sophia.

Sophia had a trunk packed full of petticoats and a few dresses all ready to go in ten minutes. She packed a few bonnets in hat boxes and felt accomplished. She would be able to go to Sunday service with them in style. Since Clive and Olive went to the Spring Creek Church then she could see a few, gentleman that she had on her 'possibilities list' in her journal. She also packed that in her trunk. She was old enough now to keep her eyes open and start thinking about the day when she could have a home of her own.

Clive was waiting for her and her mother seemed to be in good spirits.

"You bundle up from the wind." Her mother said.

"I will mother." Sophia smiled and kept her tone very light and bubbly. She was willing to concede to anything now.

Sophia went to the hall closet and got out her thick wool coat, her scarf and mittens. She tied a sturdy bonnet on her head and put on the scarf and mittens to prove to her mother that she was compliant.

Clive grabbed up her trunk and Sophia picked up her hat boxes clumsily with the mittens on.

"You have a lovely time. I will stay busy. I have a meeting with the women's group at church, and perhaps I will plan a lunch with Millie Quackenbush for tomorrow." Amelia gave a wink to Clive, which seemed out of character.

Sophia wondered what they had spoken of.

There was no wind to speak of when they got outside but the air was brisk. Sophia was cozy warm in her coat, so she wasn't worried about catching a chill.

"I have a few deliveries to make once we drop off your trunks to the house. Perhaps you and Olive can tag along?" Clive asked.

Sophia smiled broadly, she was ready for any adventure that Clive was willing to take her on.

She saw the crates in the back of the wagon next to her trunk and heard the proof of animals being in them. She was intrigued to know what Clive was up to.

This was going to be a day full of fun, she just knew it.

Violet Griffen

Violet had spent a few minutes with her neighbor Marie and

she walked the path with her back toward the ranch next door. Marie had her loaves of fresh baked bread and Violet had a loaf to give to Reynaldo.

Marie was chatting about the weather and her children, excited that her grandbabies were coming to stay for a few days. Violet enjoyed her company and also the sound of leaves as they crunched beneath her feet. The weather was bound to snap soon, for the smell of snow was in the air.

Marie gave a little wave as Violet headed toward the new barn. It was built in early summer and Violet enjoyed the look of it. Some good memories of the moments she had first realized that Reynaldo was interested in her. The glances and the awkward moments always came to her when she thought of those days. It was the start of something.

She walked the path and saw some horses being put through their paces. Then she saw him. He was a specimen, his rich tanned skin and dark coloring were easy on the eyes, but she also knew his heart and it was one the most attractive parts of him. He had a rock-solid faith in the Lord, and saw the good in people, better than anyone. He saw beyond people's scars and flaws. That is perhaps why he was so very good at his job. He had some pretty amazing patience with the toughest or meanest horse and they were eating out of his hand in no time.

Violet couldn't help but smile when she saw him wave. They had taken their relationship very slowly as he had promised her months ago. But the thudding of her heart was telling her that she was nearly ready for more.

He met her along the edge of the tall fence and climbed over with remarkable speed.

"You are looking well today." Reynaldo said. He took off his hat and gave her a grin. As always, he was the charmer.

"You are looking well yourself Rey." Violet said. Suddenly she wished, not for the first time, that they could spend every day together.

She handed over the bread. He placed a hand over hers and held it for a long moment. He was making her heart beat fast again.

"I look forward to this every time." He said sincerely. "Every time I see you, I realize I need to see you more."

"I was just thinking something similar." Violet admitted.

He took the bread and she felt the loss of contact profoundly.

53

She had been married before, and the loving connection, the kisses and the affection were something she longed for again, in her heart.

"Could I come by after supper?" Reynaldo asked.

"I would love that, but the cabin is not ready for guests tonight" Violet said. "I am staying with Chelsea and Russell Grant down the road for a few days. I'll be around the next few days off and on."

Violet saw a few of the work hands watching them. Everyone knew about them, and more than once she was teased about the slow pace of her and Reynaldo's relationship. Sometimes she wished that they would have more private time together. In her mind that meant one thing. In her heart was budding the wish, that Reynaldo was thinking what she was thinking. Perhaps she felt that change was coming, because her hopes were that Reynaldo wanted more than courting. She said goodbye and tossed a look over her shoulder at him as she waked away. It was getting harder and harder to say goodbye.

Chapter 6

Milton Vaughn

Milton Vaughn settled his bags at his feet as he watched the muddy river flow by. The steamship was coming to a stop soon. He took a glance at his gold pocket watch and saw that it was later than he had hoped for. He winked at a well-dressed woman that was nearby, who seemed to be admiring him. He knew he was handsome and he took great care in his appearance. His well-tailored tweed suit made him look European, he thought with pride. His brown polished shoes were of good quality and his bowler hat had two smart hawk feathers in the hat band that made him stand out. His intention was always to stand out in a crowd.

He hummed very quietly as he waited, trying to keep his mind occupied while he waited to leave the boat. He was not a patient soul and sitting still bothered him on most days. The woman he winked at had looked away at first, but she was starting to glance in his direction again. It amused him, and he couldn't help but smirk. She wasn't very attractive in the face, but she had a certain charm about her. The West was not well populated with decent women, so any woman under the age of thirty that was decent to look at was a pleasant surprise.

He pulled the gold watch out again and chided himself for checking so often.

He was glad to be away from the stink of San Francisco, getting his business affairs wrapped up, and his suppliers all set up for the store he had in Oregon City. His partner had been here for many months, but he was ready to make certain that the store was set up properly. His partner was really just a barber after all. Running a Drug and Sundries store was a serious business and had to be maintained properly. Milton had big plans for expanding up the Pacific Coast and making his fortune. Finding partners was his aim and this was a good place to start.

He disembarked from the ferry shortly after it landed. The woman who was glancing his way had left and was out of his mind now. He was focused on getting his trunks loaded to a wagon for hire and getting to town.

The air was cooler here that San Francisco and he was eager to get warm and then get to work. He knew that the shop he owned was on the main street.

He found a wagon and driver and settled on the price for the ride to town. He waited as the driver loaded everything for him.

He took stock of his surroundings; the trees were mostly bare and he could see the mountains beyond them. The white caps were crisp against the dark stone mountains. It was exhilarating to see it now. The bright clouds didn't look like storm clouds and he was pleased to have a little time here before the winter weather hemmed him in completely.

The driver let him know that he was ready and he smiled at him. He was ready to get to town.

<hr>

Clive Quackenbush & Sophia Greaves

"You ladies wait right here." Clive said with a mischievous grin.

Sophia was sitting on the loveseat next to her Aunt Olivia. She had recieved a warm and generous hug from her aunt when she arrived. She could feel the anxiety and heaviness leave her as she rode with Clive. She had really needed to get away.

It was wonderful how Clive and Olivia's home felt. It was peaceful and happy here. Olivia had decorated it, but it wasn't about what curtains were up, but instead it was something Sophia felt. It was hard to say exactly what it was, but a sense of welcome and other comforting things that made her love it here.

"I love it when Clive is up to something." Olivia said next to Sophia. "He may be over sixty years old, but he still has the heart of a twelve-year-old boy sometimes."

Sophia smiled again, Clive had his many charms and no one she knew could resist them.

Clive came back inside with two crates both with small wool blankets draped over them.

"Ok, ladies, time to close your eyes," Clive said then chuckled.

Olivia sighed and then laughed. "You know Clive, you are adorable when you are like this." She said with a grin and closed her eyes.

"My mother would have said I was a complete tease." Clive

gave Sophia a look.

Sophia laughed then closed her own eyes.

There was a little sound, some scuffling and a few mutterings and some chuckling from Clive.

Sophia heard him take a few steps.

"Okay, you can open your eyes now." Clive said.

He had a small dog in each hand, one was cream-colored and one was brown with blue eyes.

Sophia and Olivia both gasped simultaneously. Sophia felt her heart melt as Clive placed the cream-colored puppy in her arms. It began to wiggle, and she pulled the puppy close.

Olivia had a similar puppy reaction in her own lap.

"They are sisters, born aboard the ship right after they shipped out." Clive said.

"Oh Clive, you are the dearest man." Olivia said. She lifted her puppy to her face and was rewarded with little licks on her nose.

"These are poodles, right?" Sophia asked. She explored all the curly-haired wonder that was rubbing its head in Sophia's hands.

"Yes, miniature poodles, all the rage in New York and Europe. I have heard they are very loyal and affectionate. They won't grow too big."

He bent down and made a gesture above the floor, not even a foot high.

Sophia picked up the bundle of fur. "Is she mine?" Sophia finally asked, afraid to get attached.

"Yes, Sophie dear, she is yours." Clive smile down at her. He kneeled down in front of his wife and was rewarded by a few licks from the chocolate brown poodle on his wife's lap.

Sophia spent the next few minutes falling in love.

Milton Vaughn

Milton Vaughn looked over the Drug and Sundries shop that his partner, Ferris Noonan, had begun for him. Milton thought it had been started well. It was organized at least but Milton saw a few ways to improve it and would get started on it right away.

"The shelves needed to be set up to display items in a more prominent way." He muttered aloud, mostly to himself because his partner seemed to be focused on his cleaning task. Ferris Noonan was a fine man but he was not interested in Milton's grand schemes. He enjoyed his part of the job but the larger vision was a little lost on the man.

Milton gave a look over to his partner, Ferris was thin and tall, with a well-trimmed beard and a thick fashionable mustache. Ferris enjoyed the small-town life, according to the letters that he had sent, and was pleased to have settled in this small town. Milton did not plan to stay here forever, but learn all he could from this business, and then move on when he would build the next. He was going to create an empire and he would start right here.

The apartment above was tidy and very simply furnished. Milton would need to remedy that soon. He enjoyed finery and wanted to make his living quarters as comfortable as possible. He would need some better furniture and some fancy goods to dress up the place. It would make for a good opportunity to meet the other business owners in town as well.

He was young, being only twenty-five, but he was savvy and he desired above anything else to create a name for himself. His own father had been the same way, and still had a thriving chain of stores in Philadelphia. Milton had left home when he was eighteen with every dime he'd saved from working in his father's shops. He hustled and bought his own shop in a tiny building in Atlanta, Georgia, then sold it for a tidy profit. Then he did it again in South Carolina.

He knew when he saw thousands of men heading west that he belonged there too. He was ready to make a name for himself. These small towns would be needing what he had to offer. He found a few willing partners and it would take all his know-how to make his businesses succeed.

Ferris Noonan was a good barber, and he noticed there were several patrons waiting on the bench at the front of the store for his services. That was a good start. The shelves had a few goods on them, just the basics. Milton had brought along several trunks with more inventory and would have more arriving over the next few days by ferry. It would take some work and some shoe leather to spread the word but the first thing he needed to do was get settled in.

He looked Ferris over again, seeing his partner in detail, noticing that he looked clean. He had a thin frame and his shirt and vest were tidy in appearance but his pants weren't ironed well.

Milton would have him remedy that. No worker in one of his stores would show up unless they were pressed and perfectly dressed. It didn't matter that they were in this small town, every detail mattered.

He watched Ferris as he gave a shave to a young man, around Milton's age. Ferris wielded his straight razor with fluid motions. He moved his feet around like a dance. He was proficient and that pleased Milton.

He gave his partner praise before he headed back upstairs to his new home. The long days of travel were catching up to him, and he would be pleased with a short nap and then he would write out his goals for the days ahead.

Corinne Grant

She was packing up a few things in her bedroom to get ready to spend some time at her father's home. The sound of tools thumping and banging against the logs were adding a horrible thump to the headache that was forming just above the bridge of Corinne's nose.

This past year of her life has been full of ups and downs and of beautiful moments yet also huge changes. Becoming a mother to her daughter Trudie had been the first blessing to arrive right after Christmas. It shifted everything within her. She began to finally understand the feeling of loving someone unconditionally within a moment of their existence.

Corinne told her husband one night, when they were settling their newborn child in her crib. "It feels like God has given us this most precious gift. I feel such love, yet also the weight of the honor that God has entrusted us with, in taking of her." Her husband Lucas had agreed.

There was this new level of fear that lived in Corinne's heart too. A fear of the unknown dangers and this overwhelming protective instinct.

She felt a bit of annoyance rise up within her and she decided to get some air and see the progress of the outside of the cabin.

She stepped outside and was struck by the chill in the air. The smell was there, and she felt that inner gut check.

She walked inside and grabbed up a thicker wool coat and shoved her hands into her sleeves.

She moved with purpose and found her husband standing on the ground. She was happy to wait to speak with him until he was done with talking with his work crew.

"It smells like snow." She said and tilted her head with annoyance.

"That is does." Lucas said and looked up to the sky.

She opened her eyes and raised her eyebrows. He had semi-promised to have the project done before the snow flew.

He looked up to the cabin. The myriad of projects showed as parts of the roof were open with logs piled and wood planks strewn about the place.

Corinne could feel that part of herself, the temper and the impatient part, beginning to elevate rapidly.

"This is so wildly inconvenient." Corinne said finally.

"I know, my darling." He placed a hand on her arm. She wasn't sure she was in the mood to be comforted.

"I just am not sure that this is good timing. The roof of our home is open to the elements. How is this possibly going to work?" She sighed with exasperation.

Lucas looked concerned, which she was glad for, but the damage had been done. She knew that the only way was forward, but now here she was, with two babies and a cabin with half a roof. The air was cold and any moment the snow and wind were going to send all of its fury into her home.

Lucas pressed his lips downward in a lopsided frown. "We have everything ready to go. It will just be a week maybe ten days and all will be grand." Lucas had said.

She looked about the yard around the cabin she loved and saw the piles of logs and lumber, a woodstove and pipes under a rubber tarp.

"I am not certain how we will be able to function with all of this going on, Lucas. We have two babies in the house. The snow will be falling at any moment." She had said harsher than necessary.

"I know my love. We will work very hard and fast." He had tried to promise. Lucas was a man who was very slow to anger, but she could see that line forming between his eyebrows. It was a rare sight, proving that he too was frustrated. "I know it must be frustrating. I promise to work as fast as we possibly can to get the work done." Lucas said and gave her a look that said that he was worried also.

"What if we get an early blizzard. A simple tarp is not going to keep that out of our home. We could have mold and rot in a matter of days." Corinne said with practicality.

"I will do everything I can to make sure that doesn't happen." Lucas said and took her hand.

"You can stop a blizzard?" Corinne said and felt her annoyance rise to full boil. This timing was all wrong. She wasn't sure what she wanted Lucas to say but she was suddenly so tired and sad and mad at the same time.

Lucas sighed.

"I will do my best at what I can control, sweetie." He promised.

She nodded but still felt the frustration.

"I need to get some work done." She muttered.

Lucas leaned in and kissed her on the cheek. She felt his warm lips on her cheek and felt that prick of her conscience.

A moment later Corinne was walking to her greenhouse, just a short walk down the flagstone steps that led from the cabin. The cold wintry air bit at her cheeks and her eyes were misty with tears. She felt like a fool.

She was overcome by emotions after the discussion she had with her husband Lucas. She had not liked how she acted.

She knew in her heart that her husband was doing what he thought was best. He had been making plans for months; gathering supplies, felling logs and ordering everything he could to make an organized expansion to their cabin.

When she had rode that ferry back from Portland with baby Caleb in her arms she had known that they would be facing some serious challenges. She already had baby Trudie at home. But when she heard baby Caleb crying in that room in Portland, knowing his mother Megan had left him behind, with no thought for his well-being, she knew they had to take him. There was no other thought in her mind. In that moment, when she ran across the room to check on this abandoned child her heart had leapt in her chest and instantly filled with love and protectiveness for the little boy. It had been one of the most profound feelings in her short life. The love that she had for her daughter Trudie was the same kind of fierce love. They had taken all the steps necessary to gain custody of him and were now truly and officially his parents.

61

Corinne felt the warmth of the greenhouse envelop her. The smells of earth and growing things were a comfort to her ragged spirit and she sat on the bench nearby and let emotions overtake her for a little while.

Her mind went over and over her emotions and thoughts that had plagued her for the last few weeks. Questioning the wisdom of her husband to do the cabin expansion now. Certainly, it would have been easier to wait until spring.

He had said that the late fall would be risky but sometimes the rain in the spring was an everyday occurrence. Then the summer heat and the bugs would potentially make the house unlivable. She had reluctantly agreed, because he had been so certain.

Now, here she was, in her greenhouse crying because she was just exhausted and worn to the bone.

She knew he was trying to make things easier on them all in the long run, but right now she just wanted to cry and be angry. Her stomach was tied in knots and the stress of the morning was eating away at her middle. Her breakfast and coffee churned in her guts like a heavy brick.

She knew the plans and tried to calm herself by imagining the cabin as it would be when it was done. The small pantry beside the kitchen was now going to be the staircase up to the second floor. The heat from the brick ovens in which Violet made her bread would rise and heat the second story in most cases. The second floor would have three bedrooms. The babies would share a room for now and Debbie would move from her room downstairs to be closer to the children. Then a portion of Debbie's room downstairs would become a larger pantry and the room at the back, redone to fit the bathtub and laundry making more room. He had promised a sorting table and a place to store more linens and the water boiling pots for when laundry was done. It was going to be some good changes. The change that she was looking forward to the most was adding a porch to the front and back of the cabin. She had commented on many occasions how much she loved sitting on Angela's porch, especially in the evenings as the sun was setting and the sky would show off the magical light to the west. In the evenings she would be able to sit and look over her garden and the creek with her lavender fields beyond and enjoy all that they were building together.

The thoughts of the changes had calmed her, and she dried her tears. She took some deep breaths and let herself relax. She spoke to God about her exhaustion and asked for wisdom and patience to get through the trying days ahead. She prayed for mild weather for a few more days so they could get the work done. She prayed for God to show her how to deal with her frustrations. She felt God's peace fill her and she was thankful.

"God, you are always good. You will always be more than enough. I do not deserve all the blessings you have given me, but I am so very thankful that I can accept them without any guilt or shame. I praise your name." Corinne said these words because she was beginning to learn that praising God in all things, even struggle, can be the best way to conquer the fear and doubt.

Just a few days ago she had been reading 1 Thessalonians 5:18.

"In everything give thanks: for this is the will of God in Christ Jesus concerning you."

Corinne was going to try to remember these words in the days ahead. This was not a permanent problem. The work would get done and her home would be better off for it. She reminded herself to talk to Lucas later in the day and apologize for her attitude. She would learn to be patient and try to not take out her frustration on her husband. It may be a life-long battle but for today she had learned a valuable lesson.

She gathered up her skirts and wiped away the wetness from her cheeks. She would push through the tired and achy muscles and get back to work. She grabbed a few pails of water from the water barrel outside and gave a peek over at her cabin. Seeing the men standing precariously on the edges of the walls, she said a prayer for their safety as they used a hoist to pull the beams up to make the second floor. A man with an axe was chopping away at the top log on each side for the new logs to set into. She was glad for their skill.

"It is going to be good." Corinne whispered to herself. It is always a shock to the system to see something that looks so destructive at first. A portion of her roof is gone. Her household was in upheaval and she had no idea how things would move forward but it had to be done.

She took a deep breath and let it out slowly. She got back to her own work. She praised God all day, whenever her heart was troubled. It somehow helped her get through it all.

She would only spend an hour at the greenhouse, watering the plants took time. She suddenly realized that she should be home getting ready for the changes coming her way. She rushed through the duty and then pulled her coat back on.

She almost passed her husband by as she walked back towards the cabin but that inner gut check came. She halted and turned.

Lucas gave her a look that seemed hesitant.

She pouted a little, the tears she had dried after their discussion were threatening to come back.

She stepped closer to him.

"I'm sorry." She said and leaned in to kiss his cheek.

He smiled, and they shared a long moment.

She knew that he was busy, doing dangerous work, so she let him do it, but just saying those two words made her feel better. She was going to make sure that her family would be safe and warm for the night and then later perhaps, she could make a more thorough apology to Lucas.

She went inside and kissed her babies, got some help from Debbie and Violet and they all made a plan together. It was time to move out.

Chapter 7

Sophia Greaves

Sophia was happy to walk her new friend on the leash that Clive had given her, she was back in her warm coat and watching the poodle scuffle around in the fallen leaves in the yard in front of Clive's house.

Olivia had already named her poodle Cocoa, and Sophia was mulling over a few names for her dog as she giggled over the antics of her new acquisition. She was darling little thing, barely the size of a small squirrel. A bundle of curls all over her. She had tawny eyes and a pinkish brown little nose. Just looking at her made Sophia happy. All negative thoughts were swept from her mind. She kept coming back to Lady, she had seen an article in a fashion magazine months ago, of a duchess with a little light-haired poodle that had been named Lady. That sounded perfect.

Sophia bent down and asked the poodle her opinion.

"Do you want to be called Lady?" Sophia asked.

The poodle was excited and danced around in little circles before she bounced on a leaf that crackled beneath her paws.

Sophia couldn't help but giggle some more. "Well, Lady it is."

Lady wiggled and romped in the leaves for a little while before Sophia was satisfied that she wasn't going to make a mess inside the house.

Clive and Olivia were ready when Sophia walked in. They had to make more deliveries. Sophia kept the leash on Lady and they all went in the wagon. Olivia and Sophia kept their poodles on leashes and secured in their laps as they headed out in the surrey. Both Lady and Cocoa must have wiggled out all of their energy because they swiftly fell asleep in the women's laps.

They arrived at Angela and Ted's home after a few minutes ride. Sophia stroked Lady's head to wake her and then handed her off to Clive, so she could get down.

Clive handed her back and Sophia was rewarded with a lick to the cheek. Sophia gave Lady a cuddle under her chin.

"I just love her to pieces, Clive." Sophia had thanked him a hundred times already, but she said it again. Clive just gave her a knowing smile before he reached for the crate in the back. He had more surprises to give out.

Olivia and Sophia walked in behind him up the front porch steps. He gave a knock and before long Galina was at the door.

"We come bearing gifts for the lady of the house." Clive said.

A few minutes later they were all gathered in the parlor, Angela was sitting in a cozy chair by the fire. Ted was doting over her and it pleased Sophia to see her brother so very happy. Soon she would be an aunt.

Aunt Sophia, she thought. Sounds good.

"Your husband and I thought long and hard over this and we decided that this companion fit you perfectly, I do hope you approve Angela dear." Clive said before he removed the blanket from the crate.

The calico cat was a huge hit and Angela cried and cuddled with her instantly.

"You men do spoil me so." Angela announced.

Sophia enjoyed the moment so much more, knowing how much Ted wanted to please her.

Sophia was feeling the same as Angela now, thankful for a little distraction and something new to focus on. A bright thought before the dreary winter.

Galina was just as thrilled and went from person to person, admiring their pets.

Sophia stopped Galina a few minutes later to chat alone with her in the kitchen.

"Are you doing better?" Sophia asked. She had been worried about Galina since the relationship with Warren had gone sour.

"I am keeping busy." Galina shared. Her eyes were still a little sad, but she wasn't looking as forlorn as she had been a month before.

"Will it make you sad that you didn't get a new pet today." Sophia felt a little guilty, when she realized how many had recieved a sweet little pick-me-up from Clive.

Galina laughed. "I will get to pet and cuddle a new kitty. I am still learning how to take care of myself and Angela. I am not ready for taking care of something else just yet."

Sophia thought her friend was trying to make the best of her situation.

"Have you gotten to see your brothers any more lately?" Sophia asked. Wondering if Galina's tempestuous relationship with her father could ever improve.

"I see them during the week sometimes. Guadalupe, his new wife, is kind and sends them over to visit when my father is out working. She is actually very nice. She may be a little more strong-willed than my mother. She is making sure he speaks with the pastor every week to manage his anger." Galina said.

Sophia nodded, glad to know that Slava Varushkin was at least trying to be better. The haunting memories of Galina's broken bones and bruises from the beating he had given her was something that Sophia would never forget. It had affected her deeply and she had spent months in prayer to try to forgive him. Some days it flooded back to her, and she would have to begin the process again. Sophia's own father had been a fool and was led around by his even more foolish brother but he had never beaten her.

Sophia had been thinking for days how to cheer up her friend and now she was here, face-to-face with her and she was drawing a blank.

What would make her happy? Sophia wondered. She said a quick prayer, hoping for some Godly inspiration, she watched Galina's face. Her dark eyes even darker and sadder than usual. Inspiration dawned, and Sophia gladly changed the subject.

"Did you ever hear back about your story that we sent out this summer?" Sophia asked. It had taken ages to get Galina to agree to send out her short children's story. Sophia believed it was good enough to publish.

Galina shook her head, but there was the tiniest hint of a smile.

"You should send it to the local paper. They are always publishing poems and short stories." Sophia urged. It would be incredible to see her friend's name in the paper.

Galina blushed. "That would be so very odd. What if people didn't like it?" Her cheeks were red, and her eyes were wide and shocked at the idea.

"They could read the story to their children. It would be grand." Sophia reached out to grab Galina's hand.

"I could turn it in for you." Sophia offered. "I just live a block away from the Oregon City Gazette." Sophia grinned and helped Galina see that this could be good for her. That she needed some happier thing to focus on.

Galina sighed and nodded. "If you wish."

Sophia squealed a little and let her enthusiasm show. She

clasped Galina's hands and squeezed them. She just wanted her friend to stop being so blue all the time.

"You been writing anymore?" Sophia asked. Galina sighed and shook her head.

"I want to, but the words won't come. I am reading again. Clive brought some books over for Angela and I to share. Edith and Heidi are reading them too. It is rather fun to read them and we all talk about them together." Galina smiled a little more.

"I am so proud of your reading, you have learned so much." Sophia said.

Galina had always been told by her father that a woman being taught to read was a waste of time. The fact that Galina was a storyteller was a cruel and vicious reality, when she was denied the education because of her father's old-world ideas. At least now, Galina had a new world opened to her.

Galina had pulled away and was keeping her hands busy with getting everything ready in the kitchen. Soon everyone was going to want some coffee and some of Violet's raspberry tarts. Violet had brought them by earlier along with some more sourdough in a bowl.

"Reading is the one thing that has kept me sane these days. I've been reading the Bible more too, although, some words I still have trouble with. I always have to ask questions when the words are bigger. They are patient with me here. That is something that I still am getting used to." Galina said. She poured some cream into a smaller container to make it easy for the guests to add cream to their coffee. Then she arranged the tarts on a plate, making it look decorative.

Sophia stole a tart and Galina gave her a playful glare. Galina tried to snatch it away and Sophia ducked away quickly. They both had a shared laugh. Sophia was more than pleased.

Violet Griffen

Violet Griffen was pleased to hold baby Caleb while Corinne got herself a cup of coffee. Violet had walked over and was going to do more baking, since Chelsea was all prepared for the canning party, Violet liked baking in her own ovens and was glad that she had come back. She had seen Corinne through the foggy glass and peeked into the greenhouse.

Corinne had been working with Caleb in the sling. Both of them had been dirty from her digging in the pots and Corinne had finally decided that Caleb was ready for a change of scenery. He was still teething and wanted to be held.

Violet had offered to put on some coffee. She was impressed that the second floor was almost ready for a new roof. Violet walked in and got the stoves hot in short order. It was strange to spend time away from the cabin that was now her home.

Corinne came in just as the coffee was hot and ready. She was shaping loaves to put in the oven. She washed her hands and took Caleb from Corinne and watched her slide into a chair gratefully.

"Another night of teething. I am not sure I can do another night like that." Corinne laid her head on the table.

Violet kissed Caleb's head after she had wiped him down. He looked up to her with his blue eyes. His hand reached up to her and he touched her cheeks. She turned her face to kiss those little reaching hands.

There was that feeling, that was so powerful inside of Violet lately. An aching fullness to her heart when she held baby Caleb or Trudie. She was actually longing for a family of her own. It competed with the feelings she had with the Grants. The feeling of being needed by the Grants had been her joy for the last few years, and suddenly now, holding this child, a painful hope was building inside of her.

Could she truly be aching to leave this place? *Certainly not.* She mused inside of her head. That was the last thing she wanted. The Grants relied on her, they told her how much of a blessing she was to them all the time. They paid her so well that her bank account was healthy, and she had no imminent needs. She was well respected and cherished here. But yet, here she was, holding this child and feeling hot tears prick at her eyes.

She let the feelings wash over her and she placed a few more kisses on Caleb's sweet face.

"You are such a precious little boy." She said in a sweet and soft tone to the boy. His blue eyes wide and watching.

The questions inside of her remained unanswered but the longing and ache remained.

Corinne grabbed herself a cup of coffee and was sipping it slowly. She was quiet and tired and Violet strapped Caleb to her own chest for a little bit and finished up her loaves. Corinne took him back.

"I am going to take Caleb back to Marie's and try to take a little nap before I fall over. You know you are tired when coffee doesn't help to wake you up." Corinne gave Violet a sleepy grin.

"Marie has been taking care of Trudie today, and I let Debbie have the morning to rest. She told me to come back and then I can try to rest too." Corinne waved and left Violet.

Violet passed the rest of the afternoon doing her work, she made a delivery of sour dough to a few neighbors and she happened to run into Reynaldo. She told him that he could stop by the Harpoles after suppertime for a walk.

Later she felt that budding excitement of nervous energy when dinner was winding down at the Harpoles. John and Marie were in the parlor with Lucas and Corinne spending time with the children, and Debbie made her own evening habits of crocheting, reading in her room, or going on long walks. Violet was tidying up after the dishes were cleaned and put away when she heard the knock at the front door. Certainly, it was him. Reynaldo was coming for his promised visit. All worries and thoughts escaped her mind.

She opened the door and Reynaldo was there, with a basket of green apples. Violet couldn't help but smile at the pretty picture he made.

"These were at the market in town. They looked so lovely and I couldn't help but think of you," he said, his smile wide. "I figured they wouldn't go to waste with this full house."

She accepted the apples and let him in.

"Hello the house." Reynaldo called out.

"Hello Rey!" John and Lucas said back.

Violet sat the basket on the counter and pondered for a moment what she could bake with those lovely green apples. They would be so tart and delicious.

She had enough cinnamon left to make a pie or some tarts, she could easily go back to the Grants for a few supplies, she mused. She was hoping for another delivery of spices to come to Oregon City before the winter snows came. She used up a good portion of her stock for all of the canning she had done over the summer and fall months. The pantry at the Grants was well stocked.

"You have the energy for a walk, the breeze is mild tonight?" He offered.

Violet spun slowly and gave him her full attention. She

nodded. Her mood was always lifted when he was around.

Violet let everyone know that she was heading out and they went out the front door together.

She put a warm shawl over her head and shoulders and let him take the lead. The sky was beginning to darken, and dusk lay over the valley. The streaks of sun to the west were orange and the colors of the sky were magnificent.

"The clouds left this afternoon. I do love these last moments of fall in the mountains." Reynaldo said.

Violet agreed. He told her about his day and she told him about hers. She had made her rounds of visiting and enjoyed every minute of it.

"Angela is healing up so well from her fall." She said, all the neighbors had been praying for their sweet neighbor.

"I ran into Ted in town today. He was also buying up some of those green apples." Reynaldo said. "He is going to be helping me find a location for my new cabin." We are going to go scouting soon. I plan to start building in the spring."

"Oh, that sounds wonderful." Violet said. She knew it had been something he was planning for a long while. "Someone in the bunkhouse will be quite pleased when you move out and create a vacancy. Violet grinned. She knew some of the ranch hands were always wishing they had a bit more privacy. Reynaldo was the ranch foreman and had the perks.

"Indeed, John Harpole and I have been discussing who should be promoted. There is a name of a deserving fellow that has been working very hard and I believe has earned it." Reynaldo said.

Violet listened joyfully. Since John Harpole was such a dear friend, and Corinne's father, the ranch and Grant's Grove were closely connected. Everyone knew everyone, from ranch hand to housekeeper. Everyone worked side by side most days.

"One reason I wanted to meet with you tonight, I have news." Reynaldo slowed his walk and looked her in the eyes.

"I am heading to California for a few weeks." He said it in a cheery tone, but Violet felt her heart drop. Reynaldo was leaving?

She tried to keep her words in a happy tone, she didn't want her disappointment to show. "Oh?" Was all she could say.

"Yes, I am helping to arrange a shipment of work horses that is arriving in a week to the Port in San Diego. It is quite an undertaking. This will double the current stock we have of large work horses. We have had a need for more work stock in Oregon

71

City, Salem, and Portland, as well as some needs further north."
Reynaldo was watching Violet. "I should only be gone a few
weeks."

Violet nodded and tried to keep a smile on her cheeks. It was a
struggle. Her first husband Eddie had gone to California and had
died in a small miner's camp almost two years ago. She had some
fears about Reynaldo now. What if he never came back. Would
California steal away another precious soul from her.

"I... will miss you," she whispered harshly.

Reynaldo rarely ever touched her, just in early summer he
once touched her face as he declared his intentions to court her. It
had been a lovely summer of walks and talks together. But now
again he took her face in his hands.

"I will be thinking of you while I am gone." His dark eyes were
caring and held more than his words were saying. He had been so
patient with her. He knew her past and all the pain she had
endured.

"I promise I will return, safe and sound." He said quietly,
realizing without her saying anything that her fears were there.

Violet sighed. "You know that is a promise you cannot make."

He chuckled a little, he ran his thumb down her cheek. It did
wonders to calm her. "Well, I would make it if I could."

"You be safe and come home." She said and tried to release her
fears. Reynaldo was only going to be gone a few weeks. Certainly,
he wasn't going to be living in a squalled miners camp, half
starving and cold.

"I plan on coming home and beginning to make big strides
toward the future." He stared into Violet's eyes.

Was he trying to tell me that he wants me in his future? Violet
wondered. If she was a brave woman she would have told him.
That she had been dreaming lately about a future with him. About
grander things than just walks and talks, but something more.

When he finally removed his hands from her face she felt the
absence of them, the wind was somehow colder now, and she
wished suddenly to be cuddled up in his arms.

She had appreciated his patience with wooing and courting her
slowly, but now suddenly, she wished that he would tell her how
he felt about her and give her a chance to speak her mind.

She took his arm and felt a rush of feelings overwhelm her. She
realized in an instant that she was in love with Reynaldo Legales.

Lord help me. She prayed in her mind as he led her back home.

72

Chapter 8

November 5, 1852

The brisk fall days reminded every resident of Oregon City and those in the Willamette Valley that winter was indeed on its way. The wind gusts would come nearly every day and those souls who were outside felt the chill. The trees and landscape were losing the charm of fall colors and the bleakness was beginning to show. Woolen coats, scarves and mittens were pulled out and thick boots and woolen socks were mended. The wisest among the valley residents had stocked pantries with soups, sauces, fruit preserves, broths, and baked beans. Roots cellars would be stocked with every good thing, from potatoes to carrots, enough to keep everyone happy and healthy throughout the cold winter months. Salted pork would be hanging, and sausage would be cured and waiting to be added to winter stews and hot frying pans. The women would gather together with canning jars and make pot after pot of stews and chili to save for another day. Hundreds of pumpkins, apples, cherries, and peaches would be made into pie filling and kept in jars for a cold winter's day when a pie would cheer everyone's spirits. Men would take more time, well into dusk, to chop extra wood, making certain that the woodstoves and fireplaces would keep everyone cozy and warm through the coldest months. The barns would be full of green hay to feed all of the livestock. Oats and barley were kept stored in the high lofts of the barns to keep it cool and dry from the moist air outside.

Thanks to Clive and JQ Quackenbush the Valley had more animals to keep families safe through the cold winter months as well. Cats would keep the mice and other varmints out of the houses and barns, away from the important things. The new dogs would be invaluable as early warnings if bears or wildcats came down from the bluffs in search of sustenance. Many new homes were in the early stages of training these dogs to be helpful hunting companions, and as November continued the woods and bluffs would be full of hunters bringing home game to feed their families.

The butcher in town would be busy until December with the

fall slaughtering of the livestock as farmers sold their animals. The smokehouse would be running day and night to have meat for the families of the valley.

<hr/>

Sean Fahey

Sean had spent the last week with his new companion, Cupid, and they were beginning to get along pretty well. There had been a few mishaps in the house training, but Sean was beginning to see that Cupid was learning the way of things. Cupid was affectionate and eager to please. He found that if he made a few extra slices of bacon with his breakfast and had a few pieces in a handkerchief in his pocket that Cupid was learning that he would be rewarded with a very pleasant treat for learning to do his business outside.

Sean realized early on that Mack's warning about beagles and their nose for food was true in every way. Sean was being trained as well, to clean up his bowls and plates right away, or Cupid would find a way to clean them up for him.

Cupid had a few extra meals in the first few days when Sean wasn't paying attention. Cupid also enjoyed chewing on his socks and would steal them at every opportunity. He would have to make a special trip to town to purchase socks if any were available this late in the year. Sean's favorite wool socks were irreparable. Cupid had been ashamed and after Sean scolded him it did seem that the incidents were becoming less frequent.

Mack made him a rope toy to give to Cupid and for the last few nights Cupid had been content to chew on that in the evenings on the rug by the fireplace, his favorite spot.

Sean was feeling pleased, he was ready for the winter, he had a new companion, and all was going well for his first winter in Oregon. He was planning to go to visit with his sister and Ted later in the evening and he thought that Cupid was ready for a longer trip with Sean and Shipley, his horse.

Sean had learned from Mack that beagles were notorious for running off when they spotted something of interest and had learned the hard way during the first attempt to train Cupid to stay on command.

Mack had been with him in the yard and Sean had Cupid on a

long thin rope. Cupid had learned to sit and lay down on command, and Sean was so pleased, but the stay command was one that Cupid wasn't grasping as quickly.

Sean had seen Cupid respond to his stay command a few times on the long rope and had even let go of the rope and let it sit on the ground. The dog had sat and stayed for several minutes without budging. So, Sean was ready to try again, this time without the rope.

Cupid would come on command most times, but this time the distraction of a family of deer bounding by at the worst possible moment was just too much for him. Cupid bounded off with a bugle, his white tail straight up in the air. He was on the hunt and Sean was on the run to catch him before he made it to the dense woods. Cupid was gone faster than a wink and Mack laughed as Sean sprinted after Cupid, following the sound of the beagle trumpeting his hunt through the woods.

It had taken nearly twenty minutes to get the beagle to come back to him, and Sean realized that it would take some more training to be able to trust Cupid off leash.

"Cupid, Cupid…" Sean said to his dog in exasperation as he tied the rope back around the collar.

Cupid was ecstatically pleased with himself and did not seem at all concerned with the dangers of romping through the woods alone.

Sean took him back the long way through the woods and knew he would have to spend an hour picking the thorns and burrs from his pants and the dog's fur this afternoon.

"Did you have to run through every thorn bush out here?" He asked Cupid.

Cupid's response was his grinning pant and a happily swishing tail.

Mack was working with his own dog when Sean finally reached his property. Mack was chuckling when Sean arrived.

"Cupid seems mighty pleased." His laugh was endearing but Sean gave him a non-malicious grimace.

"Yes, indeed." Sean muttered, making Mack laugh again.

"We will get these two trained eventually. It is still early on. I will keep my gal on a rope for a while more. We don't want to lose them into the cold dark woods yet." Mack said and gave his girl and then Cupid a pat on the head.

"I was overeager. I will learn to be a bit more patient." Sean reasoned.

Sean did a few more exercises with the stay command, on the rope, and then Mack had headed home.

It had been a few days with more and more training. He had been working with Shipley his horse and Cupid to train Cupid to run alongside and Cupid was learning. Sean was eager to take him with him to visit his sister tonight. He was hoping that Cupid would be well-behaved and he would be able to visit peacefully.

Sean was happy to be visiting his sister any time but tonight he was even more pleased since it was a weeknight, and he knew that Dolly would likely be there for dinner. He had never been very experienced with wooing women and his lifestyle had not allowed him to even be around many, but suddenly he realized that Dolly was intriguing enough that he may just need to learn a few more things about her.

It was time he sought out some advice from someone wise to maybe get ahead with his wooing of a certain woman. He had no idea what the future held, but he was willing to make a fool of himself to try his hand at courting.

He had seen Clive the day before in town and he had asked Clive to stop by this afternoon if he could. Sean was ready to pick his brain and see what the old timer could offer in any way to help him get Dolly's attention.

Clive showed up promptly at 3:30 and Sean had coffee and biscuits ready.

"Hello!" Clive knocked and gave a loud greeting.

Cupid gave a bark to announce.

"Come on in." Sean yelled, Cupid barked a few extra times and Sean attempted to shush him. Cupid let out a few more barks as Clive came in and then he wagged and wiggled as Clive gave him some attention.

Sean was happy whenever Clive came for a visit. Sean had bought the land and cabin from him. The deal had been a bit too generous on Clive's part in Sean's opinion, but Sean was working hard to keep the cabin as cozy and welcoming as Clive had kept it. Between Angela and some of her friends he had new curtains and rugs, and with his carpenter friend in town he had a few new tables and cabinets up in the kitchen. Sean was proud to show off his cozy home to his friend. Clive was scrubbing Cupid's head and the dog was in heavenly bliss.

"He is a handsome fella." Clive said, he seemed pleased.

"Yes, he is, his training is going pretty well too." Sean said, but told him about the mishap with the deer and Cupid's adventure in the woods.

Clive smiled cheerfully with Sean as they laughed about it. "We are having fun with two small dogs at our home. They are keeping us hopping, though. Sophia and Olive are in love with their little cuties and I'm sure they will spoil them excessively."

"I am probably spoiling Cupid a bit too, I give him bacon as a reward for doing his business outside." Sean admitted.

"We should try that trick. Sophia is having better luck with her poodle, Lady. My wife's poodle is not grasping the concept quite as well." Clive chuckled. "It has been a long time since I trained a dog, and perhaps I am a bit rusty."

"We will all get better at it with time." Sean said.

"Alright, fella, I know that something is on your mind," Clive said, getting Sean to gather his courage. It was time to spill his guts.

"I am falling for a girl, well a woman." Sean blurted out. He felt his heart rate pick up just with the thought of having this conversation. He felt woefully out of his depth. Sean looked down to Cupid who was sitting between them. Sean chided himself at wanting to look away from Clive's absorbing gaze. He would have to stop acting like a ninny if he wanted to conquer this situation.

"Well, now, I have noticed ya lookin'. You ready to be doin' something about it?" Clive asked. His eyes could search through a soul when they wanted to.

Sean nodded and returned Clive's gaze.

"Well, Dolly is a rare and special bird." Clive rubbed at the short beard on his chin. "She will need a different kind of wooing. Most girls would take a certain kind of attention. I am not certain that she would respond with hearts and flowers." He sat back and was quiet for a moment.

Sean would let the man think things through.

"I am thinking that you probably know enough about her to start getting ideas on some ways to get her attention. You just probably don't know how to put it into action." Clive said thoughtfully.

"I agree, I know that she is not likely to want the same things as other gals. I don't even know if she is seeking that kind of attention." Sean said. A part of him wondered if he would ever break past the friendship and into anything else.

78

"She is very independent, part of that is the fact that she has her own life that she has fought to keep. She spent months in the wilderness escaping from those men from her old tribe." Clive said.

Sean knew bits and pieces about that story from local gossip. Nothing bad was ever said about Dolly, but he didn't have much in detail about her past. She wasn't one to talk about such things.

"I don't know that it is a hopeless cause. I have seen her being wooed in the past." Clive said.

"Oh…?" Sean said, startled. He wondered if perhaps he was too late. That someone else had swooped in and stolen her heart. *Who could this man be?* He wondered and worried for a moment.

"His name was Reggie, and he left over a year ago now. I think he might have had a chance with her if he hadn't chosen a different path. I do believe that he was beginning to win her over." Clive said. He reached out to soothe Sean. "They never were courting openly, but I do know from her that she turned him down when he made an offer to her. She was in a different place in her life then, waiting for her tribe to come for her."

Sean nodded, he wasn't sure if he was comforted by Clive's words. It gave him a few new worries to consider.

"Do you think she would even consider me as a suitor then?" Sean asked the question that tugged at him more often than he cared to admit.

"I believe it can be done son, but you will have to be patient with her. She comes from a different culture, and she has her own dreams and goals. She is so very quiet, you will have to be able to talk with her about things, and that is a challenge with someone like her." Clive smiled to cheer him. "If I put myself in your shoes for a moment I would probably try to win her over. You do have a prime piece of land here, iff'n I do say so myself." Clive chuckled. "You know the game and wildlife here. You can bring that up in easy conversation when you see her next. She may be willing to go hunting. Heck, I would be pleased to head out this weekend to hunt along the bluffs. Perhaps, you could invite her along." Clive gave Sean a wink. "You might just have some chances to talk to her a bit more."

Sean liked his idea his thoughts gave Sean some things to ponder.

"Only the Lord knows whether you have a future with Dolly, but if you pray and ask for God's Wisdom he gives it out freely,"

Clive offered. "You have a Bible close by?" Clive asked. Sean had his Bible nearby and handed the leather-bound book over to his friend.

"I think it in James…" Clive opened and licked a thumb and turned a few pages. "Yes, here it is. James 1, verse 5. *'If any of you lack wisdom, let him ask of God, that giveth to all men liberally, and upbraideth not; and it shall be given him'.*"

Sean let the words in, Sean was always adding verses to his journal and he gladly penciled that verse in. Clive read it to him again, so he could get the words right.

"Thank you, Clive I need to learn to trust God more with these things. A life spent out of practice for these kinds of things leaves me wandering in my thoughts and actions a little too often."

Clive stayed, and they chatted for a few minutes. Soon, Cupid needed to go outside.

"I do miss this view sometimes. There is something special here. I have a new view now though, with someone very special to share it with." Clive gave Sean a wink. "I will be praying for that for you son, when it's God's timing."

Sean nodded thoughtfully. He was glad he had been able to talk to Clive, it had given him a lot to think on. Knowing that Dolly had been wooed before made him confused and he wondered if perhaps she was pining for someone else. It gave him a strange and unpleasant feeling in his chest.

Clive rode away a few minutes later and Sean led Cupid inside, he needed to get ready to go soon.

He warmed up the water and shaved, putting on a fresh shirt and pants. He found his nicest leather coat in the wardrobe that the carpenter had built for him. It smelled of cedar and was a nice addition to his bedroom.

Cupid could tell that something was happening as he sat anxiously by the front door.

"You ready for a trip to Angela's house?" Sean asked Cupid with enthusiasm. Cupid answered with his tail thumping against the front door. It made a hollow thumping sound and Sean couldn't help but laugh a little.

Sean tied the long lead rope to Cupid and they went outside. He would have to take the road to make sure that Cupid didn't get snagged on anything. The trip started off well. His horse Shipley and Cupid were getting used to each other. Sean kept a slow pace and Cupid came along well. Cupid had his nose to the ground for most of the trip, exploring every scent along the way.

Ted was out on the front porch with his rifle and a rag. He gave a wave to Sean when he rode by. Sean was pleased that Cupid had only looked over to Ted and hadn't tried to bolt to him. Sean always worried that Cupid was going to forget his training and get tangled under the horse. That would be a tragedy.

Sean rode back to the barn and then replaced the rope with a shorter one on Cupid's collar.

"Okay fella, you behave today." Sean scratched at Cupid's ears.

"That is a pretty boy." A voice from the corner of the barn said.

Sean smiled at Warren.

"He is, I think." Sean smiled to Warren who was hanging up some tools.

"I am excited to know that there are more dogs in the valley. I will be buying my own place in the spring, I hope to have a dog someday." Warren said. He was a big lad, broad shouldered with a pleasant smile for everyone.

"My neighbor has a female—we will be breeding them when they get a bit older, I will set aside a pup for you if you like." Sean offered.

"I will be happy to take you up on that." Warren grinned even wider.

"You let me know when you buy a place. I will gladly come scope the land with you. If you ever need a hand with building a barn or a fence, you better send for me. I had plenty of help getting my place set up. I feel the need to help someone and pass it on." Sean gave him a clap on the shoulder.

Cupid got excited and tried to jump up on Warren and Sean corrected his dog.

"No jumping, Cupid." Sean said giving the rope a slight tug.

Cupid took a few steps back and looked to Sean a little shamefaced.

"Aw, Cupid... what a great name." Warren said, and he knelt down to Cupid to give him some affection.

The way everyone responded to his new dog was a pleasant surprise. Since dogs were a rarity everyone wanted to give him attention. Sean was hoping it would still work on Dolly. He would take whatever attention he could get.

"Thanks for the offer Sean, I am finding myself thinking all the time about my own little farm. I keep wondering if I am man enough for the task." Warren said, his face showed his concern. Sean knew that Warren's father had passed away a while back and he had been missing having a man in his life.

"You are a hard worker from all the talk from Ted and Earl, I have even heard Clive talk about ya." Sean said, trying to encourage him. "Not one of them is prone to exaggerate."

Warren dropped his chin a bit, probably a bit shy on getting praise.

"Hard work is the biggest challenge, and you haven't shied away from that here. You will learn as you go and get wisdom from those who have come before you." Sean said, knowing it was true for himself as well.

"Thanks for the offer for help, I will certainly need to count on my neighbors to get me started." Warren said and gave Sean a nod.

Sean was happy to have begun so many good friendships in the last year. His life with Ol' Willie had been a bit different, they had spent most of their time in the woods. They had enjoyed the solitude away from others as much as possible. Now he was in a new place, discovering new paths to take, and people who were genuine and helpful. Both experiences would make him a better man, he thought to himself.

"Let's go Cupid." He waved to Warren and headed out of the barn.

Sean was excited as he walked around the house, hoping the evening would go well and he would have a good visit with his sister. Things had steadily gotten better between them since he arrived in Oregon. He had really done badly when she came to San Francisco a few years before. He had still been so very confused about his parent's death, that he had pushed her away. It had taken a lot of courage and a trip to Ireland to visit their Great Aunt to finally break him and help him see the error of his ways. He had always run away from his problems. He had found God again, and day by day, God was showing him how to be a better man.

Galina had let he and Cupid in. Sean kept a tight grip on the leash. Cupid was responding well and sat when he was told too. His tail swished happily as he looked from person to person. Ted has a polishing rag and his rifle across his lap in a kitchen chair. Ted had set his rifle down and stood to give Sean a warm bear

82

hug.

"Good evening, brother." Ted said warmly. Sean was glad his sister had found Ted, while she had been in San Francisco looking for him. God had given her something sweet to cling to while she sought out her fool of a brother. Sean introduced Cupid and let the dog get his wiggles out. He knew that Cupid would greet everyone with enthusiasm, but every wiggle would tire him out a bit more.

"We got a cat from Clive, so we should get the introductions done. We will see if they can get along," Ted said with a smile and a raised eyebrow. He knelt down and gave Cupid a scratch behind his ears. Cupid tried very hard to lick Ted in the face, but Ted dodged it successfully, then laughed.

"Angel, you want to give the cat to Galina?" He called out.

"Alright," Sean heard his sister from the parlor.

Galina came out, holding a calico cat, with orange, black and white spots. "Meet the Duchess," Galina said with a smile.

Cupid began to whine, when Galina came in with the cat, and Sean was worried that he was going to bolt after it. However, Sean was pleased when the introductions went well. Cupid was curious and sniffed the cat. Duchess gave Cupid a half-hearted hiss and swat but was patient to let the dog give her a thorough sniffing. Galina let the cat go and she wandered back to the parlor.

"She has the run of the place." Galina smiled then went back to work.

"Clive gave us a few bags of sand and we made a pallet for Duchess, she is already scratching at the side door." Ted said as he watched Duchess walk away.

Sean laughed. "I wish that would work for a dog."

"I was hoping Duchess would like to visit the barn, to see if she would be a good mouser. So far she enjoys sitting on laps and pillows." Ted smiled. "Her name fits a little too well." Ted invited Sean with a gesture to the parlor.

Sean let Cupid follow but kept him on the leash. He wasn't ready to give the dog free rein in someone else's house yet.

Angela was on the settee next to the fireplace, the cat curled up on the pillow next to her feet. Sean was pleased to see his sister looking well.

"I like your hair like that, sister." Sean said, and he leaned down to plant a kiss on the top of her head.

Angela set the crochet hook down on her lap and took a hand and patted at her hairdo.

83

"Galina and I have been looking through all the fancy magazines that Clive shared with us. Galina had been practicing different styles in the advertisements. I was so impressed that Heidi and Galina have been looking so fine and fancy, I was brave enough to let them try it with mine." Angela smiled.

"Well, you are looking fine." Sean said as he sat across from her in the leather chair.

Angela gestured for Sean to let Cupid have a little more lead on his leash.

"Come here Cupid." Angela said with a cheery voice. Duchess reacted when Cupid approached by running away and hiding under the davenport. They all laughed.

"He is already calmer than he was a few days ago when we met him at your place." Angela said as she gave Cupid a few pets on the head.

"He definitely is on his best behavior when on the leash. My neighbor Mack has a female who resists the leash. It is so funny how each dog is a little unique in temperament." Sean said.

They chatted for a few minutes about the little incidents that had happened with Sean and Cupid, the good and the bad. Everyone was enjoying the talk when Sean heard footsteps from the other room. The gliding cadence of steps down the stairs next to the kitchen.

Sean felt like a fool, with his inner critic giving him grief over the thought of Dolly joining the talk. Suddenly he felt his heart rate increase and his hands begin to sweat a little.

Dolly was indeed there, wearing a simple gown, dark green and her hair braided back simply. Dolly smiled as she came in the room.

"Hello," she said and gave everyone a warm smile.

Everyone in the room said hello back.

"Oh, you brought your dog." Dolly said and gasped happily. She took a few quick steps closer and knelt next to Sean. He could not help but enjoy her closeness.

If he was alone he might have told her that she smelled like a flower meadow. But after the talk with Clive he thought better. Dolly would not be won over with hearts and flowers.

Cupid had a new person to sniff and wiggle for and he did his job well.

"Does he have a name yet?" Dolly looked up to Sean, her dark eyes full of joy. Cupid was enjoying her attention and leaning on her, with his tale thumping happily.

"His name is Cupid." Sean said and saw her try to figure out his name. He could tell after a moment that she didn't know that word.

Sean explained. "Cupid is like an angel, I think it came from an old, old story. Mostly he is painted as a small angel with wings, who shoots a bow and arrow, and whoever is struck falls in love." Sean was slightly embarrassed to share the name now, and it's meaning. He got through it but felt a bit foolish.

"That is a good name." Dolly said thoughtfully. "You have struck me with your arrow Cupid, for I cannot help but love you." She said to the dog, who easily accepted her affection, and gave some back to her willingly.

Everyone in the room laughed and talked about nothing important for several minutes.

Galina stepped away, declaring that she had to check on dinner.

Angela had coaxed Duchess up to her lap and they all settled in. Dolly urged Sean to stay in his chair, and she sat next to him with Cupid cuddled up on her lap. He was still on the leash but Sean gave it a lot of slack so he could settle in.

Sean was pleased that things were working out so well so far. If he could work up his bravery he would try to get more time with this mysterious woman.

"Were you working at the labs today?" Sean asked finally.

"Oh yes, for a few hours. Also I have been spending a few hours each morning trying to finish the last drawings for the book Corinne and I are having printed." Dolly said.

"I am so impressed by all of your knowledge Dolly. You have done so well." Angela said. She was seated near the fireplace and the light of the fire was glowing on her cheeks and her red hair was lovely. Sean thought she would make a beautiful painting, sitting as she was with her cat in her lap. He wondered if Ted would like that, maybe he could hire an artist to come someday. It would be a wonderful gift.

"Thank you, Angela. Corinne and I are working hard at it." Dolly was speaking more comfortably today. Sean could tell that she felt safe here. He was trying to learn her habits.

"How soon do you think it will be done?" Sean asked, to keep her talking.

"I think in the next month it should be ready to send to..." She paused to think of the word. "Boston. Yes, it is going to Boston. Corinne knows the most about where the book will go." Dolly said. She didn't seem ashamed to have to think of words, and Sean was glad for that.

"You have done well here." Sean said, hoping that he wasn't going too far in complimenting her.

"I agree." Angela said, smiling.

Ted, not wanting to be left out spoke up. "Very well indeed. Someday, I can see your name on many books, spread throughout the land. Helping mothers, fathers and people of all ages find ways to help those that are sick or wounded. You are doing God's work Dolly." Ted praised and Dolly blushed.

She looked down and focused attention on the sleepy dog in her lap. She was embarrassed by the praise and Sean found it charming.

The parlor grew quiet and Sean figured that his moment had come, to change the subject and to see if he could make his plan come to fruition.

"I was just talking with Clive earlier today. We were wanting to head out for a hunting trip along the north bluff, just a day trip, tomorrow. Would you like to come along? If you aren't too busy with your work." Sean spit it out. Dolly looked up at him.

"I would like that. I need to get back out to the woods. I have been indoors so much lately, that would be very nice." Dolly said with a smile. "You would be okay if I brought my bow?" Her eyes looked directly into his, they didn't shy away. It was not a look of affection as he had hoped, but he could see friendship there.

"Of course, bring whatever you like. You have warm enough gear? I am guessing there may be snow by then." Sean said and smiled.

"Oh, yes, I have a great coat that Clive helped me with. I will wear my hunting clothes. I hope they do not offend you." She said.

He had seen her in her leather pants, hunting before. He thought she was brave to wear them. They just added another layer to that mystery that charmed him.

"Not at all, I am not so proper. I promise you." Sean said with a small laugh.

"That is good." Dolly smiled.

"I certainly wish fashion would allow for women to dress as men. It would certainly be more practical." Angela said. "I am hoping it will be a long while before I wear those dratted hoops again."

"You could wear pants, my Angel. I would love you just the same." Ted reached out and placed a hand on her arm. Angela looked up to him lovingly.

"I am not as brave as Dolly. But, I enjoy seeing her in her leathers. It makes me happy to see her living out her life as independently as she pleases. She is rather more adventurous than me."

Ted laughed.

"You have had adventures." Dolly said to defend her friend from the implied criticism.

"I have had a few too many adventures. I am ready for some quiet adventures." Angela grinned.

"I know that someday, I will do something else, and have more quiet adventures." Dolly said seriously. "For now, I will be happy to explore the woods and streams." She smiled and looked up to Sean. His heartbeat picked up again. "I will enjoy walking the woods with you."

It was the closest thing to an endearment she had ever said to him. He let his heart beat away in his chest, and the strange feeling grew just a little more within him. He knew in that moment he was making progress.

Sean basked in that moment as the conversation moved through many topics, the local news and the state of the weather. He enjoyed the conversation more after that sweet moment with Dolly.

The conversation only continued as dinner was served and they moved to the table. Sean tied the leash to his chair, and Cupid sat obediently next to him as they ate. Eventually the dog went to sleep.

The big topic at the table was the canning party that was being held at the house the next day. The back room was full of supplies and the pantry full of food goods to be canned.

Sean left for the evening long after dusk. Wishing everyone well and with best wishes for their party the next day. Sean saddled up and tied the long lead on Cupid for the ride home. His heart was light, and he said a thankful prayer for each person there that night.

He made it home safe and sound. Soon his horse was settled in the barn with feed, his dog was asleep by the fire. He sat with his journal.

There is no greater thing than good friendship, and good company.
Thanking God for his many blessings today. - SF

Chapter 9

Dolly Bluebird Bouchard

Dolly stepped down the staircase carefully, hoping to be silent. She held a small lantern and the light cast a yellow glow around her. The world outside was dark and Dolly enjoyed the peaceful solitude. She set the lantern on the table and lit a few candles around the room giving her enough light to get around without tripping and making noise.

She knew Ted would probably be another hour before he awoke at 6 a.m. So, she got the fire burning in the fireplace and in the kitchen stove. She flinched once when the wood settled in the stove as it began to burn. She was silent, barely breathing, making sure that she didn't hear anyone stirring. Angela deserved every minute of rest, carrying her child snug inside of her. Dolly sighed and resumed her activities. There were pans and ingredients stacked up on the counter for the canning party that was happening later that morning. Usually the kitchen was spotless. Dolly was glad she had laid out the oats the night before for her breakfast.

The water was boiling soon, and Dolly poured the oats in and stirred. A few minutes of watching then waiting and she pulled the pan from the heat and set it softly on a quilted pad.

She let the oats sit there for a minute and she went over to the table to get the brush and ties that she had left there. She brushed through her long dark hair in the silence, hearing the soft crackle of the hair and brush in the quiet room. She enjoyed these kinds of moments. When the world around her was still. She said a little prayer as she braided her hair. The quiet always made her think of God, and how she was never truly alone. She prayed for a safe day of hunting, then prayed for every soul in the house and on the land. Her fingers wove through her soft hair and she tied each braid with a leather tie.

She checked her refection in the oval mirror near the stairwell. She couldn't see well in the dim light, but the outline of her face showed her enough to see that she was neat and tidy.

She added some sugar and cinnamon to the pan of oatmeal,

not bothering to dirty a bowl. She ate it right from the pan. It was warming and delicious. She ate every bite and filled the pan with the wash water that was left over from the night before. Oatmeal was a pest to clean up if it dried to the pan.

She sat in a chair and tied her tall leather boots over her feet and calves. These were the warmest boots she owned. She had made them herself. They were lined with fur and quite lovely. Dolly smiled, remembering the nights of last winter, stitching them together. She knew her mother would have praised her for the fine handiwork.

She still thought of her tribe sometimes. The things she was taught would never leave her. There would never be a day that she wouldn't remember her former life, but she was happy now.

She buttoned up her long wool coat and pulled the woolen cap on and wrapped the scarf around her neck. She slung her canteen over her shoulder. She reached for her bow and arrows. She picked up the long knife from the table and checked the sharpness then slid it back into the leather sheath. She was ready.

She was mounted on Clover within a few minutes and saw the lantern being lit at the front of the barn as she was walking slowly out of the barn. Warren was there, smiling and waving to her as she left. He would be milking the cows and getting started with the busy day of farm work. She made a note to herself to send him and Earl, the other worker on the farm, a fresh kill for their dinner table.

She broke into a faster pace once she passed the Sparks' cabin. The air was cold, and she knew she would need that warm scarf wrapped around her face soon. Clover seemed happy to be out with her and she felt him pick up the pace. The frozen ground was crunching under his hooves and Dolly felt the joy of being outdoors in the still and quiet. The stars shown above her, and her eyes saw the dark landscape beyond. The stream was showing signs of thin ice and the air smelled of winter. That earthy cold scent was hard to describe in words, but she knew that snow would fall soon.

It had been more than a week since she practiced with her bow. With all the work she and Corinne had been doing to get the book ready to be published she was aching to be in her element again. The woods were her home.

Sean's cabin was set next to a mountain bluff. It looked warm and welcoming surrounded by tall pines with smoke curling up softly into the cold wintry darkness. The yellow lantern light glowed through the windows. She was beginning to see this place as Sean's cabin finally, though a part of her would always see Clive here. Sean was making it his own, adding a small barn and some fencing. She would have teased him about how small his garden was, but she was never bold enough to say the things she thought, not to Sean. She wasn't certain why.

She led Clover to the barn as she heard the sound of Sean's beagle marking her arrival. Dolly laughed at the howl.

"He sure does make a racket." She laughed again and patted Clover before sliding off her mount.

Sean was at her side a moment later. He smiled at her warmly. "Let's get Clover in the barn." She was amazed that he remembered her horse's name but then just smiled back.

Sean took charge and got Clover settled into the stall next to his horse. "Some oats?" Sean asked. She nodded and then enjoyed the scene, watching Sean give Clover some affection, rubbing his nose and talking to him sweetly. Dolly couldn't help but grin when she heard the howling come from the cabin.

Sean joined her and laughed as a pathetic howl came from the cabin again, sounding so mournful.

"He might just die if he doesn't see you soon." Sean said and placed a hand on her shoulder as they walked inside. She felt his hand on her and the pressure of it was pleasing. She looked over to Sean, and for the briefest moment she wondered at his friendly gesture. He looked sideways at her with a broad smile, probably still in good humor from the dog's theatrics but the way he looked at her… it reminded her for a moment of a memory. Just a glimpse of Reggie and how she had caught him looking at her once. She looked away and felt a strange inner confusion, not wanting to think of Reggie again but the reminder was there. It was something to think about.

The cabin was warm, and Cupid was quick to wiggle and pounce on her as she entered. She was laughing and soothing the poor creature in his exuberance.

"Oh, Cupid…" She gasped as she knelt down and got a few healthy licks on the cheek.

"No, Cupid." Sean scolded but then laughed taking out all the fierceness of his censure.

Dolly laughed and soothed a minute more, showing Cupid that she was not to be jumped on. Cupid did calm and only his tail showed his excitement. He accepted all her love and affection very willingly.

She was getting warm and took off her coat. Sean was right there to take it from her.

"Clive should be here any time. I brewed up some coffee." Sean turned and hung up her coat, she also handed over her hat and scarf. He touched her hand as she handed them over, shocked with the charge she felt.

"Coffee would be wonderful" she finally said. She had been so very excited to go hunting today but now she was feeling uncertain. Had she been foolish to accept Sean's offer. She was going to look such a fool if she was having feelings similar to how she had begun to feel for Reggie before he left. There was nothing she despised more than looking like a fool. She sighed as Sean walked toward his small kitchen stove to get coffee. She sat in one of the soft chairs by the fireplace and let herself lose her swirling thoughts in paying attention to Cupid. She smiled down at the dog and gave him a thorough rubdown. He rolled over in merciful surrender.

"He certainly loves you," Sean said, and Dolly nearly jumped.

He handed her a cup of coffee while her heartbeat settled back to normal. "Thank you," she said softly. She was afraid to look up at him so didn't, instead looking at the cup. He had put cream and sugar in her cup already, the way she liked it. How had he known that?

She sipped thankfully and watched the fire for a moment, wishing for something to say. The silence hadn't grown awkward yet, but it would soon.

"I saw a small herd of deer along the northern edge of the property. But Mack said we can hunt on his land as well today." Sean had sat in the other chair and was also looking at the flames in the fireplace.

"That sounds like a good place to start." Dolly said finally, looking at Sean, feeling foolish for being silly. He glanced over to her again, with that look on his face. Just for a moment, but she knew she had been right in that instant. Sean's eyes said what she had believed a few minutes before. There was something more than friendship behind his eyes. She was suddenly terrified. Cupid let out a howl and ran to the door. Sean set his coffee down and gave Dolly a little smile that made her nervous.

"That should be Clive." Sean pulled on his coat. Dolly sat

inside and fretted.

<hr/>

There was something magical, about being in the woods at dawn. Dolly felt her warm breath against the scarf she pulled up around her mouth. She breathed in the frosty cold air. Even with all the experience of each hunter here, their steps were not as silent as they would be in the summer. The ground, with the layer of frost, was crunching underfoot. They went slowly beyond the bluff as quietly as they could.

Dolly was so relieved when Clive had joined them, and the strange worry she had been feeling around Sean had melted away. She looked above the canopy of the pines and saw the morning light streaking over the eastern mountains. Just the hint of light against the midnight blue. The stars were fading.

They covered the ground and went beyond any place she had hunted before with Clive.

"Be watchful of bears." Clive said as they crossed a thin stream. "There might still be a few around." He spoke just above a whisper.

Dolly watched the ground for any fresh signs of deer, but the frost made it more difficult. The morning light continued to filter through the trees as they walked through the woods. There were rocks and bushes to work around as they went deeper into the forest. The world was awakening, and it was an hour into the trip when they paused, to listen.

Dolly pointed and saw a dark owl perched high on a branch above them. The creature was still for a moment and turned its head in their direction. It took flight a moment later and Dolly was happy to watch it take flight. The powerful wings pushed it high up through the dark and dreary branches. Dolly looked at Clive and Sean with a grin. She could see that they loved the woods and all its wonders as much as she did.

They stayed there for a little time. The sounds of the forest said that there were creatures around and they stayed still. They were rewarded for their stillness as a fat hare came out from the underbrush. Dolly was able to shoot it cleanly with her bow. She used her knife and cleaned the hare quickly, then Sean shared water from his canteen for her to rinse her hands.

They began to walk again and found what they were looking

for. A small collection of bucks was gathered by a stream and Clive pointed. They all stopped and stayed still. Clive was good at giving non-verbal instructions and they each had a buck targeted. They would shoot all together. Each at their own target.

She had hunted with Clive before, and knew that when she had counted to ten they would all shoot. Clive gave the slight nod and she counted in her mind and let out her breath slowly. She pulled back on her arrow and the slightest sound of the bending of the hardwood of her bow was loud in her ears after it being so silent. The buck she was aiming at was a few years old. He was healthy and strong. He turned a little and Dolly adjusted her aim, she wanted a clean shot through the ribs and into the heart. In her mind she counted three, two, one. She let the arrow fly and within a heartbeat the sound of gunfire erupted from the men.

Clive's buck dropped, but both Sean and Dolly's bucks were on the run. Dolly watched for a moment to see what direction hers would go. She left from her crouched position and was on the run. Sean was beside her for part of the run but veered to the right to keep an eye on his buck. She watched her buck leap over a few bushes. He was bleeding heavily. She watched the ground as she ran at half speed, not wanting to get caught on a root or branch. She climbed over a fallen log and saw that her buck was ahead. He spun for a moment then fell. Dolly was at the side of the creature within a moment. She let out a whistle to let Clive know that she was safe. It was a minute later that she heard Sean's whistle.

Dolly got to work gutting the buck. She didn't want the meat to spoil. It would be the waste of a life. She thanked God for the creature he made and thought of the good meat and skins it would provide. She went forward with the messy work quickly and efficiently. The arrow had struck true and she knew that the buck hadn't suffered. He had reacted in shock but fell within a minute. Dolly was pleased.

It took some time but they all gathered back with Clive. Dolly had tied up her buck and was carrying him with his feet around her shoulders. It took some shifting, but she found a comfortable position. They all praised each other on the fine shooting and then started the walk back to Sean's cabin. Since they were no longer hunting they had a pleasant talk as they traveled.

"I need to pull my rifle out of the closet at Chelsea and Russell's house. I realize that I enjoy using my bow, but I don't want to get rusty on the rifle skills." Dolly said at they crossed the creek. The noise they made stirred up a few animals and they all watched a few chipmunks run away in a flurry of skittering leaves and critters.

"I was just thinking about how quiet and stealthy you are with that bow." Clive said with a smile. He shifted his shoulders and stopped for a moment. He seemed to find a comfortable position and then walked on.

Dolly smiled. "I would be happy to make you a bow." She immediately began to imagine how she would make it.

"Well, now, that would be somethin'." Clive said huskily. She was feeling a little out of breath from carrying the heavy carcass.

"I will be utterly jealous." Sean said and laughed.

"Well now, Dolly, as if you didn't have enough jobs. When you aren't searching the woods for plants, making medicine, and writing books, you can spend your free time making bows for all us menfolk!" Clive cackled happily.

Dolly gave Clive a sideways look, then nearly tripped on a rock on the ground. Sean leaned over and placed his hand on her shoulder to help steady her.

Dolly laughed at herself. "Well, I was going to say something about Clive's teasing, but my feet betrayed me." She said. She was feeling happy and satiated after the morning in the forest and the camaraderie between her and these men was growing.

She gave Sean a look that was hopefully thankful for his help.

"Oh, please share what you were going to say." Sean urged. He had a brown spot of dirt on his chin. Instead of making him look unkempt it made his look rather rugged. She felt silly for noticing.

"Well, I was just going to say that Clive should not be teasing anyone about having so many jobs and interests." Dolly looked over and Clive winked at her.

"As always, Dolly is quite correct." Clive chuckled. He held up a hand and stopped to shift the weight of the buck on his back again. "Ugh... I am feeling my age just now."

"You have the biggest buck of the day, Clive. If you don't feel a bit uncomfortable then you are not human." Sean said and let out a big sigh of his own.

Dolly was feeling the burn of carrying the weight in her legs and shoulders and told them so.

"Well, I am supposin' that a little hard work will keep us all fit." Clive offered.

They all agreed and kept up on the walk, retracing their path back to the cabin.

Poor Cupid was inside, howling up a storm, while they were all in the barn. Sean had enough pulleys to hang each carcass from the ceiling and set a bucket under each buck for them to finish bleeding out. He poked a hole in the ice of a water barrel and dampened a few rags for them to clean up any blood they had on their hands and bodies.

Clive suggested that Sean put a big bear trap along the back of the barn and brace the doors overnight to keep his horse safe in the barn with the carcasses.

"I always worry about the horse out here when the bears are roaming so close." Sean said as they were putting the big beam across the front barn door.

"I caught a few bears trying. That was when I started trapping them after a big kill. I ate bear stew one winter and have a nice pelt from one that tried to get in the barn." Clive said, as they walked around to the back. Clive pointed out a good spot for it, and they set the heavy trap behind the back window. Dolly had used snares for smaller creatures in the woods, but this big metal trap was quite a contraption. It would certainly break the leg of a human if anyone was unlucky enough to step into it.

Sean offered coffee and biscuits inside and they all eagerly went inside to get some warmth.

Dolly was so relaxed during the hunt but her nervous energy began again when she went back inside the cabin. She gave some more attention to Cupid to give herself something to focus on.

She stayed quiet while they drank their coffee and her mind was busy, thinking up excuses on why she had to leave. She wanted to talk to her trusted friend Chelsea. She needed some advice.

Eventually she found an excuse. "I should go. I feel the need to clean up." Dolly said stiffly. Hoping they couldn't tell that she was nervous and agitated.

Sean and Clive didn't seem to think anything odd about her and wished her a safe ride home.

She didn't want to interrupt the canning party, so she rode Clover back to Chelsea and Russell Grant's cabin. She spent a long time in the barn with Clover when she arrived, giving him a good brushing and enjoying the quiet within the barn to sort out her thoughts. She was certainly confused about her interaction with Sean. She would try to find the words to speak about it with Chelsea, but a part of her wanted to forget all about it. If she put it to the back of her mind perhaps it would go away.

Chelsea was gone, Dolly had forgotten that she was at the canning party. Dolly was slightly relieved. She spent some time boiling some water and made a bath to wash off the grime of the hunting adventure. She wouldn't think about her irrational thoughts about Sean Fahey. She would focus on her work. It was her way.

Dolly wanted to be kind to Chelsea, so she spent some time doing chores around the house. Hoping to surprise her friend when she returned. Chelsea would come home to clean house after a long day.

❖❖❖

Galina Varushkin

The day had finally arrived, and Galina and Edith were finishing up on a few treats for the canning party. The kitchen was a mess, with large pots on the countertop and a few crates of canning jars underfoot but they cheerfully worked to get the raspberry tarts and blueberry turnovers out of the oven. Galina had learned from Edith how to make a sugar glaze and smoothed it over the turnovers as they came out of the oven. Galina smiled over the scrumptious treats that were glistening in the light.

"Oh, dearie," Edith stated with pride. "Those look divine." Edith gave her a warm smile and Galina placed the turnovers on large platters while Edith put another batch in the oven.

There was a knock at the door and Violet peeked her head through the open door.

"Are you ready for me?" Violet asked sweetly.

"Always!" Edith called out. "Bring yerself in from that cold wind. I near burst my buttons running over from my cabin today. My bones do not like the bite of that wind today." Edith chuckled a little and smiled.

The kitchen was warm already and good aromas were filling the house. Galina noticed that Edith's cheeks were a healthy pink and she looked happy. Galina was hoping today would be a good day, with so many friends and lots of visiting.

Violet shuffled in with a big covered basket. She set it on the table. "I have some more stuff to bring in." Violet said and headed towards the door.

"I could ask Warren, he is in the barn today. I asked him on my way in if he would be willing help the ladies bring in their supplies." Edith offered.

"Oh, that would be so kind. But not if it's a bother." Violet said.

"Oh, it's no bother, I'll just ring the bell. Warren will come around if he is free." Edith said, then walked to the backroom. There was a handy bell by the back door to call if anyone needed help. It wasn't something they used all the time, but after Angela's last fall it had to be used a few times when she needed help.

Galina walked behind Edith, some part of her wanting to see Warren, even a glimpse of him.

Why am I so stubborn? I should just apologize and get it over with. Galina said to herself. She watched Edith ring the bell out by the back door. It was just a quick ring, not a long extended one. The cue that some help was needed but not urgent.

Galina watched out the back window and saw Warren's shape exit the barn. He walked up the small hill towards the house. Galina felt her breath catch a little. She had enjoyed his company so much. Now, it was just ruined. *I am such a fool.* She thought.

It was a slow agony watching him walk up to the back door. Galina was standing back and letting Edith handle talking with him. Galina wasn't sure if she should smile at him or just keep her face impassive. She wanted to smile at him. To make some kind of peace offering.

He was finally there, handsome as ever, broad chested and a kind smile on his face. He was a few years older than her, considered a man now by most. It was beginning to show, in the slow way of time, watching a boy grow into a man. Galina was a little heartsick, just seeing him, wishing she hadn't been acting like such a child.

"Hey, good Warren, do you mind unloading some goods for Violet? I think her wagon is out front." Edith asked politely.

"I would be pleased to help out ma'am." Warren smiled his full smile. His eyes shifted and locked onto Galina's for just a moment. His smile never faded. It was a long moment before he looked away. Galina caught herself smiling, and her cheeks were heating up. She was certain she was blushing.

"Aren't you a dear." Edith praised and thanked him. "You be sure to come by, I will send you home with some canned goods as a thank you. I'm certain your mama and sister could make a little extra room in their pantry for some treats."

"That they could, ma'am." Warren said. He laughed when Edith chided him on calling her 'ma'am'.

"You better be calling me Edith, or Mama Sparks from now on. I done told you more than once." Edith scolded happily. "Iff'n you don't I might have to take a switch to ya." She laughed heartily.

Warren laughed fuller and Galina wanted to laugh too. Her stubbornness had led to this strange existence, where she could not allow herself to enjoy things like she had before.

Warren left a moment later. He had met her gaze for the briefest moment and she smiled a little for him. Hopefully, she could say with a smile everything that she just couldn't say aloud.

Warren was in and out of the house with carrying the crates of supplies in for Violet, then a few minutes later was back in with Marie Harpole, who had a few young children in tow.

Galina stayed busy, cleaning up the mess from the morning cooking and washing up a few dishes that had gathered from breakfast. Edith was beside her and was quick to dry and get everything put away neatly.

Conversation was already flowing as Violet and Marie were making plans for the day.

Marie was always pleasing to have around. Her sweet voice was melodic as she flitted about the rooms. She got her children settled into the parlor, Heidi Sparks was there with the other Spark's children and she was going to be watching them with the help of Cooper and Lila Harpole. Galina was definitely going to be helping as much as she was needed, but Galina was hoping to spend the majority of her time learning from the women. She felt that inner nudge to learn all she could. She would soon be of marriageable age and needed to know more. Though with her ruination of her relationship with Warren it might delay that kind of thinking for some time.

"No worries, Heidi, if you need extra hands to help we all will be pitching in." Marie gave Heidi a hug and thanked her again for volunteering. Heidi was a few years younger than Galina, but they got along well. She had been adopted with her younger siblings by the Spark's family. She hadn't always been happy here, still mourning the death of her parents, but in the last months she had been slowly and steadily coming out of the dark mood and enjoying life again. Galina was glad to see Heidi smiling more over the last months.

"I will check in often too, Heidi." Galina said when Marie was leaving.

"Thanks, Galina." Heidi said with a smile. "I should be fine, unless the kids get restless. I have a few fun activities planned." Heidi settled on a chair and invited Abigail Harpole up to her lap, she was growing fast and had her mother's blond curls and sweet pink cheeks.

A few minutes later Corinne arrived with her two babies in tow. Warren was behind her, with bushels of vegetables and fruits. It took a few trips to get them inside.

"I don't know how much help I will be, but I am here." Corinne said with a tired shrug.

"You know that these kinds of events go well with many hands. If you can help with some of the prep work, then we can stay busy doing the canning work." Violet said and took a child from Corinne's arms. Trudie reached for Violet and was rewarded with a kiss on her fingers and cheeks from Violet. Galina ran over and took Caleb from Corinne and Caleb nestled into Galina's chest.

"Aw, he is a sleepy boy." Galina said softly.

"He hasn't been sleeping well at night. He has some teeth coming in." Corinne said as she was shrugging out of her coat. "Staying at the Harpole's while the cabin is getting finished has put us all in a whirl."

Galina hadn't been to see the changes in the cabin for a few days, but she hoped for everyone's sake that the cabin would be ready soon. She knew that Lucas had hired a big crew, he even had her father working to help get the cabin done before the major snow of winter arrived.

"I will keep Caleb for a few minutes, you get settled in." Galina offered. There was something so warm and comforting about holding a sleepy child.

The room filled with chaos as more people arrived. Chelsea with Brody and Sarah came in with a few other women from church. The pastor's wife, Mrs. Whitlan came in with the two foster girls near to Heidi's age. All the kids were sent to the parlor and Heidi was glad to get a few extra hands to care for all the children as the women worked.

Chelsea stood in the arch leading to the parlor. "Okay, all of the older children, I am looking at you Brody and Cooper. No rough-housing today! You will be helpful to Heidi and the other girls. They are in charge, and I better not hear of any trouble now." Galina could hear a few muttered words of agreement. "If you all behave and let the women work then you will be handsomely rewarded."

Chelsea had a husky, no-nonsense voice that carried well. It was such a strange opposite to see her, petite and pretty, and still young. Galina loved Chelsea and her blunt sense of humor too.

The kitchen was swarming with many hands and soon Galina was put to task after she passed Caleb back to Corinne, who soothed Caleb to sleep, there was a cradle all ready in Angela's bedroom, Ted had it made in town. It would be getting its first use.

Galina was handed a basket of herbs and she spent a good half an hour pulling rosemary leaves from stems. Edith and Violet were handing out the orders and soon every surface had someone chopping, sifting or sorting.

A few more people joined the party as the morning commenced. Soon the smell of a savory stew was coming from the kitchen. Galina snacked on some of the treats she had made with Edith earlier.

Corinne sat next to Galina. They were both peeling apples for the apple pie filling they would be canning after the stew was done.

"I was told that one of your stories might be in the newspapers." Corinne said with enthusiasm.

"Perhaps…" Galina said, amused. It had only been a few days since she had discussed it with Sophia.

"Well, I think that is just so wonderful." Corinne grabbed at a handful of peels and moved them over to a bowl set aside for the peelings. She then sliced the apple in half and began cutting the pieces into smaller chunks.

Galina met Corinne's gaze, she could see that Corinne was proud of her. "Thanks." Galina said simply.

"I hope that you know how much we all care for you." Corinne said and gave Galina a pointed look.

Galina nodded, suddenly feeling a little misty. There had been some hard days and knowing that people were supporting her was a sweet thought amidst the chaos in her own mind.

"I appreciate that so much Corinne. Sometimes my mind gets all muddled and I start feeling alone, when I don't have to be." Galina admitted. She looked down at the apple she had been slicing and felt the need to focus on her hands and not her words.

"I remember being young, I made some foolish choices back then. I let my mouth get ahead of me sometimes. I beat myself up pretty hard about it." Corinne said next to her. Her words rang true to Galina.

"I can relate to that." Galina laughed a little. She felt lighter after the admission.

"You know where to find me, if you ever need to talk something out." Corinne offered.

"I would never want to bother you. You have your own troubles." Galina said, perhaps a bit too quickly.

Corinne set the knife and apple down and gave Galina's shoulder a tap. "I hope you know better than that… I would be so sad if you didn't feel like you could come to me, any time, day or night. Tell me you don't feel that way." Corinne said with feeling.

Galina forced her eyes to look toward her friend Corinne, the woman who had gone out in the middle of the night to save her after her father's beating. The one who had stood by Galina even when her father had shown up at their doorstep making threats. Galina felt foolish.

"I am a bit of a mess, I am sorry Corinne." Galina admitted. She sighed and wondered if she would ever get her thoughts right. "I was thinking about you, staying at the Harpoles, and now having adopted Caleb, and your house being torn apart. I just didn't think that talking about my silly problems would… well, I would never want to be a burden to you. You saved my life." Galina finally spit it all out. Hot tears rolled down her cheeks.

"Well, my house is going to be done when it is done. Caring for babies is a challenge, but I have some wonderful helpers, as you well know. Even with all that, there is always time to bounce a baby on my knee and talk to a dear friend." Corinne smiled, and Galina nodded, hoping to tell Corinne that she understood. Suddenly her throat was tight, and she felt mute. Hopefully Corinne could tell all she felt from a nod.

The room was full, Olivia and Sophia joined the group and the afternoon was spent with everyone talking and cooking. The pots of stew were canned, and every household was given a few jars to store in their pantries. A few were set aside to give to the pastor and his wife. The apple pie filling was then canned. There was a surplus of apples, especially with this year's harvest, from Angela and Ted's trees. There would be pies all winter. A few dozen apples were then used to make apple butter, since a request had been made from several families who enjoyed that. Galina had never tried apple butter and was very pleased with the taste. Galina loved all the spices and hoped that Angela would get a jar for their pantry. Galina was hoping for a little of that on some breakfast toast, or even on a biscuit.

This day was a good distraction and she was glad to help with all the prepping of vegetables for the next canning project. The company was good, and her mind was kept occupied.

Sophia and Edith had come up with a plan, that after the canning event Galina would go back with Sophia and stay at the Quackenbush house overnight and go to church with them.

"Angela had the idea, I just made sure it was all good with them. Angela wanted you to enjoy the rest of the weekend." Edith had declared. Galina was happy to be able to get away.

Hundreds of jars later and a few sleepy children were carted back home. Goodbyes were said, and a few stayed behind to finish the cleanup.

Sophia and Olivia were lighthearted and singing silly songs, and everyone joined in as the kitchen got put back to order.

Angela declared the event a success, and they were already making a plan to do this a few times in the next year.

"If we do this every year, throughout the growing season we all will have full pantries, and less food will go to waste. I think we threw out so many strawberries this year, because I didn't think ahead." Angela lamented.

Violet agreed. "I will start working in my journal, to come up with canning recipes that coincide with the proper harvesting time. I think it should be a good challenge." Violet was writing notes down in her little notebook.

"Edith, I will come by on Monday to pick you up with the buggy, we can go to the butcher, he said he will have that order of lard ready for me by then." Violet looked up from her notes.

"I will be ready. Before I forget, thank you, Galina, for all the hard work today. You were a big part of today's success." Edith gave Galina a warm smile.

Galina smiled at everyone who was looking at her with

appreciation.

"You go pack up, I'm sure Olivia and Sophia are ready to get back home. It is already growing dark." Angela said with a smile. "You come back tomorrow whenever you feel like. You deserve a long day off after all the work you have done."

"Are you certain?" Galina said, she was surprised that Angela wanted to take on Sunday dinner all alone. She was still pretty slow with her walking cane.

"I am coming over to help her out, now you put your worries aside." Edith said with her no-nonsense tone.

Galina grinned and nodded. "I will be back tomorrow night."

Sophia went with Galina to her room upstairs. Galina and Sophia made quick work of packing up a bag for the night.

"You should wear your burgundy dress tomorrow. It is the prettiest color on you." Sophia urged.

Galina paused over the dresses hung in the wardrobe.

"Wearing those hoops in the cold… My legs get so cold." Galina grumbled, even though she agreed. Marie had made this dress for her, and it was her favorite.

"I always wear double of my underthings in the winter months. I hate to be cold too." Sophia said practically. "I'll be wearing my hoops to church tomorrow too."

Galina grabbed the dress and then the hoops. It would be cumbersome to take with her but there was no changing what had to be done. She grabbed up the winter bonnet she had that matched the dress.

"All ready." Galina said with a smile. Getting away was the perfect remedy for her messed up emotions.

They bounced down the stairs where Olivia was chatting by the front door. She was always a picture of sweetness. Spending time with Olivia and Clive would be so much fun.

Galina said her goodbyes and got on her coat. The door was opened, and Olivia and Sophia went outside to the porch. Galina grabbed up her satchel and then the hoops and turned to go out the door.

Warren was waiting there.

"Evening ladies." Warren said politely.

"Evening…" Said Sophia and Olivia in unison.

Galina felt her heart stop beating for a moment.

"Hello Miss Varushkin." Warren looked Galina right in the eye.

"Let me help you with your things." Warren grabbed for her bags and hoops before Galina could even respond.

Galina gulped.

She followed behind Warren as they all walked toward the buggy that was set up and waiting for them. It wasn't a long walk but for Galina it felt like time was crawling at a snail's pace. She felt that nudge again. The inner voice was telling her to make things right.

"Thank you, Warren." Galina said finally when they reached the buggy. He placed her things behind the back of the seat. He helped Olivia and Sophia up into the buggy.

"You ladies be careful getting home now. Looks like snow in those clouds tonight." He said. He was being so polite. Galina knew she had just a small chance to say something kind.

What to say? She wondered.

"See you at church tomorrow?" She blurted out. It was a safe thing to say, but also was a hint that she wasn't angry.

"I will be there, Lord willing," He winked at Galina, causing her stomach to flip uncomfortably.

Galina smiled at him with the full smile that she hadn't used in a while.

"You have a good night." She said finally, and he helped her into the back seat. She was feeling a little ridiculous about how nice it was to hold his hand, even for just a moment.

She watched Warren wave as they made their way out of the Greaves' drive and onto the road. Sophia turned around once they crossed the bridge.

"That went well, I think." Sophia giggled.

"Oh hush!" Galina blushed and giggled a little too.

The ride home was dark, and Galina saw that Warren had been right. As they were pulling up to the barn behind the Quackenbush house the first snowflakes began to fall.

Chapter 10

Clive Quackenbush

Clive was waiting for the women and had hot coffee on the stove.

"I'm glad you got in from the cold." He said casually as he helped his wife out of her thick coat.

"It was a pleasant ride home; the wind was only starting to pick up just as we were getting close to home." Olivia said.

The puppies, who had been sleeping in the parlor, came bounding out with excitement and a few barks as they realized that new people had arrived.

"Oh, sweet Lady." Sophia said sweetly and scooped up her toy poodle and was rewarded with a few happy kisses.

"Now Galina, you make yerself comfortable." Clive said in his usual jovial tone.

"You want a cup of coffee, Galya?" Sophia asked, using the nickname that Galina's mother had always used. It always warmed her heart to hear it.

"Oh yes." Sophia placed Lady on the floor and Galina crouched down low to give the poodle some affection.

Galina cooed and muttered sweet talk to Lady and Cocoa for a few minutes. A few happy yips and barks could be heard throughout the house as the puppies settled down from the excitement.

Clive and Olivia were laughing at the two, who were falling all over themselves wiggling and squirming to get Galina's affection.

"Oh, they are just darlings." Galina praised.

Soon, coffee was poured for everyone and they all settled in the parlor. The poodles were worn out with all the excitement and each one found a lap to snuggle into. Though, a few times they would wake and waddle over to a new lap sleepily. Galina was enjoying the cuddling immensely.

They chitchatted for a long time. Talking about the plans for over the winter months.

Sophia and Olivia each talked about lace, because they loved it. Galina talked about the Greaves household and how well

Angela was healing. After a while Sophia and Galina went up to Sophia's room and they talked the way that young girls do.

Clive sipped on the last few drops of his coffee. The evening was now quiet, with a only slight noise coming from the upstairs every once in a while from the two young ladies. It was a pleasing sound.

"I am glad that Galina is spending some time here." Clive said and looked over to his wife. She made a lovely picture, with a poodle in her lap, and the book in her hand.

"I am as well." Olivia smiled at Clive.

He was thankful for her. A companion was such a gift from the Lord. Had it truly only been a few months now of marriage? Every day felt like such a blessing that it certainly made it seem like longer than that. He mused.

"I wanted to talk with you. Now that we have some quiet time." Olivia said. She closed her book and set it on the table next to her.

"You mentioned a while back about me hiring a cook." Olivia said.

Clive perked up, feeling happy to bring up a topic that he was very interested in. "I think you are a fine cook, my love." He said emphatically. "I just don't want you to feel the need to do that plus your work, and the housework."

Olivia gave him a look. "I see you doing the housework around here more than I do it." She laughed.

"Well, I'm just makin' sure you don't go changin' yer mind about me. The slob that I am." Clive chuckled.

Olivia smiled a bit then continued, "I think you are a helpful spouse, more than I ever expected. But, I will agree to your proposal to hire on some help. I have a new project, and I realize that it might be wise. I just want to be certain that it would not be a financial burden."

Clive nodded and pursed his lips. Pleased that she had mulled over his idea and had agreed. "That is no concern. If you ever want to see the finances, you are more than welcome to it." Clive offered.

Olivia shook her head. "I wasn't really worried, that is just me being a ninny. That last excuse that was bouncing around in my head." She laughed a little. Then she had a serious pause. She looked concerned.

Clive saw the serious look that crossed her brow. He knew she had something on her mind.

"What's the project?" He asked.

"Well, I wanted to make sure you were ready for this, but there is really no way to approach it gently." Olivia sighed. "We are expecting a child."

Clive couldn't help himself and let out a whoop. Cocoa jumped from her lap and started barking.

"Oh, my sweet Olive." Clive was at her side and kissing her sweetly.

Olivia was crying, and he wiped away her tears.

Sophia and Galina were making their way down the stairs. Sophia's dog Lady joined in the barking with Cocoa.

"What is the ruckus?" Sophia asked with a confused smile.

The dogs finally stopped their barking and settled on wiggling at Clive's feet. He was still kneeling next to Olivia.

"We are expecting a baby." He said it again, and he kissed Olivia on the cheek. He put a hand to his head. "The Lord certainly has a blessed me so much." He smiled so wide that he was going to split open soon.

Sophia and Galina gushed, and Olivia cried a few more tears.

They all got settled down and sat back into the chairs around the fireplace. Clive sat in the chair next to his bride, holding her hand.

"How long have you known?" Clive asked finally.

"Since yesterday, I went to see Doc Williams, because of my exhaustion and tummy complaints. I really had no idea that I could even have children. I was married for so long before… I was certain I was barren." Olivia let a few tears fall. "I had given up on that dream a long time ago."

Clive kissed her hand. He felt tears of his own welling up in his eyes, making the room look blurry. "I have grandchildren, who have children. God is certainly been busy finding me blessings." He shook his head. "May the Lord be praised for all of His goodness."

Milton Vaughn

Milton lathered up the special shaving cream he used and

108

applied it with the soft brush over his chin and cheeks. He had learned from his father when he was young to handle a straight razor proficiently. He glided it over his own skin with smooth even motions. The sound the blade made over the skin was a long bristling hiss as it cut through the facial hair. It was something that was pleasing, if not a bit tedious sometimes, as a daily routine. He enjoyed the sensation of a barber doing it better. The whole experience with a barber was a luxury, a little bit of pampering for a man, that was acceptable, as long as the barber had a sharp blade and skill.

He wiped away the excess cream when he was done and used Kalydor, a lotion, after the shave to sooth the skin. It had a pleasant scent.

Milton dressed well, but with a thought about the society in which he lived now. He had a certain pride about being a sharp dresser, but he kept his best cufflinks and accessories to a minimum here. Being in Oregon City for more than a week he had observed his new neighbors, a lot of them sporting beards and simpler garb. He wondered what they thought of him as he went about town, meeting the other shop owners and folks strolling through town during this cold blustery week. His brown wool suit had a pleasing pinstripe and he placed the round hat on his head to keep it warm. He was off to church and felt a nice suit would always make a good impression, even in this far off place. He was certain to be the best dressed in town. It would get him noticed but he wasn't so fancy as to create a spectacle. He had visited the church in town last weekend. He did his duty, shaking hands, and singing along with the hymns. His mother would have been so pleased. In his youth he had tried his mother's patience a million times as his mind wandered throughout the service. He and a few of his pals would somehow be a disruption, even while barely doing more than making gestures across the pews during the minister's sermon. Once he was out on his own he realized the benefit of church, less about the sermon, but more about the social aspect of belonging to a community. He enjoyed a few songs, that reminded him of his childhood, and gave him some pleasant memories of his mother. She had loved to sing those songs all throughout her days at home. He didn't mind the music so much, even though some churches didn't have the best musicians. Some had no musical accompaniment at all, just the sound of the voices carrying the melody. On occasion when the singing was lackluster, he worked at keeping his smile on and his distaste for the offkey and offensive sounds until the songs were finished.

He knew that people put high stock in a man's church attendance. To him it was rather dull and tedious but it was necessary. There was truly no other place one could be more quickly accepted and welcomed in a new town or city than by plopping down in a church pew every Sunday morning. Milton considered it a part of his job, it might be the single most important part.

He grabbed the gold watch off the dresser, feeling the smooth texture of the outside against his hand. His daily habit was always to open it turn the knob, winding it for the next day. The quiet tick-tick-tick was something that he enjoyed.

This watch had been in his family for several generations. According to stories it had come across with his great grandfather, from Britain, decades ago. Every man in his family, on his father's side, had been in business. Milton felt a certain pride at finding success at his young age. He had been promised this watch when he became a man.

His father had been a steady, hard-working man. There was always food on the table, church on Sundays, and work to be done. Milton had appreciated the lessons he was taught by his father, though not always the long discussions. His father had been more religious and serious than Milton. The long days of working under his father had made Milton impatient. Milton was always wanting to be one step ahead of his father. His father was cautious and frugal with investing. Milton was always wanting to try out new schemes and ideas at the barbershop. His father had tried a few. Some had gained them customers and sales, others hadn't. Even the tiniest setback would set Milton's father back into his frugal and cautious ways.

Milton had left home at seventeen a few days before he was eighteen. He had saved his money, made enquiries and had a partner for business already set up for himself.

He packed his suits and trunks and hired a cart and while his parents were at a church brunch he left. He had taken the gold watch the night before. He sat at the breakfast table, listening to his father search through his bedroom for the watch, not saying a word.

"I am certain we will find it." Milton's mother said sweetly as she served up breakfast.

She was wearing her nicest lace collar for the luncheon and the cameo pin that Milton had bought for her birthday. She was always kind and thoughtful, and Milton found, throughout the years, that if he doted on her enough, she would champion the son over the father. He played them off each other with subtlety although never maliciously. He found he had a gift for it and used it to get his father to promote his ideas. His father was always being encouraged to pay Milton well for his many hours of work at the shop, and for all of his ideas and promotions. His mother's urgings had led to Milton's savings growing substantially since he was thirteen. She was convinced that Milton was very mature for his age.

Milton was tired of waiting to come of age and with many letters sent and contacts made he set forth. He wouldn't grow old and gray waiting for his father to pass away and give him the store, instead he would make his own way.

He left a note behind for his mother.

Dearest Mother,

I begin my journey today to prove I am the man you raised. I am borrowing the gold watch to have a reminder of the man my father has trained me to be. I have a partnership for a new shop in a new town to set up, and my head full of ideas. I will write when I get settled in.

With much love,
Milton

He really had no intentions of returning the watch, and the few times he had written to his mother over the years he had kept things pleasant. He never gave his address to them, until he had sold his last business in the East. He sent a short note that he was sailing to the west. Someday he would write and give them a return address, but not yet.

Milton took a brush and wiped away any fuzz or debris from his pants and grabbed his wool coat. It was time for Sunday service.

He rented a one-seat buggy at the livery and followed the directions he had recieved earlier in the week from a business owner.

The snow was falling softly, but it wasn't sticking to the ground just yet. Just a feathered covering so far and the roads weren't bad yet. He was uncertain of the severity of winter here in these parts, but he was well protected from the chill in his coat and hat.

The small church was down Spring Creek Road two miles from town. It wasn't fancy, it had no stained-glass windows or even a bell. Just a simple country church. Milton could imagine how charming it would look in the summer with the fields of green beyond and the mountains behind. It currently was on the verge of quaint, once there was a blanket of white the scenery would be charming. The drab brown grass was still visible, and it lost a little of its appeal.

Milton pulled forward and tied the buggy to the rail. He threw the wool blanket over the seat to keep it dry and walked slowly inside. Nodding and smiling his best at any nearby church-goers.

"Good morning, sir," a man said as Milton neared the steps.

The man was tall and broad shouldered. He was dressed in a suit, though not as fashionable as his, he mused.

"Good morning to you." Milton smiled broadly. The man waited for him at the top of the steps.

"I'm Lucas Grant." The man gave Milton a welcome pat across the shoulders.

Milton reached forward to shake Lucas' hand. "Milton Vaughn, pleased to meet you." Milton knew how to do this part well. He could easily mix in just about any company.

Milton smiled and said a few how-do-ya-dos and found a seat in a middle pew. The inside of the church was clean and bright with an obvious fresh coat of paint. The pews were nicely carved, and Milton was pleased to be there. He stood and shook a few more hands, watching people come in. Some of the women were gathering around each other. This scene was as normal as could be.

The majority of the women of the West were rather plain in his opinion. This room had plenty of examples for him to judge. He kept the impassive grin on his lips as he looked over the people of the room. There were a lot of burly men, certainly farmers and laborers. A native woman, who was an obvious half-breed was talking with the women. She wasn't a beauty, but her features were pleasant, but she wasn't his type, though as she smiled a few times and he had to amend his thoughts on her beauty. She had a broad and stunning smile, but he sensed that she was rather intense in her other moments.

There were a few attractive women throughout the room but the majority of the women who were married were plain and a little thick around the middle. This was to be expected, as most women had children and grew comfortable in their new roles. He tried to keep his eyes moving. He nodded his friendly nod to any men who caught his eye, just that unassuming and neighborly nod. Once the service was done he knew from a glance the people that he would make an extra effort to meet and whom he could just be polite to.

His eyes were drawn to the two young women at the back of the room, one was blonde with an abundance of curls, the other was a brunette with dark eyes and long dark hair. The brunette was intriguing, and he watched her hang her coat on the hooks in the back of the room. Her hair hung down her back, the sides pinned up, meaning she was unmarried. Only married women wore all of the hair pinned up. Her eyes were striking, and he had to make an effort to look away from her. The fashionable burgundy dress was cinched tight around her tiny waist, and her curves were beguiling. She was young, but was she perhaps old enough, he wondered?

He glanced around the room, making certain he wasn't too obvious, then his eyes bounced back to the brunette and blonde. They stopped to chat with the group of well-dressed ladies in the back. He could see that this was a close-knit community and the women were sweet to each other. There were no catty looks shared at all between anyone that he could see.

You can learn a lot about people from watching them interact. Milton thought to himself.

Milton shook hands with a few people he recognized. An older gentleman came up behind him and Milton reached out to shake his hand.

"Clive Quackenbush, good to see you again." Milton smiled. Clive was a pleasant man, and Milton had met him a few times at the fancy goods store. Milton would work hard to maintain a good reputation with him, because he knew from opinion around town that Clive was highly respected.

"Good to see you too. Milton Vaughn, correct?" Clive shook Milton's hand firmly, even reaching over and placing a hand over Milton's, a warm and welcoming gesture. Milton never took gestures for granted and placed a hand on Clive's shoulder.

"I heard there was a country church outside of town and had

to come see it. My mother would have been so charmed by this lovely little place." Milton smiled sincerely. Clive smiled a little broader. Everyone had a certain pride about their place of worship and Milton knew that a little praise would go a long way.

"You own the barber shop in town correct?" Clive asked. He was cordial and expressive, Milton could not help but like him. Clive had a sincere gaze that didn't wander.

Milton affirmed Clive's statement and was pleased when Clive said that he enjoyed a good shave there on occasion. They chatted for a few minutes about how Milton liked the town. The pastor was up front talking and Milton gave a final nod to Clive and sat in the pew. He heard Clive talking softly behind him.

"Come on in ladies." Milton turned his head and saw that the two young women sat next to Clive and a woman who had her arm linked with Clive.

That must be his wife. Milton mused. She was an attractive woman, though a few years younger than Clive for certain.

Milton looked back to the front and saw the pastor smiling, waiting patiently for everyone to take their seats.

A blonde woman and the man he shook hands with earlier went up to the front with a violin. Milton remembered his name as Lucas. They announced the number in the hymnal and Milton leafed through the pages to find the song.

The violin music started, and it was sweet and pure. Milton smiled, enjoying the way the music sounded. The woman began to sing, she had a talent and Milton was amazed at how it tugged at his heart strings a little.

Nearer, my God, to Thee, nearer to Thee!
E'en though it be a cross that raiseth me,
Still all my song shall be, nearer, my God, to Thee

The congregation sang along and though the church was small and simple the singing was beautiful.

The voices behind him sang the refrain in sweet harmony. Milton just knew that the young girl's voices were behind him, and he felt their presence there as they sang the refrain.

Nearer, my God, to Thee, Nearer to Thee!

Milton may not have held much respect for religion, but the music was always something that broke through his shell. He sang along and followed through the verses in the hymnal.

The last verse was sung triumphantly, and Milton was caught up in the fervor of everyone else.

There in my Father's Home, safe and at rest,
There in my Savior's love, perfectly blest;
Age after age to be nearer, My God, to Thee

Nearer, My God to Thee, Nearer to Thee!

Milton had felt the urge to clap, because it had been a beautiful and sweet performance, but he followed the mood of the room and stayed silent, enjoying the feeling the lovely melody had given him. He thought of his sweet mother, who would have loved the whole experience.

The pastor came forward and Milton kept his mind alert as he began to speak. Milton thought the man was in his late 40s and seemed fit. He spoke with conviction and even got a chuckle or two with his words, as he shared a story from the New Testament.

Milton had a way to stay alert while the preacher continued, he kept his eyes forward, not glancing around much. He didn't want people to ever think he was bored and not paying attention. He listened enough to form an opinion of the sermon so, if he was asked, he would have something thoughtful to say. He was good at this game. He would think of something flattering to say to people. He would remember to say the book of the Bible that the pastor was speaking about and a little something extra to prove that he listened. He thought about the two unmarried ladies sitting behind him, thanking his lucky stars that they would be so easy to meet since they were so close. It wouldn't take much effort at all to get an introduction.

The pastor finally wrapped up is sermon and led them all in a prayer. Milton dutifully closed his eyes and joined the community and said 'amen' with everyone at the close. The pastor made a request for tithes and offerings and Milton pulled out a dollar coin to put in the plate that passed by him. There was an announcement about a few events on the social calendar, a winter dance coming in December and some charity work for those who needed pantry goods in the lumber camp outside of town. Milton made a mental note to be a part of the events to gain more trust in this small town. The pastor finally released them for the day and Milton stood and made no pause before he greeted Clive Quackenbush again.

"What a lovely service." Milton smiled, putting his hand out again in greeting.

"It was indeed." Clive beamed his pleasure. He turned his head toward the blonde woman at his side. "This is my new bride, Olivia, and her niece Sophia. A very dear friend is here as well, Galina."

Milton smiled sincerely to each lady in turn. Olivia had a sparkle in her eye and Milton could see why Clive had snatched her up. Even being older, she was still a very beautiful woman, with a wit and wisdom behind her eyes.

"I am certain that I heard you young ladies singing earlier." Milton met the gazes of each girl. The blonde was so much like her aunt, very similar features. She reached forward boldly and shook Milton's hand firmly. Milton paused when he met the eyes of the brunette.

"Sophia," Milton said, and he looked to the blonde. "Gali…" He said as he reached forward to shake her hand.

"Galina…" The brunette said with a soft pink glow to her cheeks.

"Ah… Galina. A beautiful name." Milton said softly. He saw the blush and was so very charmed by it. She has bold dark eyes, but her demeanor was not as bold. Though both girls were lovely, he was drawn to Galina, and without a moment's pause he knew he would pursue her. He would have to be careful to not scare her away.

Milton shook her hand. He looked to all three women, ready to spread his charm around.

"When we all were singing I felt it so fully. The lovely voices behind me just made me soar with the angels for a moment." Milton said, he was pleased to see his statement work and they all smiled broader. "My mother loved to sing these spiritual songs and I always think of her when I sing about our Lord."

The women looked flushed and pleased over his compliments and he kept his sincerest smile plastered on his face.

Milton gave Galina a short gaze, just to see if she would meet it. She did for the briefest of moments and it was all he needed to move forward. She was intrigued at the least. He could work with that.

He turned to Clive. "I so enjoyed the sermon. I must go meet the pastor. I really enjoyed his take on that chapter in Acts."

"Yes, Pastor Whittlan is a fine speaker and a wise teacher." Clive affirmed.

"Pastor Whittlan, thank you." Milton spoke softly and nodded. "Olivia, Sophia and Galina… it was my supreme pleasure to have been lucky enough to sit in front of you today. It is an honor to meet you. I hope to see you in town, if the winter snows don't keep you away." He bent his chin down low and smirked a little at Galina and Sophia, it was a look that usually brought a blush if he did it well. He did, and they both blushed.

Clive gave him a clap on the back and Milton moved out of the pew to head toward the pastor. He had some time to shake hands and charm as many people as he could today. Making introductions and repeating his platitudes of the singing and the sermon to anyone who would hear it. His job was to make a good impression, and he worked the room.

Milton finally moved toward the hooks along the back wall to retrieve his hat and coat. Clive was there and the girls who were talking to a woman with lovely red hair.

"It is too bad that Warren couldn't come to service today." He saw Sophia speaking to Galina.

Galina nodded. She turned her eyes toward Milton for the briefest moment and he grinned a little, the shock in her eyes of being caught looking was so sweet. She looked away and he wanted to chuckle but kept it inside.

"I am glad to meet ya, Milton. If you like you can come to supper after service next week. Lord willin' and weather permittin'." Clive offered as he was grabbing up the coats.

"I would be honored to attend." Milton said sincerely. "Perhaps I will convince the ladies to sing for me after we eat." He laughed a little and Clive joined in.

"I think you are just charming enough to get them to agree." Clive laughed too.

Milton watched, good humored as Clive helped each woman with their coats. First his wife, then Sophia. As Clive got behind Galina Milton saw the other women were busy with their buttons, he had her gaze for the briefest moment, he gave her a bold wink and smiled. Her eyes grew wide but no one else saw the exchange.

He tipped his hat and left the church, feeling certain that he had made a good impression.

◆◦◆◦◆———◆◦◆◦◆

Galina Varushkin

She couldn't help but be flattered by the attention she had been given from the new man at church. Galina and Sophia had volunteered to make supper and had giggled and whispered about him all through the preparations.

The name of Milton Vaughn was spoken all through the prepping, cooking and then in the cleaning up time after supper.

Clive and Olivia had their own time, talking about their own exciting news.

"Do you think that Milton is staying in town?" Sophia wondered. Her eyes were lit up and her cheeks flushed from the heat of the hot stove as she boiled more water for the cleaning.

"Well, if he owns a business then that would suggest he is here to stay." Galina smiled.

Sophia frowned for a moment. "I do sort of feel bad for poor Warren today. It seemed like you and him were getting along again. He missed a chance to talk with you."

Galina paused to think on it. "Everything happens for a reason." She smiled. She had been in a cycle of tumultuous emotions lately and it was good that her heart was settling down. She felt good about the small strides she had made to make peace with Warren, but she wasn't certain that she was able to picture them going back to what it had been before. These last months had changed her somehow. She knew she had some growing up to do. She had been foolish.

She looked to Sophia and thought about speaking her thoughts aloud but then changed her mind. It was one thing to know your mistakes. It was another matter altogether to share that with someone like Sophia. She was her dearest friend, but Sophia was so good and happy. Galina sometimes wondered if she was good enough to be her friend.

Galina smiled wistfully and dropped her gaze back to the work they were doing. Her thoughts bounced around between Warren, and the handsome new man at service today. She would have never thought that the smiles from a stranger could affect her so

118

completely. She anticipated next Sunday's dinner here more than ever.

"I may need a new lace collar, Sophie." Galina said as she was washing off a spill of flour from the biscuits they had cut out a minute before. "I have a little set aside for it."

"A lace collar can be done." Sophia laughed. "But if you think I will allow you to pay for it…" Sophia let the sentence go and gave Galina a look.

Galina acted surprised and then laughed. "If you keep giving away all of your lace there will be nothing left to sell." She harrumphed a little. Sometimes it felt like charity for people to give her things. She had earned her own money. Why would no one allow her to spend it?

"Cannot happen." Sophia put the biscuits in the oven and Galina worked to get the rest of the counter cleaned off from the mess left behind. "Besides, I already started a new design and made you a collar just this last week. It is nearly done. I will show it to you before you go back to the Greaves."

Galina nodded and accepted the explanation, but she was contemplating spending the money she was going to use for the lace collar to buy her friend a gift. It eased her mind a little to do something thoughtful and her ruffled feathers inside settled back down.

Chapter 11

Dolly Bluebird Bouchard

Dolly had returned to Sean Fahey's cabin on Monday morning. She had work to do and she couldn't avoid it. The buck she killed needed to be skinned. She had never dreaded this task in the past, because she was good with a skinning knife. There was part of the job that was fascinating and she knew she had skill. It had been a big part of tribal life. She knew that if they could see her now that they would be proud of her.

Suddenly, though, this job she had to do became a distraction. What could one glance from Sean Fahey have changed within her? How could that even be possible? It had been months of easy friendship and now it wasn't.

Dolly had never had that talk with Chelsea, trying to pretend her thoughts away. Now she was certainly doomed.

Sean met her in the barn. She had dressed simply, actually wearing men's brown pants and a flannel shirt that Clive had sold her at his store. She usually didn't mind wearing these clothes, but now she wondered what Sean would think of her dressed this way.

"I have a wagon ready and can take the deer to the butcher if you like." Sean offered as they got started on the skinning.

"That would be fine." Dolly said simply. She knew that she sounded stiff and formal. She added. "Thank you, Sean." She swallowed hard after saying his name and her stomach clenched uncomfortably. Was she becoming ill?

Dolly tried not to look over at Sean, who was examining the carcass he was going to skin. He was a few inches taller than her. Dolly examined his face, trying to see if he looked anything like Angela in features. They didn't look very much alike, but he shared the same nose of his sister. His dark brown hair swung over his forehead a little as he turned his head from side to side. His brow furrowed in concentration. Dolly wasn't certain she could judge a man for how handsome he was, because her childhood was spent around men that all looked different from the men around her. She usually tried to judge men on their character, or their prowess. She recalled a young Shoshone boy she had found handsome when she was younger. She could still see his face, with a glow on his skin as he let an arrow fly. She had always been trying to get his attention, wanting all of the boys to believe that she was as good a shot as any of them.

She looked at Sean now, wondering what had led her to look at his features this way. She had read books that spoke of love. Usually the men in the books were wealthy and the women were beautiful. She enjoyed the books where the women were witty and able to perceive things beyond the simple conclusion that a woman only had worth because she was beautiful, and men were only desirable because they were handsome or wealthy.

Dolly remembered with a blush the day she read through the Song of Solomon in the Bible. When she had discussed it with Chelsea she could barely find the words to ask what it meant.

Chelsea had smiled at her charmingly. 'God is love and he wants us to find love with each other. He created us to desire love. The world does not always show us how to woo each other. I also wonder about this part of the bible. Perhaps God inspired Solomon to share these words because we all need a reminder to cherish each other.'

Suddenly, thinking about the poetic words and the images they placed in her mind. She imagined for a moment Sean speaking to her with words of love. A verse from the bible came to her.

Let him kiss me with the kisses of his mouth!

She was overwhelmed suddenly.

"Excuse me." Dolly said and ran from the barn. The cold air was so refreshing.

Her insides were churning, and she felt feverish all of the sudden. She was certainly losing all of her wits. Thinking of Sean this way was not going to lead to anything good. She was being a fool.

Sean joined her a minute later.

"Ah, here you are." Sean said. He looked concerned for her. That did not help her thoughts of him. He placed his hand on her shoulder. Dolly felt like her own skin was betraying her when she enjoyed the warmth of him.

"I don't think I feel well today." Dolly said softly.

Sean was nodding at her. "You want me to take you home in the wagon? I can tie up Clover behind."

Dolly shook her head. She wanted to be away from him. Any moment she was going to embarrass herself. "No, I think I will be fine."

"I will ride with you. I insist. To make certain you arrive safely. I will go ahead and skin your buck for you when I get back." Sean said and went for his horse Shipley. Dolly stood in front of the barn, wondering if perhaps she had eaten something foul.

Clover was tied out front, and Sean took her by the arm and led her over to her horse.

"Are you certain you do not want to ride with me?" Sean asked. "You look a little flushed."

Dolly wasn't certain if she could answer. She was watching the concern and care on Sean's face, and it was making her even more confused.

"You do not have to take such trouble with me." Dolly said and lowered her chin. What could she do in this moment. She was feeling lost and overwhelmed.

"It is really no trouble." Sean touched her face and lifted her chin. "Dolly, I am worried for you."

His green eyes, she saw them now. They were a shade darker than his sister Angela's. Angela could see into a person sometimes. She was so very caring and considerate. Suddenly she saw Sean and wondering if he was also as considerate as Angela. Perhaps he hadn't always been, but he certainly seemed so now, as he captured her gaze.

"Why do you worry for me?" Dolly asked. It was an odd thing to ask. But now, in all the confusion in her mind she needed to know. What did he mean when he looked at her the way he did.

Sean never looked away, but he did look a little confused. He was only a foot away from her. She felt his breath on her face.

The long moment seemed like an eternity, but Sean finally spoke. "I care for you."

Dolly just stood still, her heart beating fast within her. Wondering what had led her to ask such a question. She couldn't take it back. He cared for her. The look in his eyes said more.

Dolly had spent her life watching people, quietly observing them, seeing everything and saying very little.

The snow had begun to fall and there were snowflakes landing on Sean's hair and still she was quiet. His eyes never left hers. Suddenly, without a thought or a warning Sean pulled her close and kissed her.

122

She had not been ever expected to be kissed. She wondered at how it could be so pleasant when she had seen others do it. Dolly had kissed children, and had kissed her friends on the cheek in greeting. It was a nice feeling to do these things, but it had no comparison to what Sean had just done.

"That was nice." Dolly said after a long minute. Sean ran his hand through his hair. He looked as confused as she felt a few minutes ago. She was feeling much better all of the sudden.

Sean looked up from the ground. Dolly smiled at him, surprising herself. He smiled back, then he lost his composure and started laughing.

"Dolly…" He said and shook his head. "You are the most perplexing woman."

Dolly did not know how to reply but she could not stop from grinning.

Sean frowned a little. "I am sorry for stealing a kiss." Sean said. "I really don't go about kissing women without permission."

"Is that how it is done?" Dolly asked. "A man asks for a kiss?"

Sean shrugged. "I think so. I do not really know. I honestly have never really done that before."

"I will ask Chelsea. She knows these things." Dolly said. She wondered if she should go home now that she was feeling better. She had a sort of nervous happiness within her. She was aware that her insides were warm and giddy.

Sean chuckled. The snow fell quietly around them, the flakes were gathered on his hair and some were starting to melt. Dolly wanted to brush them away, but Scan beat her to it.

Dolly had not looked away from him, and she noticed a red flush to his cheeks.

"I should go, Sean. I think I will be fine for the ride home." She tried to smile and let him know that she was not ill.

He reached for her hand. Feeling his grip was wonderful and made her heartbeat pick up the pace again.

"You are not angry with me?" Sean asked, his smile was gone, and he looked genuinely worried.

"No, I am not." Dolly answered simply. She did not have the words to say what she felt. There was a sweet and wonderful feeling inside her, but she could not describe it. It would be like describing the feeling of sunshine on your face, or how it felt to watch the birth of a new life.

Sean was watching her, and she hoped that he could tell that she was not cross with him. She had no way to tell him anything, because her mind was not her own.

She gave Sean a wave and untied Clover.

"I will see you soon," she said cheerfully.

She mounted up and then gave him a happy wave before she rode off. She was certain she would always remember this moment somehow. Sean with the snow falling on his dark hair and how he kissed her with the winter snow falling around them.

Violet Griffen

It was early on Tuesday morning and Violet was pounding out the last of the sourdough to take over to the Grant cabin. Lucas said that the work on the roof would be done today, 'Lord willin."

Violet knew that having so many bodies underfoot at the Harpole's was getting under everyone's skin just a little bit. It wasn't the normal routine and that could always put everyone in a frazzled state after a few days of chaos.

Marie was braiding her daughter's hair and they were chit chatting the way that mothers and daughters do.

"Do you think my hair is pretty, mama?" Lila said. She may be adopted but to Violet, she saw all Marie's love was there for Lila, whether she was blood kin or not.

"I do, you know I always wished to have such straight shiny hair as you have Lila dear," Marie said. Marie finished the one side of the braid and began working on the other side.

"I have always wanted curly hair like you and Abigail." Lila said and pouted prettily.

Abigail was two years old and looked up to Lila, who had spoken her name. She had a rag doll in her lap and was pretending to braid her hair, just the way her mama was braiding Lila's.

"Don't we always wish for what we don't have?" Marie said. She finished the braid and gave Lila a kiss on the top of her head.

Cooper came through the back hallway, his hands swinging, and his boots dangling wildly around him by the strings.

"Cooper, you better stop that. You will hit somebody with

124

those." Marie gave Cooper a look. He stopped his boots and went to his mother who was beckoning him over to the bench where they were sitting by the front door.

"Lila already said her verse that she learned for school today." Marie said and gave Lila a smile. "Do you want to tell it to me, so that I know that you know it?"

"I know it well enough." Cooper said grumpily.

"Well, then say it." Marie said, her voice was chipper. Violet watched the scene play out, wondering how far Cooper was going to go with his mood.

How did that saying go? *Did you wake up on the wrong side of the bed?*

"I don't see why we have to learn old verses anyway." Cooper huffed.

"Because, it is up to the parents to make sure you grow up knowing the Word of God." Marie said.

"Well, I think that book is boring. Nobody talks like that. I don't see the point of it." Cooper was definitely not in the mood to cooperate.

"So, what about the part of the Bible where is says, 'Thou shall not kill'." Marie said. "Do you think that is a good rule? Should people go around killing other people?"

"Well, no." Cooper said and frowned.

"What about the part where Jesus died for your sins and you get forgiven just because he loved. Is that a good part?" Marie asked.

"That is a good part." Cooper sighed. He didn't want to admit it. Violet could see that she was slowly breaking down his argument.

"Well, if you didn't read the Bible, and learn it, how would you know about it?" Marie asked.

"I don't always understand it, mama. Sometimes it doesn't make sense to me too." Lila said.

Violet smiled, seeing Lila come to the defense of her brother.

"Well, some things in the Bible don't always make perfect sense to me either. Sometimes I read something and just wonder. You want to know what I do when that happens?" Marie said.

Both Cooper and Lila were paying attention now.

"I pray about it. Sometimes God shows me, or I talk about it with someone else, to see what they think about it. Sometimes, I consider it a mystery. God is rather mysterious." Marie said and smiled. "I have a few questions for God someday, when I get to go to heaven."

"What kind of questions?" Cooper asked. He let his boots plop to the floor and he sat. Beginning to put his boots on for school, he looked up to his mother, he was still listening.

"Well, I have some big questions, but along with some hard questions I have, I kind of wonder about things. Like, how did he make lightning? Why did he bother making pesky mosquitos?"

Both Cooper and Lila laughed at her questions. Abigail laughed too, when she heard her siblings laugh.

She wants to be a big kid. Violet thought.

"I suppose that I have some questions too." Cooper said.

"Well, you make a good list. I am certain God won't mind answering all your questions." Marie said.

Cooper stood. *"Psalm 119, verse 66. 'Teach me good judgment and knowledge: for I have believed thy commandments'."* He was trying to behave and show that he could be obedient.

"Good job Coop." Marie said with a smile. "What do you think that means?"

"Well, good judgement, means knowing right from wrong." Cooper said.

Lila chimed in. "I think the second part is about believing God's word."

Marie nodded.

"So, it is asking God to show us right from wrong, because we read His word and believe." Cooper said after a moment to pause and think about it.

"That is very good." Marie. "Does that sound like something we all need?"

Both Cooper and Lila nodded.

Marie gave her kids a hug and praised them both for thinking through the issue.

She scooped up Abigail.

Just then the front door opened and John Harpole peeked his head in. Pepper, their dog came in, his fur a bit sparkly from the damp rainy morning. His tail wagged appreciatively when he saw everyone.

"Ready for a ride to school?" John asked. He gave a nod toward Violet across the room. Violet nodded back, her hands still deep in dough.

"Have them tell you about their Bible verse today. We have

126

young scholars." Marie said and hitched Abigail on her hip.

There was a scurry of activity for a moment as everyone bundled into coats. Cooper tried to skip wearing his mittens, Marie insisted. John also insisted. Cooper finally agreed. Lila shook her head, probably wondering why boys were so difficult. Soon they were out the door.

Marie put Abigail down and walked hand in hand with her over to Violet.

"That was a fun way to start the morning." Violet said with a chuckle.

"Every day it is a new challenge. That was a pretty good one." Marie leaned against the counter.

"You do a wonderful job with your children." Violet said. Feeling that pang in her heart again. Wondering if she would ever have a chance to be a mother.

"It takes a lot of prayer and determination." Marie admitted. "I don't always have a ready solution when they get grumpy. Sometimes it goes the other way. Discipline is probably the hardest for me." Marie stepped around, grabbed a mug, and then poured the last of the coffee from the pot on the stove.

Abigail stayed where she was, having been trained to stay out of the kitchen when people were working there.

She came back around and leaned on the counter again. She sipped at her coffee once she poured some cream and sugar in it.

"I can imagine that discipline would be hard for me as well." Violet had been musing about the idea; to actually discipline someone you loved with every breath.

"It becomes obvious pretty quickly when you have a child. The first time they disobey intentionally. It starts a lot younger than you can imagine. They give you this look, sometimes before they can even walk. When you say no, you know that they understand you, and they watch what you do when they go out of their way to do what you told them not to." Marie smiled and shook her head. "I don't know who said it to me, but it rings true. We are all barbarians, until we are trained not to be."

Violet laughed, she could see how parenting teaches a person a whole new set of skills.

Marie finished her coffee, and Violet finished her chores, but the whole morning scene gave Violet something to think about. This desire to be a mother was growing inside of her. It was time that she had to face it. It was also time to talk to Corinne. Her heart grew heavy with the thought of change, but she knew that she couldn't avoid this conversation. It didn't have to happen in a day but she needed to face her future and not pretend her feelings away.

Dolly Bouchard

Dolly arrived at Chelsea Grant's cabin. The afternoon light was dimmed through the windows as a cloud passed over the sun. There was a fire crackling away in the fireplace and Dolly could hear the sounds of shuffling pans in the kitchen.

Dolly took off her coat, gloves and mittens and saw they would have to be cleaned from her hunting and animal handling. She headed towards the kitchen in the back of the cabin. It was separate room from the dining room and small parlor.

Chelsea was crouched on the ground, looking through a low cupboard. There was more clanging, and Chelsea let out an aggravated grumble.

She stood and put her hands on her hips in exasperation.

"Greetings." Dolly said softly, hoping that she wouldn't scare her friend out of her wits. Chelsea did jump a little.

"Hi Dolly." She put a hand to her heart.

"Sorry to scare you." Dolly said sincerely.

"Oh, that is fine, I am more concerned that I lost my extra bread pan. I have two loaves already proofed and cannot find that…" Chelsea huffed. "I cannot find that bread pan."

Dolly could tell that Chelsea was frustrated and Dolly thought about the last time she had seen the pan. It had been several weeks since she had seen Chelsea bake bread. Dolly was always bouncing between so many different homes, she wasn't positive that she could be very helpful.

"I have been tempted to ask my husband to build me a blueprint home like Angela's." She put a hand on the counter.

"You want a bigger home?" Dolly asked.

"Yes." Chelsea said rather pathetically. "I know it would be expensive, but I have a notion that our family is going to get bigger again."

Dolly was surprised and smiled a little. To know that her friend was perhaps expecting again was a sweet thought.

"I don't think that Russell would be against such an idea. I have heard him remark about wanting to build a bigger house for you. He was just talking about hiring on another helper here, since the purchase of all of the livestock in the fall." Dolly said practically. "This cabin could be used for something else."

Chelsea nodded. "I will pray about it. Silly me." Chelsea's cheeks were red as she wiped away a tear. "What could possibly make me cry over a silly bread pan?"

Dolly laughed with Chelsea, understanding the trials of a woman were something that just couldn't always be explained.

Dolly helped Chelsea search for the pan and a Dolly eventually found it in the parlor behind a chair. It had wooden block toys inside of it.

"That seems logical. I have a basket for the toys but a bread pan makes much more sense." Chelsea chuckled when Dolly handed it to her.

"Where are the children?" Dolly asked.

"Oh, Russell took them to the barn. The new cat we got to keep away birds and mice is very intriguing to all the young'ns." Chelsea smiled and wiped out her bread pan with a dishcloth. "I will get this bread in the oven before any more catastrophes occur."

Dolly watched her friend do her work, while getting up the courage to talk with her about Sean.

Chelsea closed the oven door with a squeak and then leaned on the counter, she sighed and grinned a little.

"I was hoping to talk with you about something." Dolly said softly.

"Well, now is a good time for it before Russell brings back the children." Chelsea said and gestured that they go sit somewhere.

Dolly walked to the parlor and sat in the chair on the right of the fireplace. Chelsea took the left.

"Well, over the last few days I have realized that Sean Fahey has been looking at me." Dolly said, she glanced over to Chelsea but then quickly looked away.

"There has been a little bit of talk about that being a possibility." Chelsea said with a chuckle.

"You tease, but I hadn't noticed until recently." Dolly put her hands to her cheeks. They were warm, and she felt like hiding in the woodbox.

"Did something happen today?" Chelsea prompted.

"Well, yes." Dolly said exasperated with herself. She finally tore her eyes away from staring at the fire to meet Chelsea's eye. "I just blurted something out, and then he kissed me."

Chelsea's eyes opened wide in surprise. "What did you say?"

"Something about that I didn't do why he cared about me. I don't truly remember it all." Dolly admitted. It had all happened so quickly, and she had felt ill and excited all at the same time.

"So, he kissed you?" Chelsea asked slowly.

"Yes, well after we stared at each other for a long while." Dolly lowered her head in her hands. It is rather embarrassing to admit all of this.

"Then he thought I was mad at him but I wasn't." She smiled, remembering the feelings that were still lingering inside of her.

"Is it bad that he kissed me?" Dolly asked.

"Not bad, or a sin." Chelsea said and made sure that Dolly understood.

Dolly let out a breath.

"Now, usually a kiss is something pretty special. Usually it is between people who are courting or engaged to be married. In some cases, I have known a few who waited until they were married to even kiss. But I am not certain I am one to go for that kind of thing. Perhaps in places where they still do arranged marriages, but I have always found that a bit barbaric. But that is only my opinion." Chelsea shrugged a little and grinned.

"Do you think that Sean is thinking about marriage?" Dolly's eyes had a wild look in them and she felt a little out of breath.

"He might be leaning in that direction, but I am suspecting that he isn't wanting to go faster than you are willing to go." Chelsea said wisely.

"I would like him to court me, I think." Dolly admitted.

"That is a good start." Chelsea reached over and squeezed her hand.

"Do you think that Sean is a good man?" Dolly asked.

"I think that Sean is extremely brave, for facing his past mistakes and making things better with Angela. I have seen him be generous to others, and I have seen him worshipping God at Sunday service. He has worked hard to make his cabin nice and he respects the land. All of these things are signs of a very good man." Chelsea smiled and squeezed Dolly's hand again. "What do you think?"

"I think I might be unable to say the words that I think about him." Dolly pressed her lips together and gave Chelsea and long look.

"Well, that sounds pretty serious." Chelsea said a minute later.

Dolly nodded, then they smiled at each other for a long time. Sometimes words were not needed.

Chapter 12

Galina Varushkin

Galina was mending socks near the fire. The wind was roaring outside and she was happy to be indoors. The cat Duchess was playing by the fire with a piece of yarn that Angela had cut for her. Galina kept giggling when the cat's strange antics would catch her eye.

Angela was in the other arm chair, her red curly hair hanging over her shoulders as she was reading her letters.

Angela laughed a little. Galina finished her stitch and looked up, wondering if Angela was going to speak. Galina was happy to catch her eye.

"I just love hearing from my Great Aunt in Ireland. It was written back in the summer." Angela smiled. "She was telling me about my cousins. A boy named Jonathan was mean to his sister's cat, by tying a ribbon too tight on his tail. He got a whuppin' from his pa and had to clean out the barn every day for a week. My Great Aunt says that she asked the barn manager to make sure the job was extra messy for him. He had to climb up the rafters and clear out all of the cobwebs and sparrow nests, as well as muck the stalls." Angela chuckled.

"Sounds like a good lesson indeed." Galina smiled.

Galina pondered the boy getting a whuppin' and felt no strange feelings about it. She knew that discipline was so very important. Her father's beating had rarely ever been about discipline though, usually beating her when she spoke up, or asked for things he didn't want her to have. Her father had used the belt on her brothers' backside. It had hurt and they had cried from them, but it hadn't been about domination or control. It was a lesson, that there are consequences.

"You look thoughtful." Angela said.

Galina looked up and saw the concern.

"Oh, just my mind wandering. Thinking of the difference between discipline and a beating. A spanking or even a harsher punishment of a belt to the backside is a way to teach a young man, or a young woman to curb their bad behavior. A beating is a whole different thing entirely." Galina said and shrugged her shoulders.

Angela nodded thoughtfully. "I often wonder if we as a society could be better at watching for the subtle differences. I recall at the orphanage, where I spent the longest part of my childhood, that if one was given the strap, usually everyone was. It was a way to control us all. If someone was doing something wrong, we would all turn on each other. No one wanted the strap for someone else's crime. I have heard stories of that here too. In a family with many children, they would all line up when one would get in trouble. We all have eyes, perhaps we could step in when things go too far." Angela said this as Duchess meowed at her feet, wanting to jump up.

Galina nodded. "I think most folks don't believe it is their place to step in. As a society we tend to let others decide what is best for their own household."

Angela had a serious frown for a moment. "It may take a long time for that to change."

Galina went back to her mending and tried to force her mind on different things. Galina finally finished her last mended sock when there was a knock at the back door.

"I will get it Angela, you stay put." Galina said with a smile. She hurriedly set the mended socks on the table and ran towards the back door. She heard the wind gusting outside and didn't want anyone standing out there in that freezing weather for long.

She opened the door to Warren, who had an armful of firewood. Galina smiled.

"Come on in out of that wind." Galina said as she moved aside to let him through the doorway. Warren was bundled up in his thick work coat. He was wearing a dark brown wool cap. He dropped the wood into the firewood box and gave a little shake to get the dusting of snow off of him.

"Sorry to leave a mess." Warren smiled brightly.

Galina gave a wave of her hand. "This room is for messes. I will be doing some laundry in here tomorrow, it will get a thorough wash down often enough." Galina said practically. She was so happy that the easy way between her and Warren was back to normal. It may never be what it once was, but she was glad for a friendship again.

"I will be bringing in another load or two." Warren said.

"Well, goodness, don't bother knocking, just come on in."

Galina said with a laugh. "Is the wood already cut?" She asked.

He nodded with a grin.

"Well, then I will just stay here and let you in so you don't have to wait." She smiled. "No need to have you standing back here freezing."

"I appreciate it. I hope I am not interrupting." Warren said thoughtfully.

"Not a bit. I just finished a big pile of mending, I have some time before I start warming up the stew for supper." Galina said.

"I think I ate some of your stew last night." Warren smiled warmly and rubbed his belly. "It was pretty good."

"Yes, I made a big pot. Dolly brought home a big buck from her hunt this weekend. Several households will be eating for days. I sent a pot over to Earl's cabin. I am glad it is being enjoyed." Galina blushed a little from the praise. It was nice to be appreciated. She was feeling rather confident lately as her cooking skills grew.

"Well, between your stew and Violet's bread, I will be well fed for the rest of the week." Warren gave her a wink. She couldn't tell if he was flirting or just being friendly, but she enjoyed the camaraderie again.

"I will wait by the door. You get back to work." Galina snapped her fingers playfully and enjoyed the wide-eyed look from Warren. She laughed and gave his back a little shove as he went out the door.

He turned and gave her a wry smile as he marched down the hill towards the back of the barn where he chopped wood.

He came back three times and the firebox was full to the brim by the time he was finished.

They chatted for only a minute before he finally went to leave.

"I just wanted to let you know. I got my own land a few days ago." He smiled, full of pride.

"Oh, my. You must be so very pleased." Galina was happy for him. He had worked long and hard for this day to come.

"I am." He said and lowered his head thoughtfully. "I will still be working here for now, but in the evenings and on Sundays after service I will be felling logs to build two cabins. My ma wants her own little cabin for her and my sister. I cannot believe how fast she is growing; almost fifteen years old."

"That will be some hard work. But I know that you will make it." Galina said sincerely. Warren was the kind of young man that

134

would accomplish a lot.

"That is kind of you." He gave her a smile and a nod. "I will be heading out tonight to start looking for good trees to fell. I think I have a good spot to build. Ted was out with me this morning early and we scouted a good place along a creek. There was some land over to the north of here. Angela's brother Sean helped me find it. I will be his neighbor near the bluff."

"I would love to see it on a day with good weather." Galina said wistfully. It was funny to know that all of her friends were old enough to get land of their own, get married. Warren was now a man. "If you want you can take my horse out. I don't want you to have to walk."

"Well, thank you. Ted is letting me borrow his own horse tonight. But if in the future I need a ride out there I will certainly ask." He smiled. "I appreciate that a lot, Galina."

She enjoyed hearing him say her name and she felt that warm feeling of friendship again.

He left finally with a wave.

Galina got busy with warming up the stew and making some baking soda biscuits. She hummed happily and tried to imagine the land that Warren would have. It was a pleasant thought.

<hr/>

Corinne Grant

The wind whipped around Corinne as she headed towards the door to her greenhouse. She was squinting her eyes against the force of cold air and snow that pelted against her and she longed for the warm air waiting for her.

"Wait, Corinne!" She heard from behind her. She whipped her head around and her wool cap was blown from her head. Her dark hair, freed from the cap, was let loose and the shorter tendrils danced around her face with the wind. It was a truly magnificent annoyance how well that hair had such perfect aim to smack her eyes at every opportunity.

Corinne's hand by instinct reached up to still the wild gyrations of her hair as she tried to see, in the gust of wind, who had called for her.

It was her husband jogging towards her. She had not seen him much over the last few days. He had been working long hours with the building crew to get the cabin finished. She watched him through squinted eyes as he changed direction and chased after her woolen hat as it tumbled away in the wintry wind. He bent and scooped up the cap without breaking stride. He was at her side in a few seconds.

"Let's go inside," he said. He came closer to her successfully blocking the wind. She smiled a little to herself, enjoying the closeness and the wind block.

They moved together toward the door and were inside the delicious warmth a moment later.

Corinne spent a long few seconds trying to shake the snow from her wayward hair.

"I must look a fright." She said with exasperation.

Lucas stomped the mud and snow off of his boots on the flagstone floor.

"You look mighty pretty to me." He smiled at her with that boyish grin that she found so charming.

Corinne gave him a steady look as she tried to pat her hair into submission.

Lucas, not to be dismissed by her look swooped down on her and gave her a kiss.

She smiled up at him after, his face still close.

"I hope you still love me after all I have put you through this last month." He said in low voice.

Corinne nodded, she was unable to stop smiling. He had that effect on her. She had missed him the last few days.

"I do." She said simply, it seemed the right thing to say. It reminded her of her wedding vows.

He took a long moment and kissed her again, telling her in his own way that he missed her too.

He finally stepped away and shrugged out of his wool coat. His dark sweater had little flecks of sawdust and debris from the building he had been doing.

"I am pleased to announce that our home is ready. I still have to move things around inside, but the roof and windows are all finished. The woodstoves are working, and the chinking is all done." He smiled with pride. He had been working so very hard. "I am a few days late, as I was hoping to get it all done before the snow flew."

Corinne smiled in relief. "Well, dear husband of mine. As you are so in control of most things around here. You cannot and will not ever be able to predict the weather." She laughed and enjoyed hearing him join her.

He nodded and reached over to run a thumb over her cheek.

"Thank you for all of the hard work." She said quietly. She felt the stress and pressure of the last few weeks lift off of her shoulders. It had been difficult, but she knew it would be worth the struggle in the long run.

"I took on this project and you have been very understanding. I appreciate that." He grinned.

"Well, don't be giving me too much credit. I had my moments..." Corinne said with a laugh. There had been more than a few tears and a few heated conversations of impatience. She had learned a few lessons as she willed herself to push aside her annoyance at the inconveniences.

"I am so please to have the bulk of the project done. I will have to wait to get the back part of the porch finished until the snow clears." He rubbed a hand on his chin. It was his usual move when he was thinking and scheming. Corinne was amused to see it.

"It might be a little while." She laughed a little.

He nodded. He looked so happy and Corinne was feeling his energy and it was carrying away the feelings and apprehensions of the week.

"My prayers were answered. No one was injured but for a few splinters, and the home is ready before you had to resort to pummeling me with a frying pan." He smiled broadly, a little over-dramatically but it was a funny gesture and she laughed again.

Corinne looked around her. Now she was torn. She had to water the plants and make sure there was enough firewood to keep the greenhouse stove burning now that it was so cold outside.

"I have to get some things done in here, but I want to start helping get the cabin ready for us all," she said. She looked to Lucas. "I am ready to sleep in my own bed again, and I am certain that father and Marie are ready for a little normalcy as well."

Lucas nodded. "I was hoping to give you a hand at getting your chores done. Then we can go over to the cabin together and put things to right."

Corinne whole heartedly agreed.

"You tell me what to do, Plant Lady." Lucas grinned and let Corinne take charge.

Lucas followed her orders and got the water barrel filled inside the greenhouse. Corinne poked and prodded at the woodstove. Lucas had hired a hand to work in the barn, but his first duty every morning was to come early and check the woodstove here first. They burned hardwoods in the stove in the winter months to make sure they burned slow and steady overnight. It sometimes would go out, but the coals usually kept the place warm enough to keep Corinne's plants alive. Oregon winters weren't usually too harsh, not compared to some states in the Union. Some of the seedlings would not survive if the temperature dropped too low.

Corinne and Lucas worked as a team to water the plants as per Corinne's instructions and Lucas did some good-natured teasing when she squealed happily over some plant that was ready to bloom. She gave her husband a good-natured elbow to his side.

They soon were walking together over the stone path to the cabin. Corinne didn't notice the howling wind very much at all.

———————◆◦◆——◆◦◆———————

Violet Griffen

Violet was excited as she packed up her few belongings and then helped Debbie gather up the children's things in the back bedroom they had been sharing. Violet bounced Trudie on her hip and Debbie had Caleb on hers.

Debbie sang an old song while they bounced.

Lucas had come a short while before and he was in and out of the room, gathering up the items as they packed them.

"I will be glad to be back to normal once again." Debbie said after she finished up the song. Caleb reached up to her chin, she made popping noises playfully at the boy. Caleb grunted and hooted happily at her.

Violet looked around and was feeling confident that they weren't leaving anything behind. Trudie seemed to be tired and was resting her head against Violet's chest. It was such a comforting feeling.

Lucas peeked his head in one last time. "You have anything else to carry?"

"Just this bag and the bucket of dirty nappies." Debbie said.

"Good. I will put the bucket out beside the back washroom." Lucas said with a grin then a grimace.

"Oh, so much laundry to do." Debbie said with a grin for

Caleb. "It was all of your doing. Wasn't it?" She bounced him a few more times the way he liked.

"I do believe that both of these rascals are equals in the dirty laundry collecting." Violet said and kissed Trudie on the head.

They both chuckled a little and followed Lucas out of the door.

John Harpole was waiting at the front door to help Lucas carry some belongings back over to the Grant cabin.

Marie was chatting with Corinne who reached out for Trudie. "I will take her and get her feeding out of the way. She looks a bit sleepy." Corinne said as she was pulling away from an embrace with Marie.

"Thank you so much again, for all you have done." Corinne kissed her step-mother on the cheek affectionately. "You were so kind to open up your home."

Marie hushed all the thanks and blew a kiss as Corinne scooped Trudie away from Violet.

"Violet, I wanted to see if perhaps you wanted to go with me to town. John is heading there shortly to pick up some items at the woodworking shop. Lucas told me that there was a slight incident with the pantry. You may have a few surprises according to him. We can see about replacing some things."

Violet hadn't heard any news about the pantry, but then in the chaos of the last few days it didn't seem to matter.

"Well, I am not certain at what to do about supper." She hadn't pulled her thoughts together yet about preparing a meal. There was a venison roast that was hanging in the Harpole shed that was designated for Lucas and Corinne from Dolly. Violet felt her mind spinning a bit.

"My cook and I can whip something up to bring over later for you all. I also heard a whisper from some other household who will be pitching in a dessert." Marie gave Violet a wink. "The day is still young. There is plenty of time to get things done, it is not even noon yet."

Violet nodded, feeling a little overwhelmed. She hadn't been sleeping well lately. Her thoughts were so befuddled thinking about her future.

"Why don't you come by when you are almost ready to leave. I can go through the pantry and see what Lucas meant. I will make a list." Violet gave Marie a hug herself and was comforted by the love she felt there. Marie had this special gift, to make you feel special and loved, just to be in her presence.

Violet bundled up in her wool coat and scarf. She searched around for her mittens but was almost certain that they were at the Grant's cabin. She shrugged and blew a kiss to Marie as she left.

Violet let out a big sigh as she headed out into the cold. The dark gray clouds were heading to the west and the thin white clouds that stayed behind looked less fierce. The wind had been howling all morning, but it looked like the weather was calming for now.

Violet walked along the footpath, her eyes glancing along the fence, wishing to catch sight of Reynaldo, but knowing that he was still gone. She missed his presence and felt that strange sensation again whenever she thought of him. She knew that her love for him had grown, and now that she knew, she could do nothing. If she saw him now she knew that there was a solid chance that she would forget her timidity and run to him and tell him exactly how she felt.

There were a few horses in the yard mostly standing around, one stood near the fence line. The brown stallion looked at her and shook his head, the way that horses do. She smiled at the horse, wondering wistfully what it was thinking.

A cold wind blew from behind her and she picked up the pace to get to the cabin. The wind wasn't as blustery as earlier, but it could certainly bite when it wanted to.

Violet took in the sight of the cabin. Now with a generous front porch on the front. The roof extended and the side where the parlor was now with a bigger window. The parlor would certainly have more light coming in. Violet smiled as she stomped her feet on the rug on the front porch. It was already a far sight better than before. The front stoop had been a bit of a muddy pit before. This would make for cleaner floors in the future.

Violet went inside and saw the flurry of John and Lucas getting things settled.

Corinne was sitting on a kitchen chair with a towel thrown over the front of her. Trudie was underneath the towel.

The parlor was in disarray with drop cloths thrown over the furniture. The kitchen was also a mess, with pantry items spread around. Violet shrugged out of her coat and gave a quiet look to Corinne. She looked nearly as overwhelmed as Violet felt.

"I will get started on the kitchen." Violet said softly. Corinne nodded and mouthed the words 'thank you.'

Violet saw that the bread she had been proofing over at the Harpole's was sitting in its usual spot on the back of the countertop. She could see some muddy footprints around on the floor but knew that there was nothing to be done about them now. The outline of the shoe prints was bigger than a woman's, so she was certain it had been the work crew that had been eating and probably drinking coffee in the kitchen for the last week.

There was a collection of dirty coffee mugs on the counter. Violet grinned and stacked them up to wash later. They did a good job on the house, she would not begrudge the men from taking a few coffee breaks in 'her' kitchen.

She made a little room on the counter and started a pot of water on the hot stove to do a little cleaning up. Being curious she headed toward the place where the pantry had been. She had been told what to expect but it was still a surprise to see the staircase going up where the shelves and foodstuffs used to be. She shook her head in amazement at all these men had accomplished.

There was the scent of sawdust in the air.

She contemplated going up the stairs, but she could tell that the wood had been stained that rich caramel coloring. She would hate to do damage to the work they had done.

She continued down the hallway. The room where Debbie had been staying was there and Violet peeked inside. The room was smaller and there was a wall of empty shelves along one side. The other side was empty. There was room for a lot in here. By the small window were some supplies under a drop cloth.

She continued down the hall and saw that the backroom, where laundry and bathing were done was in complete and utter chaos. There were pantry goods everywhere. Every flat surface had something piled upon it, whether it be tools or food. Violet felt the sudden urge to laugh.

"Well, it may be a few days before we can even reach the stove to wash the laundry." She said softly to the room.

Debbie was behind her chuckling. "I was thinking that same thing just a few minutes ago."

Violet saw that Debbie was alone.

"Ah, I just fed Caleb and he is now sleeping soundly. Trudie and Caleb are sharing a crib in Lucas and Corinne's room." Debbie placed a hand on Violet's shoulder.

The both shared a look and somehow, comically, they both took in a big breath and sighed. The urge to laugh was there, a

141

silly hysterical feeling that Violet fought when she smothered the sound with a hand. There were sleeping children nearby, but she was very amused. Debbie and Violet leaned against each other for a moment, fighting off laughter.

"Where does one even start on a mess like this?" Debbie asked in a harsh whisper. Her eyes misty from holding in her laughter.

Violet shook her head and let her eyes sweep through the room.

"I suppose we can figure that out later." Violet shrugged as she hooked her arm in to Debbie's and forcibly turned her away from the room of chaos.

"Later is better." Debbie agreed with a wide smile and nodded comically.

They got back to the kitchen and saw that Lucas and John Harpole where talking with Corinne.

"I will head back to get Marie and then we can head out," John said. He gave Violet and Debbie a nod before he turned to go.

When John was gone the house seemed quiet and still.

Corinne plopped down into a dining chair Lucas joined in next to her. He gave a gesture for Violet and Debbie to join.

"You've done some good work here Lucas." Violet said softly. She gave him a smile to let him know she was sincere.

"Thank you, but I know there is a lot more to do. It will be a few more days of chaos. But I thought that being here was better even with the mess to be cleaned." He said and reached out a hand for Corinne's.

"I have never shied away from a little work in all my days." Debbie said and patted Violet's shoulder.

"I'm just pleased to be under my own roof again." Corinne said with a sigh.

Violet saw that Corinne looked a little tired, but she looked relieved. These last few weeks had been hard on everyone.

"Debbie, your bed frame has been moved upstairs, but I will need to pull the ropes tight and get your mattress up the stairs." Lucas said. "You have a woodstove in your room and one in the children's room right next to you. There is an empty room that will be furnished later sometime, when the children get older."

Debbie nodded, "I can help with the rope pulling for the bed. I have made a few beds in my day." Debbie's smile was infectious and they all smiled to join in.

The camaraderie of this household was deeply felt by Violet. She had always wondered at how Corinne and Lucas, still being so young, had learned to be so accommodating with the help. It must have been how they were raised. They knew how to treat Violet and Debbie with respect. It was something to behold. Violet knew that they paid her for her work, and that she was expected to do her duties, but somehow, it wasn't a burden at all. She was treated as an equal and loved as family.

"I heard something about some pantry goods..." Violet was snapped out of her thoughts when the idea popped into her head. She was supposed to go to town.

"Oh, yes, one of the lads wasn't very careful with the bag of sugar and had to spend a good hour sweeping a lot of sugar off the floor. I had him carry it all out into the back woods, I can imagine there were some happy critters who got a sweet treat." Lucas said.

"Well, at least it got cleaned up and didn't melt into the floorboards." Corinne said with a soft laugh.

Violet's eyes went wide, trying to imagine how terrible it would be to clean melted sugar. "I am glad to have not come home to that."

Lucas chuckled quietly. "I have some funds for you. I know I have saddled with you with all kinds of things to do, but we will get things sorted in a few days." Lucas fished a piece of paper out of his back pocket. "I have a few things we need in town. John is picking up the items I have ordered from Amos Drays, the woodworker, and if you and Marie stop by the grocer and the butcher feel free to get whatever you are needing. Even if we already have some of these items it may take a few days to get everything tidied up. If you can get a few extra nappies as well. It may be a few more days of laundry getting dirty before it can be washed. I sent a note with John, to see if anyone is willing to come by and help with the laundry. I would ask Galina next door, but with Angela needing her help I think we can try to find someone else who can help."

Lucas looked over the list and handed it to Violet. She gave it a glance and saw that there were some good practical things on the list, they would make things a little easier while the cabin was being put to rights.

Marie came by with some bread and cheese for everyone to snack on while Lucas and John chatted in between bites. The plan was set.

Corinne, Lucas and Debbie would stay behind and quietly try to tidy the place up a bit, and Violet would have Marie's help in town. Violet had a basket of loaves made from the day before and decided to wrap one up on a whim. She bundled up again, in her dark wool coat. John got she and Marie settled in the back seat with a warm lap blanket on their laps. Violet had found her mittens finally and was glad for their warmth. There were a few fluttering snowflakes falling as John clicked the team of horses into action. The last few days had brought snow flurries on and off and the world was beginning to have the white blanket of winter showing in spots. The snow wasn't sticking to the roads yet, but it would be soon if the weather continued. Violet wondered if they would all be putting the runners on their wagons soon. One could never tell in Oregon if the winter would be mild or not.

Violet was happy to chat with Marie and John on the way to town.

"I will gladly come by in the next day or so, perhaps I can bring a few other ladies and we can tackle putting the pantry back together." Marie said thoughtfully.

Violet smiled and thanked her for the offer. It would definitely help to have extra hands. It certainly was going to be an interesting week.

They hit a bump in the road and the loaf of sourdough bread nearly flew off of Violet's lap. She gripped it harder with her awkward mittens and saved it.

Marie's giggle was charming as she saw Violet fumble around with a loaf of bread.

"Did you bring that along for someone specific?" Marie asked.

"Oh, I was just listening to John and Lucas talking about how much work the carpenter in town has done to get some furniture made for our home. I made these loaves yesterday. I made a few too many. I was trying to be thoughtful." Violet smiled.

"Amos Drays will certainly appreciate it." Marie nodded at Violet then they both laughed nervously as the surrey bounced again with a jerk.

"Sorry for the rough road." John said from the front seat. "The wet cold weather always does a number on the roads here. One day we will perhaps have fancier roads like the cities. But that may be a long way off."

They finally made it to town and pulled up to the carpenter's shop. Violet was very pleasantly surprised when she walked in. The air was fragrant with the sweet and earthy scent of sawdust and the visual splendor of seeing so many beautiful things; fancy wood cabinets, rocking chairs, a fine large table that was dark and glistening.

Amos was in the back of the shop.

"Greetings Amos!" John yelled out.

Amos Drays looked up with a happy smile. He had been using a wood plane and Violet could see little curl-shaped shavings all around the side of the piece. For some reason she found them charming, like a little baby's curls.

Amos came over, weaving around all of the stacks of furniture and cabinets in varying degree of progress. He was wiping off the sawdust that was clinging to his work apron.

"Lucas sent me to pick up the pieces you have for him." John said and gave Amos a hearty handshake.

"Oh, yes. I have his order ready to go in the back. I have a lad that can load up the wagon for you." Amos smiled and nudged his head toward the back door.

"I will bring a wagon over from the livery. I just wanted to be certain that all was ready." John smiled. "I brought the ladies over in the surrey."

"You head over to the livery, I want to peek through Amos' lovely creations and see if I perhaps need a thing or two for the house." Marie said batting her eyelashes at her husband. Everyone laughed.

"Of course." John reached a hand to her cheek and rubbed it affectionately. "You look around."

Violet was pleased to see that John was generous and affectionate as usual with her. It made her think of Reynaldo and the pang of missing him was there in her middle.

Marie clapped her hands together with purpose. "Hmmm." She hummed a moment. "Amos, you do such magnificent work."

"You let me know if anything strikes your fancy." Amos said with a pleased expression. Violet could tell that he took a great amount of pride in his workmanship.

"Oh, Mr. Drays, before I forget," Violet handed over her bundle to Amos.

He reached out with a quizzical eyebrow raised. He pulled the tea towel away.

"Oh my," he said as his eyes grew wide. He brought the loaf closer to his face. "Your famous sourdough bread." He wrapped it back up and held it closer to him, as if it was a cherished new possession.

Violet smiled at seeing his reaction. "I wanted to thank you for taking such good care on making the Grant's furniture. It was certainly kind of you to get these pieces done so fast."

He blushed a little and grinned. "Every man in town will be green with envy when I tell them I got a whole loaf of your bread. Your fame is spreading."

She had never really chatted with him much beyond pleasantries and knew him to be a soft-spoken man. He wasn't as handsome as Reynaldo, but he did have a pleasant way about him.

"Well, I don't know about my 'fame' but I do love baking, bread especially." Violet said, feeling her own cheeks flush with slight embarrassment over the praise.

"Every man without a wife in Oregon City was clearly thrilled to hear that Reynaldo Legales was heading to California. Then all of our hopes were dashed when we heard that it was just a short business trip. I bet you would have at least twenty marriage proposals next week iff'n we though there was a chance." Amos said with a laugh. It seemed very outside his character to speak so much.

Violet was shocked to hear that so many knew about the courtship between her and Reynaldo. Her inner voice chided her shock though, this was a small town. Everyone knew everyone's business eventually.

"Reynaldo was the wisest among us all. He wooed you properly, while the rest of us were scratching our heads." Amos chuckled again.

Violet wasn't certain what to say when a thought came to mind. "You know, we women sometimes talk about this subject. About how many single men there are here in Oregon City. I heard that a man in Portland was considering sending advertisements back East, for western brides." She wondered if it was rude to say, but it was out of her mouth before she could take it back.

"You know, that might not be such bad notion. I am growing tired of the bachelor life." He smiled at Violet, and she could see his sweet nature through his eyes. He really did have a lot going for him. He had a kind temperament, he was a hard worker who earned a good living. He would make some woman a very good husband.

Violet tilted her head in thought. "I wonder if Clive would know some ways to place an advertisement in a newspaper back East."

"Clive certainly seems to know everyone." Amos nodded. "I'm sorry if I made you uncomfortable. I do tend to act foolish around a beautiful woman. A downfall of mine."

Violet was tickled, feeling more comfortable with Amos. He was kind and funnier than she had expected.

"You do flatter me. I will pray for you and the other single men here more often now." She wondered what her brothers would do to find a wife. How would they eventually find a wife here where women were so scarce?

Amos turned and watched Marie perusing the furniture.

"Is there anything that strikes your fancy Mrs. Griffen?" He asked with that eyebrow raised again.

"Oh, everything actually. Your work is beautiful." Violet let her eyes sweep around the room. There were so many beautiful things.

"I hope you find something that perhaps you cannot live without, then maybe we could barter." Amos smelled the bread one more time and grinned.

Violet laughed. "Well, it might be difficult for me to get you baked goods in the winter months." Violet said practically.

"Well, I see one of your neighbors or Lucas at least once a week. A loaf of bread or something sweet would certainly be a priceless commodity to me. I am very limited in my cooking and since the hotel closed a few years ago my meals are rather drab these days."

"I might see what could be done." Violet said. "Let me look around and see what strikes my fancy." She actually had a fine little nest egg saved up at the bank. Maybe she should start preparing herself for the future and have a few things that were all her own.

She wandered to find Marie who was staring at a charming set of dining chairs.

Marie looked over to Violet, "Aren't these just so elegant?"

Violet nodded with a smile. The detailed carving on each chair was indeed very elegant, with ivy and flowers wrapped in a woven pattern through the chair backs. The legs of each chair had the woven leaves and floral design as well.

"I am not certain I care about the cost." Marie said and looked a little guilty. "I may just have to work my wiles on my husband."

"I am not certain you will have to work that hard. I was living at your home for a few weeks. He just mentioned that you needed a new table and chairs. The set he brought over the Oregon Trail has taken a bit of a beating and your family has grown so much." Violet said practically.

Marie nodded, then looked at the chairs again, then sighed.

Violet had to stifle the giggle that threatened to break forth. Marie was just so adorable. She was always so light and bubbling in her own way. It was never confused with being dimwitted, but just playful and charming.

Violet wandered away while Marie ran her hands along the chairs and table set. Violet saw some beautiful dressers and some carved decorations, bowls, and shelves, all of them lovely. In the back her eye caught sight of a wooden trunk, all golden brown and gleaming. It wasn't ornate, but it still had a pure beauty about it. She thought of the small trunk that she had in her room at the Grant's. It was a leather trunk that was falling apart, and bits of leather were always breaking away from it and leaving little pieces around for her to sweep up whenever she opened it.

"How much for a trunk like this one?" Violet made eye contact with Amos who was standing near Marie, answering a few questions about the chairs and table.

"Well, I was thinking of a solution to our barter. Warren, your neighbor has just bought land and we are working on getting some furniture pieces for him. If he is willing to come by your place once a week, for a basket of goodies, I can make you your very own trunk at no cost," Amos said. He seemed excited at the prospect and Violet bit down her objections. Certainly, there would be no harm in this kind of arrangement.

"I agree, though I have a few misgivings. Your work is certainly more valuable than a few baked goods." Violet said with her arms folded stubbornly.

"My poor stomach says otherwise." He said with a rich belly laugh.

"Well, since you put it that way." Violet smiled, completely charmed by the new friend she had made.

"When Reynaldo comes back from his trip soon I will be

certain to make it clear that I will not be trying to steal you away. Though, the thought certainly has merit. But, alas, I am not the kind of man that would do that sort of thing." Amos reached out for her hand, to strike the deal.

She shook his hand with a smile. "You know that the rumor is about town that you are rather shy. I am seeing a new side of you that most do not see, I am thinking."

He shrugged. "I guess I got so excited about eating good food that it loosened up my tongue."

She smiled and was already thinking about the baking she would do to barter for a beautiful trunk from this master craftsman. He pointed out a few different carving styles, to learn her taste, and she asked him a few questions about what his favorite kinds of sweets were.

John showed up with a wagon and with some heavy lifting the wagon was loaded down with the order for Lucas. John had hired a man to drive the load back to the Grant's home once the day of shopping was complete.

Violet and Marie said goodbye to Amos and excitedly chatted about their picks from the shop. John, of course had agreed to the table and chairs set and Amos would be busy at work to add a few more chairs to the set.

Violet and Marie made quick work at the grocers. Then they stopped into the fancy goods store to say hello to Millie and JQ.

"I need some more buttons and wanted to see if you got anything new in the last delivery. I heard that there was a ferry in just a few days ago." Marie said after they had all exchanged pleasantries.

Millie was in pleasant spirits, to have customers that were friendly and JQ went back to looking over some paperwork.

Marie and Violet gushed over the buttons, bows, and ribbons that were new. They each had a few special items to purchase by the end of thirty minutes.

Violet pulled out her coins and paid for some pale blue yarn that she had her eye on. A whistle blew in the distance and everyone suddenly seemed excited by the sound.

"Looks like we have another arrival." JQ said setting his pencil down and folding up the ledger he was working on.

"I do love the mystery of a ferry arrival. One never knows what has arrived." Millie said with a large grin.

Marie and Violet went to meet with John out front.

"I was wanting to see which ferry was arriving. I know that Reynaldo left five days ago with the first shipment of horses from Sacramento." John said enthusiastically. "Would it be a huge inconvenience for you to wait an hour or so? I want to ride over and see if this is him."

"Oh, that is no bother dear. I can certainly handle the surrey to take us home." Marie offered.

Violet was torn, hoping to see Reynaldo was suddenly like a force inside of her chest.

"We do need to stop by the butchers yet." Violet reminded Marie. "Perhaps he will know by the time we are done."

"Good thinking." John kissed his wife on the cheek. "I will ride over and find out. Then we can plan appropriately."

Marie and Violet waved and watched John jog ahead to the livery. The ladies walked over to the butcher and spent some time choosing meats and making sure that both households would be well fed over the next weeks. Marie sent the butcher's boy with the orders, over to the wagon and they got the three crates of meat loaded in and secured with their other purchases.

There was a group of men at the livery, a block down the street, and Violet felt her heart start to thud happily when she thought that she saw Reynaldo in the group. She held her composure in check, but she wanted to run to him and she felt that eager anticipation of seeing him again.

Marie gave Violet a sly smile. "Looks like Reynaldo over yonder."

Violet's legs felt wooden and stiff as she followed Marie across the street. They made their way around a few piles of horse manure, watching out for a wagon that went by. A gust of wind was cold on her face, but she barely took notice.

She saw him lean over and say something to John Harpole then freed himself from the group of men to meet her on the side of the street. Reynaldo almost always had a smile, it was something that made everyone connect with him, but now his smile was broader than she had ever seen it. His eyes sparkled as she drew up next to him.

"You are a sight to see." Reynaldo said and drew up close to her. She felt his warm breath on her cheek. She suddenly forgot about all the people around them.

"I missed you." Violet said softly. He was so close to her and she wasn't sure if she could stand it if he pulled away.

"And I you." He answered. His eyes sparkled as his smile faded. She lost all the words she had wanted to say to him as they said volumes in that long moment just with their eyes locked.

He took her hands in his. "I have to go soon, but, may I see you later. It could be after supper before I am free."

Violet nodded. "You better come and find me." She smiled a little.

"You have no idea what you do to me." He boldly kissed her on the cheek, then raised his eyebrows chuckling as the crowd around them hooted and cheered.

There is something that happens inside of a woman, a strange warm kind of pride when she is admired publicly by someone that she cares about. Violet supposed it was probably similar to the feeling a man gets when he has a beautiful woman on his arm and he gets envious stares of the men as they pass by.

The warmth spread through Violet as she walked over to join Marie. The men say their farewells and a whole crew rode off to retrieve the horses from the ferry.

"Well, who needs romantic novels when they see something like that?" Marie said and grinned mischievously.

Violet rolled her eyes a little but then grinned to herself. "That was rather lovely, wasn't it?"

Marie stepped in front of Violet and gave her a once over. "Are you ready for what comes next?"

Violet took a deep breath and sighed. She had been thinking of nothing else. "I am." She replied simply.

"Well, I feel the urge to stop by the store again. I might be in the mood to make a new dress." Marie said and grabbed Violet's arm. "I'll just take a quick look. Then we will get home and get ready for supper."

Marie and Violet chatted and giggled like young girls as they invaded the fancy goods store again.

Chapter 13

Amos Drays

Amos took a break after Marie and Violet left his shop and headed back to his office table. His mind was buzzing with thoughts. That discussion with Violet had really sparked into flame. It was a concern he had been thinking on for more than a year.

With so few women in Oregon City and the surrounding area how was any single man going to find a wife? Amos left his office and paced restlessly for a minute and then grabbed up a sign to hang on the front door. This time of day wasn't very busy, so he could go across the street.

Jacob Bowman was the blacksmith across the street and Amos would often visit him in the afternoon. Maybe Jacob had some time to talk. Amos realized that he needed to talk out all of the thoughts in his head.

The sound was a soothing one, ting-ting clang, ting-ting clang. The sound had a musical quality to it that was pleasing. Amos waited outside of the open work area, not wanting to interrupt Jacob in the middle of something dangerous. He had all the doors wide open and the fire was burning bright and hot in the forge.

He watched the burly man for a minute, shaping a nail with deftness. It was common to see him making small projects like nails and spikes in between jobs. These kinds of things were always needed. Jacob finished the nail, then with the prongs, dunked it in a bucket of water with a hiss.

"Hey friend." Amos said when the place was quiet. Jacob turned and smiled at Amos. He pulled off his gloves and set them down on a nearby table.

"Hey there Amos. You came at a good time. If I make another nail I will lose my sanity." He had a deep voice and it fit him to a tee. He had a beard that was dark brown and a shade darker than his hair. He was currently wearing a large dingy cloth around his head, to keep sparks from burning his hair.

"I feel the same way when I've made too many pegs," Amos laughed a little, but his mind was still swirling with his ideas.

"Let me grab some water." Jacob grabbed a cup and went to the nearby water barrel and scooped some out and downed every drop before scooping up some more.

Jacob gestured, wordlessly offering Amos a drink. Amos shook his head.

"You look like you've got something on your mind." Jacob was wandering back, taking a few more sips of water.

"Yes, well, nothing we haven't mentioned to each other a few thousand times." Amos scratched at his chin trying to find the words he was looking for.

"I was talking to Violet Griffen today." Amos started, and saw Jacob raise up his eyebrows in surprise. "She came by with Marie Harpole and they were picking up some furniture I made for the Grants."

"I bet that was pleasant, having some pretty ladies in your shop." Jacob chuckled and smiled broadly.

"Oh, it wasn't like that, you fool." Amos laughed at the implication behind his friend's eyes. "I feel a little guilty, because I perhaps did a little more flirting with Violet than was necessary. Especially knowing that her and Reynaldo are courting." Amos shrugged, feeling like a fool for how much he did enjoy having women in his shop.

"Rey is one lucky dog." Jacob took a big swig of water.

"Indeed." Amos agreed. "We did actually talk a little about how few unmarried women were in town."

"You and Violet?" Jacob asked.

"Yes," Amos was getting to the part of the conversation that was making him uncomfortable, but he had no choice. He had to talk out this problem or perhaps it never would get solved. "A few days ago, I saw Sophia Greaves walking through town and though she is a young beauty, however, I realized that I just didn't have any kind of inclination or attraction. I mean she is attractive, but…" Amos paused, he felt like a fool.

"You and I are not alike in that department. I see just about any woman and can find an attractive feature if I concentrate on it." Jacob chuckled.

"Well, I can usually find something in any woman that is beautiful or endearing, unless she is mean as a snake or something." Amos said. He was flustered that he wasn't making much sense.

Jacob laughed, and it rumbled through him. Amos smiled and

waited for his amused friend to stop laughing.

"The point I am trying to make is this. If there are two or three young women in all of Oregon City that are single, either we have to travel to find one, or maybe try to get some to come here." Amos offered. He sighed and felt better that he was coming to the point.

"I can see that." Jacob was serious now, considering what Amos said. "I was reading about Sacramento the other day and wondering if there were any opportunities for finding a wife there." Jacob admitted.

"Really?" Amos was surprised to know that his friend had considered something like that.

"Yes, but it seems a fool's errand. With the numbers of folks still pouring into California and the stories of the saloons and wild situations that are reported in the papers..." Jacob scratched his arm and paused. "It just seems like swimming in a swamp."

Amos nodded. "Perhaps the papers are reporting only the bad."

"That always could be, but my guess is that the few women that are there are not the kind of women we are looking for." Jacob said thoughtfully.

Amos nodded. Amos had been raised in a conservative Christian home. He would be embarrassed to even contemplate what his parents would think about trying to find a bride at a saloon.

"Violet made a suggestion, and I am thinking about how I could put it into action." Amos said after he fought off the urge to blush about his previous thoughts. "She suggested that we talk with Clive about doing some advertisements back East for brides."

"It isn't a terrible idea. I know that Clive is always sending off correspondence to papers back East looking for goods for his stores. He would know how to do it." Jacob scratched at his arm again, obviously a repetitive action he often did while in thought.

"I was thinking before I came over that perhaps there is a simpler way, or maybe I am just a little apprehensive about trusting an advertisement." Amos had a few unpleasant thoughts about strangers commenting on the sad state of affairs when a man was so desperate that he had to trust a stranger who would answer an ad in the paper.

"What are you thinking then?" Jacob asked. He seemed interested, so Amos continued. He felt like a fool but then he had nothing to lose at this point.

"I often write to my grandfather, Wallace Drays. I was always close to him growing up and learned a lot from him about my craft. He has always been the example of a good Christian man. If I wrote to him I could ask him to start spreading the word that women are needed here, instead of just trusting anyone who answers the ads. That way we might have someone who could meet the women and make certain that they knew the benefits but also the hardships. Life here is different than life there." Amos was pleased to see Jacob nodding.

"That isn't a terrible idea. I still write to my uncle in New Jersey often. I could do something similar there. He is very active in his church, and my aunt would know which young women might be up for a new start. When I was a kid I remember my eldest sister was teased unmercifully because she was called a spinster when she turned twenty-one without being married. She was the sweetest thing, but she wasn't as pretty as some of the other girls in town." Jacob smiled and had a faraway look.

"She did eventually marry, but I recall that some of her close friends didn't. I wonder how many other good women are slighted because they aren't as good looking or outgoing and they are overlooked." Jacob added.

"That is something to consider. I don't know that I am gravely concerned about the beauty of a woman's face as I am about the beauty in her heart." Amos said thoughtfully.

"Aw, that was rather precious of you Amos." Jacob laughed. "But I actually agree. Thinking back about my sister…. I just wonder if this couldn't work."

Amos smiled, feeling relieved that Jacob thought his plan had merit.

"I could start working on a letter tonight. Maybe if I share the address of my grandfather with you and you share your uncle's address with me they could coordinate a plan. I have some money saved, I can send that along in case some women don't have the funds to travel here." Amos added as a thought popped into his head.

"I think we are thinking a bit small. We might have some other men to talk to. If half the men in town write back East, and we all send funds for a woman to come west, it's more likely to have many brides in the bargain. It would be a sad state to bring over two women and some dapper dandy or two comes along and marries them as soon as they land. If you add up the single men in Oregon City, Salem, and Portland alone I could see an army of men ready to pounce at the mere suggestion of marriageable women arriving here. I think we should spread the word. If we each send enough money for a woman or two to come west, perhaps then more and more women would come as our idea takes purchase. We just might populate Oregon in no time." Jacob gave Amos a slug in the arm.

Amos knew that Jacob's idea was good. Suddenly the idea grew. He would get busy writing the first draft of his letter. "It is November already. If we send off letters soon then by spring we could have some women on wagon trains or passenger ships. By this time next year, we could be all fighting over who gets married first!" Amos laughed at the thought.

"I have a feeling that you would be winning that bet." Jacob shook his head and rubbed his fingers through his scruffy beard. "The thought has definite merit. I may still be willing to talk to Clive, though to see if he wants to write to some of the men he knows in other towns, to suggest our idea. He always has good ideas on how to get things done."

"A worthy plan." Amos agreed.

"I am glad you stopped by. I might just spend the afternoon distracted thinking about a letter I need to write." Jacob gave Amos a friendly slug to the arm.

<hr>

Corinne Grant

Corinne looked up from her sorting and saw the dark gray clouds looming over the valley.

"Yuck, it looks like more snow is coming. I hope everyone gets home safely," Corinne said to Debbie, who had her arms full of jars to put on some of the pantry shelves.

Lucas had industriously been putting up the rest of the shelves in the pantry and was now watching the children while Debbie and Corinne could get a few things put away. It was a beautiful mess in the backroom.

"I've been praying as I gather," Debbie said and then made a whoomph sound as she almost tripped on several things in her path.

Corinne stood and was there to catch Debbie, but she had righted herself.

"Perhaps we need prayer for safety too." Corinne said and giggled a little. She was tired, and everything was a little funnier than it would be normally. Debbie chuckled a little too.

"Lord, bless us crazy women!" Debbie said and hooted a little. Her humor was always infectious. Corinne thought again how glad she was to have her here. She reminded her a bit of her Grandmother Trudie, who always had a way of making people laugh and feel right at home.

Corinne and Debbie found as much as they could and loaded up the shelves for a little while until they heard the wagon outside. The jangling harnesses were always a good sign that there was an arrival. Corinne heard Pepper the dog next door, announce the wagon a moment later. Pepper was her father's family pet, but Corinne noticed that he was the protector of her own property as well. He was still making his daily visits when her brother Cooper was in school. That dog certainly put a few miles of walking in every day. One day she wanted a dog of their own. When the children were a little bigger, she mused. The pleasant image of her two little ones playing chase with a bundle of fur was a pleasant thought as she walked to the front door. The house was in a shambles with things to trip on and weave around. Lucas made more space, but it wasn't feeling bigger yet. Right now, it seemed as if a mighty windstorm had come through her home.

The wagon with furniture had arrived and behind it were Marie and Violet. The man driving the wagon was one of John's work hands and he was willing to help bring in all the goods.

It was all hands getting busy. Marie came inside and took charge of one of the babies and Debbie the other.

Violet's cheeks were flushed pink and she had a different countenance about her. Corinne wondered if something had happened in town.

Marie filled her in. "Reynaldo is back from his trip. John stayed behind to organize the new horses that came on the ferry."

Corinne nodded and smiled. It sparked that inner nudge inside of her. She had a feeling that Violet was going to be leaving soon. It was hard to think on. Corinne loved Violet so very much and her heart would resist the change. She knew though, she would never deny her friend her own happiness. Someday Violet may want her own husband and children. It gave Corinne a bitter sweet heartache.

Violet was unloading the food from the wagon and lead the charge to get the pantry goods put away. The meat would have to be dealt with as well. Lucas stored the meat in the root cellar where it would stay colder. Next on his agenda was to build a small shed out behind the house. It would work for storing the meat in the winter months. His brother, Russell, had made one the year before and it had worked well.

Corinne felt her arms and shoulders burning over the next few hours as she did all that she could to get things put away, moved or shuffled around in her home. Lucas had stopped a few times to give her encouragement. He had even given her a kiss on the cheek once or twice. He had this permanent look on his face that seemed to apologize for the mess that the house was in. She was trying to make sure he knew that she wasn't perturbed at him. But the more exhausted she got through the afternoon and into the evening the more she wasn't sure if she would be able to comfort him at all.

She stopped for a moment when her shoulders were tensing up. She went into the parlor. She glanced around and saw the bigger window and the extension had made much more room. The furniture was jumbled around and a new sofa and rocking chair had been added, it was shoved into a back corner for now. Debbie was on the chair with Trudie in her lap.

"Lucas came in here a little while ago. He was so excited by this fence type thing that Amos Drays had designed," Debbie said when Corinne sat. Corinne reached over and stroked her daughter's fluffy dark hair.

"He mentioned it to me too a few days ago. But my brain has had a bit of a stir lately. I am not certain I know what it is all about." Corinne said with a sigh. She was rubbing the tense muscles of her shoulders. There was a knot on her right shoulder and it was burning incessantly.

"Corinne, could you take her on your lap for a moment." Debbie offered, and Corinne took Trudie gratefully. Trudie reached up with her chubby arms and cuddled under her mother's chin sweetly. Her eyes were glassy and sleepy and for just a brief moment she stared into Corinne's eyes and locked in. It was a much-needed reminder of why she was working so hard.

Debbie was behind Corinne a minute later and giving Corinne a much-needed massage.

Corinne groaned in pain and pleasure.

"I am not certain why it feels so much better when someone else's rubs your shoulders, it must be some kind of magic." Corinne said after a few minutes. Trudie was cuddled against Corinne's chest and Corinne had her arms loosely around her daughter, as Debbie worked on the knotted muscles.

"I have never told you, but my people were blessed with magical abilities long ago." Debbie said with a chuckle.

"I believe it." Corinne sighed happily. It was a strange sensation, to feel the stress of the day just lift off of her like that. The squeezing pressure was floating away under the skillful hands of her friend.

"You need to remember to get a good rest tonight. You will get sick if you keep overdoing it." Debbie wasn't usually bossy, but Corinne knew that it was good advice.

"I agree, let's hope the babies sleep well tonight. No teething or crying but just blissful silence all night long." Corinne's eyes were closed still lost in the sensation.

Debbie finished her ministrations and gave Corinne a friendly kiss on the top of her head. "Mama needs rest."

<hr />

Violet Griffen

Violet did her work with a flurry of lifting and sorting. The bags and boxes on the wagon had been dealt with efficiently.

"Thank you, Jason" Violet said to the ranch hand that was helping to unload the furniture. Little by little she was learning the names of all the workers on the ranch next door. They were a group of mostly polite men.

John gave her a lopsided smile and lifted the tarp covered table that was made for Debbie's bedroom upstairs. Violet slipped in behind him and grabbed a heavy bag of meat from the butcher's shop.

She delivered it to the cellar and shuffled a few things around to make certain everything was well organized. Her mind was torn between her task at hand and the man that had promised to come and see her.

She was trying to stay focused but noticed that her hands were shaking a few times with the excitement that was building inside

159

of her.

She went back to the wagon and met with Corinne and Lucas who were grabbing crates that were full of goods from the grocer.

"I got the meat in the cellar." Violet said.

"You are such gem." Lucas gave Violet a grateful smile. She felt it down to her toes, how much they appreciated her.

Violet smiled back and grabbed the last visible crate.

"I think the rest is furniture." Corinne said. She blew her breath out in a huff to blow a wayward tendril of hair out of her eyes. Corinne gave Violet a long look. "I heard that Rey is back. You excited?" Corinne asked a hint of teasing behind her eyes.

"Yes… and nervous." Violet said and lifted a shoulder in a half shrug. The bag full of potatoes was heavy in the other arm.

"He will be happy to see you." Corinne said to be a comfort.

Violet smiled as they walked back to her house. She kept looking towards the road, hoping to see a sign of the ranch hands back with all the horses. It was going to be a spectacle when they arrived.

"Let's get this all settled inside. We can organize it all tomorrow. We made some progress on the back room, but it is still a mess. One more day of messy won't do any harm." Corinne chuckled.

"I think we will all sleep well tonight." Violet added. She was tired earlier, but now she had that nervous energy rushing through her, which she knew would eventually fade and she would be asleep on her feet.

The next hour Violet stayed on task, shuffling around pantry goods and helping Lucas get the shelves put back up in the new pantry. It was more than a little chaotic and Violet's shoulders were burning from the load.

"You take a little break." Lucas suggested when he had caught her rubbing on her right shoulder. She felt bad for showing her discomfort.

"I'll be fine." Violet said with a grimace. She was determined to get as much done as she could.

"No, no…" Lucas said and waved a finger at her and smiled. "We all have to set limits, or we will have injuries. I am taking a break myself after this. I asked Corinne to get some coffee on. I am betting that it will be done any minute now." His green eyes were sincere. Violet decided to listen, if Lucas was taking on the task to make sure his household was not overdoing things then who was she to disagree with him.

Violet was surprised to see Cooper and Lila from next door standing with Corinne in the kitchen.

Cooper and Lila both waved at them as Lucas and Violet entered the room.

"Mama sent us over with the zucchini bread and told us to tell you that they will be bringing supper, I mean, dinner over soon." Lila said, her face showing her nervousness. Violet was pleased to get to know her better but she was still shy while speaking in groups but she was delightful one on one.

"We brought some butter over too." Cooper added not wanting to be left out.

"Thank you for that." Lucas said sincerely and gave Cooper a tussle to his head and Lila a pat on her shoulders. Violet was pleased to see the respect and love that this extended family shared.

Lila ran over and gave Violet a hug around her middle. They had a special little bond and Violet felt a rush of warmth as she placed a hand on Lila's warm head, smoothing her silky hair affectionately.

Corinne served up a few plates of zucchini bread and started up an assembly line of mugs for coffee.

Cooper and Lila headed back home to help their mama get everything ready.

It was a flurry of activity with Debbie hustling in with two babies in her arms. Lucas took Caleb and he snuggled right in on his chest, his cheeks pink and his eyes sleepy.

"They have been fed and they are both tired from all the ruckus." Debbie said and patted Trudie softly on the back.

Corinne was doctoring up the coffee the way everyone liked it and was handing out the cups and people sat at the bigger table that had been delivered and set up.

"The table looks nice," Debbie said as she sat down. "We can finally all fit now." She took a sip of coffee and closed her eyes to savor it for a moment.

Violet sat with her mug next to Debbie and then ran a hand along the wood of the table. "It is very nice. Amos Drays does good work." She told the group about the trade that she had made with Amos, to make him treats in trade for a new wooden chest.

"That sounds pretty fair." Lucas said. "I know that I get ribbed quite often in town that I might be the luckiest man in the Valley, with the bevy of talented women living in my home."

The women appreciated his statement and chatted about it for a few minutes. Violet also told them about Amos' talk about the lack of women in Oregon City.

"I have thought about that. It is a common topic now in town. I wonder what will be done about it." Lucas said and sipped on his coffee again then dunked a piece of his zucchini bread into the half-filled cup, a piece broke off and was floating around the top. Everyone found this amusing.

Lucas grinned boyishly and took another big swig to try and catch the piece of floating zucchini bread which added a new round of chuckles.

"Delicious!" Lucas said and grinned.

"I do love it when you act silly," Corinne said with a tired smile.

They finished up their snack and were chatting about plans of what to do until dinner. They all looked up suddenly when there was a loud commotion outside.

The horses were coming in.

Everyone, including the children were bundled up and they went outside to watch the procession. They walked up past the greenhouse and lab to be able to see the horses coming in down the road. There were two ranch hands at the front. One section of the fence was opened, and they had a wagon blocking the road. They could see through the trees to the west a long line of horses of every color traveling up the road towards the bridge. Corrine took Caleb from Lucas and she was pointing out the horses to him, as Debbie was doing for Trudie. Both of them were instantly awake and curious.

Soon voices could be heard as the horse neared the bridge and wanted to stop or turn around. There was yelling and some coaxing but the first few went over the bridge with a lot on whinnies and protests from the large beasts. The line behind them was long and it was amusing to see the struggle between man and beast. There were a few young horses who were not convinced that the bridge was not an evil force and they played a merry game of chase with one of the ranch hands.

Violet could see a few horses off in the distance that slowed down and wandered off toward Corinne's empty lavender field, probably looking for something to munch on. A ranch hand rode over quickly and forced the few lazy horses to get back in line and get back up the road.

Violet was fascinated by the process, and she felt that strange child-like fascination with these majestic creatures once again. The line was moving forward as the ranch hands forced the horses to go into the fenced in area. A few tried to turn into Angela's front yard to get around the wagon blocking the road but were thwarted.

Caleb was making excited noises and Trudie was saying "Ooo, ooo."

Violet couldn't help herself and was laughing amidst all the chaos. Between the horses, the ranch hands, and the crowd that was gathering around to watch it was quite a spectacle. Corinne and Lucas were waving to all the neighbors that were gathered around. Angela and Ted were on the front porch with Galina and Dolly, Earl and Warren were behind the wagon that was blocking the road. A few neighbors that lived farther on were showing up on horseback. It was a gathering.

"I can't believe that all of those horses fit on one ferry. That would have been quite a feat!" Corinne leaned over to say to Violet.

Violet agreed, trying to imagine the mayhem aboard a ferry with all of that livestock.

"We have to give these men the proper respect. I cannot imagine how to manage this much muscle and determination." Violet said in awe.

The long line of horses were making their way up the road and Violet could see the end of the line, about a quarter mile up the road. A line of about eight ranch hands with John Harpole were corralling the rest of the horses. A few more slower horses tried to escape into Corinne's field again, but they disliked the whistles and yells from the ranch hand and the barks from Pepper who kept running around like a mad thing, working just as hard as the men to keep the horses in line.

"Goggy!" Trudie said with a heart-warming laugh.

Everyone nearby whipped their head around and gave Trudie a serious look. She had never said a word before and the Grant household was amazed to hear her speak. They all gave her a pat on the back and Lucas and Corinne could not contain their smiles.

Corinne wiped away a tear of joy.

"Oh, her first word." She looked over to Lucas, who was beaming with pride.

"I guess that means we need to get a dog." Lucas laughed.

Corinne nodded. "Once the house is put back together. I think so." Corinne smiled and rubbed Trudie's back. "Yep, Trudie, that is a doggy, good girl!"

Corinne was talking to both of her children as the last of the horses came up over the bridge then into the corral. Caleb's little chubby finger was pointed at the horses and his eyes still wide with delight.

The horses ran around the corral, still agitated from the journey. A few were nuzzling their noses into the snow looking for grass to nibble on.

A few ranch hands went in on horseback and were guiding them toward the barn where a bale of alfalfa was waiting for them. Violet could finally see Reynaldo, riding beside John Harpole, deep in conversation and pointing and gesturing. He probably had more work to do before he could come to see her but seeing him was good. She was glad to have him back, safe and sound.

Marie gave a little whistle and they all turned to see her behind them.

"I got some stew on the stove warm and steamy, and some bread." Marie said as she got closer.

Cooper and Lila were further down along the fence, standing on the first board, pointing, clearly fascinated with all the new horseflesh to admire.

"Much ado today." Lucas said as he thanked Marie for her hard work.

"Doesn't it always come like that. A bunch of days of nothing, then one day everything happens all at once." Marie said smiling, her dimples were deep into her pink cheeks.

Her daughter reached to be picked up by Marie. "Mama I am cold."

Marie gave her attention to Abigail. "Where did your mittens go?" Marie looked all around.

"I don't know." The little girl said with a pout.

Violet chuckled a little.

The next minute they all stood around chatting, watching the new horses get acquainted with their new home at the Harpole ranch. A few curious horses in the other fenced area came to see the new arrivals. They were sniffing the air and whinnying in the way horses do. Violet wondered with vague curiosity if they were welcome whinnies or not. She wasn't one to understand the language of animals, but it amused her to think on it.

Marie called Cooper and Lila away from the fence and they whined and made a few attempts to stay and watch, but Marie took charge. "No more lollygagging from you. Dinner is on the stove and Papa will be in soon. I want hands washed and toys put away." Marie gave everyone a wave and took charge of her oldest children who were still mildly grumbling about the interruption of their fun.

Lucas and Corinne decided that they should all head in and get cleaned up for dinner as well.

Violet started walking back up the road also, watching Cooper drag his heels and complaining.

"Cooper Harpole, you get your act together or you will go to bed without your dinner." Marie stated firmly.

Violet remembered being young and her mother scolding her own brothers. It was getting easier to sort out the good memories of her childhood from the bad.

Everyone was washed up and Violet was busy serving up plates of food while Corinne and Debbie got the children set up in the high chairs by the bigger table. Caleb had the wiggles and Violet commiserated with Debbie, who was trying to get the little fellow to settle down.

"He doesn't want to sit in his chair tonight." Violet said.

She set a plate on the table and clapped her hands together a few times, and Caleb and Trudie both looked up to her distractedly. Violet made a few silly faces at the kids to keep them still while Corine and Debbie finished getting them settled in.

Corinne gave Violet another appreciative glance.

Lucas said a prayer, blessing the food a few minutes later, thanking God for all the women in his life that worked so hard and made his life a blessing, then everyone dove into the food with abandon.

Caleb was trying to eat a little piece of soft bread that Corinne had pulled out from her own plate. He tasted a few and spit them out a few times before attempting to chew with his few baby teeth. Trudie, who had said her first word earlier was back to babbling nonsense the same as before.

They all decided to keep working with both Caleb and Trudie to understand more words.

The chaos of the day faded a little as the Grant house enjoyed the good stew and bread.

Chelsea arrived while they were eating to deliver some vanilla cake and warm apple cider for them to enjoy after dinner. Lucas gave his sister-in-law a big hug. She hugged everyone else and then had to leave.

"Dolly is coming back with me, so I best not keep her waiting." Her husky voice was apologetic to have to go so soon.

They all thanked her for the dessert and waved goodbye when she stepped back out into the cold.

The dinner was leisurely eaten after that, with the chaos of the day over they were all enjoying the simple pleasure of being back home. Dinner at the Harpole's had been wonderful, like a holiday feast every day, but there was something special about being back home.

Violet was stuffed full once she had cleaned out the bowl of stew. She pushed back in her chair to relax a little. She was planning out her evening in her mind. Hoping to get the dishes done before Reynaldo showed up. She would take a lantern with her to the pantry and see where everything was and get a start on thinking what she would make for breakfast in the morning. It might be simple fare for a day or so until she got the lay of the land again.

Lucas excused himself and went into the larger parlor and poked a stick in the fireplace and lit a few lanterns to brighten the space as the sun was fast going down outside. The cabin was beginning to glow with the warmth of firelight as he put new logs in the fireplace. The crackling was a warm and homey sound that pleased Violet.

Trudie was a bit of a mess, with little bits of food up her arms, all over her face and in her hair, as she was learning to eat like the grownups. It might be a while before she was proficient, Violet thought.

Trudie made a bit of a fuss when Debbie took a warm wet rag to her arms and face. She made a little cry that was not very sincere but she was bright as a new penny when Debbie was done with her. Caleb took his cleanup with much less ado.

Violet got up and started working on the cleanup while Corinne and Debbie sat with the two children in the parlor. Corinne was going to read them a story and get them good and tired with a little play, so they would sleep well.

Lucas went back to work in the back of the cabin and Violet got busy.

Within an hour the dishes were drying on a tea towel. As she was wiping down the table there was a knock at the door.

Reynaldo was there, dark and handsome and smiling that charming smile.

She could have asked him if he wanted a coffee, or a piece of vanilla cake but she said nothing. Instead she just let her eyes drink in the sight of the man that she was falling in love with.

"I missed you Violet." He had said that earlier. But she didn't mind hearing that again.

She should have responded with something coherent, but she just couldn't speak, her nervous energy collided with her emotions and she just launched against him with a hug that she needed so badly. She felt him chuckle as he put his arms around her. It was exactly what she needed, and she held on for a long minute.

She pulled away reluctantly and blushed crimson to the roots of her hair.

"I'm sorry," she muttered softly.

"I didn't mind at all." He said placing a hand alongside her arm. The warm presence of it made her feel rather giddy.

She gestured for him to join her at the table and she got him a cup of coffee and a piece of cake without even asking if he wanted any.

She wondered absently if he was hungry for dinner.

"You want some stew?" She looked up to see him watching her intently.

"I could definitely eat some stew." He said without ever losing the grin.

She grabbed him a bowl of stew and served him a feast. She grabbed herself another mug full of some left over cider.

"That was quite a show with all the horses coming in." Violet said as she watched him eat his dinner quickly. He must have been hungry from the long day of activity.

They chatted about the horse's arrival for a few minutes until his plate was cleaned off.

"It was good to get this job done. I will probably have to go at least once a year to do this again, now that we have suppliers from Kentucky and Georgia sending us new breeding lines." Reynaldo said. "Good supper." He winked at her.

"Oh, I didn't make it. Today was move in day, and we had some help from Marie and Chelsea." Violet said. She cleared away his dishes then sat back down. She hoped that he would stay as long as he wanted. The family was in the parlor so they had a good chance to talk, while still being proper. She wanted him all to herself for as long as possible.

"It was nice to be back in California again. I went to visit my family while I was there. My brothers actually helped me get the horses on the ferry. It worked out rather well." He smiled and reached for her hand.

"Was it good to see the family?" She asked, hoping that it was.

"Yes, it brought back good memories to see my brothers and sisters. It was rather shocking to see them all so much older than before. But they said the same about me." He chuckled. "Juan, my eldest brother, said that I had left as a scrawny good for nothing kid."

"Sounds like a brother." Violet laughed.

"My father has retired from the ranching business and split up the land and cattle between us sons." Reynaldo said. "That was shocking to me at first, but after I spoke with him briefly he explained it all." His eyes clouded for a moment.

"Fathers can be complicated." Violet said with sincerity.

"Yes, but the conversation with him wasn't a bad one. He was proud of me." Reynaldo squeezed her hand and looked a little distracted. "I must say, I cannot quite figure out something." He paused. "When my father said he was proud of me, I felt anger instead of feeling accomplished."

Violet could see that he was struggling with complicated emotions. She knew from talks they had shared that his father was not kind or easy to get along with. "I can understand. Perhaps it made you angry to hear now the words you needed to hear when you were young." She had her own issues from when she was young. She decided to share. "When my father said that he loved me, it began to change as I got older. I wondered for a long time if I would ever be able to hear those words without having them mean something terrible or tainted. But I thank God that it never happened that way. I can feel love and accept love from others without having his warped actions affect me as much."

Reynaldo squeezed her hands again. "You are wise, Violet. I am always amazed by you."

She locked her eyes with his and lost herself in them.

"Did you see your mother?" She asked, she was trying to distract herself after that intense gaze from him. He was not making this easy.

168

"Yes, and I told her about you." He grinned at her slyly.

"Good things I hope." Violet said, feeling a strange sense of pride that he thought enough of her that he spoke to his family about her.

"All good things." He winked. "I talked so much about your bread that they were all jealous to taste your cooking."

"You are silly. It is just bread you fool." Violet said and flushed with pleasure.

"Not when you make it." He added. "My mother made a feast for me the first day, and I was spoiled with all of my childhood favorites. I was useless after that meal." He patted his belly.

"A good feast usually requires a good nap." Violet said from experience. They both laughed.

"My baby sister, Esma, is almost thirteen. She is a pretty little thing and has everyone wrapped around her little finger. She was only four or five years old when I left. All of my other siblings are married and working the ranch." He smiled and told her all about the land. She couldn't help but smile seeing the place he grew up through his eyes.

"I hope to take you someday." He said, and she could tell that he was a little embarrassed to say it. "Actually, I am hoping for something more." He met her eyes again. "I brought something back with me, I wonder if you would like it."

Violet gulped nervously and felt her stomach knot up with nervous energy. She stared at him dumbly as he reached into his pocket then pulled her up to stand.

"I cannot imagine living another day without knowing that you are a part of my future." He said seriously and reached for her with his free hand. He knelt before her and her heart pounded quickly in her chest. "Violet Griffen, will you marry me?"

Violet was speechless and still for a long moment; just looking at the man she loved, she was overwhelmed to know that he wanted her. She felt warm tears on her cheeks.

She finally found her voice and whispered "Yes, I will." Then it was his turn to hug her. She was so wonderfully happy, her heart was full. This promise to marry him was going to change everything about her life, but she knew it was the right decision. God had shown her over the last months that she could accept that things would be different, but she was still going to be blessed.

The group in the parlor heard Reynaldo when he picked up Violet and she laughed and squealed a little. They joined them and started in with congratulations and cheering.

"I remember a day over last spring when this young woman was certain that you had no interest in her." Lucas gave Reynaldo a poke to the ribs. Reynaldo laughed and nodded.

"That took some work for me. But my mother always taught me to try and try again." He smiled to Violet and she blushed.

She was so very happy and seeing that everyone else was supportive really helped to calm her fears. She wasn't sure how everything was going to work out in the end, but she was certain about Reynaldo and his steadfast heart.

Corinne and Debbie both gave Violet big hugs.

"You are going to be a wonderful wife and mother, Vie, you deserve this!" Corinne whispered in her ear then looked into her eyes for a long time. Corinne was such a dear friend and having her approval was a sweet balm.

The night passed and Reynaldo held her hand while they sat in the new parlor that now had plenty of seats for everyone. The hearth crackled with warm fire and the conversation was sweet and inspiring. Corinne and Lucas shared stories of the first few months of marriage. These were all things that Violet had heard before, but it was amusing to hear them again in context. Debbie talked about her marriage that started out happily but then turned when he went running off. It definitely reminded Violet of her first husband Eddie who was such a sweet and loving man, but who just couldn't stay to make things work. He had been lured away. Reynaldo was not that kind of man and Violet was relieved that she had a second chance at marriage.

It was nearing midnight, the babies had long been in their beds and everyone finally was getting tired, the day had been a long one. Violet's shoulders were stiff and sore from all the heavy lifting, but she had forgotten about the discomfort in the thrilling conclusion of the evening.

"I should be getting on back to my cabin." Reynaldo said as he pulled Violet up from the davenport. She moved her stiff arms around and gave them a little stretch to get the blood moving again.

Reynaldo gave her a curious look.

"Oh, just my arms and shoulders are a bit sore from all the work today." Violet smiled at him and felt like she wanted to hug him again or lean against his chest and just rest there a while. "I will ask Debbie for a rub down before I go to sleep, or maybe just wait until morning."

"Ah, well, someday that will be my job." He put a hand to her cheek. She blushed to the roots of her hair again.

"You better get on out of here Reynaldo, you get to save all that sparking for another day." Lucas scolded. "Violet is under my protection now." Lucas chuckled and gave Reynaldo a little poke.

They were both laughing as Reynaldo headed to the front door and put on his wool coat. Everyone said goodbye to him and went about getting the house ready for them all to retire.

Violet put on her own coat and walked outside with Reynaldo. He immediately pulled her close. She was finally able to do what she wanted and rested her head against his chest. He rested his chin on the top of her head and she felt so very warm and protected.

He finally let her pull back and she looked him in the eyes. She didn't need anything else but knowing he was there for her.

"You know that I love you." He said in a whisper.

"And I am in love with you." She answered simply.

He kissed her softly. It was all the promise that she needed.

Chapter 14

Sean Fahey

Sean's heart was pumping. He felt the crisp damp air hit his cheeks as he jumped over a small bush. His lungs were burning from the sustained running. The air was cold, but he was sweating rivulets under his coat. He thought of shrugging it off, but he might lose it in the woods.

"Cu-pid!" Sean called, his voice was getting raspy.

The day had started so well. The snow had fallen overnight, soft and wispy. Sean had enjoyed the peaceful serenity when he took Cupid out for his evening walk. He was doing so well with his training, not needing a leash when he was in the yard by the house. The moon had peeked from behind the snow clouds and Sean let the silent moonlight fill him up.

The morning was bright with sunlight and the cabin was brighter than usual reflecting sunlight off the snow showing bright white light through his home. He was think about adding an addition to the cabin with a den for books and a nice big paned window to see the mountains. He had so many plans and the bright light of the morning had him humming with the possibilities.

He had spent a little time with a cup of coffee and his Bible, he meandered his way through Psalms. His stubby pencil was jotting down verses in his journal.

Cupid was fed and soon needed to go outside. Sean made the obviously boneheaded decision to let him out without the leash to do his business.

The large ten point buck was standing there, rather proudly, just beyond the barn and made eye contact with Sean first. Sean loved seeing animals in nature and was pleased to see this tall buck, standing boldly, well-muscled with his darker winter coat. His nose twitched a moment and his eyes went wide and shifted to the wagging dog at Sean's side. It had only taken a split second for the buck to bolt up and leap away. He turned and headed east into the dense woods for cover.

Cupid was after the buck at lightning speed. Sean was left

there, with obviously slower reflexes that any of the creatures that were running through the woods.

It had been ten minutes already and Sean had no notion whatsoever of where Cupid had run off to. The trail was cold, but Sean kept running in the direction he hoped his dog was.

Sean tripped on a tree root and flew down to the ground. "Whoomph…" Sean let out involuntarily.

He mentally checked himself over and stood up. Staring off in a few directions as he patted himself. He wasn't injured but he was out of breath from sprinting through the woods. He couldn't see any hoof or paw prints. His dog was lost.

Sean felt a pang at his own stupidity.

He let out a shrill whistle, hoping maybe that Cupid would hear it. He wasn't good at responding to his whistle yet.

"Stupid Cupid." He muttered under his breath. The rhyme not amusing him as it usually would.

Sean stomped around in a big circle, trying to see if there were any tracks. After a few minutes of feeling like a fool Sean whistled again. He yelled until his voice was hoarse.

Sean could imagine the worst-case scenarios well. His dog, starving and alone in the snow, freezing to death, or sniffing his way into a bear den, or finding a mountain lion. This was the wilderness after all. Cupid was certainly not the apex predator to be able to fend for himself for long.

Sean whistled a few more times and turned around. He was wondering what to do next. He would walk back and see if he could find some kind of trail. He may need to go back to the cabin and grab some better gear. He might need to go tracking to find the dog and need a few supplies. This was not a good start to the day.

The sun was shining brightly, the air warmer than expected and Sean could see the sunbeams shining through the branches, melting the snow a little bit.

Sean was stepping through the underbrush still searching for the signs of his pet or a big buck anywhere as he traveled back in the direction of his cabin.

He heard a far away bark and his hope was kindled. He yelled for Cupid again, then whistled.

It was about two minutes later another happy bark gave away the direction. Sean turned a little and walked back eastward, hoping that his dog was trying to find him.

Sean finally saw him, he then leapt over a small creek and was bounding toward Sean. His tail was whipping the tall weeds and brown leaves of the shrubbery around him. He certainly made a racket as he bounced and spun up to Sean. He had the stupidest grin on his doggy face.

If dogs could talk, Sean mused, Cupid would be telling him 'I had so much fun!'

Sean wasn't sure if he should chastise him or scold him. It probably wouldn't do any good. Sean knelt down and attached the short-braided leash he had in his coat pocket. He would never make that mistake again. This dog needed a leash.

Cupid wagged his tail happily for the next half hour as they walked back towards the cabin. Sean was shaking his head. In one way he was glad that his dog was safe. In another, it still annoyed him to have had that much exercise so early in the day.

"I still have chores to do dog." Sean said to Cupid, who was oblivious. "I wasn't needing to go traipsing through the woods, what if we had found a bear who hasn't started hibernating yet?"

Cupid just looked at him with those soulful eyes and Sean huffed.

They were almost to the barn when Sean saw a buggy parked out front. Cupid must have seen it too because he was pulling on the leash and Sean was one second away from losing his grip on it. Sean reached forward and caught the braided cord with a second hand to make sure the dog didn't escape again.

Dolly was outside on the porch.

Sean smiled, he couldn't help himself. Her long dark hair was down, and she was smiling prettily there. He would like to see her standing on that porch every day if he could.

"Good to see you." Dolly said, with her slow and careful way.

He wasn't sure how me managed it, but his smile broadened.

"You are a bright spot in my day. I just chased this hound through the woods for quite a while." Sean said with a laugh. Cupid was pulling hard on the leash, Sean gave a little tug of warning and Cupid took the cue and slowed his pull.

Sean climbed up the steps and Cupid was a furry ball of wiggles trying to get Dolly's attention.

"I told Angela to wait inside." Dolly said as she kneeled to give Cupid affection.

Cupid was euphoric and rolled over so Dolly could scratch his belly, which she did with abandon.

"Oh good. I'm glad you both came for a visit." Sean said and felt that nervous tug of energy he always had when Dolly was around. He thought about that kiss and was tempted to do it again. *I am such a fool.* He thought.

"I wanted to say, before we go inside. That I talked with Chelsea Grant." Dolly said and looked up to him bravely. Her cheeks were pink.

"Oh?" He gave her his full attention. His nerves suddenly tightened in his gut.

"I think we should start courting. If that is still what you would like." She said boldly.

Sean nodded dumbly and swallowed before he spoke, he suddenly imagined that if he uttered a word he would squeak like a young boy. "I would like that... very much," He muttered.

She smiled, and he lost his train of thought. She stood up in front of him and tilted her head just a little bit and looked at him with a look that seemed to be sizing him up. It was utterly charming.

Sean stood there dumbly while she assessed his worth with a lift of her lips to the tiniest grin she finally relaxed her stance. "Let's go in."

Sean agreed and followed her inside the house as Cupid did, with total adoration.

Sean had to shake himself out of his stupor as he saw Angela inside at the kitchen counter.

"I brought you a few jars of venison stew, Galina made a large batch. We wanted to be certain you weren't out here starving." Angela gave him a wink. "Though I see you have plenty of food in your cupboards."

"Sister, have you been snooping around?" Sean asked with a chuckle.

"Absolutely, isn't that a sister's job?" She walked over and gave Sean an embrace.

"I suppose so." He said with a grumble. He was enjoying the new banter between them.

"This cabin isn't so bad, but I would always want a bigger pantry, especially with the long winters." She added practically.

"I have plans to add on. I saw a cabin closer to town that did it well. I was thinking of talking to a few folks around to get a working design." Sean said then gestured the two women to come and sit by the fireplace. He put another log on the fire then he sat

175

on the stool near the hearth.

"Be sure to talk with Lucas Grant, he is pretty good at designing anything. He has the brains for that kind of thing." Angela said, she was obviously proud of her friends.

"I will do." Sean smiled.

They all chatted away for the next hour. Dolly joined in too and they talked about weather and small talk for a good while. There was nothing serious but just good visiting. It really did confirm his wish to make the parlor bigger, so he could invite people over more often. He talked it over with the women and they had their own ideas. Dolly thought with a new parlor he could have a dining room table instead of the tiny table in the cramped little kitchen. They had good ideas. Most of the cabin was taken up with bedrooms. With more space he would have room to stretch out.

"It is a strange thing for me to know I have that inheritance sitting in the bank. I often forget about it. I actually had the thought the other day that maybe I couldn't afford to make the changes around here. Then it dawned on me a few minutes later." He laughed.

"I sometimes do that too." Angela said. "Perhaps because we spent so much of our lives with nothing we just fall back on that feeling that nothing will ever change. I recognize that feeling inside of me."

Sean agreed with his sister.

"For me, I fear making plans sometimes." Dolly spoke up. "I spent so much time waiting for my tribe to return for me that I still haven't put down any roots. I am trying to put those feelings aside though." She said and clasped her hands together nervously. "I feel God telling me to be still and stay in one place. Though, I am not certain what place that is yet."

Sean felt his heart jump in his chest, wishing she would stay with him. But he knew that he would have to bide his time with her. They would have to find out if it was God's will for them to be together. At least that is what he felt that God was telling him.

Soon the visit ended. Sean said goodbye to Angela, then said an awkward goodbye to Dolly.

"Would you like for me to call on you someday soon?" He asked.

"I will be at Chelsea's the next few days." She said and smiled becomingly.

He nodded and fumbled around with his hands, not knowing what to do with himself.

"You are always welcome to come visit the greenhouses at Grant's Grove, I am usually there or in the labs." Dolly suggested.

Sean knew he would be doing that soon. It was a good suggestion. He felt that a change was coming about in his life and he liked the change.

⁕⁘⁙ ⁙⁘⁕

Galina Varushkin

The new hardwood floors were smooth and chilly against her feet and were a little shocking to Galina after the warm bed. She reached for her woolen stockings. Sophia was next to her, reaching around and looking rumpled, her curly hair was in frizzy disarray around her. Galina couldn't judge Sophia too harshly on her morning appearance. Galina was pretty sure that she had forgotten to remove a hair pin and reaching up, felt around to find it. She fumbled around blindly with her hand through her hair and finally pulled the pin out. She bent over the bed awkwardly and found the second wool stocking had traveled in the night nearly halfway under the bed. She would have to crawl around on her hands and knees to retrieve it.

All the commotion of getting up had excited Lady. The poodle was curious and perky and was right there yipping in Galina's ear. Galina laughed as she got on the ground and with several awkward sleepy swipes, tried to reach the stocking. Lady, who had an affinity for fitting under the bed and finding socks, was able to help and hinder the process. The poodle snatched up the stocking and wiggled herself out from under the bed.

Galina had to crawl around the bed, chasing the poodle and quietly coaxing the furry creature to let the stocking go. Sophia quietly giggled, no help at all.

Galina put on her stocking while glaring playfully at Sophia, who was trying hard to not have the giggles.

They padded down the stairs together, Lady bouncing up and down the steps watching them carefully, making sure that they were coming.

"I wish I had her energy every day." Galina said quietly. She yawned and stretched a little, wishing that she was still in the warm and cozy bed upstairs.

They peeked out the window and it was hard to tell what the weather was doing. The window was frosted over.

"I will take Lady outside to do her business." Sophia said in a loud whisper.

"I will make the coffee." Galina smiled and knelt down to give Lady a scratch on the head. Lady sniffed her hand and then allowed the cuddle.

Galina quietly found the coffee pot in the Quackenbush kitchen. She poked at the red coals that still smoldered in the bottom of the cookstove. Clive must have put some slow burning hardwoods in the night before. Galina found the stacked wood and put some fresh kindling in to get the fire to catch.

Sophia came back inside, looking rather silly in Clive's big coat. "Oh, it is so cold." She shivered.

The coffee took a few minutes. Galina and Sophia stood over the pot and the hot stove to warm themselves. They poured out two cups of coffee and sat by the fireplace, planning out hair and dress choices. Since they were a similar size Sophia had brought a few of her own dresses to try on the night before.

Galina had liked the midnight blue one with bright white lace on the edges. Sophia had really liked her in the emerald green print with cream-colored pinstripes. Sophia's mother made it a point to be certain that Sophia was well provided for when it came to her wardrobe. Sophia enjoyed dressing in the latest fashion but would have gladly had fewer dresses in her crowded wardrobe. Sophia had begun to store more of her clothing in Aunt Olivia's old wardrobe which she had left behind when she had married.

"I honestly don't know why my mother wants me to dress so nicely. She is afraid for me to ever be seen in public. She nearly swoons if a man even looks twice at me. I will certainly be a spinster if she has any say in the matter. The lectures I get daily on the kind of man that would want to wed me. The way she acts it's as though we have come to the land of wild men bent on stealing a woman and heaving her over his shoulders." Sophia giggled.

"That would certainly be interesting." Galina's eyes went wide.

"I have read stories about the Scottish highlanders. Some have stolen brides and then just announced to their tribe that they are married. According to one book I read, that was all that was needed." Galina laughed.

"Is it strange that I find that somewhat scandalous but also slightly romantic." Sophia grinned a crooked smile.

"It probably only seems romantic in a story. If you were stolen, then dragged kicking and screaming through the night, then married to a savage stranger you might think otherwise." Galina said practically.

"You really should write a story like that." Sophia said with her eyes wide. She gripped her hands in front of her chest, almost pleading.

"You silly girl." Galina took a big sip of her coffee, shaking her head.

"You should." Sophia insisted.

"I like writing children's stories." Galina stuck her tongue out at Sophia playfully.

"For now…but life can make us change over time." Sophia stood and gave Galina the gesture to turn in her chair. "Time for me to start braiding your hair. Otherwise we will look a fright for church."

The hair was done, elegant and beautiful with her thick dark hair pulled up nicely on top and hanging with heavy curls in the back. Galina felt older and more elegant than ever before.

Galina had been practicing hairstyles quite a bit with Heather Sparks and Angela. She had Sophia's hair done with deft fingers. Sophia's natural curl and lovely blond hair was always beautiful, but with the braids and curls it was stunning.

"We will turn heads for certain." Galina said as they stood next to each other and looked into the gilded mirror in the parlor. The firelight in the room was a glowing warmly and made them feel romantic and lovely.

They giggled like the girls they were and went upstairs to get dressed. They heard stirring from Clive and Olivia and made haste to finish getting ready before breakfast. There was a hustle of bustles and petticoats and a few hasty changes made but they appeared downstairs as breakfast was getting set on the table.

"You ladies are lovely as always." Clive announced. He was pouring coffee for his wife as she scooped out scrambled eggs for all the plates.

"I will need some more eggs after tomorrow." Olivia said to Clive as he slid up next to her to peck her on the cheek.

"I will get some from the grocers." Clive said and tried to slide in a hand to her side.

Olivia wiggled away from him playfully. "I have a hot pan and you are going to get burned." She laughed and hustled a few steps to the kitchen.

She came back out with a jar of strawberry preserves and butter for the toast.

They ate breakfast with efficiency and Clive was talking with Olivia about getting Amos Drays in town to make them a cradle and a crib for the empty spare room. Sophia talked about making lace for a christening gown. Everyone was in a lovely mood.

Clive pulled out a large beef roast. Olivia got it seasoned and in the oven before they all headed out for the church service. Olivia fretted that the beef would not be done in time, but Clive calmed her fears.

"I am certain we can keep ourselves entertained while the roast finishes up. Milton seems to have a gift of gab and will keep us all busy for a spell." He gave Olivia and the girls a wink.

"We made that coffeecake last night. We can have some coffee and cake when we get back home. That will tide us over." Sophia suggested.

"See there, Sophia has a grand plan." He gave Olivia a wink and patted Sophia on the shoulder.

The air was cold as they rode over in the surrey. It was only a mile up the road but Galina was happy for the warmth of the church when they arrived. There was a nice warm fire in the woodstove at the back of the room and many of her friends were gathered around it when they arrived.

She was thrilled when she heard the good news that was spreading like wildfire.

Angela was hugging Violet and Reynaldo was looking so very pleased with himself.

"Violet and Reynaldo are engaged." Angela told her once she was done with Violet.

Sophia and Galina both squealed and congratulated Violet and the merry mood spread around the room.

Violet's ring was a beautiful green emerald and she blushed so very prettily every time she was asked to show it off.

It took a long time to get everyone into their seats but finally Galina saw Milton sitting in the row in front of them. He greeted them all quickly before they sat down.

Galina was fidgety and distracted through the entire service. She could not say at all about what the sermon had been about, because of Milton sitting so close.

180

Certainly, he would know that she was watching his every move. She felt silly and girlish, but he was so very handsome and interesting. He was a mystery for her to solve. She did try to give herself a warning, that she did not know the man very well. She could easily say though, that she was intrigued by him.

The service ended, and Milton followed behind them in his own little buggy. Galina had to force herself to not turn around to watch him coming up the road behind them.

Sophia was just as distracted, and they giggled and fussed over each other a little more than was necessary.

The house was beginning to have all the good smells of a fine supper as they all shrugged out of their coats, commenting on the wonderful aroma.

"It might be an hour or two before it is cooked through." Olivia said. "But the girls made a fine coffeecake last night. I can get some coffee on."

Milton turned to the girls. "Is there any cinnamon on that coffee cake?" Smiling that charming smile of his.

Galina spoke up. "Yes, it has a crunchy cinnamon crumble." She tried to smile charmingly back at him.

"Oh, that is indeed my favorite." He gave Galina a sweet and appreciative look. Her heart beat a steady thump in her chest.

"Why don't we go into the parlor and chit chat for a spell." Clive gave Milton a wave with his arm to lead the way.

Clive's parlor had a nice big paned window that looked over the fields and mountains to the south and the white blanket of snow lay soft on the fields, showing off the valley pleasantly.

"Oh, you do have yourself a fine view there." Milton said and sat down in the winged back chair that Clive offered.

Galina pulled herself away from the doorway and back into the kitchen to help get the coffee and cake served. She was reluctant to miss anything that was said but knew that she had to help out. It was the proper thing to do.

Sophia and Galina helped Olivia get a few things prepared up for supper. The potatoes were peeled and soaking in a bowl of water, so they wouldn't brown. Olivia set up some bread rolls to rise the night before and she got them buttered and ready on a tray to go into the oven when the roast came out.

They served up the coffee and cake a few minutes later and everyone had a nice little chat. Milton was very entertaining, sharing stories of his first days in the West. He had shared a little about the boom town of San Francisco, and Galina found it very closely resembled the experience that Angela had of the place. A stinky and chaotic town square with muddy roads and gangs causing trouble.

"I liked Sacramento a far sight better and the lovely culture of the Latino people there was charming. I had quite a few men that were of Spanish descent in my barber shop and they were lovely folks. I was invited to a fiesta once by a gentleman named Guillermo, an odd name on my lips, but the food was so delicious. I have never in my life tasted anything like it." Milton was a good story teller and gave them all a glimpse into the day he spent at a fiesta in the house of a wealthy landowner. "There was this one thing, tamales…" He laughed and grinned. "I hope I am saying it correctly. They were wrapped up in a corn husk and didn't look appetizing at all. I had no idea how to eat the thing and almost bit into as it was. I finally figured it out. Oh…" He sighed and held a hand over his belly. "It melted in the mouth and tasted of corn and spices." He grinned. "Whenever I go back to Sacramento for business I will find a way to eat one again."

Everyone was charmed, and he was very enthralled to hear from everyone, asking all the ladies to participate and talk about themselves.

The time passed quickly, and Galina had to leave again to help get the dinner prepared. Clive and Milton went outside to bring in some firewood. Milton insisted on helping even when Clive told him it wasn't necessary as a guest.

"I never shy away from a little work." Milton jumped right in and made himself a part of the work force.

While Galina was setting the table for supper Milton stood right beside her for a long moment, making her feel nervous. "You need any help with those plates, Galina?" His voice was low and just above a whisper. She was perplexed at what to do with herself. She looked to the side and caught his teasing glance. He was enjoying that she was so nervous. It gave her a little jolt of gumption.

"Here are some plates then Mr. Vaughn," She raised an eyebrow and handed over a stack of two plates. He seemed to enjoy the look on her face.

"Aw, I was hoping for you to say my name." He pouted a little and set the plates in the empty spots.

Clive carved up the roast and everyone dove into the meal.

Milton gave high praise to Olivia and her helpers for making such a fine meal. Declaring it to be as fine as his mother's home cooking.

After the meal Clive brought out his checkerboard and everyone got chance to play a round.

Milton really tried hard to distract Galina while she was playing against him, but she won the round, feeling rather proud of herself.

It was after four o'clock and Milton and Clive were both looking outside.

"I probably should head out. It will be getting dark soon enough." Milton said with a sad face. "I have enjoyed the hospitality so very much."

"I should be getting Galina back home with the Greaves as well." Clive said and got up with a lazy Sunday stretch.

"I would be honored to give Miss Varushkin a ride back home." Milton said with smile. He turned from Clive to look towards Galina to make sure that she was open to the idea.

This day had been full of such pleasantries, but Galina wasn't sure if it was appropriate. She had gone on walks with Warren in the past and no one had told her that was improper. She gave a glance to Clive. He smiled and nodded.

"You be sure to get her home safe and sound. Looks like more snow is coming our way." Clive said practically.

Galina sighed in relief, he must have approved to agree. She felt her cheeks flush for the thousandth time of the day.

"Let me grab my coat and other things." Galina said and darted off with Sophia right behind her.

As soon as she was in Sophia's room Sophia gave her shoulders a squeeze from behind.

"I think he likes you." Sophia said breathlessly.

"I don't know, perhaps he is just being polite, and a flirt." Galina said as she gathered up her clothing from the day before. Her hands were shaking with nervous energy. "Clive is a bit of a flirt, it's harmless really. It makes people feel at ease."

"The way he was looking at you over the table wasn't just being a flirt." Sophia said and laughed again. She was bounding around the room gathering things to help with the packing.

Galina did think that he had been very attentive, and there was that secret thrill of being admired. It was more exciting than any other feeling and she remembered how it had also been with

Warren. She had read once in a novel about it feeling like butterflies in the stomach. It was a good description. He was rather mysterious and so very charming.

"We will see what happens." Galina said. She took a deep breath and sighed, trying to calm herself.

"Oh…" Sophia sighed loudly. "It is going to be impossible to not know what happened. I may have to walk over if the weather is good to hear how the ride went."

Sophia was staying for another few days at the Quackenbush home before going back to town. Galina was going to miss having her closer.

"Don't you take any risks. I don't want you getting sick." Galina was trying to be practical, even though she knew that she would love for Sophia to come by. It would break up the tedious work days to have a visitor. Ted and Angela loved having Sophia around as well. Ted still doted on his sister, as much as he teased her, as was his job. Galina smiled at the thought.

Galina was ready, Sophia gushed one more time. "You make sure he holds your hand to help you into the buggy, and again to get out." She giggled.

"I declare, Sophia, you are just ridiculous!" Galina laughed and picked up her satchel.

"I have to be ridiculous sometimes. It feels like a relief after all the tense days at home in town. I need to feel silly and foolish sometimes. Otherwise I will lose my temper and explode sometime at my mother. Then, everything would get worse." Sophia said with a moment of levity. "Spending this last week with Clive and Olivia, and also with you." Sophia's eyes misted over. "It was so needed to take my mind off of all of the pressure I have at home."

Galina had rarely seen Sophia be so serious and she gave her a long hug.

"I am sorry that things are hard for you." Galina said with sincerity. She knew what it felt like to have pressure at home. Though their situations were very different, she understood the need to just feel carefree sometimes.

"Thank you, Galina." Sophia pulled away from the hug. "I feel rather foolish sometimes. I don't have it so bad really. I guess I am just wanting a bit more freedom."

Galina nodded as she patted Sophia's cheek affectionately.

They finished up the packing and Galina said her goodbye to Lady the dog, who was curious about everything.

Galina was ready to go. Her boots thumped down the steps and she looked up to find Milton looking at her expectantly from across the room.

"Let me…" He said and took her satchel.

Clive helped Galina on with her coat and she gave hugs to Olivia, Clive and Sophia, as well as a pat on the head of Lady and Cocoa who were excited about all the activity.

Galina followed Milton out to his shining black buggy. Milton put the satchel behind the seats and then helped her up into her side then darted around the back and got up into the other seat. He looked over to her with a mischievous smile.

"I was hoping to give you a ride home. I was thinking about how to ask for days." He said and lowered his head shyly. He was so handsome and sweet that he took her breath away.

"Truly?" She asked. Wondering why someone like him would even notice someone like her.

"Yes truly." He smiled broadly. He took the reins and gave a cluck for the two horses to go. "I was thinking about those dark eyes of yours all week."

Galina was flattered . The butterflies were busy dancing away inside of her.

He reached below and grabbed a wool blanket and she took it and smoothed it over her lap.

"I don't think you realize how lovely you are." He said as he got the buggy turned and facing the roadway towards the Greaves' home.

"You are quite good at flattering a girl." She said, feeling a little overwhelmed at his level of charm.

"I don't mean to be forward. I just believe in saying what I feel." He gave her a look that she felt was sincere.

"Honesty is good." Galina offered.

"I am determined to get to know you better." He said as he pulled out onto the snow-covered road. He was going slow to be safe. "If you allow me to come sometime to visit you I may have to turn this buggy into a sleigh."

Galina thrilled at the idea of gliding through the snow with him, though a warning was ringing in her heart to take things slowly.

"Well, perhaps you will get to know me and find out that I am rather boring. Promises of sleigh rides are rather special." She said, knowing it was a little flirtatious but fun to tease him a little.

"Well, I already know from your friend Sophia that you write stories. I know that you sing like an angel. That you love the Lord and that you can cook and keep a house." He said without taking his eyes from the road.

"All of those things are true. But there are other things about me that you don't know." Galina said. It was nice to hear him say these sweet things, after the last few months of feeling like a fool.

"I want to know all about you. What about your family?" He asked. Galina was glad that his eyes were on the road. She felt her happy feeling fade, trying to think of a way to simply explain her family.

"My family cabin is just up the road a way." Galina said, trying to make her tone as cheery as it was before, but she knew that she had failed.

"Oh, should we stop in so you can say hello to them?" Milton asked her and looked at her with expectation.

She shook her head fiercely. "No, no that is..." She stammered. "No, please."

He slowed the horses to a stop and turned to give her his full attention. "Is everything alright?"

He placed a hand on her shoulder. She wished that she could have felt the warmth of it while she tried to still the panic that rose up inside of her.

This happy feeling of being flattered was soon going to come to end if he found out about her father and all the terrible things that had happened to her.

"Galina?" Milton was still watching her face and she wanted to hide. Even the sound of her name on his lips made her heartsick. It was all going to end.

"My brothers are there, and though I would love to see them..." Galina took a deep breath and then let the words fly. There was no hiding her secrets when everyone in town knew it. "I am not welcome there. My father and I... well we... I..." Galina was frustrated that she couldn't find the words to say.

"I understand complicated fathers." Milton said softly.

"You do?" Galina's voice was barely above a whisper. She was afraid that she was going to cry and ruin a perfect day.

"Yes, I do." Milton smiled at her. "No more talk of families then." He took his gloved hand and patted her cheek.

"I will tell you about it someday." Galina said and sighed deeply, feeling the tension lift.

"When you are ready, Galina." He said her name again. It felt like warm honey on her wounded heart.

She was surprised to see the kindness in his eyes before he turned back to drive the buggy. He had such a swagger that she expected it to always be there, but this side of him was nice too. Perhaps he wasn't just a flirt.

He asked her about the Greaves family, and she told him about everything she could think of that was interesting, including the cat Duchess who was the new addition. The time passed too quickly, and they approached the bridge before the Greaves' property.

"Just turn left after the bridge." Galina said, slightly disappointed that the ride was over so soon.

The horses whinnied a little after the first step on the bridge, their hooves clattering on the wood.

She watched his hand expertly handle the horses with a firm grip.

He pulled into the drive then called for the horses to stop.

"Galina, I had a pleasant drive with you. I rather wish it was springtime and I could have taken you out for longer." He smiled then told her to wait where she was.

He leapt down and circled back to come to her side. She had placed the lap blanket below the seat and then took his hand to help her down.

"Thank you for the ride and the good company." She said feeling nervous again.

"I was enchanted." He said as he boldly placed a hand on her cheek again. He had taken off his gloves . His hand was warm and slightly calloused, not at all what she expected as a shopkeeper.

She smiled at him and blushed again.

"If I may be so bold to ask if I may come to call again?" He lowered his chin again, looking vulnerable and sweet. Sophia had been right. He was interested.

"I would enjoy that. Though I will have to ask Angela and Ted. I want to respect the rules in their household." She answered, hoping he would understand.

"I completely understand, I will come by sometime and make my introductions, so they can let me know what is expected." Milton said and smiled broadly. He helped her with her things to the front door.

Galina was hopeful and happy as she waved goodbye to him a

minute later.

Inside Edith and Angela were at the kitchen counter. Galina hung her coat and placed her bag on the bottom steps of the staircase and joined them.

"Oh, you look so lovely." Angela declared. "I noticed it at Sunday service, but I was all distracted this morning and forgot to mention it."

"I know, there was many distractions this morning." She had been distracted more by the intriguing Mr. Vaughn. The good news about Violet had slipped her mind already. "I should go over and visit with her sometime this week if I can." Galina said. She felt bad that she had barely said a word to Violet. Violet had been so very kind to Galina over the last few years and she needed to be certain to hear all about Reynaldo and what Violet was feeling about everything.

"Oh, we can stop over tomorrow afternoon if there isn't too much snowing and blowing outside." Angela said. "The Grants just moved back into the house, so we can lend a helping hand while we find out the goods on the engagement." Angela smiled brightly, and Edith agreed. They spent a few minutes of chatting about what kind of food they would take along. Everything here always revolved around food. It was the normal part of daily life around here. Food, work and visiting.

Galina finally brought up Milton after they had exhausted the idea of the visit.

"I was just wanting to let you know that Mr. Vaughn drove me home today." Galina said with apprehension. She hoped that they would like him and that she would be allowed to court him. She had read in some books that maids and housekeepers in fancy homes were not allowed that sort of thing.

"Oh, that was kind of him. What kind of man is he? Clive said the other day that he had invited him to Sunday dinner." Angela asked. Galina felt both Edith and Angela's gaze and she tried not to blush too much while she told them about the dinner.

"He sounds a bit like Clive." Edith said with a smile. "He likes to tell stories and owns a business in town."

Galina nodded. "He asked if he could come to call." She admitted.

"Oh, my!" Angela's green eyes widened. "That was quick."

Angela and Edith took turns teasing her.

"I know it is quick, but I told him that I needed to ask you and

Ted first. I wasn't certain that you would be… well that you would appreciate inviting a young man to come call at your house." Galina was nervous to ask.

"Oh, I don't see any trouble with it. I could send Ted to town to invite him to supper. Ease a little of the awkwardness out. That way we can all get acquainted." Angela put an arm around Galina's shoulder. Galina wondered if she had looked worried.

"That would be very nice." Galina said letting out a nervous sigh. "I do rather like him. I have not known him long, but it is rather flattering to be noticed."

"I will have that talk with Ted about inviting him to supper. He is outside in the cold, chopping wood with Warren. He will be frozen through if he doesn't come in soon." Angela chuckled.

Duchess, the cat, was tired of being ignored and she meowed and caught their attention.

"I guess that means you are hungry." Angela reached down and gave Duchess a pet to the head.

Edith grabbed up a few pieces of leftover chicken and filled up a saucer for Duchess.

Galina went upstairs and unpacked her bags and changed from her clothes into a regular day dress. She sat down at the little corner desk and wrote a bit in her journal. She needed to get her thoughts out on paper. She stood for a little while afterwards just watching out the back window, she saw Ted and Warren carrying firewood to Earl's cabin and then stacking some for the big house. She wondered about the time she had spent with Warren and felt a little guilty about her budding feelings for Milton. They were total opposites in personality and she wondered about that. Warren was steady and dependable, and Milton was like a windstorm bustling his way about town.

She wasn't sure what she felt, but she was apprehensive about deciding anything just yet. When she was quiet and listened to God, then she would know what to do.

Chapter 15

Milton Vaughn

Milton was working the barber chair on Monday. His barber was down with some sort of flu and Milton had sent him back to the boarding house. No one wanted to be shaved by a sniffling barber.

The first few hours of the morning had been busy. He had some nice chats with a few men who needed their beards trimmed and a haircut, and two men who needed shaved. It had been a few months since Milton had done any barber work, but it came back to him without a pause.

He had a little down time over the lunch hour and walked to the little restaurant and got a roast beef sandwich from the proprietor. The husband and wife that ran the family restaurant were nice enough and he was sure to compliment them on the food and the nice service by his young daughters. They were all under twelve years old, but he lied and said they would all be beautiful young women someday. They looked a little too much like their father to be prizes in the looks department, but in the West that was certainly not going to be a problem for them.

He knew that the restaurant was a new business here. He wasn't sure how most folks in town could afford the expensive prices of the restaurant, but Milton didn't mind splurging.

He thought about Galina as he walked across the street with his sandwich wrapped in waxed paper. He had known about her family history before he had even gone this past Sunday to church and before the dinner at Clive Quackenbush's house. There wasn't much you couldn't find out about in a town this small by asking the right questions.

He knew all about the Quackenbush family and Sophia and Galina, even the Greaves and their neighbors the Grants. People loved to talk and the gossip about Galina and the troubles with her father was troubling to be certain. It made him even more intrigued by her. Everyone in town had only good things say about her. How she had taken care of her family when the yellow fever came through, and she had been doing a good job of it. Her father sounded like the worst kind of hot headed fool. He felt a small pang that he had even suggested stopping by to visit her father's cabin, especially after seeing the look of pain on her face, but he had been curious to see how she would react. He was interested in the girl. She was beautiful and sweet, but he wasn't sure if she was done healing from the incident with her father. Seeing her reaction, though a little pained, was not so agitated or emotional enough to make him take pause. She did fine, and he went ahead with his plans of courting her. If she had turned into a weeping and inconsolable mess, then perhaps he would have forgone asking to call on her. She had been flustered but not so much that he found it distasteful.

He was rather looking forward to the challenge of winning her over. Those dark eyes of hers had a little fire behind them and he was looking forward to spending more time with her. It gave him something to do over the cold winter months. There was also the social aspect. He knew that gossip about courting a local girl was good for business. It would make people curious, and curiosity brought people into his store. He had used this trick before.

Milton finished up his lunch, throwing the wax paper and crumbs into the woodstove in the back of the store. The small bell dinged a minute later, and he greeted the next customer.

He was pleasantly surprised by Ted Greaves who paid for a shave and invited him to dinner on Friday. Ted was a little younger than Milton, but Milton liked him enough. He seemed a little dull and quiet the first few minutes, but he was a little more talkative by the end of the visit.

Ted had tried to be the guardian of Galina and Milton found it amusing, but Milton had said all the right things to earn his trust.

Milton chuckled a little to himself when Ted left. People were so very malleable. They will believe anything if you say it with a nice smile and use the right words.

<hr />

Sophia Greaves

Sophia got her trunk open and was taking out her dresses to hang in the wardrobe of her bedroom back home. She had been so happy staying with Aunt Olivia and Clive and now the happy feelings were slipping away as she felt the pressure of being back home. She was not a big fan of winter here in town, being so isolated and stuck inside day after day.

Lady wandered around her bedroom, sniffing everything and investigating the room.

"You like your new room?" Sophia asked Lady in a sweet tone. At least she had Lady with her now. A happy go lucky little playmate. Lady wagged her tail and looked up to her with a puppy smile. Her little pink tongue was sticking out as she panted happily.

It was going to take some work to keep an eye on Lady while she was working, over the next week or so, but Sophia was determined to not have any puppy accidents in the house. She had a feeling that her mother would get a bee in her bonnet about it.

Amelia Greaves was waiting for Sophia at the bottom of the stairs when she was all done.

"You get your clothes hung up properly?" Amelia asked.

"Yes, mother." Sophia said and gave herself a mental warning to watch her tone.

"You certain they won't get wrinkled now?" Amelia asked with her own distrusting tone.

"Yes, I am certain." Sophia brightened her tone. *I will not lose my patience in the first five minutes.* Sophia thought to herself.

She had eaten lunch over at the Quackenbush home before Clive drove her back home. They stopped by the butcher on the way back to town and bought a few venison steaks to make into dog food for Lady.

"You can throw some peas and carrots in the bowl too." Clive had said as they made the quick trip from the butcher to her home. He had given her a list.

Sophia was going to talk with the housekeeper and see what she should do. She didn't want Lady to be a burden on anyone, so she would make the dog's food and gather up the food from the root cellar herself.

Lady followed Sophia down the stairs happily. She hesitated on the landing unsure if she should trust the next step.

"It's okay Lady." Sophia coaxed a little. Lady was happy for the prompting and shuffled herself down three more stairs to the bottom.

"Well, she is a cute little thing." Amelia said, hands on her hips.

Sophia noticed that her mother had lost a few pounds and was looking less full around her face.

"You are looking nice Mother." Sophia said, she was a firm believer that if you saw something nice about someone, then you should say it. Her mother had taught her that. She wished that her mother would remember it more often.

"Oh, thank you dear. I thought I would cut back on the sweets." Her mother smiled. When she smiled she was just as pretty as Aunt Olivia. Sophia smiled back.

"Well, it looks good on you." Sophia was warming up a little and the dread was lifting off of her.

She had spent the last days talking with Aunt Olivia, almost daily, while they made lace together. They discussed at length about the right way for Sophia to deal with her mother's moods.

It was simple really. Romans 12:18 said it all.

"If it be possible, as much as lieth in you, live peaceably with all men."

She needed to find a way to keep the peace. Though, Olivia had given her some good advice about speaking up when the right occasion arose.

"She needs to know that she is being irritable. I reminded her often enough." Olivia had said.

"Yes, but you are not her daughter." Sophia had replied.

Sophia had been praying daily about the subject for many months and she felt that she was beginning to understand what God wanted from her. She would be peaceful. On the other hand, she could stand her ground when her mother was going overboard on the dramatics and the nitpicking. If Sophia couldn't do that then she wasn't ready to be an adult.

"I am going to talk with the housekeeper and see about making Lady some food for tomorrow." Sophia said.

"You keep your on eye on her. I don't want any messes in the house now. It will breed disease." Amelia said in a softer tone.

"I was thinking of that while I was unpacking." Sophia smiled. She was trying to prove to her mother that she could be responsible.

"That is good, dear." Her mother bent down and gave Lady a little scratch on the head. Lady was pleased to have a new admirer and wiggled and pawed at Amelia's skirts. Sophia turned to walk to the kitchen; her eyes sparkled a little with mirth when she heard a giggle coming from her mother's direction.

This was going to be good for them both. Lady could be a

bright spot to clear the air a little.

The housekeeper, Beatrice, was thrilled about Lady and left the kitchen to come get a peek. She was instantly in love with Lady and gave her plenty of attention too. She was thrilled to help prepare the dog's food and Sophia gave her the paper from Clive.

"Oh, this in no problem at all. I have plenty of dried peas and canned pumpkin in the pantry. This venison is good and I can make up some gravy. When I was a girl we had a pack of dogs on my father's sheep farm. They loved having some gravy in their food bowls." Beatrice said with a happy grin. Her round face was all smiles. "If you are in the shop or working on a lace piece I can take the little gal on a walk or two to do her business as well. She can keep me company on my trips to the butcher shop." She made a few kissing noises in Lady's direction and sent the puppy into a frenzy. Lady barked once in her excitement and did a spin. They all had to laugh at her antics.

The pans were laid out for the evening and Sophia put Lady's leash on and led her to the back door. At Clive's house, every time she took the dog to go outside, she bent down and took her little paw and scratched at the door so that it made a little hiss noise. She would then open the door and let the puppy out. Sophia was hoping that Clive's book on dogs was right, and it would train the dog to scratch at the back door if she needed to go outside. Earlier in the morning Lady had stood at Clive's door and whined to be let out. Sophia was counting that as a positive sign that they were on the right track.

Sophia was sad to see the dark clouds rolling in and feel the cold wind whipping around her. Lady seemed oblivious to the cold and sniffed around at everything she could see. Sophia walked along the edge of the roadway and made sure to listen for wagons coming by as she walked. She wasn't sure if Lady would know enough to stay out of the way if a team came by fast.

As the walk continued Sophia had to work hard not to shiver. She wasn't even certain if Lady needed the walk, but she was determined to give it a few more minutes. Her mind began to wander as she got to the safety of a group of trees just past the group of main houses. Lady was sniffing around.

Sophia was wondering how Galina had done with Milton, and if they were officially courting. Sophia also had a strange feeling about poor Warren, and how he must be feeling. She wasn't certain that Warren had ever stopped caring for Galina and was just giving her some time to grow up a little more. Galina was her closest friend, but sometimes she did overreact to things. She had tried to convince Galina a hundred times to just talk to Warren about what happened. Sophia shook her head. Galina could be stubborn and drive in her heels about things. Sometimes Sophia wished that she had a little of Galina's backbone. But she wondered if her friend didn't get herself into trouble because of all that extra gumption she had about everything.

Sophia watched Lady start sniffing in a circle and knew the time was coming closer to the end of the journey for her and Lady for this round. She hoped that Cocoa was doing well this evening and not missing Lady too much. That made her think about Olivia and her good news.

Sophia was wondering when her aunt was going to come to visit with her sister. Then Sophia could talk about the coming child with her mother. It was definitely a big surprise and Olivia was still finding the change a little shocking. Sophia could tell that Olivia was happy about the news, but she had put it far outside the realm of possibilities. It was proof that God doesn't forget our dreams, even if we give up hope a little.

With the happy thought of Clive and Olivia's fortuitous news in her heart and knowing Lady was done with her business, Sophia could finally turn back and face away from the cold wind and head back home.

A wagon did drive by a few moments later, but Sophia heard it in plenty of time and cut the leash short and Lady stayed obediently by her side without pulling. Lady was a little shaken by the rattling of the wagon and the whinny of the horses as they went by, but she recovered and followed Sophia to the back door of their house soon enough.

The evening was spent getting the rest of her trunk items put away, and her bobbins and lace projects back in their proper places. The cozy parlor was her domain again. She was hoping that the walls weren't going to start closing in on her again for a while.

Amelia spent some time letting Lady get to know her. Sophia was pleased to see Lady on Amelia's lap and Amelia rubbing the soft fur contentedly.

"I see you are getting along together just fine." Sophia said brightly.

"Oh yes, we are." Amelia's eyes were gleaming a little as she

195

looked up. "She is a little angel." She turned to look at Lady. "Yes, you are." She said that last part like she was talking to a baby. Sophia laughed a little.

"Yep, we gals are all in love with a tiny little poodle." Sophia said and sat in her blue velvet chair by the hearth. Suddenly being home wasn't so bad.

They ate dinner with Beatrice, the housekeeper, promptly at six p.m. and then she headed off to her own room.

Sophia and Amelia spent the rest of the night getting back into their old routine. Sophia gave Lady a walk before bedtime and then gladly went back upstairs to get some sleep. It had been a full day, and it gave her a little hope that her home was a little more peaceful than it had been before.

Chapter 16

Amos Drays

Amos placed a new table into the front area of the store. A dark cherry sided table. He was very pleased with it. He knew it would sell quickly. He had another two just like it in the back that were ready for staining.

He kept the first one he made in storage along with the others he had made for the house he was going to start building in the spring. He had purchased a little chunk of land from a landowner just a few blocks away from main street. It had a nice view over the Willamette River and a nice stand of trees in the backyard. He could see a nice future there. The landowner had been wise and got permission to sell off little pieces of his land to shop owners in town. Eventually they all would want to live in a house that wasn't above their stores. He had suggested it to Jacob, the blacksmith, and he promptly purchased the plot right next to Amos' before the plots were gone.

Amos had ordered a kit house plan he found in a catalogue suggested by JQ down at the fancy goods store. It would be a nice four-bedroom house when all was said and done with a front and back porch.

It had been a week since his discussion about the letters and he had finally sent his letter off. Several men in town had agreed to write back East, and a fellow named Drew included instructions for the women traveling west. It had some very practical information. A good hotel to meet up at in Independence Missouri, and good advice to the women who were traveling by land. They all shared the names and addresses of the family members to share and communicate. The meeting between the men had been earlier in the week at Amos' shop. They all sat around the table tossing out ideas to add to their correspondence. The hope of having women in town was giving them all a little spring in their step.

Amos had written then re-written his letter at least five times before he was happy with it. His grandfather back in Indiana could do with it what he would. Amos wasn't certain if this plan would work at all, but it was worth a try. He sent along twenty dollars to help with traveling expenses for anyone that agreed to travel west. It was a large sum of money to send off on a gamble, but he had high hopes.

In his mind Amos wasn't sure that any women would agree to this foolhardy plan. What woman would travel for months on end just to get a husband? He had prayed so much about it, but he felt in his heart it was the right thing to do. He would just have to prepare himself as best he could and see what would happen. A few thoughts had entered his mind over the last few days, that maybe he would have to travel back East to find a wife and come back, but that seemed a pretty drastic move on his part. It would take at least a year to do that kind of thing. A year without working his business was just not something he could imagine.

He saw the young lady, Sophia Greaves at church with her mother, and tried to summon up some kind of feelings, but beyond thinking of her as pretty he just didn't see her as a potential mate. He heard through the grapevine that Violet Griffen was engaged and was glad for her and Reynaldo, although a little part of him was sad. She had been sending him a few meals and treats since they had made an agreement. Tasting her food had made his bachelor cooking seem so much more pathetic.

Would there ever be a day that he wasn't alone every night? Was there someone out there that was meant for him?

Only God knew...

<hr/>

Violet Griffen

With the aid of neighbors and some hired help from town the newly expanded Grant house was put back together. The children's room upstairs was painted. The rugs and curtains made it rather charming. There were the two rocking chairs from downstairs that were moved upstairs, and the new rockers were in the parlor.

All of the laundry was done and the back room cleared out with a lot of sorting. Since the back room was larger, a new sorting table was put in the back corner with some shelves to keep all the cleaning supplies up and away from the little hands of the growing babies. That had been Marie's suggestion.

"They may be little now, but someday they get bigger and toddle their way into trouble in the blink of an eye." Marie had stated while she was helping. They all took her advice to heart.

Violet was pleased with the pantry once it was finally put back together. All of the cans goods she had made were stacked in neat little rows. All the hard work was on display. It did make her rather proud to see it all. The small window casting morning light through it made it much easier to see into all the corners.

Debbie was taking charge of organizing the parlor. There were plenty of little hideaway baskets and boxes for the children's blankets and toys. There was now a wooden pen in the corner for Trudie and Caleb to play in safely while Debbie cleaned. It would work for quite a while, until they were old enough to climb out. They were all hoping that would be a long way off.

Lucas finished up the chinking on the south side, where the wrap-around porch was added, and the cabin was warm and cozy again. There was now a big wood storage box inside the back door by the kitchen that would be handy throughout the winter months. They could keep it full and not have to go out to the woodshed as often. It was a rather chilly business to go that way.

Lucas had been pretty wise and added a wind block wall to the outhouse and Violet was secretly thanking him again and again when she had to use the outdoor building. The cold winter wind was especially cruel at night.

Reynaldo had been by to visit her nearly every night, even though it had been a busy and chaotic week. Tonight, Corinne and Lucas were going to have dinner with Chelsea and Lucas; Debbie had promised to make herself a proper chaperone.

"I'll be at the table, writing letters and you and Reynaldo can talk about the future in the parlor." Debbie had given her a wink.

Violet was making a pork roast and garlic buttered red potatoes for dinner and was hoping that he would like it. She added thyme and rosemary herbs to the bread dough and was enjoying the scent of them baking. The aroma in the house smelled so good that Corinne and Lucas were threatening to stay behind so they could eat it.

Lucas gave her a teasing wink when she had looked a little flustered.

"You and Reynaldo will have a good chance to talk while we are gone. Though, I am glad that Debbie is here. No need to have tongues wagging." Corinne said.

"I have had enough of that." Violet said with conviction.

Corinne laughed and agreed about herself as well.

The day flew by and babies woke up from naps, and Corinne and Lucas were busy getting everyone ready to go out. The was snow falling softly outside but there was no wind to speak of.

They left around 4:30 and that gave Violet an hour to get ready herself. She changed into a Sunday dress, feeling a little silly with the voluminous skirts to finish making dinner.

The time passed painfully slow as she worked in the kitchen. She felt a little ridiculous in the fancier dress while working, but she wanted to look nice. She felt rather drab day after day when he came to visit, and she was always in her work clothes.

Debbie kept herself busy, putting away the children's clean clothes that had been hanging in the back room to dry. Violet was getting used to the new sounds in the home. The thumping sound of going up and down the stairs was new. Violet had been apprehensive about the plans to add a second story to the cabin, but she was very pleased with the results. Lucas had thought through all the options and he had made the best use of every inch of the existing cabin, with the addition. Now the family had more elbow room.

Since Corinne was expecting another child, the family could grow without everyone on top of each other.

She knew of some families in the valley that had three or more children all bunked together in a small loft room. There was a family that Pastor Whittlan's wife was telling her about where all the family was in a small two room cabin, two adults and four children.

Violet finished up her work, thinking about how thankful she was for her cozy home, the good food, and all the blessings she had in her life. There were so many that were less fortunate.

Debbie's steps could be heard on the stairs and Violet removed her apron.

All the food was laid out on the countertop. She grabbed up three plates to set the table.

Debbie gave her a smile.

"All the clothes are put up." Debbie slid her hands together. "Those vittles look mighty tasty." She said with a sing song voice.

Violet laughed a little at Debbie's excitement.

"It's nothing fancy." Violet said.

"Oh, Violet, you make nothing fancy seem pretty special."

200

Debbie and Violet got the table set just in time for the knock at the door.

———————◆◦◆———◆◦◆———————

"I was hoping to have the house done by late spring. Would an early summer wedding be good for you?" Reynaldo looked up to Violet and she nodded with a grin.

Dinner had been wonderful, they talked a lot. Debbie was funny and perky throughout the conversation. She hadn't made the situation awkward at all.

Now, Debbie was at the table in the next room, and Reynaldo and Violet were talking about their future plans. Violet had been nervous, but once they were together her nerves settled down and she just felt warm and cozy, happy to be near him.

He looked vulnerable and Violet wondered for the thousandth time why he cared for her. She wanted to remember every time that he looked at her this way. His dark eyes were focused on her face.

"A summer wedding would be just fine for me." Violet said. She could imagine it in her mind.

Reynaldo had shown her the plans for the house that he had put together with John and Lucas.

"I want to have a nice kitchen for you, and a bread oven." Reynaldo smiled broadly and pulled out a paper and showed her.

Violet looked over the drawing and saw that he had done some really good planning for the space that would be her domain. If the dimensions were correct she could bake at least two to three loafs at a time in the wide brick oven drawn on the page.

"That is very sweet of you." Violet said and looked up shyly to Reynaldo.

He laughed a little. "Sweet maybe, but I think a bit selfish. I do love your bread."

Violet laughed too. "With an oven like that I could feed everyone in the Valley." She wondered if perhaps she could make enough to do something that had been nagging in the back of her mind for a while.

"I wonder, if I made big batches, if I could sell some to the grocer?" Violet said, then gave Reynaldo a look that questioned if he perhaps had that very idea.

"You mentioned that once, you know." Reynaldo said and set

the paper down in his lap.

"I did?" Violet was trying to remember. She vaguely remembered talking about that once with him on one of their long walks over the summer.

"Yes, you did. I was listening." Reynaldo was sitting in the winged back chair looking pleased and relaxed as they talked about the future. It was such a wonderful and calm way to spend the afternoon and Violet was soaking up the good feeling she had.

"I am lucky to have you in my life." Violet said, feeling the love she had blooming inside of her growing a little each day.

"I feel the same way." Reynaldo said and reached a hand to her.

Her hand in his was such a simple pleasure. Knowing that he had been willing to be patient with her and to earn her trust was something that stuck with her in the quiet moments over the last few months. Now that they were engaged he wasn't in a hurry but was making sure that she was comfortable moving forward one plan at a time.

The look that passed between them made Violet feel safe and treasured. She suddenly couldn't wait the long months it would take until they were finally man and wife.

"The wait is going to be torturous I think." Violet finally said.

"I can agree to that." Reynaldo lifted his head and looked skyward. "The Lord will help me, or I shall be doomed." He laughed.

"Okay, before I lose my senses, what other plans do you have?" Violet felt her cheeks flush with her confession and squeezed his hand.

"Okay." Reynaldo shook his head a little, regaining his focus. He brought out the drawings again and they dove back into planning out a life.

Violet was seeing Reynaldo for the kind and thoughtful man that he was. She found him handsome but that was fleeting. The real treasure was finding someone to love that had a good heart, and Reynaldo had that. She was proud to know that she had not been charmed at first by his handsome face. She had slowly and steadily learned to know him before she had let her heart fall.

Chapter 17

Galina Varushkin

Galina had finished sweeping the floors and rugs and was tidying up the kitchen when Milton arrived early for the dinner.

He looked handsome in his tweed suit and he had roses in his hands. Galina grinned as she answered.

"You, Mr. Vaughn, are early. Dinner will be nearly an hour away." Galina said without being too upset.

He handed her the roses and took off his coat. "I got these from Corinne at the greenhouse. I was pleasantly surprised by her business. I have set an appointment to talk with her on Monday about ordering some of her oils and other medicines for the store." He gave her a big smile.

Galina gave the roses a sniff and loved the rich scent. "These are lovely."

She gestured Milton to sit down as she headed toward the kitchen to get a vase. "I do love Corinne. She saved my life, after all." Galina hustled back with the vase and got busy arranging them.

"I would love to hear that story someday." Milton said. He was watching her intently.

"We have to be quiet for a little while." Galina said and gave him a little whisper. "Angela is taking a short nap. She is in the family way, which can make a woman extra tired. She wanted to be awake and alert for dinner later." Galina gave Milton a conspiratorial grin.

"You are so very pretty today." Milton said softly.

"Aw, you are too kind." Galina said and flitted around with the flowers. "Oh, they need water."

She came back a minute later with the water pitcher and poured water into the flower vase. She set it on a side table.

"There, it looks just lovely." She turned to see the admiration in Milton's eyes. "Thank you."

"I can only visit with you for a few minutes, then I will have get busy in the kitchen, unless you want to talk to me while I work." Galina didn't want to be a bad hostess, but he had arrived an hour early. "The turkey will be done soon, but the dressing and the gravy still has to be made. I have a lot to do." Galina looked at herself, still in her work dress. "Oh, bother. I haven't even changed yet." She gave Milton a withering look. "Well, I must be making such an impression when a young man comes to call."

"You look just fine by my eyes. I can keep myself busy and I don't mind visiting while you work." Milton said with an easy tone. His eyebrows were raised and he had a ready smile that played upon his lips, like he had a little secret.

She gestured him over and set up a stool on the opposite side of the counter. She hustled around gathering up all the things she needed. "I am so glad I went to get the dairy earlier today. I would be out crawling around in the snow right about now if we were out of butter and milk." Galina was feeling silly. Her nerves were causing her to babble. He was going to think that she was magpie if she didn't take a few deep breaths and calm herself.

"Why don't you tell me how Corinne saved your life. While you get your things together." Milton suggested.

"It is a hard story to tell, but I will." Galina said and gave him a lopsided smile.

She told an abbreviated version as she got the potatoes in boiling pot. She got to the part where her mother and baby brother passed away, then she checked the turkey and put the dressing into the oven while she let the bird rest. She asked him for a little help with the turkey drippings because the bird was heavy. He knew just how to be a good helper. She told the story about her father and the beating she had received that last day she had lived there.

"I went back to the house one time, when I knew my father was working." Galina said. "I gathered up a few of my mother's things, and my little stash of books and savings and never looked back." Galina said, feeling proud for telling the story without getting too emotional.

"It is hard to believe that Lucas Grant didn't fire him on the spot." Milton said with a frown.

"Oh, we talked about it quite a bit at the time. They had several heated discussions. Lucas made some pretty serious threats, and my father got a bit out of control and punched Clive." Galina's eyes were wide as she remembered it. It was pretty horrible. She shook her head.

"That man is out of control." Milton pressed his lips together in a tight line.

"Lucas had a few talks with some other men and all of us women, and we all decided together that if my father agreed to talk to the pastor weekly about his anger then he could keep his job. But if he ever laid a hand on me or my brothers again that he would lose his job and be blackballed for any future jobs in this community," Galina said then turned back to the gravy, it would scorch if she looked away for too long.

"That would be a hard choice to make." Milton said. "I am going to have my own devil of a time not pounding down his door and making him eat his own teeth for what he did to you."

Galina wasn't sure what to feel about the protective statement. It was nice to be cared for, but she wasn't sure if getting Milton stirred up would help anything. "I am in a good place now. His new wife sends the boys over a few times a month. In the summer months they come over and play in the creek. My father dutifully goes to see the pastor every week. Guadalupe, his wife now, keeps him in line." Galina pulled the gravy off of the stove and set it on a thick pad on the countertop. "I think she is stronger willed than my mother. He probably had no idea who she was when he married her. I am not certain a man can really know a woman fully until he has lived with her." She shrugged.

Milton laughed a little and agreed.

"I better go make sure that Angela is awake and change into my dinner dress. Ted will be in any minute now." Galina said and was surprised when she saw Angela standing at her doorway.

"Oh, sorry I slept for so long." Angela said giving a little smile and nod to Galina.

"That is no concern." Milton went over to her and gave her a hand to help her through the room.

"Thanks for the help. My leg was throbbing pretty terribly this morning. I declare, I sound like an old woman." Angela laughed a little, her green eyes were bright and cheery though. Galina had been worried about her earlier.

"I heard that you had a mighty big fall a few years ago. Sometimes it takes a long while to heal." Milton said to make Angela feel better.

"It doesn't help that I was a fool and broke my ankle over the summer months." Angela gladly sat on the stool.

"I am glad you are here Milton, everyone is buzzing about you. I feel rather avant garde being one of the first to have you over to dinner." Angela laughed and teased a little. "I expect to hear all of your best stories at dinner."

Milton gave Angela a nod. "I will certainly do my best."

Ted came through the back door and Milton shook his hand when he came in.

"I will let you all chat. The food is nearly done and I am still in my work dress." Galina said. She turned and hustled up the stairs to change quickly.

It only took her five minutes before she was back down the stairs in her dark burgundy dress that was a favorite.

Milton's eyes were praise enough. She felt like she was floating on a cloud.

She put the apron on over her dress and finished the dinner prep by making the mashed potatoes.

She gave the carving knife to Ted and he did a pretty good job of carving the turkey. Galina had Milton's help to set the table and get all of the food placed.

The meal passed wonderfully. Galina was so thrilled to have everyone getting along so well. She was setting all of her worries aside and just enjoying the stories and laughter as the evening passed. Galina tidied up the table after supper and Ted and Angela took care of the dishes so that Milton and Galina could talk in the parlor.

Galina had fresh nerves when she and Milton were alone.

"I am so glad that you came here tonight." Galina said nervously.

"I am as well. I am glad to see that you are happy here." Milton was watching her intently, making her stomach tighten up and flipflop uncomfortably.

He suggested that they play a game of checkers, so he could have a chance to beat her. She laughed when he crowed over his first win. She was enjoying the surroundings, him seated across from her, looking so casual now with his tweed jacket on the chair seat behind him. He was wearing a vest with fancy brass buttons and was a handsome picture. His chin was set determinedly while he focused on his moves. He kept giving her flirtatious looks as they played. It was so much fun to be playful and flirt back a little. Once, she was biting her lip in contemplation over a move and she caught him staring at her mouth. He had wanted to be caught and the little dare he made with his eyes made her stomach jump. Knowing that she had caught him staring created a delicious butterfly fluttering again.

She did try to put more focus into the second game, but she lost again. She was glad to see that he was a good winner. She laughed as he tried to compliment her on her strategies, but she knew that she was rather hopeless. His flirting was more than a little distracting.

Ted and Angela joined in on the fun and the games were swapped around. There was a lot of laughter as the competition grew. When big moves were made then people would laugh or call out in victory. The evening passed in a light-hearted fashion and Galina felt a calm peaceful feeling as she passed through the night. Somehow in her mind the whole business with Warren had made her feel like she was unlovable again. The way her father made her feel when she lived with him. Seeing everyone smiling and having good time was good medicine for her. Whether or not she was intending to court Milton any further, having a carefree evening was good for her.

Galina sat with Angela for a few minutes together by the fireplace watching Ted and Milton play a round.

"He seems to be very attentive." Angela said softly leaning in close to Galina.

"He makes me nervous, but he is very understanding, and he listens. He is easy to talk to." Galina said. She was feeling a little more vulnerable, hoping that Angela liked Milton. It really mattered to her that others could see if Milton was the kind of man that she should continue to see.

"A good listener is a good thing." Angela said and patted Galina on the hand. "You both have plenty of time to get to know each other. It is always a good thing to take the proper time to court."

Galina knew that to be true. She had been watching the relationships around her for a long while. Knowing that her example growing up and the example of her parents' marriage was not what she wanted. She didn't just want a husband someday, but a partner. Someone to go through life with and not just someone you live with. She had lived with Corinne and Lucas for a time, and had seen their marriage, then Angela and Ted. Galina wanted to find a man who would cherish her. She was beginning to hope that Milton was that man for her.

The darkness closed in on the valley and the evening drew to an end. Milton was getting ready to go outside and get his buggy when he asked Galina to come talk with him on the porch. Galina slipped into her coat and followed him outside.

Milton took her to the far side of the porch where the light of the windows was the dimmest.

"I just wanted to tell you that I was so very impressed by you tonight." His smile was gone, and he was serious and looking at her intensely.

"Why, thank you. I had such a lovely time with you. I think you really impressed Angela and Ted." Galina said, she was starting to feel more comfortable talking with him.

"I am only concerned with your opinion of me Galina. I came here tonight for you." He removed his gloves and placed his fingertips on her chin. The effect was rather chill-inducing and Galina felt a shiver run up her spine. "Angela and Ted are nice people. But I believe, the more I know you, that *you* are an extraordinary woman."

Galina was speechless. He ran a thumb along the edge of her cheekbone.

"Every time I look into those dark mysterious eyes of yours I feel like I am drowning." He said softly. His face drew closer to her and she felt that magnetic pull to him. He was mesmerizing.

"You are so…" Galina started but he hushed her with his finger on her lips. She forgot every word she was going to say.

"I think I am falling for you, Galina. I think I am rather lost." He whispered then tortured her senses when he ran his thumb along her cheek again.

Galina was wondering if she had forgotten to breath, his eyes were so intense. She felt herself getting lost in his eyes.

Then he kissed her. It was a long minute and his arms were around her, pulling her close to him. He pulled away from her, letting her catch her breath. His face just an inch away from hers.

"My Galina…" He said breathlessly. Then he kissed her again.

The lights were low in the house when Galina finally went inside. Her cheeks were crimson, and her mind was floating on a cloud.

———◆·◉·◆———◆·◉·◆———

Corinne Grant

209

Corinne had finished watering the plants in the greenhouse and was walking through checking over the seedlings and plants. She snipped off the edges of brown leaves, and clipped off flowers that were withered, collecting their seeds for more plants.

There was an entire row of fruits trees that were growing well in the back, and would continue growing nicely; pear, apple, and peach. She would be able to sell them in the next year to eager farmers. They would benefit everyone in the valley eventually flooding the valley with fruit. She was always happy to get new arrivals of seeds from back East and the varieties were always good to have. She had a section of squash and melons growing in another area. She knew Edith Sparks and a few others would be thrilled to have more variety in their gardens next year.

It always gave her a good feeling when she had quiet time in her greenhouse. She kept an eye on her pendant watch closely. She had only a few minutes before Milton Vaughn arrived for his appointment.

Corinne decided to sit on the bench by the door for a moment, a wave of illness coming over her again. It had been happening for the last week. Just a wave of nausea and dizziness. If her suspicions were correct then she was expecting a child again. She had that nervous jittery feeling going through her, remembering the doubts from before. She hadn't even whispered her suspicions to anyone else, but she knew that soon people would notice. Women seemed to have the ability to notice any subtle change in a woman and they just knew.

Corinne thought of the challenges that lay ahead, with Violet getting married, and having Trudie and Caleb still so young. Corinne had long been wondering if she should hire on another person to help in the greenhouse. Perhaps she should contact some people back East. She knew of some qualified individuals who would perhaps jump at the chance to manage her greenhouse. It would be a long journey, but it could be a great stepping stone for a young botanist to have a few years of management. Corinne let her mind go through scenarios. It was hard to run a household and run a business. She felt that with her family growing, and with this new realization of a child on the way it was the encouragement she needed to get help. She wasn't as afraid of that as she had been in the past. She was growing up, she thought. She was learning to let others show their strengths as well.

Corinne knew that in a few months their book of herbal and plant remedies would begin the process of publishing, and then she didn't know what to expect. The crops were constantly expanding as Lucas cleared more land. There was also a discussion about expanding the lab and getting more equipment. Her business was growing. Clive had told her recently when she had chatted with him that every business, if it is successful, has 'growing pains.' There is always that precipice that demands a business owner to decide; move forward or to stay put. There is always risk of doing too much too soon, but the wise person listens to God and has the patience to know when the timing is God's and not just a matter of 'wanting it to be so.'

Corinne had a few minutes to pray, asking God for His wisdom for her life, her family and her business.

She checked her watch after her quiet time and got up to find her coat. Milton would be arriving any minute, so she would brave the cold after the warmth of the greenhouse.

The sky was bright overhead, but a few dark clouds lingered over the mountains to the east. Corinne adjusted her scarf to protect her neck and chin from the cold wind. She walked up the path to the laboratory and was pleased to see Milton Vaughn's buggy pull in.

Corinne gave a wave and watched him get out with a spring in his step. He tied the horses to the nearby fence post.

"Good morning to you Mrs. Grant." He said pleasantly.

"Good morning, Mr. Vaughn." Corinne smiled pleasantly. Word around the Valley was that he was courting Galina, and he had confirmed it a few days ago when he had purchased some red roses from the greenhouse. "Let's get inside, the wind has a bite to it." She said and nodded her head in the direction of the lab.

Dolly was inside affixing labels to bottles for shipping. She smiled up from her work.

Corinne hung her coat up on the coat rack and welcomed Milton to do the same. She noticed his fine dark suit and thought that he was a snappy dresser. He seemed to be a fashion plate and Corinne smiled a little to herself. Every business owner she knew had a suit in his wardrobe, but none that she had seen were cut as fine as this. Corinne wondered if Milton Vaughn was going to create a need for all the grown men to start dressing in finer threads. It happened with women. Corinne had noticed that as soon as one lady was wearing a new style of dress, or finer lace collar, all the women would start caring a bit more about whether that old dress was good enough.

"Welcome to my lab. This is Dolly Bouchard. This is Milton Vaughn." Corinne gave introductions.

Dolly shook his hand politely.

"Dolly is the one who runs my labs so efficiently. I have a few other employees during the harvest months but mostly through the winter months it is her and I handling the orders and keeping the greenhouse producing." Corinne said.

"It is a pleasure to meet you." Dolly said slowly. She was still shy around strangers, but she was always professional when they had a new client.

"I am hoping to purchase a few bottles of oil and some of the salves and medicines you have made. The apothecary was raving about your deft hands with herbs and plants." Milton said smoothly. He took great care to give them both eye contact respectfully.

Corinne gave him a tour of the building and he had some questions about how the oil production worked. Both Dolly and Corinne took a chance to explain the process. He nodded appreciatively, and Corinne was glad to lead him forward to the shelves in the storage area to show him the products that she had available.

Corinne went through the products that she had made that might be a good fit for his store.

"I have a liniment for sore muscles and back pain." Corinne pointed to a section of bottles.

"What are the ingredients?" Milton asked.

"It has alcohol, olive oil, peppermint oil, and is also infused with ground rosemary and pepper." Corinne said. "It has a scent, but it does work well."

He perused a few other items and his order list was coming together.

"The camphor lip balm, and the burn cream with lavender." Milton was tapping his lip in thought as they went through the items on the shelves.

"I heard from the apothecary that you had jasmine oil that you produced. I was looking forward to creating a product. I was able to make a sample toilet water from the small amount I was able to buy from the apothecary." Milton smiled at Corinne with an enthusiastic look.

212

"I am sorry, but we have no spare Jasmine oil at this time. All of our bottles have already been purchased." Corinne said. Corinne turned to ask Dolly a question.

"So, you have a few still on the premises?" Milton asked and placed his palms together hopefully.

"It will be mid-summer before we have more available for sale. We only have a small crop." Corinne had the story on the tip of her tongue of how she had collected the first Jasmine pods on the Oregon trail. She saw the look of frustration on Milton's face.

"I really wanted that, that was a big reason why I am here today." Milton said with a tense edge to his voice. Corinne understood his need but there wasn't anything that she could do.

"Yes, the few bottles we have are all for an order that was received more than a week ago. I was just waiting for the packing crate. With the busy week we had I hadn't gotten Lucas to make the shipping crate until this morning. I am sorry." Dolly spoke slowly and precisely but Corinne could tell that she was a little nervous because her hands were fidgeting.

"I would think that a local business would take precedence in a case like this." Milton said. Corinne did not like the tense set of his jaw. Perhaps in his world he could try to get his way with pressure, however, she felt that inner gut check and dug in her heels.

"I am sorry, but that is not the way I run my business." Corinne stated firmly. She could feel heat rising in her cheeks. She did not appreciate Milton's body language.

"Well, I just don't understand why you cannot make an exception, since I am here attempting to pay good money for your products." Milton said as his voice began rising, making Corinne even more uncomfortable.

She heard a knock at the door and was hoping beyond all hope that Lucas was stopping by to visit the lab for some reason or another.

"Come in!" Corinne yelled out. Feeling strange and anxious after the tense scene with Milton.

Sean Fahey peeked his head in and Corinne gestured him to come in.

Corinne was glad for another male to be in the building. Sean ran his hand through his hair to shake out the flakes of snow that had gathered there.

He smiled sheepishly. "I should have worn a hat."

Corinne smiled tensely. "We are finishing up with a client order, come on back." She gestured for Sean to follow.

"I am sorry for inconveniencing you, but I cannot fulfill your request at this time." Dolly was telling Milton firmly. Corinne was proud of Dolly for standing her ground.

It was hard to stand firm with someone when they were putting high pressure on a situation. It was making Corinne's stomach churn uncomfortably. She suddenly wished to end this visit by Mr. Vaughn.

"Well, I guess I have no choice. But I consider this rather rude when a customer is standing here, and the product is here. I don't think I am out of line to demand to have this batch. The other client will certainly have to wait since it is being put in the post." Milton said stiffly. He had puffed out his chest.

"Are you still wanting the other items you ordered, or should we just put those back on the shelf?" Corinne asked. She felt strange and awkward with Sean in the room but in a way, she was glad for a witness.

Milton turned and saw that Sean Fahey was standing at the doorway.

"Oh, another customer." He huffed. "Don't bother asking for what is on the shelves. Not everything is available." He smiled sarcastically. He pressed his lips together then rolled his eyes. "Yes, I will just take the items I ordered." He started pulling money out of his billfold. Dolly totaled up his order and he handed over the money. She put his bottles and jars into a crate and he bent down quickly and scooped it up.

"Ladies… sir." Milton nodded stiffly and made a hasty exit.

Corinne let out a puff of air, trying to let the anxiety go out of her shoulders and stomach.

"That seemed a bit tense." Sean said and grimaced.

Dolly laughed a little nervously. "Yes, that was unexpected." She gave Corinne a wide-eyed look.

"I just had supper with him last night, with Angela and Ted." Sean said and frowned.

"Yes, Milton Vaughn, he owns the new barber shop." Corinne frowned.

"He is courting Galina." Dolly said and frowned as well.

There was a moment of silence. "Some people are just high pressure when it comes to business dealings." Corinne said after a minute.

"I guess I can see that, but I would not want my sister dating someone who could be that rude. If I was being honest." Sean stated. "He was very polite last night, but perhaps he was on his best behavior."

"Perhaps it was just a bad day for him." Dolly said. Her eyebrows were furrowed. "I think I am… what is the word." She paused. "Making…" Her face brightened. "Making excuses."

Corinne and Sean nodded in agreement.

"I hate this feeling. Now I am questioning him as a viable partner for Galina. That is a shame." Corinne sighed. She would hate to say something to Galina about Milton's behavior today if it was just a onetime issue. He may have had a good reason for being frustrated.

"I will probably just mark it down as a bad day." Corinne shrugged.

"I could use a distraction." Dolly said, and everyone agreed. "Would you like to take a look around the greenhouse with me, Sean?" She smiled, and her countenance lightened. Corinne was glad to see that tense situation hadn't affected Dolly for long. Probably a nice chat with Sean would be good for her. Suddenly Corinne wanted to go back home and see her babies. A bright and happy thought after a tense situation.

Corinne watched Sean and Dolly leave and followed them to the door of the greenhouse. She invited Sean and Dolly over to lunch at the house and then went over to help Violet with lunch preparation.

Trudie and Caleb were playing in the wooden pen in the parlor and Debbie was folding the laundry that had been hanging in the back room. Corinne got right inside the pen with Trudie and Caleb and they both crawled in her lap for attention. It was like being smothered with love and Corinne soaked it in. She gave kisses and hugs and made faces and felt the tension leave her fully for a few minutes.

The children got distracted and she climbed back out after a few minutes.

"I invited Dolly and Sean to lunch, so I will help Violet get things ready, since I gave her some extra work." Corinne shared. Debbie gave her a smile as she patted the finished laundry pile.

"Well are finally caught up on the laundry with that last little bit." Debbie said triumphantly. Corinne took the small pile of some of her own clothing and went to put it away as Debbie went to put the nappies and children's clothes away in the new dresser upstairs.

Corinne was growing accustomed to the new changes in the cabin. Having a second story was a bit odd at first. But now with more room and a larger parlor the place felt more spacious. There were more windows and the light was brighter. It felt less like a frontier cabin and homier somehow. She was looking forward to the spring and summer months and finally having a porch to sit on in the evening hours. She had a suspicion that it was going to be a favorite place for the family to be once the weather warmed.

Corinne joined with Violet and they worked together.

"I had a strange happening at the lab today." Corinne told her about the situation with Milton Vaughn.

Violet frowned. "That doesn't sound very polite." She was slicing bread and paused. She tapped a foot on the floor. "I am tempted to give him a piece of my mind. But I know that wouldn't help the situation."

"There is a part of me that accepts that sometimes people do business differently than I do. He was frustrated. Perhaps that is just the way some men are. They overreact, then they get over it. I can imagine that sometimes Lucas, or my father have to get heated with their employees or even with a seller who made a deal and then it doesn't go the way he expected. We all have situations we regret, after the heat of the moment is passed." Corinne wondered.

Violet nodded. "I do recall something like that happening at the mill when I grew up there. My father would say that a person would want a cheaper price and get mad when my father wouldn't give the rock bottom price for them."

Corinne wondered if remembering her father would cause Violet to have bad memories.

"I will talk with Lucas." Corinne said. She was struggling with the idea of Galina courting someone with a temper. He had not acted violently in any way, but the tension felt like it could have led to that. It bothered her to know that her dear friend could be getting attached to man who might be rude or have expectations of perfection all the time. It was on her mind through the rest of the day.

Dolly and Sean came by after a few more minutes and Corinne and Violet served bacon sandwiches and soup that Violet warmed up.

Sean and Dolly were sweet and the smiles and looks between

them were the beginning of something special.

Debbie, Corinne, and Violet chatted about the new budding relationship excitedly and came to the conclusion that Dolly and Sean were a good match so far. Sean was opening up more now that he was making better acquaintance with everyone, and Corinne wanted to encourage the friendship between Lucas and Sean. She would have a few things to discuss with her husband this evening and looked forward to it. It was her favorite part of the day, the evening time they spent together with sleepy children in their laps and talking. Every time she had any doubts about anything her husband was the calming place for her to land.

Chapter 18

Galina Varushkin

Monday morning began with the bright sun in the windows. Galina sat in the chair by the second story window in her room and saw the mist hanging over the snow. The snow was dripping off the roof. It looked like the weather was warming up. Her heart was light as she pulled up her stockings. Perhaps she could get out of the house today.

She was in a pleasant mood after she had another evening with Milton. He had been invited to Sunday dinner and he was as charming as ever the night before. This last week since the first dinner had been a wonderful time for her. She was feeling so special and cherished.

He had brought her two new books of poetry and she had gone to sleep dreaming happily of the kisses and his sweet words that he had told her on the porch the night before.

"I believe I am in love with you." He had told her after he kissed her silly. Her heart had been tumbling down that same path herself and she had shyly told him that she was falling for him as well.

Galina carried her shoes down the stairs with her and she skipped rather happily down the staircase with a ka-thump, ka-thump. It matched her happy heartbeat, thinking of the way Milton had looked at her.

Sean and Dolly had come to dinner as well and Galina wondered at the quiet and reserved way that Dolly was with Sean. Galina was certain that she could never have been that shy around Milton, or even Warren for that matter. She wondered if Dolly and Sean would have to court for a year before finally being able to open up to each other.

Milton had been by the house every few days, even just to bring her a present, and they had taken a ride around the land on horseback together on Saturday afternoon. She felt that she and Milton were a perfect match and she knew him so well already.

Galina was excited to be a part of Ted and Angela's new tradition based on Ted's family practice of giving gifts on the

Christmas holiday and Galina was eager to spend a little of her money in town to buy small gifts. Angela was almost finished knitting the stockings to hang on the chimney, and Ted was thrilled when he received the holiday poems book he had ordered with a favorite childhood poem by Clement Moore, The Night before Christmas.

Ted was now reading a Christmas Carol aloud each night before they retired, It was putting them in a mood to create some new traditions. Galina enjoyed the discussions Ted and Angela had about how they wanted to create lovely family memories with their new child that was coming in a few months.

Everyone was all abuzz about the Christmas Ball to be held in the church in town and Galina was going to see if she could borrow one of Sophia's fancy dresses.

Galina was warming up the stove when she heard Warren at the back door and felt the familiar pang of uncomfortable guilt she always had when she saw him now. He had seen her this last Sunday at church when Milton had been helping her into his buggy and he had stolen a quick kiss from her when he thought no one was looking. She had looked up as soon as she was settled in the buggy and saw Warren looking at her with some confusion. She was certain that everyone knew that she and Milton were courting. She was surprised by the look of hurt and confusion. Certainly, after all of these weeks he couldn't still think of her as an unattached woman.

Galina tried to smile pleasantly as she took the two buckets of milk from Warren. His face was neutral.

"The weather seems a bit warmer today." Galina said, trying to make the moment seem less awkward.

Warren met her eyes and held for a long moment.

"We don't have to do this, Galina." He said quietly. "You don't need to try to make light of things. You don't have to pretend."

Galina was filled with dread when she saw the hurt look on Warren's features. She didn't know what to say.

"I wish you all happiness. I won't interfere in any way." He said and gave her the slightest smile and it tugged at her heart a little. He was trying so very hard to do the right thing.

"Thank you, Warren." Galina finally said. She wondered if they ever would have that easy friendship that they had before, but a part of her wondered if that was the way it should be.

She was in love with Milton now, she had to let the silly

infatuation with the farm boy go for good. Warren had his own future, and she had to move on to live her own life.

After seeing Warren, she was a little less enthusiastic and had to work through her morning chores. She was slightly annoyed that Warren had to make a scene. Well, it wasn't a scene really, but it made her feel uncomfortable. He could have just let it go. Instead he had to make her feel bad with those kind eyes of his. Galina rolled her eyes several times while she was rolling her biscuits.

Angela was up while Galina was finishing up with bacon and eggs.

She looked bright and perky and Galina was glad to see it.

"Looks like the snow is melting." Angela said cheerfully. She was running a brush through her long red hair. Galina could tell that Angela's figure was filling out a bit more with her pregnancy, but she was really quite pretty with the glow in her cheeks again. Galina absently wondered what pregnancy would feel like. Someday she might also have that glow in her cheeks as well.

"There does seem to be a break in the weather." Galina put the bacon on the plate and then poured the bacon fat in the jar she would use for later.

"I was thinking, if you wanted to go to town today. Edith is coming by in a little while to do some baking with me. You could go and visit with Sophia and run those errands you were mentioning this weekend." Angela grinned and then grabbed a few plates from the cupboard.

"You are moving well today." Galina said and watched Angela walking with little to no limp.

"I feel like I am getting stronger, day by day." Angela said. "I have to be patient with myself and know when to pay attention to my leg and if it starts hurting then I have to sit down for a spell." She shrugged. "It is a tough thing sometimes, being a grown up." Angela laughed a little. Her laugh brightened the room and Galina couldn't help but feel lighter. A day to ride to town, she knew just what she was going to do.

Angela set the table and rang the bell for Ted to come in for breakfast. He was at the back door a minute later.

"The weather is fine today, but the cow pasture is knee deep in mud." He laughed as he came in. His dark pants were muddy up to the knees, indeed. "I think we need to dig a trench for the water to go somewhere else." He walked holding up his pant legs, so

220

they wouldn't make a mess on the floor. Angela was laughing, and Galina was trying not to snicker herself. He looked rather ridiculous waddling.

After breakfast Galina and Angela made quick work of the cleanup and Galina headed up to her room to get ready to go to town. She was so happy to get outside again, even for a day. When the weather breaks you have to make the most of it.

Within the hour she was bouncing down the muddy roads to town in the one-horse buggy. Warren had prepared it for her, but he was on the far side of the barn when she arrived. She was happier for it.

She had a free day to go about her happy errands, and she just didn't have any desire to feel sad over the lost friendship with Warren. She had just too many happy dreams to focus on the past.

She parked the buggy at the livery. Her day of fun was beginning.

◆•◎•◆━◆•◎•◆

Galina stopped at the fancy goods store and Millie Quackenbush was at the counter and helped Galina find a few gifts. She found a lot of special items and was pleasantly surprised with her little treasures. She thanked Mrs. Quackenbush and then made her way down the street to Milton's barber shop, hoping to see him for a few minutes. She would peek in and make sure that he wasn't busy with customers.

The sign above the door said Vaughn's Barbershop and Sundries. In the window there were advertisements for toiletry goods. There was a small table in the window with different fancy bottles of perfume sprays and shave creams. Galina was proud that his window display was so well thought out. She was excited to go inside and explore.

She peeked in the window and saw a few people inside and the barber was giving someone a shave. She didn't see Milton, but she went inside anyway. She could explore the shop at least if he wasn't currently in.

The scent of shaving soap was pleasant as she heard the bell tinkling over the door. To the right was the barber chair and the man with a hot towel wrapped around his head comically.

Galina got the full picture of the room. The shop had an expensive cream wallpaper that she knew had to have been imported from back East. Wallpaper was a luxury in these parts. Angela and Ted had to place an order from Philadelphia and wait six months for their order to come in for the wallpaper in the parlor and dining room. Everyone who came to visit commented on how nice it was to see, since it was so rare.

Galina walked to the left where all the toiletries were available on shelves. She found a few more gift options and was carrying around a few things and reading bottles as she was surprised by a whisper in her ear.

"You look rather ravishing, Miss Varushkin."

Galina felt the back of her neck tickle from Milton's breath on her skin as he whispered. She turned and gave him a sly smile.

"I hope you don't mind. I had to take advantage of the pleasant weather. I am shopping for Christmas gifts today." She bit her lip, hoping he wouldn't be displeased that she had come.

"Oh, I am happy to see you my dear." He said. His facial features and low voice said more than his words. He seemed very pleased that she had come to see his shop.

Galina felt that thrill to hear him call her 'dear.' He looked so handsome in his brown tweed. His hair was slicked with a shiny glossy substance and he looked like he belonged in an advertisement.

"I think your barber shop is smashing. Everything is so well placed. I was drawn right in." Galina gushed praise and he preened a little.

"Thank you. I am pleased that people are taking notice in town. Today, with the warmer weather the morning has been busy." He smiled. "Our barber has appointments all day and my sales for sundries is doing very well. Better than I expected actually." He smiled and showed her a few things on the shelves that were popular.

"Oh… Ted has one of these." She picked up the tooth cleaning brush box. "He likes it very much. He was trying to convince us that we all need one." Galina smiled.

"Oh yes, I think it will eventually replace the chew stick. I was working with a fellow in Atlanta on this design." Milton seemed proud. "You should try it with the toothpaste." He picked up a jar and then opened the box, so she could smell the scent.

"It has a hint of cinnamon." She smiled and was delighted. Her arms were filling up with items and she began to wonder if she could afford it all. "I should put a few of these items back. I definitely want to try this out, since you suggested it." She said with concern. She was looking through her items that she had collected.

"Don't you dare. You keep everything in your arms." He winked at her.

She shook her head and rolled her eyes at him. "You cannot give away the store, Mr. Vaughn."

"I can make an exception for the most beautiful girl in town." He whispered close to her ear. She felt the gooseflesh rise against on the back of her neck. She felt a bit flustered and knew that her cheeks were heating up.

"Oh, you make the prettiest picture when you blush that way." He laughed a little.

He continued to show her pretty things and kept adding items to her arms. She was soon going to have trouble holding all of it.

He then led her to the front desk and got her a little linen sack to carry it all.

"You are a bit of a fool Mr. Vaughn." Galina teased.

"A fool in love." He smiled his charming smile and she had nothing more to say about his generosity. He was certainly winning her over.

"Are you heading back home, or do you have more shopping to do in town?" He asked as he glanced around the store at the few customers who had come in and were milling around.

"I was going to head over to see Sophia for a visit before I ride home." Galina said. She was so very happy to see him in his environment and felt lucky that he had chosen her, even over the pretty and bubbly Sophia.

"Why don't you give me a few minutes to help these customers and I will walk you over." He placed his hand over hers for a moment and squeezed it affectionately. He wasn't shy about showing his affection for her in public and she felt rather proud to watch him talk to the customers for a few minutes. Galina saw that a few men were sitting on the bench near the barber, waiting for their turn in the barber's chair.

Milton was smiling and charming to the customers and was answering questions about products. Galina had seen Clive and JQ in the fancy goods store helping customers and saw the similarities between the interactions with people. It takes a special kind of person to be able to be able to run a shop. Galina didn't think that it was something she could do well. She would get tongue tied or take it personally if a customer didn't take her suggestion.

Galina watched and waited until his last customer had paid and was leaving the store. He helped her on with her coat and they went outside.

They walked along the boardwalk. The street was bustling with wagons going by and people taking advantage of the warm snap of weather. Milton grabbed her arm beside him and tucked it securely in the crook of his arm.

"It is so nice to be out today with my girl." Milton said as they walked slowly toward Sophia's house. He kept looking over at Galina and then suddenly he stopped her and pressed her against the side of a building and kissed her quickly, causing her to giggle.

Galina turned back facing forward and saw the shocked gaze of Millie Quackenbush who was placing something in the window display. Galina blushed furiously, Milton was laughing, and Galina was trying to walk faster away from the fancy good's store window. The more she blushed the more Milton laughed.

Galina sighed as they got around the corner.

"You crazy man! You just kissed me in front of the biggest gossip in town." Galina was wide eyed and panicked.

"Oh, don't worry so much my dear girl." He kissed her on the cheek again and Galina was giggling and laughing at his antics and she tried to run away. Milton was more than happy to chase her all the way to the doorstep of Sophia Greaves.

Galina said her goodbyes to Milton and went inside, feeling a bit silly from her chase with Milton, she went through the front room, the Lace Shop, and gave a knock to the glass fronted door next to the parlor.

Sophia greeted her.

"You will not believe what happened today!" Galina said with enthusiasm. She gave Sophia a look that spoke volumes.

"Mother, I am going to take Lady for a walk and talk with Galina." Sophia gave her mother a warning and then scooped up Lady and the leash.

They went for a long walk, and Galina filled her in on all of the details.

◆◆◆ ◆◆◆

Galina headed home after her visit with Sophia, she had a

dress folded tidily in a bag that she was borrowing for the
Christmas Ball and her bag of items that Milton had given her.
She retrieved the horse from the livery and begged a little help to
attach her items to the back of the saddle. She would have to hang
the dress promptly when she arrived back to the Greaves house.
She did not want to the dress to get wrinkled.

She had an inkling of dread that worked through her as she
rode home, wondering if Millie Quackenbush was going to spread
rumors about Milton and her behavior in the street.

It was just a kiss. Galina thought with a little anger, it wasn't like
they had been indecent. But she knew that it was frowned upon
and admitted to herself that she would find it rather shocking to
see that if it had been someone else.

The wind was picking up and Galina could tell that the
warmer weather was about to change. The scent of snow was in
the air and the wind bit at her cheeks. Galina gave her horse the
proper encouragement to pick up the pace. It was time to get
home.

Chapter 19

Sean Fahey

The last few weeks had been a pleasant passing of the time as Sean was learning how to handle a courtship. It was a strange and wonderful new ritual to plan out how he would see her next. He found himself visiting at least once a week to Dolly at the lab. Usually they would have a nice chat while they walked the greenhouse. There were a few trees in the back of the greenhouse that he had put on hold after he had been given ideas from Dolly about what to plant on his property. He was daydreaming a bit that perhaps she was starting to imagine herself someday being a part of that land. He felt a little silly when his mind wandered to those kinds of thoughts, but he seemed helpless to stop himself. Those pleasant thoughts would sometimes battle in his mind with his doubts, but some days the hope lingered, and he enjoyed it.

Chelsea and Russell Grant were also quite helpful in Sean's courtship with Dolly, inviting him to supper a few times over the last weeks. Little by little they were both overcoming their tongue-tied state and finally he felt that she was comfortable sharing her life story with him.

Dolly was such a fascinating woman and he was understanding more as time passed. He had no desire to rush anything with her but was pleased to take his time getting to know her. Clive had given him some good advice early on. To take courtship at a slow and steady pace.

With the change in the weather, the rain and mud had made Dolly adjust to make her travel to work a little easier. She was now staying with Angela and Ted and he was looking forward to the late lunch he was invited to at his sister's home. Sean was still wearing his Sunday suit when he rode back home to take care of Cupid.

Cupid was waiting for him and made a howling welcome, he headed up the steps. He took Cupid out on a leash and was careful to stay away from the muddiest areas of his front yard. There was little snow left after the thaw and the ground was spongy in most places and thick with mud where the water had pooled.

Sean had made arrangements with Mack, his neighbor, to take Cupid for the afternoon and evening, since he wasn't certain how long he would be visiting. He wanted to focus on visiting, and not keeping Cupid from chasing around his sister's cat, Duchess. They had a rather tempestuous relationship, the dog and cat. Sean was still remembering a moment or two from previous visits, though mostly it had gone well. Sometimes Cupid got a little more enthusiastic about their friendship than Duchess was comfortable with. There were a few standoffs between them that had been entertaining.

Sean rode over to Mack's with Cupid and Mack gave him a good-natured ribbing about his dinner with Dolly. Sean took it in stride.

"We'll be doing some more training this afternoon with the dogs. I am hoping they will both be ready for some hunting practice come spring." Mack said as he gave Cupid a good scratch behind the ears.

"That sounds like a worthwhile plan." Sean said. He was anxious to get back, but he appreciated the friendship with his neighbor and wanted to make sure he cultivated that as well as his relationship with others.

He was finally off a few minutes later, riding towards his sister's home. He was happy that he had managed to avoid a mess to his new gray suit pants. This warm snap was nice, but the mud was quite the nuisance.

He had crossed the wooden bridge and was turning into the property when he heard the sound of a horse and buggy over the bridge behind him. He saw that young man, Milton Vaughn, behind him and felt an annoyance rise in his chest. It only took a moment for him to realize that this other man was probably coming to dinner again.

Sean was still remembering his rudeness from the lab that had happened several weeks past. It had not made a very good impression. Sean reminded himself to be civil, but he was not amused to share the day with him. He would make an effort to give him a wide berth as much as he could throughout the visit.

Sean got his horse settled in the barn and saw Milton on his heels, handing the reins over to Warren.

Sean could sense the man right behind him as he walked up the porch steps.

"Are you here to see Galina?" The voice behind him asked.

Sean turned. Milton was there, his eyes a bit hard and tense.

"I am here to visit my sister Angela, and my brother Ted." Sean kept Dolly out of the conversation for now. The reminder to be civil was still playing in his gut.

The light dawned in Milton's eyes.

"Oh, yes. I remember now." Milton smiled tensely, the emotion not reaching his eyes.

"Yes, well, whomever I am here to see I hope to see you in better spirits than the last time we had the opportunity to meet." Sean said.

Milton nodded and had the decency to look chagrined. "Yes, well, that was an unfortunate business misunderstanding."

Sean frowned. "Unfortunate indeed." Sean was making eye contact with Milton and a few moments of tense male bravado passed between them.

Galina was at the door a moment later and her genuine smile for them was good to see. Inside Sean had that gut check. He wasn't sure that he liked that the young and impressionable Galina had anything to do with Milton, especially after the way he had seen him treat Corinne and Dolly at the lab. He suddenly had a protective feeling for his sister's friend and was determined to keep an eye on Milton Vaughn.

Dolly was inside, and he gave her a smile but made his way to see his sister first. She was looking healthy and blooming with pink cheeks and a sparkle in her eye as she talked with Ted.

"You are looking well, sis." He gave her a kiss on the cheek.

She smiled, and gave him a comedic once over look. "I wanted to tease you on your appearance, but you look nice yourself."

"Well, I wanted to dress to impress today." Sean smiled broadly for effect. Both Ted and Angela laughed.

"You go practice your charms on Dolly." Angela gave him a push and he willingly obeyed.

He did just what his sister had so wisely suggested and spent some quality time talking with Dolly while Ted and Angela took charge of setting the table and setting the food out for dinner.

The time he spent with her was growing more precious with every time they talked.

Today was no exception and he enjoyed hearing about her day. He had found her mysterious before and had wanted to know more about her. As he was getting to know her more, he felt that stirring within himself wondering if perhaps someday they could have a life together. A part of him believed that it could happen. The feelings were certainly growing for him. He could admit to himself that the more he cared for her the more he felt that inner voice telling him that he was perhaps not good enough for her. He worked hard to push the negative thoughts away. Even now, as he looked at her and listened to her speak he could feel that negative voice telling him that he was not ready to commit or shouldn't be.

"You seem quiet today, Sean." Dolly placed a hand to his shoulder. She smiled pertly, "That is usually what I do." Her smile stayed, and her eyes teased him a little.

"Oh, I was just a bit distracted by those eyes of yours." Sean said. He was feeling like a fool for entertaining those negative thoughts while he had this precious time to spend with this wonderful woman.

"That is flattering." Dolly said and stepped a little closer to him. It was a comfort to him that she was beginning to trust him.

Ted and Angela were announcing that dinner was ready to serve. Sean let Dolly take the lead and picked out a chair next to her at the table after he pulled out the chair for her politely. Milton and Galina were on the opposite side.

The meal was a good one, but Sean was repeatedly getting annoyed when Milton was interrupting people while they were talking.

"The way I see things…" Milton liked to say before he spouted off his opinion.

Sean met his sister's gaze a few times when Milton got long-winded and they shared a secret smile of shared annoyance. He even got a look from Dolly, who had the patience of a saint, that said that she had noticed Milton carrying on what seemed to be a long dialogue with himself at a few points in the conversation. Sean found it odd that Milton was even interrupting Galina upon occasion as well.

Sean was trying very hard to let his annoyance slip away, and instead focused on being a good guest. One thing he had learned from his mentor William Shipley, was that when you saw someone behaving in a way you didn't like, try to do everything in your power not to make yourself as big a nuisance. It wasn't poetic, but it had stuck with Sean and he was using all his self-control not to snap back at the sharply dressed young man at the table. Funny, but Milton might actually be older than Sean, he mused, but he acted like a young pup sometimes.

"I heard that one of your short stories is going to be published in the papers." Sean finally said when Milton was done talking about California politics. He wanted a subject change.

Galina blushed and smiled, and Sean was happy to give her some praise. He knew from Angela that Galina was a special friend and they all were trying to build her up.

"Yes, Ted's sister Sophia was the one who urged me to do it. She even sent it in." Galina smiled broadly. "I am not certain I would have been brave enough."

"We all have…" Angela started to say but Milton chimed in.

"You should never have any doubts about your skills, Galina. I do hope that your friends give you the proper support you need to flourish." Milton said with an eyebrow cocked up.

Galina pulled her chin back a little defiantly for a moment. "Milton, my friends have always been very supportive. You take back that tone of yours." She eyed him and teased a little with her voice. Milton backed off a little. He held up his fork in mock surrender.

"Oh, perhaps I am just a jaded city boy." Milton laughed off his accusatory comment. Sean's nerves were a little frayed even hearing him talk anymore.

Galina turned to Angela who had been interrupted. "What were you going to say Angela?" Galina smiled apologetically.

Angela shook her head a little. Sean could tell that Milton's comment might have upset her a little. "Oh, it was just how proud we are of you, and how well… Oh… I don't remember exactly what I was going to say. But that is the main gist of it." Angela gave a half-hearted smile to Galina.

Galina turned and gave Milton a nudge. "See now Milton, you interrupted Angela." Galina was smiling but Milton gave an apologetic nod to Angela.

"I do rather run away with myself." Milton said smoothly. He had the smile on his lips, but Sean wondered at the cold look in his eyes sometimes. Perhaps Sean should just admit it.

I don't like Milton at all! Sean thought. *Not one little bit.*

After supper Sean and Dolly volunteered to do the cleanup and Ted and Angela entertained the other couple in the parlor.

Sean was glad for some time alone with Dolly and they chatted about hunting and the woods and other small things while they washed up the dishes. Sean took over washing the pans and Dolly put things away after she dried the rest of the dishes, since she knew where things belonged.

"You are not afraid of washing up I see." Dolly said as Sean was scrubbing the roasting pan.

"Well, I am not afraid of a little soap and water." Sean gave her a teasing smile.

"Well, some of the men in my tribe would challenge your warrior status for your helping the womenfolk." Dolly said with a little respect in her tone. He enjoyed when she shared the differences of her life in the tribe and outside of it. It made her a very unique person to talk to.

"Would they challenge me to a duel?" He asked.

She looked confused for a moment. He could tell that she was pondering the meaning of the word.

"Like pacing with guns... or..." She paused and placed the towel on the counter. She held out her hands like two revolvers. "Pistols!" She smiled as she got the word correct.

"Yes, it is a very European tradition, pacing across a stance and facing off with guns." Sean laughed. "I once saw a version of that down near San Francisco, two men in a showdown in the street. It didn't end very well for one of them." Sean grimaced.

"My tribesmen would tease certainly, and perhaps a different kind of showdown. Words and fists weren't unheard of. In that way I don't think that my tribesmen were much different." Dolly was thoughtful but went back to her duties.

"I think some men have a little too much of something that makes them feel like lashing out. I cannot separate myself altogether. That internal struggle of manhood probably always be there a little. Certain people..." Sean paused and gave Dolly a look then nudge his head toward the parlor. "Certain men can get under my skin a bit." He shrugged, since his arms were covered in soapy dishwater.

Dolly raised her eyebrows, questioning him. She mouthed the word 'Milton?'

Sean nodded slowly.

Dolly covered her mouth with her hand to keep from giggling out loud.

"I agree." She whispered and smiled sheepishly.

One more reason to fall for this beautiful and mysterious woman.

"Bluebird..." He said, using her native name. "You are one smart lady."

She set the towel back on the counter and leaned in close to his ear. He felt his blood pressure rise a little with her closeness.

"I think I like to hear you call me that." She whispered. The slight push of air and that sound of her voice was a teasing and as tempting as a sip of fine Irish whiskey. Sean couldn't help but smile a bit.

He was tongue-tied for a moment or two, but finally was able to respond. "I was hoping you would say that."

After the chore was done and they had dawdled in the kitchen a little longer than necessary Sean and Dolly joined the others in the parlor.

Angela and Ted were in the chairs and Galina and Milton were on the loveseat. Sean was way too happy for a while to care what Milton was saying, especially after having such a fine time talking and enjoying Dolly's smiles. Sean pulled up two footstools and Dolly and Sean each sat upon one of them.

Angela was telling a story about Corinne when they had been hiding from the mean and cantankerous Auntie Rose in Boston when Milton leaned over to whisper in Galina's ear.

Sean found it to be rude but kept his attention on his sister who was talking.

"Rose Capron put me to work cleaning the cobwebs from the attic after I was caught in one of Corinne's dresses. Corinne had dared me to try it on. I knew better but we were having a bit of fun. Corinne felt so bad about that." Angela frowned and shook her head in a playful manner. "I will never forget those days." She smiled to everyone. Sean gave a glance and Galina and Milton were in their own little world.

"I am thinking about making some hot tea." Galina stood and gave acknowledgement to Angela and Ted. Then in an afterthought. "Anyone else want some tea?" Her cheeks were flushed.

Everyone politely declined and Galina and Milton headed toward the kitchen and out of earshot.

Sean was glad for the release of tension from his own shoulders, but he could tell between the glances of Ted and Angela that they had concerns. They were polite hosts though and Ted suggested they share the loveseat and they continued to share stories throughout the evening.

Angela got up a few minutes later when the tea kettle whistled and then came back.

"They are cuddled up in the window seat." She raised an eyebrow a little before she slowly sat back down. Ted held her hand for a little extra support. She was moving better, but now with the weight from pregnancy she was a little more awkward.

"I will check on them off and on." Ted smiled conspiratorially.

Sean was glad that they were protecting Galina and taking the guardianship of her seriously. There was something about Milton that made Sean protective of the young girl, though he did not know her very well.

The conversation flowed and there was a lot of laughter as the night progressed. Sean kept peeking out of the side window to make certain he could ride back home safely, but he had no desire to leave for many hours.

He was feeling more at home here, in his sister's home, and Ted… he was becoming a brother slowly but steadily.

Sean was trying to imagine a life where he could see this group together often. With Dolly on his arm, and his sister and Ted and their children around.

It was a pleasant dream that he was growing in his mind and he wanted to hold on to it. The nagging doubts would be there, but for now he wanted to enjoy every moment of happiness.

The time finally came that Angela was yawning and Ted was looking to Sean to help him in convincing her to head to bed. Sean willingly got up and made his goodbyes.

"You were such splendid hosts to us all tonight." Sean smiled to his sister. He helped Dolly up from her spot beside him. He already missed the warmth of her presence there next to him. "I must regretfully depart back to my humble cabin in the woods." He gave Ted and Angela a short bow. "Thank you for the good food and excellent company." Since he was in a jolly mood he reached for Dolly's hand and lifted it gently for a slight kiss, and then enjoyed her blush.

"Oh, he is cheeky." Angela said and laughed a little.

Sean laughed with her.

"You get some good rest." Sean made her promise.

Angela nodded.

Dolly walked with him towards the door.

Milton and Galina must have had the same idea for they were both putting on their coats.

Sean wondered why Galina was getting bundled into her winter coat, but he turned his attention to Dolly.

233

"I had a wonderful time with you tonight." Sean watched the flickering lights from the candles in her dark eyes. Her darker skin was glowing in the warm light and he was struggling to find his sanity for a moment.

"I think I am growing rather fond of our time together." Dolly said, surprising him.

Sean could not have put it better. "I agree."

"See you at church on Sunday?" She asked.

He nodded slowly. He was enjoying the eye contact a little too much. He wanted to kiss her again, but he held back. He was taking it slow. He was trying to be certain that he wasn't being pushy or foolhardy any longer with her. That first kiss had been sweet between them. He wanted to make certain that before he kissed her again that she was certain about him.

"I will be coming by to visit again soon, Bluebird." He said again, and he found the pleasant response she had to her name on his lips was intoxicating again. The curve of her light brown cheek, and the pull of a smile that hinted on her lips.

He used all the reserve willpower he had to say goodbye and go out the front door. He pulled his coat tight against his face and pulled his hat on his head as the wind reminded him of the state of the weather. It was rather rude to interrupt the pleasant thought of Dolly's sweet smile with a cold wind down his jacket to his neck and face. He turned off to the side for a glance to see if it was snowing and he saw the shape of Galina and Milton in a fiery embrace.

He turned away and opened his eyes wide.

Well, they certainly were on a different romantic path. Sean felt a bit foolish and forced himself to move forward and off the porch to get to the barn.

He was feeling a bit of a fool, waiting to kiss Dolly again. He wasn't sure what he truly was waiting for. But he wanted to be respectful, and perhaps prove to himself that he had self-control and patience. He knew a little bit of it was that nagging, negative thought that persisted in his mind. It was telling him that he better not hurt her, and also that he was bound to, because that is the kind of man that he was.

Sean pushed away the negative thoughts and walked faster towards the barn. His dark gray dress slacks were not nearly as warm as his dark blue denim pants. He found Shipley in the stall and he was rewarded with a nuzzle from him against his hand.

"You ready to leave your nice warm spot to go back in the cold with me?" He asked of the horse. Shipley seemed willing enough and Sean got the blanket and saddle back in place.

The ride home was cold, but the moon peeked from behind a cloud and lit the way. Sean's mind was at battle between the pleasant memories of the night, and the doubts that plagued him.

* * *

Galina Varushkin

The house was quiet as Galina stepped through the parlor, she was tidying the room. A throw blanket was on the chair and Galina folded it neatly and placed it back in the corner basket. The fire was low, so she set another log on it, so it would keep burning through the night. She slid the metal gate in front of the fireplace to make certain the sparks wouldn't fly through the room. She blew out the lanterns that had lit the room with the warm glow of soft yellow light throughout the evening.

It had been strange to be there with Milton while Sean and Dolly were there this time. It had changed the dynamic and she wasn't sure that she liked it. Perhaps with Sean, being Angela's brother, it made it feel like a family dinner. Milton had been a little talkative at dinner and she could see on Dolly and Sean's face that they hadn't been very impressed by Milton's comments. Galina actually rolled her eyes over their responses even now.

What makes them think that they are better than Milton? Galina thought with irritation. Galina knew about Sean's past, and he was no angel to be judging Milton's words at every turn.

Milton had said as much when they had their private time to talk finally.

Galina felt herself warm, thinking about the time when they were cuddled up in the window seat by the dining room table. His words played out in her mind.

"You are such an incredible and accomplished woman already at your young age. I see you will be far and above all of these people soon. Not one of them has the ambition to write stories, or to look at the world as you do." Milton had said. He had stroked her hand affectionately as they sat and watched the snow fall softly in the windows that surrounded them.

The view over the valley had been lovely and Galina pointed

235

out the neighbor's lights in the windows of their homes that they could see.

She had told Milton that Angela had been extremely supportive of her desire to read and write and had been instrumental in her education, especially when the word spread that Galina's father didn't want her in school.

"They may have been supportive then, but now they just use you for cleaning up." Milton had stated and then squeezed her hand. "You are better than that."

Galina had tried to defend them. "I volunteered for the job when Angela was hurt. Since I knew that I needed an occupation. They pay me well, even though I am still learning."

Milton shook his head. "I am certain that someday soon they will start to criticize our relationship. You mind my words. They have only their needs in mind. With Angela expecting, they will see your relationship to me as a hindrance to them. They will hem and haw and tell you that you should slow down, and that you are so young." He kissed the back of her head. "I see you as a woman, and they still treat you like a child who doesn't know her own mind."

They had spoken of many things tonight from their cozy spot on the window seat but the words about Angela and Ted were still lingering in her mind.

Milton was bringing up some valid points.

Galina went up to her room and got a fire laid in the small woodstove then sat on her bed while the room warmed up. In her thoughts she was reviewing every word that Milton had said.

She finally changed into her nightgown and crawled under the covers saying a quick prayer. It took a while for her to fall asleep though. She was wondering if perhaps Milton was right about her employers.

Chapter 20

Corinne Grant

Corrine's eyes drooped a little with the ever-present exhaustion as she padded down the stairs with Trudie in her arms. Trudie's head was snuggled against her chest. Caleb was already seated in his chair by the table, being fussed over by Debbie, but Trudie had needed her clothes completely replaced after an unfortunate incident with her nappy.

It was one of those things that couldn't be explained; how much a person could be so thoroughly exhausted, and also love the little routines of a life so completely. It was a mystery. Those few steps down the stairs with Trudie cuddled against her, were precious. She felt it earlier also, when she had entered the children's room and had seen Caleb, sitting up so proudly and looking at her with those sweet eyes in the soft morning light that came through the window. All the work and worry and love mixed together filled the heart so beautifully. It pushed past the exhaustion and made Corinne thankful for the precious little children that God had given her.

The second story of the cabin had been wise plan of her husband's, and though Corinne had struggled through the chaos of it all she knew that in the long run it was going to make things easier. The bigger windows and rooms made the cabin even brighter through the days. The house was so full of extra space it made them all feel much less cramped.

Trudie reluctantly went into the chair by the table next to her brother. Caleb was making a mess while Debbie was happily spooning him some thin oatmeal.

Trudie was wanting her own oatmeal and Corinne got a bowl from Violet who also cut up a few slices of buttered toast and cut it into small fingers for Trudie to try. Corinne delivered the pieces of toast to Trudie and then Violet beckoned Corinne back with a mug of hot coffee.

Corrine gave a look to Violet that hopefully expressed her complete and utter gratitude. Corinne sat at the table and sipped on her coffee like a lifeline. It had cream and sugar and a sprinkle of cinnamon that was a bit decadent. Corinne moaned appreciatively.

"Violet, you are a saint." Corinne said softly and saw Debbie nodding from her place across the table. Debbie had leaned over and tied a bib around Trudie's neck as she wiggled. She was happy to try and eat the toast that Violet had made, some of the pieces were eaten, and some made their way to the floor to be swept up later.

Corinne sipped her coffee as there was a knock on the door. Violet answered it.

"Hello, the house." Clive's voice was a happy sound.

The three women all greeted Clive and Corinne welcomed him inside.

"I saw your husband outside, dutifully cleaning up the path out front." Clive smiled. His face was clean shaven except for a mustache and Corinne though he was looking very happy.

"You look well." Corinne said.

Violet offered him some coffee or tea.

"I'll take some tea, I've had two cups of coffee already, another and I will pay for it fer' certain." Clive chuckled a little and his eyes went wide dramatically.

Violet asked about Olivia.

"Oh, my bride was up early, starting to work on some creation that she is excited about. She had a bit of morning sickness early but has rallied. That raspberry leaf tea you suggested to her Corinne has been a blessing. I have already got more from the apothecary in town to be certain she doesn't run out."

Corinne nodded, suddenly aware that she was a mess, her hair not even brushed and hanging down her back. She reached up to feel if any parts were sticking out in unbecoming ways.

"Ah, don't fret yerself'. You look wonderful. It brings back some good memories seeing you so." Clive smiled warmly. "Makes me see you as I first knew you, sitting by the campfire in the dawn's light with the wilderness all around us."

Some of those memories flooded Corinne at the suggestion and she smiled wistfully.

"That seems an age ago, but it has only been four years." Corinne said and pondered the amount of living she had done these last years.

Violet served Clive some hot tea and he joined them at the table. Violet sat with them.

Clive commented on the quality of the new table and then they all chatted and sipped their coffee and tea a few minutes while they watched the entertainment of the two young children try their hand at eating.

"I think Caleb had more oatmeal on him then in him." Clive cackled a little.

"You will get your turn at this soon enough." Corinne warned, a small bit of laughter bubbled out, feeling good.

Clive placed a hand over his heart. "It warms my heart to think so. But I am trying hard not to get my heart too attached to the idea, the doctor warned us that in older women sometimes… well…" Clive gave a look to Corinne. She knew that not all pregnancies ended with delivery from her own experience.

"I am praying for you and Olivia." Corinne said, and the other women said the same.

Clive let the moment grow silent as they watched Corinne feeding Trudie, who was ready for her oatmeal. She took her bites a little better than Caleb, being a few months older, and having had a bit more practice.

"That's a good girl." Clive said and was rewarded with a bit of mimicry by Trudie.

It sounded a bit like 'oog earl' but it was close enough to get everyone excited.

"Before I forget. Corinne, if you like I can take you back to town iff'n ya like and you can peek through my crates from Australia and China before I let the apothecary have a crack at it." Clive lifted his eyebrows, knowing that she would be interested.

"Oh, yes!" Corinne felt the excitement of new goods from far off lands sink in and give her a needed boost. "If you don't mind waiting for me to get tidied up." Corinne put a hand to her hair again.

"I'm in no rush. Let me switch places with ya. I will take on the feeding, and you eat a few bites yerself." Clive stood and swapped spots with her.

Violet got up as well and served up a plate of breakfast for Corinne after a minute of bustling around in the kitchen.

Corinne gratefully ate her fluffy scrambled eggs and toast while watching Clive and Trudie bond over oatmeal.

Caleb seemed fascinated by Clive and his wide eyes never looked away.

Corinne soon was scuttling off to her room and Violet followed behind with a pitcher of warm water.

Corinne did a quick clean up, making certain that all remnants of sticky oatmeal were off her arms and hands. She found a clean suit that was fashionable and sensible and was pleased that it still fit. Since having Trudie Corinne noticed that she wasn't shaped exactly the same as before. She was still thin, but her curves were a bit more pronounced than they used to be.

Violet came back a few minutes later and offered to help pin up Corinne's hair and Corinne was thankful for the moment, to let Violet be kind. Violet's hands were swift and comforting as she ran her hands over Corinne's scalp and soon Corinne was pleased with her reflection.

Corinne pondered again at Violet's new plans and knew that the day would come when Violet would no longer be here every morning like this. It was a bittersweet pain in Corinne's heart, but she was so very happy for Violet and Reynaldo. They had a chance at their own happiness like she herself had found. Corinne would never, ever deny that to anyone.

"You are so wonderful." Corinne took Violet's hands sincerely. It had been said a thousand times. But Corinne wanted to be certain she said it a thousand more before Violet moved on to her own home with Reynaldo. Violet met her gaze and they shared a wordless moment of understanding.

Corinne came back out to the kitchen and dining room and saw that Caleb was now on Clive's lap reaching up and patting Clive's cheek. His eyes were filled with awe. Clive seemed to be having a bonding moment with the boy, so Corinne grabbed up her mug and refreshed it with a bit more coffee and cream. Violet slipped in next to her with a cinnamon stick and a metal rasp and a delightful dusting of spice wafted down to land in her coffee. Corinne smiled.

"You spoil me so." Corinne gave Violet a little elbow bump and then sat back down at the table.

When Corinne's cup was down to the bottom and after a few funny stories that Debbie was telling for the entertainment of Trudie and the rest of the company, Clive and Corinne were ready to go.

Clive stopped to say hello to Lucas who had just finished shoveling the previous evening's snow from the path all the way from the cabin to the greenhouse, and also to the lab.

Clive was headed off to get the wagon and Lucas swooped in

for a quick goodbye kiss.

"I love you, wife." Lucas whispered in her ear. His cheek was chilled from being outside and his unshaved stubble was sweet and rough against her skin.

"And I love you, husband." She said back. Every once in a while, she saw Lucas with fresh eyes and this moment was one of those as she pulled away. Perhaps Clive's suggestion earlier had stirred up the memories of when she first began to know Lucas Grant, the sweet and wonderful man who was her husband. With his hardworking spirit, and quick wit. Although now having known him longer she knew all the other things that made him such a special person. He was beyond loyal and that feeling of love was refreshed inside her.

It was a happy and warm feeling to take with her on the ride to town.

Clive was superb company. The pleasant way the morning had progressed and the two cups of coffee, Corinne forgot about the tired state of her body and looked forward to the rest of her day.

The road was a bit rough in places and the wind had a biting chill that her bonnet did little to prevent. They quickly got the buggy parked at the livery and Clive escorted her to the post office first, since it had been a few days since anyone had been to town. She had several crates and packages for the lab, as well as a few letters for herself and her husband from back East. Corinne sought the mail for her father's household next door, and also Angela's household as well. Clive had summoned a worker from the fancy good's stockroom to go back to the livery and rent a wagon for the return ride, since all the goods wouldn't fit in the back of the buggy. Corinne insisted on paying for the rental with her reduced family price, since her father owned the livery. Clive only huffed a little.

With quick work the crates and letters were packaged neatly and safely into the back of the wagon and Corinne followed Clive over to the warehouse for the goods that had come the day before by ferry.

Corinne was lost in her own little world when Clive opened up the boxes.

There were jars and small tins full of all kinds of good things. She squealed with glee over the ten small brown bottles that had eucalyptus oil from the crate from Australia. She was down the last drop in the one bottle that had traveled all the way from

Boston with her. It was impossible to get those last drops out and now Corinne was so very happy to add this to her personal collection. She bought them all, keeping in mind that she would split the order with Doc Williams, since he was more likely to need it. She would gladly show him how she had been taught to use it. Doc Williams was humble enough to appreciate her input, which endeared him even more to her. She was always available when he needed an extra hand and enjoyed every chance she had to help people. It was a part of her.

Clive chuckled as Corinne named off the items that she was most excited about.

"This box of white willow bark is such a treasure. I will definitely take half of that. I know that the apothecary shop will take the rest." Corinne was pulling out everything sniffing and reading labels, even if they weren't in a language that she could read. "I think this is green tea leaves. Oh, China has the best tea!" Corinne said excitedly. She found so many other treasures in Clive's crates and had a large selection that she ordered by the end of it all.

"Do you mind if I make a quick trip to the bank and the grocers before we go?" Corinne asked Clive as they were packaging up the last of her purchases.

"I will add these purchases to my ledger, and get a few things done in my office. You come back to me when you are ready." Clive gave Corinne a wink and she surprised him with a hug.

"Oh, I will never tire of that kind of thing." Clive patted Corinne's back.

Corinne was feeling a bit sentimental, with all the memories that Clive had stirred within her that morning. Just mentioning the trip they had shared made Corinne more aware of how much she had to be grateful for. Clive was a big part of the reason she had survived to have such a happy life.

Corinne bundled back into her warm coat as Clive promised to get her purchases to the wagon waiting at the livery.

Corinne walked across the busy street, first getting some money at the bank, and then making a stop at the grocers. She found a few things there that had been shipped from southern California and Corinne happily plunked down her coins for a box full of oranges and a few bags of onions. Corinne had something she wanted to do with the oranges, with the Christmas holiday coming. She gave the clerk a tip and had him deliver the goods to the wagon for her.

She made a quick stop to Doc Williams office and only spent a few minutes visiting with him and his wife before she headed back to the fancy goods store to find Clive.

The bell tinkled overhead as Corinne walked through the front door. Millie Quackenbush greeted Corinne with a smile and Corinne walked up to chat with the woman. Millie had been running the front counter for more years than Corinne had been here, and she was dressed in a warm red plaid dress that was cinched as tight as it could go around her generous frame. Her husband JQ, was Clive's son and though Corinne and Millie had a checkered past with some clashing of ideas, it had been a peaceful friendship for a few years since the early struggles of their acquaintance. Both Corinne and Millie were respected in their own way, and eventually the ruffled feathers had ceased to be thought of.

"I think you may be the only soul who braved coming to town today." Millie said and looked around her store, grimacing at its lonely state.

"Oh, that wind is cold enough to make anyone think twice." Corinne said with sincerity.

"I will certainly be happy to stay in today myself, though it does get rather dull, when so few come to the store in these winter months. A few days ago, the place was full of customers, now I fear that you may be my only customer all day." Millie shook her head in disappointment. Millie frowned for a moment, like she had a thought and gave Corinne a grave look. "Corinne, since I have you here, I wonder if I could share a concern I have."

Corinne wasn't certain what confidence that Millie would have with her, but she nodded. "Of course, Millie."

"I will heat up some water for tea and we can talk for a few. I need to get something off my chest." Millie gestured for Corinne to follow. She had never been upstairs and was intrigued at least with wondering what in the world that Millie would want to confide.

———◆◆———◆◆———

"I am concerned about our dear friend Galina!" Millie said as she leaned over the table to serve the tea.

Corinne had been spending her time waiting perusing the

parlor upstairs and was impressed with the nice home of JQ and Millie Quackenbush. She had never thought she would be invited there. Millie's words took a moment to soak in.

"You are worried about Galina?" Corinne picked up her teacup and paused just holding it as she thought about Millie's words.

"Yes, that poor girl has been through so much already. I fear that she might be attaching herself to a young man that is undeserving." Millie sat and picked up her own cup of tea and took a sip then sighed a little dramatically.

Hmm... Corinne thought. Have I officially become someone that Millie wants to gossip with? Corinne wasn't sure where this conversation was going to go, but she wasn't certain that she wanted to be a part of it.

"Galina has been through a lot." Corinne cautiously agreed. She wasn't going to add anymore to the story if that was Millie's intention.

"Yes. So sorry. I am being so vague. I will get to the point." Millie groaned a little. "I have seen Galina and Milton in town and they seem rather affectionate. That is no crime, though perhaps to others it was scandalous. I saw them kissing in front of my store just last week, but I kept it to myself, for the Lord is working on showing me that gossip is a foul sin in His eyes. We all have our cross to bear, and my mouth has gotten the best of me quite a bit in my lifetime." Millie lowered her head for a moment, looking chagrined. "You know that yourself, over some of my past actions with you. I still bear the shame of that sometimes." Millie gave Corinne an apologetic smile. "Well, I was not the only one that saw them that day, and the gossip began to run around from doorstep to doorstep. When they came to me I tried to downplay the public affection as much as I could, reminding people that we were all affectionate and impetuous when we were young. I am not certain that I helped with stemming the flow of wagging tongues, but I did try. But the other gossip in town was the main concern." Millie placed the teacup down and there was a hint of a rattle against the saucer. "Milton is developing a reputation with other business owners and I fear that it isn't a good one. He had been rather pushy with several vendors and his temper has been on display in many cases. Several vendors who were pressured by Milton to sell him goods are now claiming that he is refusing to pay them. I have been into Milton's store and he seems to be running a very nice business there. I have no issues with him personally, but I think of Galina, and the trials she has had with her family and I wonder if she is getting herself entangled with a young man with a temper." Millie did look concerned and Corinne was analyzing what Millie had shared.

"I can see how that could be the case." Corinne said, the recent memory of her own experience with Mr. Vaughn had not been a good one. The comparison between the stories was something to consider. She knew for a fact that only herself, Dolly and Sean knew of that previous incident.

Corinne had mentioned it a little to her own household, but had felt guilty about potentially gossiping and didn't bring it up again.

"With Galina's mother in heaven it seems to me that we all have to do our Christian duty and look after those that needs some extra care. If she was my daughter I would try to talk with her, and just make sure that she knew the young man a bit more before allowing feelings to continue to grow."

Millie sighed, as if the information had been a burden and now that she had shared her feelings she was feeling lighter.

"I do care about Galina deeply, and I can see that you care as well. " Corinne said thoughtfully.

"I don't want you to just take my word on it, I am just the messenger. I created this reputation with my own actions in the past, to want to be involved in other people's business. Now, with fresh eyes I can see how much time I spent on such endeavors when people come to me. It is truly rather ugly how gossip turns people into something that is also ugly. I can see it now, and I am thanking God that even at my age that I can learn a few things about myself."

Corinne though that Millie was being rather brave in her confession. It was a good thing to know, in God's timing, when we have crossed the line.

"It sounds like you have made some good strides forward." Corinne said and tried to convey that she was in support of Millie's change of attitude on gossip.

"The Lord and I have been having some talks together." Millie sipped her tea again. "I like to think of the story in the Bible of the vineyard. If the Lord is there to prune the branches so that vine produces good fruit, then I want to be willing to allow God to do that. No matter how painful the pruning process may be. I cannot say that I won't falter, or fall back on my bad habits, but I know that I am forgiven, and that makes those tearful moments of self-reflection a bit more bearable." Millie's voice was showing a bit of emotion and Corinne could feel her sincerity. Corinne knew that she would be looking up those verses when she was home. Sometimes in life you get a lesson from unexpected sources.

"I will be praying about what you have told me. I will see what God tells me to do with this information." Corinne said after a few moments to think. She sipped the warm tea and let her mind go through all her words.

"I had JQ talk to a few of these business owners, making certain it was just gossip but had actually happened. Business owners in the town have a pretty good relationship with one another, since there is not much competition with each other. We each have our own kind of product, perhaps in a bigger town it would be more cutthroat. I have a list of the business owners that have actually made formal complaints to the town council about invoices going unpaid. JQ did speak to those that claim that Milton has a temper and JQ wrote down the particulars." Millie handed over a few pieces of folded paper. "I want to see Galina happy, and I just don't know..." Millie sighed. "I don't know how to describe the feeling. Just a sense of bad intentions on his part. I have met him on several occasions, and he has a charm about him. He can be quite personable. But..." Millie shook her head.

"There is perhaps something behind his eyes." Corinne said finally, voicing the words that had been in her own mind about the handsome and charming Mr. Vaughn.

Millie nodded miserably.

The next minute was quiet and they both seemed to be lost in thought before Millie spoke again. She seemed a bit more determined.

"I have spoken at length with Clive, because he is probably the wisest man I know." Millie said. "Don't tell him that." She smiled a little. "Clive has had him over to his home. When I pressed him for his character assessment he used the word 'slick'. I just hope that I am wrong, and Milton is just young and a bit headstrong and pushy in business. It does happen, especially if he is used to working in a bigger city perhaps. But, I think Galina should know, in case she... well in case things are moving towards an understanding between them."

Corinne agreed that further thought should be taken. With

everything in her mind from this already busy day Corinne felt the need for a nap, but she knew from experience, if she tried, it would have been an utter failure. Her mind would play over and over every word and deed of the day and she would get no rest.

"Thank you, Millie, for sharing with me. I will definitely talk to God about this one."

Corinne stood, and Millie came around the table and gave Corinne an unexpected hug.

"May God bless you, my dear." Millie said as she pulled away.

As Corinne went down the stairs towards Clive's office she knew that she would need God's blessing for certain. Her heart was heavy.

<hr />

Corinne sat on the chair by the door and laced up her boots. Her mind was made up. She had spent the afternoon in prayer as she worked with Dolly to put away the goods she had bought from town.

Dolly had been just as thrilled as she over the amazing treasures that Clive had offered. The medicines and ointments section of the labs, with the tall shelves in the back corner would be growing with all the new raw material to work with.

Corinne had gone to go back home but then turned mid-step to go to the barn where Lucas had been working and found him in the loft.

Corinne stared up in the dusty barn and saw the disturbance of Lucas with puffs of dust that were visible in the air near him.

"Lucas!" Corinne sang out.

He peeked his head over the edge, giving Corinne a few heart palpitations of fear.

"Don't lean over like that!" Corinne said, wide-eyed.

Lucas was laughing the entire climb down the ladder.

"Did you think I was going to fall?" He was teasing her, and she gave him a fake slug in the stomach.

"I think you men try to scare us women into an early grave." Corinne huffed and pouted playfully at him.

He kissed her to sooth her. It had worked.

The feeling was playful between them, but it turned serious when Corinne told him about the talk she had with Millie.

Lucas was thoughtful as they sat on a haybale for a few

minutes while Corinne let him think about it.

They talked a little, but he was hesitant to give her advice.

"I think we should pray about it." Lucas said finally. "My prayer is that God shows you what to do. I feel like you and Galina have a bond, and if anyone was to tell her about this, then it should be you. I think if a man would tell her it could come across as condescending, and that would just send the wrong message."

They had prayed together about the situation and Corinne had spent the rest of the afternoon with the children. Praying and letting God lead her in the right direction while she played with Caleb and Trudie.

Now as she prepared to walk over to the Greaves house her mind was resolved to do what needed to be done. She had a few knots in her stomach and a lump in her throat as she stepped out the front door. She stopped to let Lucas know what she was doing.

"I am so proud of you, my darling girl." Lucas had kissed her on the forehead.

It was a comforting gesture, but it did little to calm her from the trepidation she felt at the forthcoming confrontation.

The fluffy white snow had put a blanket of quiet over the landscape, dulling the sounds around her. The world was still and Corinne prayed for peace as she took the short walk to the road. She looked up at Angela's house, in the quiet of the dusk, and hoped that she wasn't going to stir up a hornet's nest with her talk with Galina. She knew she was doing what had to be done.

A minute later she walked up the front steps and knocked on the door.

Ted answered and gave her a welcome smile.

"Is Angela around?" Corinne asked when Ted welcomed her in.

"Yes, she just woke up from a nap." Ted said and led her to the parlor.

Angela was settled into a winged back chair by the fireplace and was knitting. She looked up with a smile.

Corinne tried to smile kindly but felt her nerves hit her and wondered if she was going to look stressed instead of happy to see her friend.

"Come sit by the fire with me friend." Angela set her knitting in her lap and made a gesture with her free hand to join her. Corinne did.

Corinne let out a sigh. She didn't waste any time and told Angela a shortened version of what she had learned in town from Millie, and also about her own experience with Milton.

Angela frowned and sighed. "I was worried that something like that was lurking in the background." She shook her head from side to side slowly. "Galina is rather attached, this isn't going to be easy on her."

Corinne's heart was saddened to hear that. Hoping that the relationship hadn't progressed very far.

"Well, I just wanted you to have the basics, so if Galina comes to talk with you then you know to what it is she is referring. I have no intention of any of this going any further, but I do apologize if this causes a storm in your home." Corinne was dreading the next step, but she was determined to get it over with.

"Is Galina in her room?" Corinne asked, feeling like she needed to get on with her plans.

Angela nodded soberly.

Corinne wasn't sure what she could say but she got up and Angela stood up as well. Corinne gave her a hug, feeling the swelling child against her middle. She was reminded about the visit she had made to the doctor in town earlier and realized that she had never spoken to her husband about her suspicions. Once she was done with this dreaded errand then she could focus on herself.

"I am praying." Angela said and kissed Corinne on the cheek.

Corinne smiled at Angela and headed out of the warmth of the parlor and went up the staircase to the second floor. She knocked on Galina's door.

Galina answered with a smile.

"Corinne!" Galina said with enthusiasm.

Galina's room was tidy with a chair next to the small woodstove in the corner and an oil lamp burning.

"I came to have a chat with you. I hope you are free." Corinne said nervously. Wishing her words were already spoken and done with.

"Let me grab another chair from Dolly's room, she isn't coming back for a few more days." Galina smiled.

Corinne sat in the chair by the fire and waited with the lump in her throat growing with every passing second.

Galina placed the chair next to Corinne and sat down with a pleasant and peaceful expression on her face.

It was time for Corinne to talk.

"I want to begin by saying that I love you like family and I never ever want to do or say anything that would hurt you in any way." It sounded so cliché and stupid when she said it. *Isn't that what everyone says right before they hurt someone? I don't want to hurt you but*....

Galina started to look a little concerned, however, she was listening.

"There are some concerns about Milton, some of his business dealings, and a few interactions he has had with people..." Corinne took a deep breath. Then said slowly. "Including myself and Dolly... that shows he may have a temper and may even be attempting to deceive people." The words were said, the hardest ones. Now if she could make Galina know how much everyone cared for her.

"Deceive people?" Galina's eyebrows furrowed. "That is not possible." She shook her head in disbelief.

Corinne felt her cheeks heat and explained about the business that hadn't been paid for services or products by Milton.

"I am certain that Milton is aware. I know people in business have their little squabbles, I am certain Milton knows and will handle it appropriately. He is always talking about his business and cares for it deeply. He wouldn't risk a reputation shift for something like that. Perhaps they just didn't invoice properly." Galina seemed to know more about Milton and his business than Corinne would have guessed.

"That may be the case, but some of his actions and attitudes have been witnessed and..." Corinne was interrupted.

"Well, I never expected you to listen to gossip Corinne." Galina said with a huff.

Corinne felt her cheeks flush again.

"It isn't gossip when it happened to me." Corinne said with a little more defensive posture then she wanted to. "He was forceful and rude to Dolly and I when he couldn't purchase something from me at my lab. It was already sold to someone else. He looked ready to strike. If Sean Fahey hadn't arrived he may have." Corinne said and felt the weight of the words land on her like bricks. This was not going the way she wanted it to go.

She had all of these words in her mind. How they all loved her and wanted to be certain that she was loved by a good man. Now it was just turning into an argument at who was to blame.

"I am certain that he was just passionate, you are probably overreacting." Galina said then she turned to look Corinne in the eye. "Did you come here to hurl accusations in hope that I would break my courtship with him?"

"That was not my intention, no. I just wanted you to know that Milton may have a few unsavory habits that you should be aware of." Corinne was trying to remain calm and she forced herself to speak calmly. Trying to remember what it was like when she had been courting Lucas, and someone had accused him of something bad. She had defended him back then, as Galina was now for Milton. In Lucas's case though, the accusation had been by a rival suitor who had lied. Corinne did not believe these people were lying about Milton.

"Unsavory habits..." Galina stood and paced around a few steps. "Don't we all have a few unsavory habits, Corinne? Don't we?" Galina was angry, and Corinne let her have the floor to say what she wished.

Corinne nodded in reply.

"Honestly, Milton is a bit different, he is passionate and a bit outspoken sometimes, but he has never had malice for anyone. I am sure he will not be pleased to stay here in Oregon City, knowing the entire town is probably gossiping that he is some kind of monster."

Corinne wanted to correct Galina, but she didn't.

Galina turned to her. "I never thought that you would want to betray me like this. I had wondered if I was truly on a path to happiness, to finally have found someone that sees me more than the girl to wash laundry, and clean up messes, but to be cherished instead. That is what Milton does for me. But now I can see. I think you all believe that I am not good enough to be connected with someone like him. I need to keep to my place, don't I?" Galina's cheeks were bright red, and she looked to Corinne accusingly.

"I have never felt that way Galina. You are..." Corinne had so much more to say but Galina cut her off.

"You know, I think I have heard enough. I may just be a servant, but this is my room. I would like to ask you to leave, now that you have had your say." Galina pointed to the door. She had tears in her eyes.

Corinne was stunned but she stood obediently. She wanted to say that she loved her and only wished that she was happy, but her words were locked behind her teeth.

Corinne left the room and walked slowly down the stairs. There was nothing in that conversation that had gone the way she had wanted it too. It was one thing to plan out your words carefully, but Corinne knew that sometimes the intentions could never be matched when speaking to someone. Corinne felt her heart breaking a bit when she saw Angela and Ted downstairs.

"I am sorry." Corinne said feeling a few tears rolling down her cheeks.

Ted and Angela tried to console her, but she wasn't in the mood for any more talking. She was so sad and tired suddenly. She needed to get home.

She went through the motions and was back in her coat and bonnet in a few moments. She said goodbye and left the Greaves' home and was on her doorstep in under a minute. She didn't even remember feeling the cold wind on her face as it blew on her tears.

She needed to be held, and Lucas was there for her when she went inside.

Her home was her sanctuary. The place where she could let all of the outside world melt away. The scent of something baking, and fresh brewed coffee.

Her husband's chest as she laid against him was warm and supportive as she shed a few extra tears over her disappointments. He smelled of chopped wood and the hint of the lemongrass soap she had made for him.

She settled into the rest of her evening trying to focus on her family.

❖──◆──◆──◆──❖

The weather turned bitter as more snow and wind howled through the valley that night.

It was long after dinner when all of the adults were gathered in the parlor that Corinne shared a little of the confrontation with all of them. They were sad along with her, but no one had any thoughts on how to repair the damage done. The conversation eventually turned and Corinne decided to share the bit of news that had been pushed to the back of her mind since Millie had shared her story.

"I did go to see Doc Williams today." Corinne confessed to them.

They all had been quiet for a little while. The mood had been somber, and everyone had been dwelling on their own thoughts. They now turned to Corinne with their full attention.

"He confirmed my suspicions, that I am expecting again."

Lucas took her hand and squeezed it affectionately.

Violet and Debbie both silently came to Corinne and gathered around her. The love in the room was a soothing balm to Corinne's heartbreak from earlier.

Corinne and Lucas went to bed soon after and they talked for a long time. She promised Lucas to slow down and Lucas promised to cherish her in every way. She fell asleep in his arms, thankful to be loved.

Sophia Greaves

Sophia could have kissed Clive when he had shown up in the early morning to pick up a box full of lace collars and other finery they had been working on order.

"Your work is getting a lot of attention. Stores in Portland, Salem, and even a new town up north called Seattle. I will need more lace for some stores in California in a few months, since the ferries and steamers won't be running as much during the next few months." Clive had said as he was looking through the orders and checking his list.

Sophia's mother clucked around him like a mother hen asking about Olivia, and how she was fairing.

"My Olive is doing just fine. We are sending out some adverts for a cook and housekeeper in the paper, and I hope to hear something in the next few months about it." Clive shared.

Sophia was antsy to get out again and she pestered Clive.

"You have any reason to go see Angela and Ted today. I was hoping to see what they were planning for Christmas and see if I could help with anything for the baby's room." Sophia asked.

"Oh, I could head on up there, Olivia was wanting to stop in to see Angela as well. The weather seems mild today and I do have the sleigh runners on the conveyance. It will be nice and warm in there too if I put a bowl of coals in the back." He gave Sophia a wink and they both had turned to Amelia Greaves, who pressed her lips together.

"I don't see why not. But Clive dear, you better bring these gals back home if the weather turns foul. I will hold you responsible." Amelia said.

Sophia had squealed a bit and on impulse kissed her mother's cheek.

"You be sure to talk with Galina a bit about that Milton fellow." Amelia shook her head. "He may be running a successful business… But he dresses so sharp and has an air about him. I don't know what he is thinking going after a sweet girl like Galina." She tsked a few times.

"I will mother." Sophia promised and ran up the stairs to put on better clothes for going out.

Christmas was only a week away and Sophia was feeling all cooped up from the last week of snow and wind. She had even kept her trips with Lady outside short. Her poor little poodle was struggling in the deeper snow. Sophia had hired a young man to shovel a path in their small backyard so Lady wouldn't get lost in a snow drift.

Sophia was happy to be ready and out the door with Clive a few minutes later. Lady was cuddled up in her lap with a small warm wool blanket. Her pale beige fur curly and soft under her finger tips as they rode along.

The pantry at her brother's home was stuffed full of pantry goods, sweets, and jars of every good thing. Sophia was already looking forward to Christmas dinner. There was raspberry cordial, and the promise of apple pie, and so many delicious promises for a feast. Sean and Dolly were going hunting with Clive and Ted in a few days. They were planning to hunt for geese and a turkey. Sophia was grinning as Galina went through all the plans for Christmas day.

"Ted has been making cheese in the barn and we all got to try a bit yesterday. It is very good." Galina said with a smile. "I had never tasted goat cheese before, but I was very impressed."

"Oh, I cannot wait." Sophia was peeking through all the jars of fruit preserves. The pantry back at her home in town was not nearly so big. They relied a lot on the grocer in town. She told Galina about the pantry at their home.

"Edith and Angela have been working all summer and fall to fill up the pantry. The root cellar is stuffed so full it is hard to walk in there." Galina laughed.

Galina grabbed up a few items to start making lunch. She had her arms full and Sophia took a few things to help.

"You don't have to help." Galina said.

"I want to." Sophia smiled.

Galina frowned a little, but she followed Sophia out of the pantry and they both headed for the kitchen.

There was a large chicken sitting on the counter.

"Uh oh, one of Angela's chickens?" Sophia asked.

"Yes, a hen has stopped laying. Angela is coping." Galina shook her head sadly. "I plucked it this morning in the other room. "This hen was a present from Ted to Angela before they were married. She is trying to be practical. But I could tell it bothered her." Galina said and picked up the bird.

"How can I help?" Sophia asked.

"If you would like to cut the celery and carrots into chunks, I will get the water going on the stove. We can get the chicken and vegetables in the pot to boil. Later I will make some egg noodles."

Sophia let Galina instruct her on what she needed to do and got busy. It was nice to be doing something different and to be in a new environment. Being with Galina was a good distraction, a lot like her visits with Clive and Olivia.

She was missing her Aunt Olivia more now since her wedding to Clive. Before getting married she had lived with Sophia and her mother and her presence down in the parlor made the days go by faster. She was always trying to make everyone happier. She was good company. She loved to read similar books to Sophia and they would talk while they worked. They even challenged Amelia, her mother, to talk about subjects that we outside of her comfort zone. Even talking about politics and news was interesting with Olivia. Sophia knew that she was struggling with the changes in her life. When did she start to care about so many things? She felt that the cares of her childhood were melting away, and now she needed her aunt more than ever. She should be able to confide in her mother, but Sophia had tried that so many times, and had been disappointed.

Her father's death profoundly changed her mother, and Sophia wasn't sure if it would ever improve.

Sophia enjoyed helping Galina and she tried to think about the happy days ahead, instead of the dull winter days of work and tension that she would face at home.

It didn't take long to get the water boiling and Galina showed her what to do to get the broth started on the stove.

"This will need to boil for an hour, then I can work on the rest of the ingredients." Galina said, as they were washing their hands and the counter. There were more vegetables on the counter, but Galina said that they would be chopped when the chicken broth was done.

Sophia had never made chicken soup before, so she was logging the instructions away in her mind. With her job, she had never spent much time in the kitchen, but she knew that someday she would like to know more about these things, just in case.

Everyone was seated in the parlor, talking about the upcoming holiday. Angela had the cat in her lap. Duchess seemed to be very content to let Angela stroke her for eternity. Sophia smiled at the sight.

Galina and Sophia pulled up extra chairs.

"I declare we need another davenport in here, I never expected to have so many guests so frequently." Angela said and frowned.

"I can look into that for you, my dear gal." Clive said. "There is a man in Salem, he has a fine shop of goods there. Stuffed chairs and what not. I have a few folks that are looking. I got a few pieces from him when I built my house." Clive smiled.

"Well, that is good to know. The parlor is big enough for another few pieces." Angela smiled and looked about the room. Sophia could tell that she was thinking about how the room would look with more furniture.

"I also need to order a new rug, the baby crib is ordered from Amos Drays, but we haven't a rug for the back bedroom yet." Angela said with a sigh.

Clive pulled out a small notepad from his front shirt pocket and jotted a few things down with a stubby pencil.

"I heard you and Sean are taking my husband out hunting in a few days." Angela said.

"Yes, he has talking about it for days, I washed up his long underwear, so he won't freeze to death." Olivia said from her chair by the fire. She laughed.

"Ah, my darling wife, you shouldn't be talking about a man's underclothes. It isn't fittin'." He chuckled, and everyone laughed.

Angela smiled. "Well, I had to dig through some trunks to find Ted's." Angela laughed. "Do try and make certain he doesn't fall in the creek or get shot." Angela said with a smirk.

"I promise to try. My dear wife would smother me in my sleep iff'n I let her beloved nephew get hurt on my watch." He gave

Olivia a wink and she nodded to agree with his statement.

"He is about to be a papa, it is only fitting to let him live long enough to hold his firstborn." Olivia said and grinned.

"Dolly is coming along?" Angela asked. "I haven't seen her in a few days, I am not certain of her plans."

"Oh yes, she will be bringing her bow. I bet you she bags more food than all of us." Clive said. "Though I have a bit of a head start with some traps set along the creek." He wiggled his eyebrows to emphasize how competitive he was.

"I am so pleased to see Sean and Dolly together. Having them over to supper a few times let me get to see them up close. I do love how they are together. I am praying that God blesses their courtship." Angela said.

"I have seen them sitting together at Sunday service. They seem so sweet together." Olivia said with a smile.

Sophia had heard about them courting and had seen them together when she would go to service with Clive and Olivia, but she didn't know them too well. She felt like she was missing out sometimes. Town was only a few miles away, but it felt farther somedays.

She looked over to Galina, her cheeks were pink, and she was frowning a little. Sophia could tell that she was upset about something.

Galina hadn't said a word since they had sat down, and she wondered if something was on her mind. Sophia kept an eye on her friend while everyone continued to talk.

The hour passed, and Sophia was happy to help Galina with the next phase of the chicken soup.

Now the the chicken was boiled Galina has Sophia chop up more vegetables.

"Why am I chopping up the same vegetables I put in the broth?" Sophia asked in confusion.

"The boiled ones are all mushy, these will taste better. I thought it was strange at first but it does taste better with fresh vegetables." Galina said with a grin.

Sophia nodded and kept chopping.

Galina scooped the chicken and boiled vegetables out of the broth. The scent was incredible, and Sophia was looking forward to sharing lunch with everyone later. She would be proud that she was able to help.

Galina strained the out all the small bits and pieces in the broth and then got it back on to simmer. She told Sophia that she would let the chicken cool off a bit before she pulled it apart.

She cleared a spot next to Sophia at the counter and started making a dough. Sophia had to focus on her chopping, but she was fascinated to watch the process of the few ingredients all coming together to make the noodles. She patted the ball of dough and cover it with a towel. Sophia was finishing up with the last of the vegetable chopping when she saw Galina's face. Her eyes were welled up with tears and her face was red.

"Do we need anything from the pantry?" Sophia asked as she set the knife on the counter.

Galina nodded, and Sophia followed her to the pantry.

"What is wrong?" Sophia asked as she shut the door behind them. The small window cast snowy white light through the cramped room.

Galina glanced up to the ceiling and two fat tears fell down her cheeks. She had a little flour on her hands and wiped at them, streaking white across her face.

"I am just feeling rather pitiful." Galina confessed.

Sophia put a hand on her shoulder for support, she found a handkerchief in her skirt pocket and handed it over to Galina. She was mopping up the flow of tears.

"I am just realizing that no one has once said that they were happy for me and Milton, they gush on and on about Sean and Dolly, and no one cares one whit about me." Galina said.

"I am sure that isn't true…" Sophia tried to think of anything to comfort her. There were people that didn't trust Milton, Sophia had heard things in town, but gossip is gossip. Sophia didn't listen to much of it, though her mother participated more often than Sophia would like.

"They all give each other looks, I can see it." Galina said and frowned. "Everyone keeps telling me to slow down and take time to get to know him better."

Sophia thought that was wise advice that everyone gives to courting couples.

"My mother and aunt both had unhappy marriages, they say that to me all the time, and I don't have a beau." Sophia said and hoped that would calm her. Perhaps Galina was just feeling emotional.

"You will have it so easy, Sophia, I am the hired help. I am beginning to wonder if they don't want me to leave, so they will discourage me from seeing him anymore." Galina said with a huff.

"Angela and Ted would never do that." Sophia said slowly and thoughtfully. She understood that Galina cared for Milton, but she didn't understand at all why Galina would suddenly have such an ungracious attitude about her brother and sister-in-law.

Galina took a deep breath. "I don't know, I just love him, and I can feel everyone's disappointment." She let the air out in a ragged breath, her chin had a tremor of emotion and Sophia feared that she would begin to sob.

"I know that your father was disappointed in you. But not everyone sees you that way." Sophia said and placed her other hand on her other shoulder facing her straight on. "We all love you and want you to be happy."

Sophia felt Galina's sadness as she tried to calm herself. Her dark eyes showed every emotion. Sophia could tell that she was struggling.

"I just wish that people would say a kind word about him. He loves me and is so very understanding." Galina hiccupped a little, it surprised her and she laughed a little. "Ugh, I am such a silly child sometimes."

Sophia smiled at her friend, wishing that she knew the right words to say.

"We all get silly and emotional sometimes." Sophia said and watched Galina recover. "You go to the back room and splash some cold water on your face. God will work all of this out. Remember to lean on God when you have doubts." Sophia said practically, then felt a little foolish. Perhaps Galina didn't want platitudes just now. "When I am struggling, I pray a lot, and read the promises that God made in the Word. It helps me through the struggles."

Galina nodded and smiled. Sophia could see that the main issue had passed.

"I'll meet you in the kitchen in a minute. I will head out to the outhouse then come back in and wash my hands and face. The cold wind can explain away my red face." Galina said thoughtfully.

Sophia nodded and kissed her friend on the cheek. "We all love you."

"Thank you, Sophie, I love you too." Galina slipped out the door and Sophia walked back to the kitchen. She was torn between two loyalties. Galina was her friend, but she was certain that Angela and Ted were not intentionally doing anything to keep Galina from being happy.

She was beginning to wonder if Milton was everything that Galina thought he was. Perhaps she couldn't see past his charm.

It was a dark topic to think on, but it threaded through her thoughts the rest of the day. She sat at the lunch table eating the soup she had helped to make and watched the interaction between Angela and Galina closely. She saw no tension there. Angela was praising her fine work, and they were talking about the upcoming Winter Ball after Christmas, and the excitement of all the activities of the coming days. There was nothing there that showed any kind of troubles between Angela and Galina.

She knew that she would go home and pray for her friend. There was something brewing under the surface and Sophia was beginning to wonder if Galina was falling for a man who didn't deserve her.

Chapter 21

Sean Fahey

The slow and steady drip in Sean's back bedroom had been getting on his nerves overnight and he removed the bucket from under the leak in the morning then put down another empty tin bucket.

The sound of dripping continued. Ting-ting-ting.

It was like the steady feeling that was nagging him in the back of his mind. Ting-ting-ting.

It was a voice, steady and unending.

'You are not a good man.' The voice seemed to say. 'You don't deserve to be happy.'

It was a problem and he was feeling tortured throughout the last weeks as the voice continued to invade his thoughts.

When he spent time with Dolly as they continued their courting, he found that the voice within him became stronger, and he wondered if perhaps God was telling him that his relationship was wrong.

He was reliving his past mistakes in his mind over the last days. That fateful decision long ago, to run away from the work orphanage. The pain of the beatings from the other boys and the stench of the place was still there. Sean was positive that he would never get those memories out of his head. The night he had escaped, he had tried to get to Angela. He had crouched against the back wall and watched the guard, wishing and praying that he would walk away just long enough for him to sneak into the girl's room and snatch up Angela. But the opportunity never came. He had been caught trying to escape before and that very scenario had caused him to get caught. So, he had left her behind. It ate away at him still, even with her forgiveness, and a promise that she had never felt that he had abandoned her. That didn't matter at all. He felt like he had done that very thing.

Perhaps these thoughts and memories were because he had not made proper atonement for his mistakes. He wondered if he would ever deserved happiness after what he had done.

Sean poured the water into the water barrel by the back door.

Cupid was at his heels trying to push his way out.

"No way, Cupid, you aren't running free in the woods again." Sean said. His mood was foul. He dreaded what had to be done.

He grabbed up his work coat and closed the door on Cupid, who immediately began his mournful whining at the back door of the cabin.

Sean found a wooden ladder in the barn and lugged it across the muddy yard. The slushy snow was sloppy under his boots. The snow melting on the roof was causing the leak, and he knew that there was no way around what needed to be done. Sean wasn't certain that a patch would do the job, or if the entire roof needing replacing, but he would have a look. He placed the ladder on the edge of the northern corner of the cabin and climbed up. He was shaking his head at the pathetic moaning from Cupid, who was lonely and probably dying (in his mind) inside the cabin.

Sean peeked over the edge of the roof and saw the problem right away. Some of the shingles had blown off and he knew what he needed to do. He also saw a large branch further up the roof that had a bunch of leaves and debris stacked up behind it. A pile of snow had gathered up and Sean knew that needed to be cleared away. It would only get worse if he left that there.

Sean reluctantly climbed up on the roof. Spreading out his arms and legs to spread his weight. It was not a comfortable feeling, to be so high off the ground. Sean felt a strange sense of panic, being at an odd angle and not having the ground solidly beneath him.

Sean crawled forward over the roof, feeling the shingles move, some of the them covered in sloppy snow which was shifting beneath him. Several of the shingles gave up under Sean's weight and slid off and away, falling to the ground.

Sean grumbled as he inched his way forward towards the large branch, every shingle that crackled and loosened under him was one that would have to be replaced. There were patches of moss growing and Sean was realizing with more dread that the roof really would need to be replaced, at least all the shingles.

He had planned to add on to the cabin in the spring and the idea of replacing the roof now seemed a fool's errand right before he was going to be chopping into the roof to expand the space in the cabin. Sean grumbled a little more.

He was nearly within reach of the branch when his right foot slipped on some moss and his body lost all purchase. Sean scrambled to grab onto anything to stop the slide, his left foot caught on the edge of something and his body slid sideways. The one shingle that was holding him up gave way and Sean slid over the surface of the roof through the slush and leaves and broken shingles and went over the edge, almost head first.

It was a long panicky moment until Sean landed on his left arm and he heard his wrist making an unpleasant crunching noise right before he yelled out in pain.

He laid there for a minute, letting the wet earth and snow soak into his clothes. He felt a strange rush of adrenaline take over. He analyzed whether or not anything else was hurt. It wasn't that terrible of a fall, it could have been worse. He could have fallen off the barn. He felt like he had been so stupid. There were probably twenty ways he could have taken care of the problem without crawling on the roof with the snow and slop up there. He knew there was moss. Moss was slippery and hazardous to walk on even while on the ground sometimes. With the angle of a roof and broken shingles and moss combined, it was a recipe for disaster.

Sean sat up and winced. He tried to wiggle his fingers and couldn't move them, and they were numb. His hand was basically useless. It was not a normal feeling and he felt his heart start to pound a little. He would have to figure out what to do.

He pushed himself up with his good arm and did another body assessment. He was a little stiff and sore. The majority of the impact had been on the arm that now was useless. The pain had been intense but now it didn't feel like much of anything. He felt a rush of energy, a strange and painful burst that happens when you are injured or frightened.

It would be so much simpler if he could ride his horse. But He definitely could not get the saddle on with only one hand.

"Ahhh." Sean yelled out in frustration. The dog was full-on howling in the house.

He could take Cupid with him, but the hassle of trying to put the leash on him was going to be impossible. Cupid would bounce around him for a few minutes then be a general nuisance underfoot, and with Sean's heart beating and that strange energy he felt thick and clumsy.

He would just have to walk to Mack's cabin and see if they could get him to the doc in town or maybe to Corinne Grant's house. Angela had told him all about her healing skills. She would be a bit closer.

Sean considered that a few articles of clothing had a bit of slush and snow still clinging, but he wanted to get help fast, so he just started walking. Mack's place was on the way toward Corinne's house. Maybe he would get lucky and Mack hadn't used this warm day to go to town like everyone else in the valley.

Sean was kicking himself that he hadn't gone inside for a scarf or a hat as the wind picked up. Sean was shaking after a few minutes. His heart was not pounding as hard, but he felt strange and tired. If he really was wishing for anything it was for a nap on his couch in front of the fireplace.

Sean had been in a few rough scrapes in his life, but he had avoided a lot of injuries in his adventures. He had always considered himself pretty steady and agile in most situations. He had hunted for mountain goats on the side of rocky cliffs and climbed over slimy moss-covered river stones, but a silly shingled roof was teaching him a lesson or two.

He held on to his useless arm and kept walking feeling like every step was stealing away at his reserve of energy.

Isaiah 40:31 popped into his mind and as he climbed over the uneven ground and marched around the brown winter bushes he mumbled the verse aloud over and over.

"But they that wait upon the Lord shall renew their strength; they shall mount up with wings as eagles; they shall run, and not be weary; and they shall walk, and not faint."

He was counting on God getting him where he needed to be. He was thankful that the day was a little warmer, even with the wind picking up and having a bite to it, it wasn't snowing. Sean knew that if it had been in a blizzard he would be in trouble.

It took much longer than it should have but he finally arrived on the edge of Mack's yard. He saw the smoke curling up from the chimney and movement inside. He heard Mack's beagle let out a howl, announcing Sean's arrival.

Mack peeked out the front door and let out a hoot of alarm.

"My goodness, Sean, you okay?" Mack yelled out and ran outside without even putting on a coat.

"I fell off the roof." Sean said weakly as Mack got closer.

"Well, bless my biscuits, let's get you inside. You look a fright. Pale as a ghost." Mack said and came up on his good side and put an arm around Sean. He was a warm wind block and Sean felt an undeniable urge to lean into his friend.

Mack gave a shrill whistle that was loud enough to hurt a little in Sean's ear. Darryl peeked out of the barn.

"Get the wagon hooked up, Sean is hurt." Mack said to his son. Darryl nodded and opened the barn doors wide.

"Let's get you warmed up."

Sean heard his feet clomping up the wooden steps in front of the cabin and felt the heat of the warm air inside rush over him and welcomed him better than just about anything else he'd ever felt.

<hr />

Corinne Grant

Corinne patted Lila with her clean hand on the top of her head. She was looking up to Corinne with her sweet hazel eyes.

"You see those shriveled brown tops on the flowers, you can pull those petals off softly and look." Corinne said and pulled one off and showed her that behind the brown petals were small seeds that looked like they could float away with a stiff breeze.

"Those are seeds." Lila said with excitement.

She looked over to her brother, but he seemed less excited. Cooper had been happy for the first few hours of the morning but now he was ready for a new adventure.

Corinne smiled, remembering being in her mother's garden when she was young. Corinne had loved it, even back then, but the wandering interest of children happens often. She would have to find him something more active to do, otherwise she might find him sleeping under a shrub soon.

Corinne showed Lila how she handled the removal of seeds from the flower pods.

"Don't start on a new kind of flower until you put all the seeds from one into the paper envelope. Each flower has an envelope with a name on it." Corinne gave Lila the attention but was already thinking of something for Cooper to do. Marie had sent them both over since there was no class this week, because the teacher was traveling to see a family member. Marie was sewing and the children were getting underfoot. Corinne knew a day in the greenhouse would give her some time to herself. Debbie was watching Sarah, Marie's youngest. Corinne was going to give Debbie the next day off after being such a willing volunteer to help Corinne's stepmother.

"Cooper..." Corinne was going to tell him to see if Lucas needed help chopping wood but there was a noise outside and the creaking of wagon wheels stopped right nearby.

Corinne couldn't tell who it was through the steam and water streaked glass of the greenhouse, but she held up a finger to Cooper. "One moment... I am going to see who is here."

Corinne had Lila and Cooper at her heels as she went quickly to the greenhouse door. It creaked open and she could see that Sean Fahey was in the back.

She responded quickly. A large barrel-chested man that she had seen at church before was there with a younger version of himself helping Sean from the wagon.

Sean was looking pale and Corinne was already preparing for the worst.

"What happened?" Corinne asked as she reached the wagon. All other thoughts were out of her mind and she knew she would need to deal with this emergency. Sean winced a few times as the younger man was helping him from the wagon. She could tell that he was shielding his right arm.

"He fell off the roof." The older man said.

Corinne was trying to remember his name, but it still escaped her.

Corinne turned, saw Cooper and Lila still standing by the door, the look on their faces serious.

"Cooper, could you quickly go fetch Lucas. Then go to the lab and fetch Dolly, please." Corinne gave Lila a look and wondered what she should do with her.

"You can go to the cabin if you like." Corinne tried to give the young girl a smile to calm her, but she turned quickly back to Sean to do her work.

She finally felt the cold and was concerned when she saw the pale look on his face. She needed to get him inside.

"Let's get him to the cabin." Corinne took charge and the two men helped Sean walk up the path. Sean was a little shaky, but his legs seemed to be working fine. Corinne was relieved to see that. He had a wool coat draped around him. The wind was cold and he was without a hat. Corinne was hoping to get him inside and warm very soon.

The cabin was cozy. Debbie and Violet were shuffling the children out of the parlor as Corinne came inside.

She got Sean settled on the couch then got him out of the coat, so she could see what the damage was.

"I was so stupid…" Sean said through gritted teeth. Corinne could tell that he was not enjoying the jostling of the coat removal at all.

"I am sending my boy Darryl back with the wagon. He will get Cupid and make sure the fire is low and your cabin is locked up tight behind." The man said.

Sean nodded calmly. "Thanks Mack." He said quietly.

Corinne was relieved. "Thanks Mack for bringing him." She was glad to have the reminder of the man's name.

Corinne asked Sean to let her see the arm that was bothering him. There was something definitely wrong in the wrist area and the swelling was starting.

"Mack, would you be willing to gather up some snow? We should get the swelling down a bit." She gave the man a look and was glad to see that he nodded and turned to go without pause.

She heard him asking Violet in the next room for a bowl to gather the snow. It was nice to have competent people who could think on their feet.

"How is your shoulder?" Corinne asked.

Sean had a grimace on his face and seemed very uncomfortable.

"It hurts buts not as bad as my wrist." Sean said quietly.

"We are going to get your shirt off, so I can see what we need to do." She said then took a few steps over to Violet's basket by the chair where she kept her sewing and knitting supplies. She grabbed a pair of scissors.

She didn't bother asking but started snipping away at the edge of the shirt, neatly cutting the arm away. She had to work hard at a few sections but got the rest of the shirt off after cutting at a few angles.

His right side had some scrapes and there was a little bruising starting along the ribcage, but she checked his ribs and they all seemed to be fine. He hadn't winced at all when she probed in the scraped areas.

She grabbed a lap blanket and wrapped it around his middle, so he would stay warm. She would focus on his arm and shoulder now.

She picked up a cloth doll from the toys and held it in front of Sean. "How exactly did you fall?"

Sean described it and then took the doll with his left hand and awkwardly showed her the angle he had landed using the doll to show how the event occurred.

"Did you hit your head at all?" Corinne asked. She was beginning to wonder about other injuries.

"No, I am not certain how I avoided that. I think as I was falling I tucked my head in. Most of my weight landed on my wrist." Sean was frowning as he let out a slow breath.

As moments passed Corinne began to gently feel along his shoulder and it didn't take long for her to see that his shoulder was out of socket a little. There was some swelling and Sean hissed a little. He was holding himself in check but also growing pale. Corinne knew she would have to cause a little more pain before he was out of woods.

"This is going to hurt a lot but it will help in the long run." Corinne said and gritted her teeth willing herself to be strong for what would come next.

Sean paled even more but gave her a look that proved that he had been preparing himself.

It took a few minutes of probing and prodding, but Corinne could see where the bone needed to go. She gripped his arm and twisted his wrist a little to get a feel. Sean grunted a little but didn't resist. Corinne let her strength go into the twisting motion and there was a loud snap. Sean let out a muted yell then closed his mouth and it sounded like an angry hum for a second. The wrist was no longer misshaped and Corinne probed again. It felt a bit swollen, but the bone was back where it belonged.

"Now for the shoulder." Corinne said with a frown.

Sean took a few deep breaths and nodded.

"Do what needs to be done."

◆◦◦◆◦◆ ◆◦◦◆◦◆

Sean Fahey

The next hour passed in a blur of pain but Sean was settled in comfortably on the couch as Dolly sat next to him.

"You look like a pale frightful mess." Dolly said as she placed a hand over Sean's cheek.

"You look beautiful." Sean said and smiled weakly.

Sean had a rubber bag full of snow resting over the swollen

wrist. It was almost numb, and Sean was happy that it was back in place.

Doc Williams had been fetched and he deemed Corinne's work to be excellently done.

"Couldn't have done it better myself." He had chuckled and whistled a little in appreciation.

"Well, my mother learned from a local doctor years ago, and I've got her journals. She copied down everything she read in the doctor's books he loaned her." Corinne had admitted.

Sean wondered if Corinne couldn't have been a doctor if the schools would have allowed her to. It really gave him pause to think about the strength of women. His painful fog was lifting as the minutes passed by and he was being fussed over by Dolly.

He watched her as she tucked a blanket around his feet, feeling rather spoiled, despite the pain that radiated in his shoulder. His wrist was fairing far better with the cold.

Dolly was so beautiful, Sean mused. Not just in the dark honey skin, but also in the way she moved and the quiet wisdom she had about her. She was caring about others in everything she did. From the game she hunted for families who were in need, to the medicines she made with Corinne in the lab, to the words she spoke when she wanted to encourage.

The last months had shown him so much more about her character and it was all the little things about her that made a pain in his chest. How could he possibly ever be good enough for her?

"You are too good to me, Bluebird." Sean said softly.

"I am not." Dolly said simply and looked to him pointedly. She hadn't said it with any force or indignation. Just a simple statement. Her eyes asked him questions and he so desperately wanted to answer all of them.

"I feel like I am the kind of man that doesn't deserve to be happy sometimes." Sean admitted, wondering why her gaze always made him have this need within to be painfully honest.

"We all are sinners." Dolly said and kneeled next to his place on the floor. She was only a foot away from him and her presence was comforting. She took the ice away from his wrist.

"Does not the Bible say that we are all sinners?" Dolly asked. Sean nodded slowly.

"And does the Bible also say that we are forgiven through Jesus Christ?" She finally had the hint of some kind of humor as she lifted a brow.

"It does." Sean sighed. She made things sound so simple.

"Then you are feeling things that are contrary to a promise that God made." Dolly placed a hand on his arm gently, so as not to hurt him further.

Sean nodded. "I wondered if perhaps someday you will realize that I am not a good man. That will see all of my flaws."

Dolly pressed her lips together in thought. She was looking at him and her eyebrows lowered in concentration.

"I am not a normal woman. I do not cook much, nor do I have a great desire for dome…" She pressed a finger to her lips. "Domestical… Domestic. I do not do domestic work much, though I keep things tidy as much as I can." She was pleased to have found the word. "I am what some have called a half-breed."

Sean shook his head and grimaced with that statement. Dolly held up a hand for him to let her finish. "I can worry sometime, that you will someday see me as not a good woman, because I do not bake the way that Violet does, or that I do not wish to stay all day in the home the way other women do once they are wed." Dolly looked down, she had tears in her eyes. "I think of these things."

Sean was stunned to hear her confession.

"I know those things about you, I knew before I courted you." He said to ease her worries. "I am afraid that you do not know all about me, that I have run away from problems, and I was hurtful to my sister on more than one occasion."

"I knew of your sister and the struggles you both had." Dolly said and didn't look away from him.

"I abandoned her at the orphanage in Boston." Sean said the worst thing, it was hard to say but he had to say it. She had to know the worst thing he had done. It wouldn't be fair of him to hide it.

"I abandoned my tribe." Dolly said with a pained look.

There was a long moment of quiet. Sean was lost in her words and his. He had felt so much guilt and shame for his actions as a boy, to leave Angela at the work orphanage. When he couldn't rescue her it was easier to forget it. To run far away and escape had been his only recourse. Now, he was working through all of that pain.

"You had your reasons." Sean finally said. He hated the look that Dolly had. He didn't want her to carry that weight.

"So did you," Dolly said. She seemed to be thinking and Sean wanted to let her have the time to consider her thoughts. Perhaps now she was considering his flaws, the ones he knew would surface someday and cause pain to everyone he loved. Dolly would not want to continue on with their courtship and that is what he deserved.

"Do you mind Sean, that I do not always speak well?" Dolly asked.

"Of course not, and you speak very well!" Sean said emphatically. He was speaking quietly, trying to keep their space alone in the parlor and their conversation as private as possible, but he said it with conviction.

Dolly shook her head. "Do you mind the color of my skin?"

Sean shook his head vehemently, though it caused his shoulder to ache. "I find your skin to be beautiful, a gift from God." His lips lifted in a grin when her cheeks brightened.

"We all have shortcomings Sean, I am beginning to know you, the strengths, and the weaknesses just as you are getting to know mine." Dolly surprised Sean when she leaned up and kissed him softly. "I accept you as you are."

It was Sean's turn to have a few tears in his eyes. He knew in that instant that he was in love with Dolly Bluebird Bouchard.

Chapter 22

Clive Quackenbush

"There is nothing better for it." Clive said and cracked a wry smile. "Violet's fresh sourdough bread has to be the best thing on earth besides the smile of my bride." He cackled a little and set the bread on Sean's countertop.

Sean gave Clive a raised eyebrow. "You are in chipper spirits."

"Oh, I am choosing today to be thankful for a few things." Clive was looking through a few of Sean's cupboards. He found the bowl of butter and then the knife he was going to use to slice off a piece of bread for the invalid.

"Oh, please, give me a few items from your list." Sean said as he was twisting to find a comfortable way to sit.

"Well, first off, I am glad I didn't go throwing myself of a roof yestermorn," he chuckled. Cupid was curious about the bread and stood below Clive expectantly.

Sean was smiling. "He begs, just tell him no."

Clive tsked and let Cupid pout in the way of dogs, lowering his ears. The dog yawned strangely, like the idea of not getting bread was something exhausting.

Clive plated up the piece of bread and slathered a heap of butter on it, the butter melted instantly and soaked in. He made another for himself, because he just couldn't pass it up.

There were a few knocks overhead and Clive looked up as he was carrying the plates from the small kitchen to the parlor.

Sean smiled and shook his head. "I hired Warren Martin to fix the roof. Since I have no way of fixing it now."

Clive gave Sean a plate and sat in the chair next to him. "Warren's a good lad, he will get it fixed up proper."

Sean nodded, then took a bite, then closed his eyes. He made a few appreciative noises as he chewed.

"I know… that woman can bake some bread." Clive took a bite for himself.

Clive sat and enjoyed his bread and let Sean do the same. It was a long minute and Sean began to speak.

"Dolly was talking about Violet yesterday." Sean said. He set the plate on the little table beside him awkwardly with his left hand.

Clive raised up and eyebrow. "Oh?"

"Yes, she was responding to some issue I have about my past, by telling me that she may never bake as well as Violet." Sean was frowning.

"There are few in this world who do." Clive said, he was thinking about the comparisons that humans are always doing to themselves, wondering if there would ever be a day when that habit would just fade away.

"She…well I am struggling, and I think she was trying to make me feel better. She did in a way." Sean shook his head in frustration. "I am not expressing myself well today."

Clive gathered up the plates and set them on the counter and was giving Sean some room to gather his thoughts.

"You ready to try again." Clive asked and sat down with a little huff of air.

Sean nodded.

"I am in love with Dolly." Sean stated. Clive smirked.

"I know that." Clive had known that for a while but sometimes it was a big surprise to the parties involved.

"She is determined and has said that she has accepted me for who I am." Sean said.

"She is a good woman." Clive answered back.

Sean nodded. "I am not a good man."

Clive took a slow breath and let Sean's statement sink in.

Lord, please give me the right words. Clive prayed silently.

"Well, now, that is a bold statement." Clive said after a few moments.

"It is true. I have some dark flaws and I feel like I will hurt her in the long term if we continue with our relationship." Sean said, Clive could tell that he meant it. "I don't want the guilt of hurting someone else on my conscience."

Clive shook his head from side to side a few times. "If only we could live our lives out and never, ever hurt anyone." Clive scratched at his chin. "I've been married a few times, and never once intended to hurt a woman I wed."

Sean was shifting around again. Clive was ready to talk again once Sean sat back and looked more comfortable.

"One time, after a hard day, I got a little too free with my humorous banter and teased my first wife on the wrong day. I

273

watched her cry for two hours straight." Clive shook his head at the memory, the helpless feeling he had watching and listening to her sob. "We always were teasing each other, and I just got carried away. I cannot remember the words exactly, but my timing was off and she was hurt. That wasn't a serious one, but a common man mistake, I'm thinking." Clive could see that Sean was listening, so he kept going.

"I have been cross with my kids a time or two and overreacted. I have yelled upon occasion when I got frustrated or just stinkin' mad when in a heated argument with a son." Clive frowned a bit and was feeling a little uncomfortable in his own seat now, facing some of his own flaws. "I spent a few Sunday mornings squirming in my pew, feeling like I let God down so much that the weight was crushing me." Clive could see that Sean was feeling that weight. Sean was nodding.

"I want to go deep with you Sean, because that is where I think we need to go." Clive said. He glanced around and found Sean's Bible nearby on the table.

He thumbed through to Ephesians, chapter six, found verse eleven with his finger. He started reading and kept going until verse eighteen.

"Put on the whole armour of God, that ye may be able to stand against the wiles of the devil. For we wrestle not against flesh and blood, but against principalities, against powers, against the rulers of the darkness of this world, against spiritual wickedness in high places. Wherefore take unto you the whole armour of God, that ye may be able to withstand in the evil day, and having done all, to stand.
Stand therefore, having your loins girt about with truth, and having on the breastplate of righteousness; And your feet shod with the preparation of the gospel of peace; Above all, taking the shield of faith, wherewith ye shall be able to quench all the fiery darts of the wicked. And take the helmet of salvation, and the sword of the Spirit, which is the word of God: Praying always with all prayer and supplication in the Spirit, and watching thereunto with all perseverance and supplication for all saints." Clive looked up from the Bible and chose his words carefully.

"You Sean, are in a battle. You have decided that your sin is greater than anyone else's and that you cannot be redeemed." Clive said flatly.

Sean took his left hand and rubbed it over his chin. "That sounds fair." Sean looked rather miserable to Clive and it made him try a bit harder.

"I think in our walk as a Christian we get caught up in the pretty parts of the Bible. These parts are the ones that lift us up and give us strength when the times get tough. But something that rarely ever gets talked about is evil." Clive pointed to a line and read it again.

"Put on the armor of God, that you may be able to stand against the wiles of the devil." Clive said again, simplifying the words for himself.

"I don't know much about that." Sean admitted.

"I think it is a topic that people feel troubled talkin' about. In 1st Peter it says… *"Be sober, be vigilant; because your adversary the devil, as a roaring lion, walketh about, seeking whom he may devour:"* Clive shook his head. "Now, I am no Bible scholar, but that verse seems pretty straightforward. If the word says it, then I need to watch out for it."

Sean seemed thoughtful, still frowning. "I don't know about thinking that the devil is walking around. Bears, and wildcats, yes. But I have always thought that people use the devil to make excuses. Some calling whiskey the 'devil's brew'." Sean was shaking his head.

"Well, it says that Jesus was tempted by the devil. There is some interesting stuff in Job about the devil. I don't know if I say that I fully understand it. But I do know that sometimes I feel like my thoughts are not my own. Like I have some dark creature whispering in my ear, especially my failures." Clive admitted.

"Well, if I think on it real hard, I do know that I believe in angels. Though, I never saw one. I can think of them and just know that I don't know everything that God is up to." Sean said and sighed. "It is just hard to completely comprehend 'the wiles of the devil' when it seems a bit fantastical."

Clive smiled and nodded. "Sometimes when I read the Bible I can do a bit of head scratchin'. Some of the Old Testament is pretty fantastical. Walls falling down over trumpet blasts, and the seas parting, and God speaking from a burning bush." He chuckled. "What I do know is that, over time, as I sought out the Lord, I felt like I could hear from God when I listen hard enough. That is real enough for me. If the Lord can speak to me in the quiet way that He does, then my guess is that the devil will try his hand at it too."

Sean was nodding. He sat up a little and winced, then shifted around.

"You are looking uncomfortable." Clive frowned a bit in commiseration.

"I got some bruises that are pestering me, that and the topic." Sean lifted one side of his mouth in a lopsided smile.

"I don't have to talk on it anymore…" Clive said and closed the Bible in his lap. He wasn't sure that Sean was ready for the deep discussion, especially feeling poorly.

"No, I need to hear it. I am perhaps just feeling a bit pitiful. I know that God has helped me make some big changes this past year. I know what you are saying, about hearing from God sometimes. It is hard to describe, but I know when it is God somehow." Sean took a deep breath and he seemed a bit lighter.

"Now, just knowing that God is there for you, that proves to you that God's presence is here with you all the time. Now, we just gotta figure out how you can deal with your mistakes." Clive said. He folded his hands together.

Sean perked up. Clive was glad to see it. Sean may be ready. His eyes were seeking out the answers.

"Now, I shared earlier about the armor of God. When I imagine this I see myself, the old coot, tinkering around trying to put on my armor. Looking rather silly and trying to be a knight but I think it is important. All these pieces of armor are important in their own way. The breastplate of righteousness, well that one perplexed me for a long time. Since that word was a bit of a boggle for me. But, once I was talking with Pastor Whittlan's wife at a supper and the topic came up. She said that righteousness to her was a gift from God, so it couldn't be earned. If we are saved from our sins, and forgiven as a gift, then we are in the book of life. That made me think about the great families in Europe, the royal families. When you are important over there your name gets to be in the genealogies. Every name is written in these long lists and if you are from the right families then your name is there as part of the royal family. Now, there is a lot of mention about crowns and kingdoms in the Bible, and maybe he was trying to tell us somehow, that once we are saved, we get on the list. Even if I am a sinner and a cantankerous old coot who loves to get lost in the words, I am on the good list in heaven. I am a righteous man, and the only thing required was to accept that I need Jesus."

Sean looked down. His shoulders dropped a bit and Clive could feel the tension leave the room.

Clive took the Bible and stood up then walked over to Sean.

"Sean, do you believe that you are saved?" He placed a hand on Sean's head, like he would a son.

"Yes." Sean's voice was thick with emotion.

"Do you believe that you are forgiven?" Clive asked.

"Yes, I do." Sean said.

"Then you are a righteous son of God. You were bought at a price, and precious in the sight of the Lord." Clive said with conviction and felt a bit of his own emotion remembering some of the times in his own life that he had to be reminded of these truths. It was crippling to feel the weight of sin and Clive knew what had to be done.

"Lord, I ask that you help Sean to put on his armor today. Please show him how to have faith in your truth and promises Lord. Help us both to resist the wiles of the devil. Help us lift up that shield of faith so that when the arrows of doubt and shame come flying at us that they will not take hold of us. Thank you, Lord for saving us from our own mistakes. Thank you for the gift of your Grace and the mercy that you give us fresh each morning. I ask all of these things in the sweet name of Jesus Christ. Amen"

Clive felt a few tears on his own cheeks as he leaned down to comfort Sean in his broken moment with God.

Chapter 23

Galina Varushkin

The wind rattled the windows as the dark clouds rolled in. Angela fussed with Duchess, the cat, who wanted to go outside and then immediately wanted back in again.

Galina was pacing at the windows. The snow which had been coming down slow before, was now coming down at a faster rate.

"I don't know if Milton is going to be able to come tonight." Angela said as she drew up behind Galina. Angela placed a hand on Galina's shoulder in support.

Galina felt that inner annoyance, knowing that situations were always happening to ruin her plans. There was nothing she could do to stop the weather, but she really wanted to see Milton again. She had had a frustrating and boring day of work, and she had done everything she had to do to get ready for his visit, only to be thwarted by the weather.

"This always happens to me." Galina said quietly and flipped her hands up in frustration.

"Everyone else gets to have someone that cares about them, but not me." Galina leaned closer to the window. Her stomach was tied up in knots and she was getting angrier as she watched out the window. The snow was beginning to come down in a slanted angry hurry.

Warren and Ted were at the back door and Galina turned in anger to see them. They were not who she wanted to see.

Warren was there stomping his boots off carrying an arm full of firewood. He was still the same Warren, hardworking and dependable.

Galina huffed out an angry breath.

Why is it when she wanted to see Warren he was nowhere in sight? Now that she didn't want to see him, he was everywhere, all the time.

Every time she went out to feed the chickens, or go for milk, or go outside on the porch for any reason, there he was. It was infuriating.

Angela laid a hand upon her shoulder again.

"You have time Galina." Angela's voice was all sweetness and understanding. In most situations it would have calmed her, but lately all of Milton's words had been making her think.

Perhaps they *were* trying to keep them apart.

There was always a look that went between Ted and Angela lately when Milton was around.

It had happened at Sunday service. Milton had reached for her hand and there was the look between them.

Galina turned to Angela, feeling a little defensive.

"So, when you and Ted were courting you didn't get frustrated about your plans being canceled?" Galina said with a little more edge to her voice then she intended.

Angela, who normally was all peaches and cream took a slightly bold edge to her look.

"When Ted and I were courting, Ted went overland from California to New York for a year to go get his family. Then they traveled by boat back to California. That was quite a wait I had to do. More than just a snow storm." Angela said and pressed her lips together.

Galina could tell that Angela was a bit annoyed.

"Well, I am just saying, that I should be allowed to be annoyed to have my plans affected by the weather." Galina sighed, the look on Angela's face wasn't calming at all.

"I don't think you are very levelheaded when it comes to Milton." Angela said finally. "I think you both are moving far too fast and you are so young."

Angela was wringing her hands. She looked around the room nervously. "I am not saying that Milton is not the right man but I think you both should slow down. Folks in town came to us worried, after seeing you kissing in the street." Angela said, her voice was tense.

Galina's cheeks flushed in some unknown emotion. She wasn't sure if she was embarrassed or something else.

"I think those people should mind their own business." Galina said, her voice was raised. "Millie Quackenbush needs to pay attention to her own problems and stop worrying about me."

"It wasn't Millie Quackenbush…" Angela tried to add but Galina gave her a glare that interrupted as well as any words could have.

Ted was in the back room and peeked his head around.

"Everything alright in here?" Ted asked, his eyebrows up and he was looking straight at Angela. Galina, for a moment, had an inkling that she needed to slow her anger if she wanted to keep her job. Angela and Ted were friends, but how much of her attitude could she toss around before they, like her father, kicked her out.

Angela gave him a dismissive wave. Ted watched for another moment and then went back outside with Warren.

"I don't think you fully grasp how many people care about you Galina." Angela said. She had this exaggerated patience in her voice that grated on Galina's nerves.

"You care so very much. You care about what people think of me more than anything else." Galina huffed, she marched back to the window, turning her back on Angela.

"That is a bold statement Galina. I do care what people say about you, but not for the reasons you think. I was just the servant girl for a long time. People didn't think much of me. I want to make certain that you are happy and have a great life." Angela was trying to stay calm. Galina could hear it in Angela's voice. She was trying to keep Galina from overreacting again.

Galina felt like a fool, but she seriously just wanted to have her say.

"I think you and Ted don't want Milton and I to continue together. I have already heard from Corinne, who had slanderous things to say about Milton." Galina turned around again and gave Angela a pointed look. "I think you asked Corinne to do that, to drive a wedge between Milton and me. You are worried that If I leave before the baby comes then you won't have the servant you need to keep the work going." Galina felt the air leave the room after the statement.

Angela's green eyes were open wide, and they were not angry or frustrated, they were deep and sad.

"I cannot even form the words to reply to that Galina." Angela shook her head slowly.

It was a painfully long minute of silence in the house. The sound of the wind whistling through the trees was ominous.

Galina turned her gaze away from Angela and watched the flame flicker in an oil lamp.

Duchess meowed nearby, searching for some attention.

Galina looked back to Angela who seemed a bit unreadable. A tendril of Angela's red hair had loosened away from the braid pulled up and pinned. It hung over Angela's pink cheek. There were misty tears lingering in Angela's eyes. From anger or sadness, it was hard for Galina to tell, but she wasn't going to speak first.

No! Galina thought. *I will not speak first. Everyone does not get to try and ruin my relationship with Milton and then I have to apologize. I cannot always be wrong.*

Galina was wishing that dinner wasn't ready and resting on the countertop. She was desperate for something, anything, that would bring about some noise or distraction in this long and threatening silence that lingered in the room.

Galina didn't move, instead fidgeting with her fingers and wanting to go back to pacing. The agony of the moment lingered on and just when she thought her mind would burst there were footsteps on the front porch.

Galina turned and focused her eyes on the person getting ready to knock.

"It's Milton." She clasped her hands together and bolted for the door.

It was a strange meal at the house, just the four of them eating quietly. Angela was more quiet than usual, and Galina felt like the whole interlude between them had been a waste of time, especially since it was nonsense. Milton hadn't let the weather slow him down.

Angela didn't volunteer to do the clean up this time, so Milton helped her by drying the dishes. They talked quietly while Galina washed the dishes. She was feeling awkward now with Angela and Ted in the parlor.

The house was far too quiet tonight and she felt that inner tension building up again.

The last dish was put away and Galina looked around at the few things to put away.

"I need to carry these things to the pantry. I'll just be a minute or two." Galina told Milton.

"No need, I will help you." Milton offered with his sly smile.

Galina huffed a little and picked up the pantry goods and pointed to a few things for Milton to carry.

Milton was slick, and as soon as Galina was through the pantry door he scooted in behind her and shut the door until just a sliver of light was showing through.

Galina stood there, her hands full of items and Milton was kissing her silly. She pulled away after a minute.

"You fool, you are going to get me into trouble." Galina said with a gasp. He was so good at making her lose her wits.

"I just wanted to make you smile." He said softly.

"Open the door a bit more, so I can see to put these things away." Galina pursed her lips together, knowing he could see her in the dim light of the doorway. He obliged her wishes and cracked the pantry door open an inch more. There was enough light to see finally and she put her items away, then snatched at the items in Milton's hands causing him to laugh.

"You are a fiery woman. I like that about you." He smiled again.

"I am going to be a fired woman soon at this rate." Galina said in a whisper.

"What happened?" Milton looked so concerned and thoughtful that Galina couldn't help but tell him.

"Angela feels like we are moving too fast. We quarreled right before you arrived." Galina said. She needed someone to talk to about this, and Milton was such a good listener that she couldn't help herself.

"Well, they are a different kind of couple than us. They had a long courtship and had other circumstances that kept them apart. I don't believe that they truly know how much we care for each other." Milton kissed her on the tip of her nose.

He always knew just what to say. Galina told him more, standing in the dark of the pantry. It all quickly spilled over and every worry and concern just tumbled out.

Milton consoled her fears and soothed away her anxiety.

"You do not need anyone but me. Soon, I will show you a better life. Don't you fret anymore." Milton promised.

The night was cut short when Angela and Ted grew tired after Milton and Galina had retreated from their hiding place in the pantry.

"I had better start heading back home before the snow gets deeper." Milton said and kissed her hand at the door once he was bundled up.

Galina knew it wasn't wise to follow him outside in this kind of weather and she reluctantly watched him leave. He promised to see her on Christmas day and gave her a wink before he closed the door behind him.

Chapter 24

Galina Varushkin

The snow lay softly on the ground and Galina could see the sun peeking over the mountains to the east, splashing the bright white light over the Valley. The snow sparkled, and she smiled seeing the roll of the hills from the window. A few horses at the ranch next door were running through the snow, picking their knees up triumphantly showing off a bit. It looked to be a mild day to start the holiday.

Galina could hear Angela and Ted shuffling around in their room and knew that they would soon be up. Galina checked the stove that she had just started a fire in a few minutes before and the stovetop was hot and ready for the pot of coffee, and a teakettle. Angela was drinking her herbal tea every morning now instead of coffee since it upset her tummy since her pregnancy started.

Galina got busy preparing a few different items for breakfast, slicing bread for toast and getting some water on to boil for oatmeal.

There were two chickens and a duck, plucked and prepared for the lunch with guests. There was going to be a feast today, so many good things served, with the help of Edith and others throughout the day.

Corinne had brought by some fresh herbs from the greenhouse a few days before and Galina had felt awkward and stilted when talking with her. Corinne had been polite and Galina had fought off the inner nudge to make peace with her. She was still so angry that everyone was collectively trying to gently convince her that perhaps Milton wasn't a good man. It just wasn't fair that they all got to be happy and that she was not. For now, Galina just kept quiet and kept her opinions to herself. If anyone else said a word she would say nothing.

"Happy Christmas Galina." Ted said as he came through the bedroom door. Galina handed him a pitcher of warm water and he took it back to the bedroom, so they could wash up. Galina smiled at his happy greeting and kept busy.

Ted came back out a minute later with Angela walking slowly behind. She was using her cane and her limp was noticeable again. Galina gave her a look of concern.

"Oh, I just slept on my side and flopped around quite a bit last night. The little person was kicking all night. Once I stretch out a bit it should be fine." Angela said with a tired smile. She came over to Galina and reached for an embrace with one arm. "Happy Christmas friend." Galina accepted the hug and felt the love there no matter what had been happening over the last weeks.

Ted stoked the fire in the parlor and got busy setting the table, so it wouldn't have to be done later. They all ate a hasty breakfast a few minutes later at the countertop. Angela pushed aside all protests when she offered to wash up the few dishes.

"Oh, stop your fussing, I am fine." Angela gave Ted a playful shove when he was trying to nudge her away from the bin of warm soapy water that Galina had prepared.

Heidi showed up while Angela was putting the dishes away. She had a few ribbons and hairpins and wanted Galina to do her hair if she had free time.

The next few minutes was all about hair as Galina did Heidi and Angela's hair for the day, then Heidi and Angela fussed over Galina's thick hair.

Edith and Henry arrived with Fiona and Peter in tow and the house got more boisterous as presents were placed under the tree. Fiona and Peter found Duchess still sleeping lazily in the bedroom and successfully chased the cat under the dining room table to hide. Edith was setting her baked goods out and the countertop was beginning to show the signs of a festive day.

People were going to be in and out all day. Galina and Angela set out the baked goods that they had been working on for the last few days. There were fresh coffee cups passed around while they waited for more guests to arrive.

"The weather is almost balmy compared to the gusty winds of the last week. I think some of the snow will be melted by this evening if the sunshine holds." Henry Sparks said jovially. Everyone was enjoying the warmer weather and the bright sunshine was putting the household in good spirits. There would be a full house.

Ted gathered everyone around.

"I wanted to say a prayer before we start the day."

Everyone reached out and held hands as Ted led the prayer.

285

"Lord, I ask for your blessing over our house today Lord. As we gather on this day we think of your promises that you sent to us through the birth of your son, Jesus. We thank you for everything that you have done to save us. As we come together Lord I ask that you give us a fresh knowledge of your goodness and mercy. Forgive us Lord of the mistakes we have made and show us Lord how to live lives that give you glory and honor. I pray a special blessing over every person that enters this home today Lord. Let us speak of your goodness today as we celebrate together. Bless our children, every man and woman. In Jesus' name I pray."

Galina said amen with everyone.

The warm spiced cider was passed around and Fiona and Peter wanted to sing the song they had been practicing at school in the weeks before. Being twins, they sang together beautifully.

Their sweet voices were so very pure, and Galina was grinning through the whole performance.

Fiona, who would usually hid behind Mama Spark's skirts was showing signs of growing out of her shyness.

"We are going to sing Hark, the Herald Angels Sing, by Charles Wesley."

Galina chuckled, glad that the school teacher was teaching Fiona so well.

> *Hark! the herald angels sing*
> *Glory to the newborn King;*
> *Peace on earth and mercy mild,*
> *God and sinners reconciled:*
> *Joyful all ye nations rise,*
> *Join the triumph of the skies,*
> *With the angelic host proclaim,*
> *Christ is born in Bethlehem:*
> *Hark! the herald angels sing*
> *Glory to the newborn King.*

The adults joined in on the last line.

There was a round of clapping and cheering for the children and they were adorably embarrassed over all the attention. Peter got his hair rustled about a few times by the men and Fiona gave a few curtsy's.

It was beginning to feel like a festive day. Conversation was flowing.

Galina was telling Fiona how pretty she looked when she overheard Ted opening the front door.

"Welcome Milton. Happy Christmas." Ted said.

Galina's heartbeat picked up happily and she gave Fiona a pat on the cheek then swiftly made her way over to welcome Milton in.

He was dressed in a new dark blue suit and looked smart with a black bowler hat tipped on his head. Galina took his hat and coat and took them to the bedroom quickly to get them out of the way. Milton was waiting by the door for her, making certain his shoes were wiped clean on the rug.

"You are looking fine today." Milton said and took her hand and kissed it gallantly like in one of the novels she enjoyed, with English gentlemen, and fair ladies.

"You look dashing in your suit." Galina said and hoped that he knew how much she appreciated him coming. Even after knowing that Angela and Ted weren't perhaps that thrilled with him. Galina had a few regrets that had been swimming through her mind about sharing a little too much with Milton. She didn't want to make him despise her friends.

The children were clamoring for presents and Ted announced that they could get started.

"My mother and sister will probably be a bit longer, so we can let the children be entertained while we wait." Ted picked up Peter and hauled him up, causing a riot of hooting laughter.

Every extra chair in the house had been set up in the parlor and the stockings were brought down from the chimney.

Once the children each had a toy from their stocking Ted went through and handed each woman a little box, including Galina. They all opened them together and every woman each got a silver chain with a small silver cross. The gushing and cooing over the gifts began. Milton helped Galina on with hers. Galina ran her fingers over the smooth cool metal of the cross as she watched every other female in turn put on their own.

"We are all sisters in Christ. What a special gift Thaddeus." Edith said with a warm smile and her eyes glistening.

Everyone agreed. Angela was not the only one to kiss Ted on the cheek. Ted was blushing a bit and laughing after the fuss was made over his gift.

"Well, gosh Ted, how is a man supposed to top that kind of

gift?" Henry gave Ted a good natured teasing elbow to the ribs before he shook his hand.

"Well, perhaps it is a challenge." Ted laughed a bit.

There were more gifts handed out and the children were thrilled. Fiona had a new dress for her favorite doll, and bright ribbons to tie in her hair. She also got a new knitted sweater with pearlescent shell buttons from Angela. The soft cream color was so pretty against her pale blond hair. Fiona primped and twirled to show it off for everyone.

In the midst of the presents there was a knock at the door and Ted went to open it. Sean and Dolly had arrived.

Dolly was carrying a platter of bread pudding and Galina rushed to the door to help her by taking the platter, so she could remove her coat.

Galina noticed that Dolly was wearing a new dress coat, a dark burgundy wool.

"Your coat is beautiful." Galina said enthusiastically.

Dolly smiled prettily, Galina noticed that she had such a beautiful broad smile. Lately she had been smiling quite a bit. She must be happy in her new courtship with Sean, and Galina was happy for her. Though she wondered if perhaps Dolly was a bit shier with Sean than Galina was with Milton.

"Sean and Chelsea picked it out for me. I do find it lovely." Dolly said.

Galina agreed that is was very attractive and unique. She swiftly put the bread pudding on the countertop that was ready for all the good food.

"Come over to the parlor, we have gifts for you." Ted invited with a scooping wave.

Sean and Dolly were greeted heartily. Sean was dressed in dark slacks and a white collared shirt with his splinted arm looking bulky and uncomfortable. But Galina thought that Milton looked more polished and refined. According to gossip Sean was a wealthy man after receiving an inheritance. But he didn't dress the part. Galina had been to his cabin a few times with Angela. His home was far simpler than it needed to be. She wondered if Sean just wasn't the flashy kind of man that her Milton was. Ted and Angela were wealthy, the house was one of the nicest in the Valley, but they lived frugally in many ways.

Galina pushed aside her thoughts on material things and sat beside Milton while more folks opened presents. Galina felt

Milton's hand on her shoulder and her skirts were spread around her. She felt like they would have made a handsome portrait sitting next to the fireplace together.

Dolly had a present for Galina. She was thrilled to find two new books inside. Grimm's Fairy Tales and Jane Austen's Persuasion.

"Since you write children's stories I thought the fairy tales would inspire new stories for you." Dolly said, her face showing that she hoped the Galina would like the gift.

"Oh, I just love this." Galina gave Dolly a kiss on the cheek and then found her present for Dolly. She had Sophia make her a special lace collar, with embroidered bluebirds along the edges.

Dolly was so very pleased. Galina could see that her eyes were misted as she thanked Galina. Dolly was not one to show emotions very often, so it meant a lot to know that she was touched by the gift.

Sean handed out presents one handed and everyone was pleased, for he had found some unique gifts.

For Angela, he gave a silk shawl that was exquisite lace. It was a pattern that Galina had seen Sophia practicing once while she was staying with the Quackenbush's. Sean must have ordered the silk special. Ted got a dark gray bowler hat that looked sharp.

"Now, I will need a new suit to match." Ted said as he cocked the hat jauntily on his head.

Sean gave everyone a silver dollar, and the children cheered at having their own money.

Galina was surprised when Sean handed her a thin package. There were fancy writing pens with fancy silver tips.

"For your writing." Sean smiling warmly to her. She felt bad for judging him so much lately and tried to warmly thank him for his thoughtful gift.

Angela had knitted something for everyone, whether it be a scarf or mittens everyone was pleased.

"I am so slow at it; the presents took me half a year to get finished. If everyone keeps having children I will have to start in January to get them all done it time." Angela said while people were thanking her. Everyone laughed with her.

"You did fine work. My knitting is rather a mess. I will stick with my gardening." Edith said before handing out her special jars of blackberry preserves to every household. Her recipe was delicious and all would cherish every bite.

The room was in a jovial mood and many conversations flowed over each other as everyone was talking about their gifts. Milton gave Galina's arm a squeeze and stood and unceremoniously pulled her up.

"I have a gift for Galina." Milton announced. The room hushed to a quieter tone. He stood in front of her and gave her his charming smile while he waited for everyone's attention.

"I believe that Galina is so very precious and talented, and I am just not certain I can spend another day without her by my side." Milton knelt, and Galina heard a gasp or two from women in the room. He pulled out something from his jacket pocket. "Galina, would you please make me the happiest man alive and become my bride?" He held a golden ring with a blue sapphire.

Galina had a rush of thoughts, wondering what everyone would think of such a quick engagement. She could not believe that Milton could be so bold, but then, it was his passion and impulsiveness that had attracted her attention since that first day she had met him, only a few short months ago. Her mind was swirling with her thoughts but somehow in the midst of certain madness she felt herself nodding frantically.

"Yes." She said, surprising herself. Milton let out a hoot and slipped the ring on her shaky hand. He stood and kissed her, respectfully on the cheek. She was thankful that he hadn't kissed her on the lips in front of everyone. Her cheeks were warm as she turned to see if all of her friends were going to show any signs of disappointment. Angela was standing and smiling. She had a hand placed over her belly and she was walking towards Galina. Galina was preparing herself for a lecture, but Angela also kissed her on the cheek.

"Congratulations sweet Galya." Angela said in a soft and sweet tone. Using Galina's nickname had been a special touch and Galina felt her anxiety lift. A round of congratulations was being said to both of the newly engaged when there was another knock on the front door.

Clive, Olivia, Sophia and Amelia were welcomed in.

The house was bursting at the seams and there was no end of presents and declarations of happy tidings as the morning continued.

The babies were truly too small to enjoy the simple pleasure of a holiday, and they needed their afternoon naps the same as always. Debbie and Violet left right before the babies were ready to be put down. Reynaldo took them over to the Greaves' house next door to peek in on the party. Corinne had sent Violet with the letter she had been working on for days for Galina.

> Dearest Galina,
> I don't know if I can say it properly face to face, because sometimes I act a fool. Please forgive me. I don't ever want you to think that I would ever want you to feel unloved or that I didn't believe in you. I am sorry if my words came across as cold and accusing. I just want you to be happy, and I trust you to go to God for His council.
> Please believe me, I never want to be without your friendship.
>
> Sincerely,
> Corinne Grant.

She had made several versions of this letter over the last week, but this simple and short version was the one she had finally sent.

Corinne watched her babies in their cribs for a few minutes and rocked in the rocking chair near their cribs in the upstairs bedroom. These last months had been exhausting but now, in the cozy warmth of the new room she knew that her husband had been right to do this addition.

Thank you, Lord, for my family. Corinne thought in quiet prayer to God. She had felt a burden lifted with sending of the letter to Galina and now in the quiet she was at peace.

Lucas was down in the parlor, probably napping, Corinne thought with a smile and wondered if he would mind if she snoozed a little too.

She didn't think about it for too long because soon she joined the rest of the household in blissful sleep.

Galina Varushkin

A few days had past and Galina felt a growing within her heart as she dreamed of her wedding day. Milton had wanted a quick wedding. He said that his love was too great for prudence. He wanted to be her husband and to lavish care and luxuries on her.

She wasn't sure when the happiness had come upon her so greatly but it was there now. This overwhelming love was like nothing she had ever had before. Not even the affection she had for Warren had come to be this great and passionate feeling.

Milton accepted her, wholly and completely. No one had ever done that before.

Milton knew her from their long talks about her past. He had allowed her to talk and talk, and he listened as no one ever had. Perhaps because she had never trusted a soul so completely, except for maybe Violet. Violet knew from her own experience the shame of abuse and neglect of a parent.

Milton had never looked down upon her or treated her as a child.

"You are a woman, and I worship you!" He had said the night before last. She let his words soothe her over and over as she handled the criticism of her friends.

She was so very angry that so many only had negative things to say about this romance that she had found. Why could they not be happy for her? Why could they not see as Milton did, that she was meant for more than cleaning up after others? If Milton could see that she had value, why then could they not see it?

Perhaps they were all jealous of what she had found.

Perhaps these marriages of her closest friends were not so passionate as her own would be. That had to be it. They saw that she had found something that was beyond what they themselves had.

Galina grasped ahold of her courage and would do what she must until the day she could leave this world behind. She would do her work for the next few weeks and then she would be free. She would become Milton's wife and live the life she had never thought possible. A man to love, that was only for her. A man who saw her as more than a servant, or a worthless girl. But a treasured woman who was beautiful and precious.

She held her arms around herself as she lay in the bedroom above the kitchen at the Greaves' farm and was pleased to dream the night away. Her heart melted over his sweet words and fiery kisses. Certainly, there was no man like her Milton. He was heaven sent.

Chapter 25

Galina Vaughn

"What God has brought together, let no man put asunder." Pastor Whittlan said and Galina felt a rush of happiness. The ceremony was almost over. "I now pronounce you husband and wife. You may now kiss your bride."

Milton kissed her sweetly and placed a hand on her cheek.

"You are mine now." He spoke in a whisper.

Galina nodded and felt so loved.

Milton turned and led her back down the aisle and all of her friends and a few members of her family were there.

All weddings had to be done in the mornings, so they had decided to make it before the church service.

It had made for an early morning, but Galina was grateful now as she stepped forward in Sophia's dress, pale blue with embroidered lace flounces. It swished happily like weddings bells as she walked beside her husband.

It had only been a few weeks since he proposed but Milton wanted to get married as soon as possible.

It had created a few weeks of bustling about, but everything was ready.

Galina smiled to her brothers that sat next to Angela and Ted.

Angela gave her a smile and her cheeks were pink. Galina wondered if the happiness she was showing now was her true feeling. Galina may never know.

Corinne was behind her, with her husband Lucas, and Violet. Everyone was standing and smiling for the newest married couple.

It had been a whirlwind courtship, Galina knew that, but she also felt like she was happier than she had ever been.

Milton was going to give her a wonderful life. She just knew it deep down inside.

There were a few minutes of conversation as everyone made their way to the front of the church and then a few people who hadn't come to the wedding started arriving for the church service.

"You look so very happy." Corinne stepped up to Galina.

Galina reached out to hug Corinne to let her know that she still cared for her.

It was hard to stay angry at friends, especially when Corinne had never meant any harm in her warnings.

The apology letter had been sincere, so Galina was determined to let it go.

"I am happy." Galina finally said when she pulled away from the embrace. It was a needed point of contact and Galina was relieved to finally have that chapter of her life over and done with.

No more doubts and accusations to think about. Now she was a wife!

She had Milton and he had her.

She knew that a good marriage was teamwork and she was determined to make her marriage a good one.

The line of people was a little overwhelming as everyone was trying to congratulate them on their marriage.

Clive and Olivia, Violet, Edith and Henry Sparks. The children wanted hugs and Galina was feeling so loved by the end of it all.

Sophia finally was last, and they embraced for a long time. She was so happy to have Sophia as a friend. Knowing that Sophia would always be honest with her and support her, even when she didn't agree. It mattered a lot and Galina was so very excited that Sophia was only going to live a street away.

Galina looked forward to many visits once the honeymoon was over.

Galina felt a heat in her cheeks pondering the new realities of marriage, but she accepted Sophia's urging to find a seat for the Sunday Service.

Milton was holding her hand through everything. They sang boisterously to the hymns and called out 'amen' together after the prayer.

She thought Pastor Whittlan had done a fine job of praying for them in the journey of their newly married life.

The time passed quickly as the service came to an end. Galina could not have said much about the sermon, because her mind was in a whirl of thoughts on what came next.

"Come along wife." Milton leaned in to whisper as the church pews began to thin out.

It was nice to hear the word and Galina felt a bit giddy.

She was a wife.

She was certain that she would never tire of hearing it.

The weather had been brutal earlier in the week, and the topic had come up more than once that if the weather got worse the wedding would have had to be postponed.

Galina waited and prayed. Finally a few days before the wedding the skies cleared and the pale blue sky of winter shone bright above.

The snow sparkled in the sunshine and Galina knew that their special day would be as planned.

There was nothing to stand in her way now.

Clive Quackenbush was hosting a party at his home for friends and Milton and Galina headed there in Milton's conveyance. The sleigh glided through the snow swiftly and Galina let out a laugh and squeal as Milton let the horses pick up speed.

Olivia and Sophia had arrived first and were setting out the drinks and food that had been baked for days.

Violet had brought over sheets of tarts and cookies. She had begged the grocer for the last of the cider of the fall season.

Clive had decorated the house with pine boughs and little bows of lace made by Amelia for the occasion.

Soon the house was full to the brim.

Clive gathered everyone around and prayed for the couple.

"Lord, I ask your blessing on Milton and Galina. We ask that you always guide them in your perfect wisdom, that you teach them to walk in the path that you have made for them." Clive let out a little cough to clear his throat. "I ask you a special blessing on your sweet daughter Galina Lord, please tell her mother, Magdalena, how much we all love and care for her. Please give this new married couple a wonderful life together, with their eyes always focused on you."

Galina cuddled up close to Milton's shoulder as they rode back to town. The back of the buggy had some leftover cider and a few treats for them to take back to their home.

Galina could not believe that this was her life now. She had her own home with Milton. She felt like her life had been this painful story without a good end in sight. Now here she was, with her very own romantic hero that swooped in and saved her.

The sun would be setting in an hour or so. The mid-winter the days were so very short. Milton had promised that he would have a fire going in their little place above the barbershop.

He had made her big promises, with houses and servants someday. For now, they would share in the simple things of spending every day together from now on.

That was all she wanted, truly.

Chapter 26

Violet Griffen

Violet was listening to Trudie babble nearby at the dining table as she pushed and pulled against the bread dough on the countertop. She had a few bread deliveries to send to town with Warren later in the day. There was a basket of goodies for Amos Drays, the carpenter for barter, and also a few treats for Galina and Milton as a surprise.

Violet had some mixed feelings, seeing them get married a few days before. The wedding had made her have doubts about waiting to marry Reynaldo, but after some prayer and dealing with herself she knew that the timing of her relationship was in God's hands. They had a good plan to marry in the summer.

Reynaldo's new house, well she can almost say it is hers, will be done and they will have all summer together for their honeymoon. She was imagining the long walks through the Valley that they would enjoy together.

She was trusting God with her journey.

By waiting, she was giving Corinne and Lucas the time to find a new cook, since Debbie had taken over much in the way of cleaning duties, a cook was practical for them. She was already praying that the Grant's would find just the right person to welcome into their family.

It was going to be so difficult to leave, probably more than she would like, but she knew in her heart that God was calling her to a new life.

Violet looked up from the bread dough to see Debbie wiping a soft cloth on Caleb's face and he broke into a big smile, with his little baby teeth showing off charmingly. She felt that tug at her heart knowing that she would have to come and visit often once she was married. She would bring bread and visit, to see the friends that she loved so dearly.

God had been so faithful helping her through these last years. The tragic way that her life had started did not have to dictate the rest of her life. She could see a future that was full of love and acceptance now, and not be so afraid of changing.

She set the bread to rise and gave each child a kiss on the top of their head while she chatted with Debbie.

"I have been putting something off for a long while and I feel the need to do it now." Violet shared.

Debbie raised her eyebrows with a question.

"Oh, I just have a letter to write." Violet smiled wistfully. She felt that bittersweet feeling swell within her.

She walked to her room and let herself be caught up in all the feelings that bubbled forth. It was difficult, but she willed herself to do what must be done.

She sat at the small table and pulled out the pen and a fresh piece of paper.

Dearest Mother,

I know you will be settled by the time you receive this letter. I have prayed for you on the long boat journey. I do hope that you were able to travel safely and without harm. I have heard from friends that traveled by boat that sometimes the food aboard such vessels can run low, and I pray that you are well supplied.

I do hope that your new life will be kind to you.

After these few months I hope that you are filled with the Lord's peace and you can let the tragedies of the last few years out of your mind. For me, it has been a long journey but on most days, I can live in the moment, instead of the past.

I know why you felt that you had to leave. The whole situation here was uncomfortable and awkward in many ways. I still sometimes struggle with my own thoughts and fears about what happened. Aware that the whole of Oregon City knows, and can discuss my past, is not easily dismissed. However; I endeavor every day to trust in God's providence. To know in my heart that I am the daughter of a living God, it is a thought that comforts me daily. My father God has never abused or misused me.

My prayer for you is that you find true happiness in the Midwest and that you find joy in the simple things again. I can see you baking bread in a farmhouse kitchen, with cousins, nieces and nephews running about the house.

Tim Jr. and Harold are doing well. They were busy during the harvest season with so many bushels of wheat and corn coming through the mill. There is a joy in knowing that all the work they do will feed so many mouths over the coming winter. The old farmers think this will be a cold winter for Oregon. I hope that we avoid the big storms though. I see all the people I love and wish an easy winter for all of them.

I am in such a good situation with a warm hearth and every need met, yet I know that not everyone has those things. There are still new families arriving and claiming land every year here and in the nearby towns. The cost of food goods is still so very high. I would not be certain that a young family starting out could afford to survive the winter months unless they had a hefty account set up for it.

I think often of Eddie, my husband, when I see the young couples in town. He was a bright moment for me and I remember him fondly. But now, I can see a bit more clearly. I am not certain he would have been able to afford to build up a claim with his wandering mind and carefree ways.

Over the last year a new man has been courting me, Reynaldo Legales, the ranch foreman next door. After a long courtship he has proposed marriage and I have accepted. It has been a struggle for me to trust any man with my heart, but I am now willing to consider love and marriage again. Reynaldo Legales is a good man with a solid faith in God and a hard worker. I no longer have a fear that I will go unmarried for the rest of my life. I am waiting to see what God has in store for me.

I will keep writing to you as time allows. I pray that you will be able to write back and let me know how you are settling in. You are in my prayers.

Sincerely,

Violet Griffen

Violet sighed when she had finished. She waited for a few minutes for the ink to dry and for her heart to settle. *Every letter will get easier,* she thought to herself.

She was going to visit her brothers soon, hoping for a good break in the weather so she could walk from town if she couldn't find a ride there.

Violet felt such a sense of regret in having been denied the relationship with her brothers for all of these past years and would endeavor to make up for it now.

In her mind the idea bloomed to make up a feast and take it, along with Reynaldo, to have a dinner there at the Watermill house. It was time to make some new memories there.

Chapter 27

February 1853

Galina Vaughn

The first two weeks of marriage passed by like a dream. Every day was a new discovery for Galina as Milton pampered her with gifts and his charming attention.

She enjoyed all the of the gifts of food and presents that her friends brought by over the first week. Then the special times spent with Milton.

They had gone to the local carpentry shop and purchased a fine set of chairs to go with the new dining table in their apartment one afternoon. Milton had taken great care, after the first week to take her around and introduce her to all of the shop owners and people in town.

They had afternoon tea with Sophia and her mother Amelia. Milton had paid the seamstress in town to make Galina a few new dresses and he splurged and bought her trinkets and sweets nearly every day.

She was feeling utterly spoiled.

Milton made sure that her kitchen was supplied for the next few weeks and she was given an allowance to go to the grocer for whatever foodstuff they needed.

"I can do some canning over the summer, purchase some fresh goods from farm stands and stock the pantry next year." Galina said one evening while they were sitting in their cozy little parlor. Milton was quick to praise her ideas.

"You are going to be such a fine wife." He said often. "One day soon, though, you will have a big fine house and a cook, and you can focus on raising children and neighborhood activities, like a socialite." He was always giving her glimpses of the future. She could imagine that with Milton's determination there was nothing that he couldn't accomplish.

She was enjoying the domestic chores more than she ever had before. It was a completely different feeling to spend hours preparing dinner and washing up when she was doing it for a husband instead of being hired. Though, she chided herself on thinking too negatively about working for Angela and Ted. She had volunteered for the job, and she had learned a lot from Edith and Angela, as well as Violet. Milton was quick to mention how they treated her, but she wasn't sure that he understood the situation well enough, and Galina did not like talking about her past with him. She was far too happy to go into her old troubles.

Milton had mentioned that a few parcels of land were for sale down the street along the river and that he was gathering funds to build them a fine house in the next year or two.

He talked about his different business ventures and after the first week, where he barely worked at all, he began working more. In the evenings after dinner he usually spent an hour or so writing letters and keeping up with his other business partners in Sacramento and San Francisco. Galina was so impressed by his driven determination to succeed that she didn't mind the time he spent in the small office downstairs behind the store. He always came back upstairs and gave her his full attention.

Galina spent that time cleaning or reading. Someday soon she planned to try to write another story. Milton was promising to take her soon to purchase a writing desk.

She was rather giddy about all the changes in her life and she was so very happy.

She was meant to be a wife. Milton had been right.

<hr />

It was nearly three weeks into their marriage when Milton had an announcement.

"It cannot be helped. I have to go." Milton said and he kissed her a few times to try and ease away the pout that she had.

Galina wasn't sure why, but the thought of him leaving after a few weeks of marriage was just not fair.

"Well, I should go with you." Galina said with a determined frown.

"I am sorry darling but not for this trip, I am hoping to make this as quick a trip as possible. I will visit my other shops and take care of several business orders all at once. I will be staying with a few of my business contacts and it will not be the kind of comfort that you deserve my dear. I will probably have a cot in a corner room in some instances." Milton took her hands and kissed each one. "I will make it up to you my dear girl. Perhaps a fur coat when I come back would make you feel like the lady that you are." Milton smiled charmingly and then pulled her close to him. The scent of his cologne was alluring as he leaned in to nuzzle against her neck. Galina laughed.

"You are impossible, Mr. Vaughn." Galina placed a hand on his head to push him away from tickling her anymore.

He did not dawdle in his decision and packed up his belongings that night.

"I should only be gone a few weeks but in case the weather keeps me away I will give you some extra money for the grocers." Milton said and handed her an envelope of cash.

Galina tried to smile but she was so sad to see him go. The apartment would be so lonely without him.

"You be certain to visit with Sophia often and pass the time pleasantly." Milton kissed the tip of her nose.

Galina nodded obediently.

The next morning he was off early to the ferry. He had kissed her awake before he left in the darkness of the morning hours.

"I love you my dear girl." He had whispered to her.

"And I you." Galina said sleepily.

He left. Galina shed a few soft tears on her pillow before she fell back to sleep.

Corinne Grant

Corinne had planned this visit for days and now that it was upon her she was nervous. Corinne followed Galina up the stairs to the apartment. She had met the barber downstairs and gotten a tour of the store from Galina and was pleased to see her so happy. She was trying so very hard to be supportive of her friend, especially after that unfortunate incident that had caused them to quarrel before Christmas. A little time and apologies had mended the fences a bit but Corinne was determined to keep them mended.

"Oh, your place is charming." Corinne smiled as she saw the layout of the cozy apartment.

"It is small, but we are enjoying the coziness." Galina smiled prettily.

"Well, you look so happy and glowing." Corinne enjoyed seeing Galina in the new environment and gave little compliments on all the choices that Galina had made, from dishes to curtains.

Galina put a kettle on and got out a cup and saucer for each of them to have some tea.

"It feels so odd having such a small pantry. After being at your house and Angela's with your big stocked pantries. I have had a few moments of panic wondering how we will get through the winter, but then I think about the grocers nearby and call myself a ninny." Galina laughed as she poured the tea.

She had fresh sugar cookies and she served those with the tea.

"These are good." Corinne said after taking a bite.

"They are Violet's recipe. She gave me a handwritten cookbook as a wedding present." Galina said warmly.

"Well, you made them better than I would have." Corinne laughed.

Galina nibbled on her cookie and chatted about her plans, to can fruits and vegetables. Corinne agreed with Milton that that was a good idea.

"I am just sad that Milton had to go and take care of business now, so soon after getting married." Galina pouted a bit when they got talking about how much she enjoyed being married.

"Oh, I would feel the same way. I bumped into Olivia Quackenbush the other day, and Clive had to do the same thing. Some business in San Francisco that needed his attention a few weeks ago. He had told her that he would rather go now, than closer to her delivery." Corinne commiserated.

"I guess that is the life of a wife." Galina said and grinned. Corinne nodded.

"We all make our little sacrifices over time but God shows us how to cope." Corinne reached a hand over to Galina to comfort her.

Galina paled for a moment and took a sip of her tea. She put a hand to her chest for a minute and took a deep breath.

"Are you alright?" Corinne said, suddenly concerned.

Galina shook her head for a moment. "Oh my…" She bolted from her chair and ran to the bucket in the back corner.

Corinne did not pause a moment to follow her and it only took a few seconds to realize what was wrong with Galina.

"Galina… You are expecting."

Corinne had walked with Galina down to Doctor William's house when she was done being ill. The doctor said it was early to tell but all indications were that Galina was very likely expecting a child.

"Oh, my goodness." Galina was shocked and overjoyed. It seemed like proof to her that she had made the right decision to marry Milton. God was blessing them with a child. He was going to be so thrilled.

Corinne walked back with Galina to make sure she was settled.

"I will get you some raspberry leaf tea at the apothecary next door." Corinne said and gave her a smile. "It will help the tummy some."

"Be sure to keep this a secret. I want to tell Milton first, before everyone else knows." Galina sat in the chair by the crackling fireplace and fretted, wringing her hands. "He has been gone a week now and it could be a few more weeks before I see him. I have never been good at secrets."

"Oh, the post between here and California is so much quicker now. I read in the paper that Portland to Sacramento mail only takes four to five days now. Do you have an address to send to?" Corinne asked.

Galina smiled at the news of improved postal delivery and nodded happily.

"I will be back shortly. You settle in with your happy news and I will be back shortly." Corinne gave Galina a kiss on the cheek and left down the stairs.

There was a gentleman getting a shave in the barber's chair with a towel piled comically over his face. Corinne nodded to a few other gentlemen that were waiting on the bench for their own turn in the barber's chair. For all of Corinne's earlier doubts about Milton, he did have a fine establishment, and she had every wish for his continued success.

She found what she was looking for at the apothecary shop and chatted amicably with the shop owner. There was something delightful about knowing a secret, Corinne thought on her way back to Galina's little apartment. She was already praying for Galina's future and the health of her child. Corinne thought happily of the child that was also growing inside of her and felt a bonding to know that Galina would share in the joy of motherhood.

Galina had found the box in the small closet that had her new silver-tipped pens and the ink well. She had to go downstairs to Milton's office to fetch the address and some paper to write to him. She sat happily at the dining table and started her letter off to Milton.

Corinne had been so very kind to sit with Galina for a while and give her some good suggestions on what to eat to try and keep her belly happy over the coming weeks.

She was finally ready, and as she pondered her words, she dipped the pen into the ink and gave it a light tap on the edge of the bottle.

Dearest Milton,

I have indeed kept myself busy this past week since you left on business. I have had a few visitors, and sat a few afternoons with Sophia, practicing my needlework while she made lace ribbons and collars. Watching her work is truly inspirational.

I am bursting with good news and I cannot contain it any longer.

I know it has only been a few weeks since our wedding, but I am fairly certain that I am carrying your child. I am overjoyed, and my prayer is that you are as well. I saw Doctor Williams today and he is as certain as he can be at this stage.

I was feeling a little ill this afternoon but I am fine now and was able to eat a healthy dinner.

I cannot help but think that God is blessing our union and knowing that by this time next year we could have a son or a daughter.

God is so very good, and I have been thanking Him all evening.

I do hope your business in California will not keep you away for long. I am thinking of you every moment. I am sending you all my love.

Sincerely,

Galina Vaughn

Galina smiled as she signed her name. It was the only time since her wedding day that she had signed her name as Galina Vaughn. She placed a hand over her belly, flat and undisturbed now. Someday soon she would start changing and growing. There was always a little joy mingled with the fear of change within nearly every woman certainly. It was a strange and wondrous miracle that was growing inside of her. Perhaps her child was no bigger that a speck of dust but it would grow.

She folded the letter when it was dry and addressed it simply, to Mr. Milton Vaughn. She printed out the address very carefully and set it on the table.

"Tomorrow, I will make a trip to the post office." She said to the room. She realized suddenly, that with the child inside of her that she was not alone and she smiled.

She thought of the wise words that Violet had spoken to her once.

'When you know the Lord, you are never alone.' Violet had said. Galina smiled as she amended the thought inside of her.

"The Lord God is with us." She said to the baby within her. She was content.

Chapter 28

March 1, 1853

Amos Drays

He had a spring in his step despite the blast of cold wind. He had just put his payment down for the order of lumber he needed to build his new home.

JQ down at the fancy goods store had helped him plan everything according to the house plans he purchased.

It would be a few months until the spring and he could break ground, but everything was arranged. He had a crew hired to help him, and he felt that stirring of excitement to know that he was moving forward. Even if his plans for the future did not include a wife, he would prepare for it. In the times he had poured his heart out to God he felt that small voice inside that told him to 'get ready.' Sometimes real faith means to step out without having a guarantee.

Amos was ready to move away from the small apartment above his business. His new house would be a blessing, even if he was alone. Though he truly and sincerely hoped that wasn't going to be forever. He was young enough to know that he had time.

Amos stopped at the grocers and bought a few supplies, extra coffee and more potatoes. They promised to deliver them to his apartment later.

He gave a nod to a few men passing by when he stepped into the post office.

"The wind has a bite to it," The Postmaster said with a grin. The man was tall and whip thin with a fanciful black mustache that curled up around his lips in a perpetual smile. Amos always liked the look of him.

"It does, but the sun had peeked through the clouds a bit. Perhaps the chill will lessen as the day progresses." Amos smiled.

"You Amos, are an eternal optimist." The man chuckled.

"You have a few pieces of mail and also a telegram." The man said.

Amos plunked down the money for the telegram and

accepted his pile with a mixture of confusion and excitement.

He resisted the urge to read it in the post office and made a quick walk to his door. He felt some trepidation in his heart about a telegram. There were only two outcomes for a telegram, good news or very bad news.

He plunked up the steps, his heartbeat felt louder in his chest than the sound of his boots on the hardwood steps.

He opened the door and took the few steps to his table and could wait no longer. He set the rest of the mail on the table and found the telegram. With a prayer under his breath, asking for good news, he opened the telegram.

5 or more women. Leaving in spring. Wallace Drays

<hr />

Galina Vaughn

The worry and waiting had been easier the first few weeks after Milton had left. She kept herself busy, the little secret within her was the joy that kept her going through the long days.

The evenings were so very quiet.

She had expected to see Milton a few days before but she hadn't heard from him. The weather had been windy, and the snow drifted along the edges of the boardwalk after a few snowfalls. Galina was certain that the ferry would come any time.

She had dutifully followed the instructions that Milton had left. Every day and deposited the funds at 4:50 p.m. in the afternoon at the bank from the register.

The barber had been paid for the time that Milton would be gone ahead of time, so she had no need to spend any of the money. She still had money in the allowance that she had received.

The raspberry leaf tea was soothing on her belly when the early afternoon sickness came every day. She had felt some nauseous and had to visit the waste bucket a few times but she was learning to manage.

The ferry whistle had blown in the early morning and Galina was anxiously listening for the sound of Milton's footsteps up the stairs.

At 4:20 she gave up on waiting for Milton and prepared to handle the bank payment.

She brushed her hair and got dressed in a warm wool suit and heavy skirts.

She emptied the register with her key and gave a barber a wave and a smile as he left for the day.

She walked through the dreary town. The sky was dark and threatening to storm again. She passed by the post office and on a whim went inside to see if she had mail.

She was so very pleased when she had a package and a letter.

She thanked the postmaster and hurried home.

She decided to open the package first.

She ripped open the brown parchment paper and saw inside was two spools of pale yellow yarn and a few knitting needles.

A note was on top, folded neatly.

My dearest wife,

I adore you with my every breath. I am also overjoyed at the blessing.

I may be a few more weeks, but I hope to have this business settled soon. Until then, you can practice knitting booties.

I promise to shower you with kisses when I return.

Milton Vaughn

Galina smiled and felt the fine texture of the wool in her fingers. Her knitting was still a bit elementary, but she would indeed practice while she waited for him to return. She knew she would keep the note for always. She loved him so very dearly.

She sighed and set the wool on the table and then picked up the letter and unfolded it and broke the seal.

To Galina Vaughn

You probably are not acquainted with me in any way, since I have never been north of Sacramento on this side of the world. I came from New York State and only came west a few years ago.

I happened upon a letter written by you to Milton and thought it wise to write to you, once I realized your acquaintance with him. I confirmed a few facts in your letter before writing to you, to be certain you indeed, were the person I was trying to reach.

I know of no other way of saying this but to just be blunt. Your marriage is not a legal one. Though I did find out from your local magistrate that a marriage certificate was filed there in Oregon Territory. I hate to be the bearer of bad tidings, but I have been married to Milton for six years.

Since I have very little ability to ascertain if Milton was previously married before me then I have to assume that I am his legal wife.

It seems there are many secrets hiding behind the charming smiles of the man that has stolen our collective hearts. Currently Milton is in the Sacramento County jail here for some embezzlement charges. He also will have an added charge of bigamy added to it.

I have spoken to the local magistrate, and the charges that have already been laid upon Milton prove to have ample evidence, it seems that he will not be out of jail for some time unless he can convince a judge to release him on bail. If he does get bail, he will certainly leave without a trace.

I did see within the letter that I found that you are expecting a child. I have shed a few tears for you, since you seem a very loving woman. In my years of reading the Bible and going to church it has not prepared me well for the situation I, and now you, have been placed.

I do hope you have set aside some small funds to get resettled once you recover from the shock of this news. I have whittled away enough funds to allow my son and I to sail back to New York state, with hopes that my family will take pity on me and allow me to stay with them. I do not know exactly how I will cope otherwise.

I will endeavor to finish this letter with dry eyes, since my heart has broken every time I have attempted to say all that I can to you.

I want to encourage you, with all vehemence possible, to put all love you have for Milton Vaughn aside. He does not deserve it in any way. His arrogance and ruthlessness knows no bounds. He spins lies with every breath he takes, I know that now. He has no scruples. I think we both need to accept that.

I am so very sorry for everything you will suffer because of him. I will be praying for you and your child every day.

I expect the newspapers to run the story of his misdeeds soon. Circumstances are certainly going to get worse for us both if the story of your marriage breaks as well. I dread that for us both.

I wish you no ill will. My heart recovered from any thoughts of that after I read your letter more than once.

I have never before leaned more fully on the Lord God for His guidance than I have in these past few days. The verse I have shared below with you has been my constant comfort. I pray it will be to you as well.

Sincerely,

Sheila Anne Fisher - Formerly Vaughn

Psalm 37:1-4
"Fret not thyself because of evildoers, neither be thou envious against the workers of iniquity. For they shall soon be cut down like the grass, and wither as the green herb. Trust in the Lord, and do good; so shalt thou dwell in the land, and verily thou shalt be fed. Delight thyself also in the Lord: and he shall give thee the desires of thine heart."

Galina read the words in horror. In her chest she had a pressure and sharp pains. She ran to the waste bucket and dry heaved until her stomach clenched painfully. She sunk to the floor.

"Oh God. Please help me. I don't know what to do!"

Galina laid herself down and sobbed. All of her dreams were shattered.

To be continued...

Character List

Wildflower Series – Character List

Corinne Grant – (nee Harpole) Married to Lucas Grant. Born 1832. Started a business making medicinal oils from plants. Also, has built a greenhouse for the cultivating of plants and herbs. She was married to Andrew Temple for a few months before he died of Cholera on the Oregon Trail.

Lucas Grant - Graduate of Yale Agricultural School, thrives on farming technology and making improvements in the agricultural field. Married to Corinne.

Chelsea Grant - Married to Russell Grant. Granddaughter of Clive Quackenbush. Mother of Brody and Sarah Grant.

Russell Grant - Lucas Grant's brother, owns a farm nearby. They help each other often on each other's land.

John & Marie Harpole - Corinne's father, first wife Lily (Corinne's mother) - deceased - 2nd wife Marie Harpole - Mother to Cooper and Abigail, they adopted Lila (Delilah)

Megan Capron -17-year-old daughter of Arnold Capron - granddaughter to Rose Capron. She enjoys painting, singing and flirting. She ran away from the Grant's cabin in the summer of 1851 with a ranch hand.

Clive Quackenbush – Born 1782 - Mountain man, fur trapper, Hudson's Bay store owner, Government liaison for Indian Affairs, hunter and business man. First wife Christina – they had three children, Jedediah, Thomas and Greta. Second wife- Martha. He currently owns two fancy goods stores in Oregon Territory and a Hudson's Bay store in San Francisco. He is also a business partner with Angela Fahey with a family legacy project.

Jedediah Quackenbush - (nickname JQ) son of Clive, works at Oregon City store.

Millicent Quackenbush - (nickname Millie) married to JQ. Works the counter in the store but is active in her community and church.

Dolly Bluebird Bouchard - (Indian name is Bluebird) half-Indian, half-white. Mother was Hopi and father was a French fur trapper. She was sent by her adoptive tribe to learn from Corinne about plants and medicines to bring back and teach the tribe. Her father's name was Joseph Bouchard.

Angela Fahey Greaves - Irish immigrant orphaned and sold into a workhouse at a young age with her brother. She became a maid in Corinne's aunt's home and they were fast friends. She attempted to cross the Oregon Trail and was injured early on and had to recover before continuing her journey. She bought land outside of Oregon City and the boarding house in town. She is Corinne Grant's neighbor. She received an inheritance from her deceased parents after Corinne found a Boston lawyer. Married to Ted (Thaddeus) Greaves

Sean Fahey - Irish Immigrant who ran away from a Boston work orphanage. Older brother to Angela Fahey. Currently moved to Oregon City to reconnect with his sister Angela.

Thaddeus Greaves - (nicknamed Ted) – married to Angela Fahey. They met in San Francisco, he traveled back to upstate New York to retrieve his family. He traveled back by boat with his family to the West and settled in Oregon City.

Amelia Greaves – Mother to Ted, widow. She is a skilled lace maker. She joined her son to get a fresh start and a guaranteed business. They live in a townhouse in Oregon City with a storefront in their home. She also has a daughter, Sophia.

Olivia Greaves Quackenbush – Sister to Amelia. She is also a skilled lace maker and has a yearning for adventure. Currently married to Clive Quackenbush and living outside of town.

Sophia Greaves – (age 16) Sister to Ted Greaves. A highly skilled lace maker. Lives in Oregon City with her mother Amelia Greaves.

Warren Martin Jr. - Hired as a spare hand, does milking and odd jobs. Stays with Earl in his cabin during the week.

Earl Burgess – Works as the land manager for Angela Fahey. Also does maintenance for Orchard House, the boarding house that Angela owns. Lost a hand in an accident years before but is a hard worker with a lot of farm knowledge.

Henry & Edith Sparks - Henry is the Captain at Fort Kearney, they took Angela in after an unfortunate accident. Edith and Henry nursed her back to health. They adopted three orphaned children from a wagon train passing through Fort Kearney. When Henry's post as Captain was completed they left the fort to travel west on the Oregon Trail. Living on Ted and Angela Greaves property. Raising 3 children they adopted. Heidi, Fiona and Peter.

Galina Varushkin – age 16 – lives outside of Oregon City. Currently working as housekeeper for Angela & Ted Greaves.

Slava Varushkin – Russian Immigrant married to Magdalena (deceased)-Father of Galina, Miloslava (age 12), Pavel (age 10), and Radimir (deceased). He was injured while working for a logging camp and left for the Gold Rush the year before, leaving his family starving and with no resources. He came back with nothing, to find that his family had been given a cabin by the Spring Creek Church. He is currently working for Lucas Grant, clearing lumber for more crops. 2nd marriage, Guadalupe, widow from Mexico who moved up to Oregon City before her husband passed away from yellow fever.

Magdalena Varushkin – (deceased) Polish immigrant. Married Slava when she was 16. Mother to all the Varushkin children.

Violet Smithers Griffen – Housekeeper for Corinne and Lucas. Married to Edward Griffen, left for gold fields. (Deceased)

Tim Smithers Jr. –brother to Violet, five years younger.

Harold Smithers – youngest brother to Violet.

Oregon City

Doctor Vincent Williams – Oregon City doctor. He works with Corinne and the apothecary to take care of the Oregon City citizens.

Persephone Williams- the Doctor's wife and friend to Corinne. She helps with birthing and assists her husband in his duties.

Mr. Higgins - runs the local apothecary.

Gomer Hynes – Runs the Oregon Gazette, a weekly newspaper.

Pastor Darrell Whittlan & wife Helen – run the Spring Creek Fellowship Church outside of Oregon City on Spring Creek Road. They adopted orphans and minister to the rural community.

Marshall Crispin - Schoolteacher outside of town.

Reynaldo Legales – Ranch Manager at Harpole Ranch. His father owns a ranch in the California territory. Hard worker and righthand man for John Harpole. Currently courting Violet Griffen.

Amos Drays - local carpenter in town,

Mrs. Gemma Caplan- former owner of Oregon City boarding house, hired on as manager and head housekeeper.

Sherriff Nigel Tudor – Sherriff of Oregon City. Acts as Judge, Sherriff and county law.

Governor John Pritchlan – resident of Oregon City, governor of Oregon Territory.

Jedidiah Prince – head of the town Council in Oregon City.

Effie Prince – wife of Jedidiah Prince. Head of the Christian women's group in town, headstrong advocate for the poor - Mother of Sydney Prince.

Meredith & Timotheus Smithers – Parents of Violet, Tim and Harold. Timotheus Smithers was hung, by decision of Oregon City after finding him guilty of abuse to Violet Smithers Griffen as a child. Meredith had sided with her husband and believed him instead of her children.

Tim and Harold Smithers – Brothers to Violet, currently running the watermill in Oregon City.

Beatrice Glasner - Housekeeper and cook for Amelia Greaves, owner of the Lace storefront in the home.

Portland, Oregon Territory

Gabriel Quackenbush - Son of JQ and grandson of Clive, runs the Hudson's Bay store in San Francisco, California territory, they moved to Portland when San Francisco became a dangerous boomtown.
Amber Quackenbush - Married to Gabriel, Irish immigrant came over as a child with her parents. Helps her husband run the fancy goods store in Portland.

Kevin & Sadie Landers – proprietors of Portland Boarding House.

San Francisco, California Territory

Brian Murphy - Manager of Q & F Distillery, runs the distillery for the Irish whiskey recipe that Angela found in an old family diary. Currently being run secretly by Clive and Angela in a partnership.

Wildflower Series

Book 1 – Finding Her Way
(previously released as Seeing the Elephant)

Book 2 – Angela's Hope

Book 3 – Daughters of the Valley

Book 4 – The Watermill

Book 5 – Love In Full Bloom

Book 6 – A Kiss in Winter

Coming soon... Book 7 – The Namesake

Also by Leah Banicki

Runner Up – A Contemporary love story,
Set in the world of reality TV.

IMPARATOS Series:

Book 1 – Aurora
Coming soon – Book 2 – Savagery

This is a young adult contemporary series,
full of action and adventure.

Connect with me online:

https://www.facebook.com/Leah.Banicki.Novelist

Please share your thoughts with me. leahsvoice@me.com

The self-publishing world is very rewarding but has its marketing
challenges. Please remember to spread the word about my books if

you like them. By using word-of-mouth!
You can help to bless an author.
Like – Share - Leave a review

Thank you, Leah Banicki

My Biography -

I am a writer, wife and mother. I live in SW lower
Michigan near the banks of Brandywine Creek. I adore
writing historical and contemporary stories, facing the
challenges that life throws at you with characters that are
relatable. I love finding humor in the ridiculous things that
are in the everyday comings and goings of life. For me a
good book is when you get to step into the character's shoes
and join them on their journey. So climb aboard, let us share
the adventure!

My writing buddy is my miniature poodle Mr. Darcy,
who snuggles at my feet while I write until he must climb
onto my chest for dancing or snuggles. My beagle Oliver is
more concerned with protecting the yard from trespassers –
squirrels and pesky robins.

I love hearing from my readers and try to answer every
email personally.

I am always on Facebook and let my readers know about
how the next books are coming along.

I have a slew of books in the works and plan on
releasing a new series soon. Keep your eyes peeled for news!
My health does not always allow me to work as fast as I
would always like but I am so thankful for every day that
God lets me continue to do this work that I love so very
much.

I am in the last year of homeschooling my high school
daughter. (My sweet girl!)
After that, Lord willing, will allow for more books and
research trips.

I plan on continuing the Wildflower Series for many more years.

https://www.facebook.com/Leah.Banicki.Novelist

Please share your thoughts with me.
leahsvoice@me.com

Mr. Darcy – my writing buddy!